His eyes met those of Denker for a brief moment, a tell-tale interjection of time which could no longer be held in check. He saw the irrevocable movement of Denker's hand, the slow swing of the gate as it fell open under its own weight. Then only the initial charge of the ostrich filled his vision.

The female hurtled into the paddock, a plumed beast intent on nothing but the preservation of her offspring. Pent-up frustration carried her cloven feet like wind over the oozing earth.

GW00707834

adjust to the kind of labour I'm talking about. Also, the man who'll hire you will know you're desperate for work. But the main reason will be because it'll take time to strengthen your body.'

'I'm pretty strong!' objected James. 'I've been working the fields since I was a child!'

'I can see that, lad. But this will require more than strength.'

'Just what kind of work is it?'

'Building roads. In the Karoo. It's like working in hell, James. Nothing but sun, sand and dust. The earth is hard and dry, and you'd work with pick and shovel from early morning till sunset. You'll get to hate the heat and the land and the men you work with. There'll be no women, little to drink, and you'll share a tent with many other men. After a while you won't know which you hate more – them or the work.'

James laughed nervously. 'Sounds as though you're trying to talk me out of it. I thought they used convicts for that kind of thing?'

'They usually do, but right now they use what are called "distressed men", men without work. There's a depression on, remember? But believe me, you won't get treated much better than a convict.'

'You think you could get me placed there?'

'I know the foreman, and you can tell him I recommended you. He's a hard bastard, though,' he added.

'I'll go and see him.' At least it was a start, something to keep him going for a few months.

'Better get you fixed up with something to sleep on,' Pat said and stood up.

It was some time before he returned from the rear of the warehouse, his arms piled high with large black and white feathers. James watched curiously as he spread the feathers on the hard floor. 'As good a mattress as any,' the old man said. 'You can use one of my blankets.'

'What feathers are they?' asked James as he knelt to feel the soft down. 'They're beautiful!'

'Ostrich feathers, lad. A major export of the Cape. Seen them before?'

'No, but I know what an ostrich is.'

'Do you now? How do you think these feathers got here?'

'I suppose the birds were hunted. How else? Hell, I don't know!'

The old man smirked with superior knowledge. 'What if I told you these feathers came from tame ostriches – from farms?'

'Tame? Like cattle?'

'Oh, they still hunt wild birds, but more and more of them are being kept on farms. That means more than one crop of feathers from a bird. Makes sense, doesn't it?'

'I'd always thought of them as wild creatures.'

'So did most people. They thought the farming thing wouldn't work. It's been tried in Algeria where it failed. They said the birds were too timid to breed in confinement, that the feathers wouldn't match the quality of those taken from wild ostriches. They're being proved wrong.'

James touched the soft down again. 'A farm bird,' he whispered in disbelief.

'There are still problems,' Pat said quickly. 'The birds are prone to disease when they're grouped together. And they break their limbs when they run against the fences. But it is working. You'll see some of the farms if you get to work on the roads. Most of them are in the Little Karoo.'

'Is this the only country where this is being done?'

Pat shrugged. 'The only measure of success is taking place here, but they're sure to try elsewhere. I know that in North Africa they keep the birds in individual cages. They actually pluck them bare every four months or so, whereas out here the feathers are clipped. Most people talk of it as plucking, though.'

'You seem to know quite a bit about it.'

'I talk to the feather buyers who export the crops. Believe me, those dumb-looking birds are going to make many men rich before long. Just you wait and see!'

James could not help touching his feather mattress again. When he finally lay down and closed his eyes, he felt as if he were resting on a bed fit for a king.

WINGS OF GOLD

Neville Sheriff

WINGS
OF
GOLD

Pan Books
in association with Macmillan London

First published 1990 by Macmillan London Ltd
This edition published 1991 by Pan Books Ltd,
Cavaye Place, London SW10 9PG

1 3 5 7 9 8 6 4 2

© Neville Sherriff 1990

ISBN 0 330 31275 8

Typeset by Macmillan Production Ltd
Printed in England by Clays Ltd, St Ives plc

This book is sold subject to the condition that it shall not,
by way of trade or otherwise, be lent, re-sold, hired out,
or otherwise circulated without the publisher's prior consent
in any form of binding or cover other than that in which
it is published and without a similar condition including this
condition being imposed on the subsequent purchaser

To Alet, for being there
To Desmond who would have

CHAPTER ONE

The warmth of that March day in 1865 was the first sign of another long English winter coming to an end. As the sun broke through the clouds, dappling the farm lands with light, James Quenton removed his shirt to let the rays touch his bare skin.

He was dark for an Englishman. The years spent working the fields at his father's side had added to his natural duskiness, intensifying his brooding good looks and hardening his strong body so that he looked older than his nineteen years. His eyes, too, were a dark brown, set wide apart under a broad brow. He was of average height, broad-shouldered, with a hard, flat stomach.

James stopped working and raised his arms to ease his tired muscles. The year was well under way, but so far offered no more promise than those which had preceded it. It had always been that way, starting with the despair which had gradually become a feature of his father's character. The land would never be theirs, and the endless labour only benefited the man who owned it. The tenant farmers continued to live in poverty. James sighed, reached for the pitchfork and struggled with the large stack of hay.

Now that he was older he came to realise it was that same despair which had made his father prone to violence – often beating his son when there was nothing else to strike out at. The land felt nothing and the landlord was beyond reach. At fifteen the boy had turned into a man, strong enough to resist and fight back, so the beating ceased. The only other outlet for his father's frustration was himself, and that inner target, as much as his sudden illness, had sent him to an early grave four years ago, leaving James the sole supporter of the family. The narrow strip of land he worked as a tenant farmer provided barely enough to feed and clothe his mother and younger brother and sister; there was little left which allowed them to raise their standard of living.

As far as James was concerned, it had been the tenant farmer's way of life which had killed his father, and he feared it would one day do the same to him. He could not change the system he had inherited; that was beyond his power. Power, he thought bitterly, it always came down to that. It made him determined somehow to escape the endless routine and futile hopes of a tenant farmer. Perhaps that was why he subconsciously resisted forming close bonds with his neighbours, as if their acceptance of that way of life would taint him or sway him from his goal of finding something better. Bennett was the only person he could call a friend, and he lived some hours' walk away. As a result they saw each other only once or twice a month. If their contact became more regular that relationship, too, might change.

James frequently had to fight the resentment he felt towards those who depended on him; he could not just leave and abandon his responsibilities towards his family. Perhaps one day, when his brother Timmy was old enough to take over his role – but by then it might be too late.

He was sweating by the time he stacked the last bundle of hay, and glanced longingly at the cool water of the river. But it was already late afternoon with plenty of chores to be done around the home. He hoped Timmy had already chopped some kindling for the fire; the younger boy was habitually lazy.

Wiping off the worst of the sweat on to his shirt, he pulled the grimy garment over his shoulders. As he bent to collect the small cloth bundle which had contained a simple lunch, he heard the approach of a galloping horse.

He straightened and squinted into the fading sun, cursing when he recognised Clinton Amersforth, the landlord's son. His presence on the farm both intrigued and unsettled James, for Clinton had long ago demonstrated he had little interest either in the estate or the people who toiled on the land.

As the horse drew to a brutal halt he was forced to move swiftly aside. 'Master Clinton,' he said and bobbed his head respectfully at the brawny youth. The horse kept moving, forcing him to turn with it as it snorted nervously around him. Clinton watched him with a superior grin on his thick lips.

'I have work to do,' replied James, blinking his eyes against the dust thrown up by the milling of the horse's hoofs. He felt his natural dislike of the horseman blend with his mounting anger at the unnecessary display of arrogance. Clinton, looking down at him from the loftiness of his saddle, emphasised his elevated station in life. Like his father, Morgan Amersforth, he had a reputation of being a bully, often striking a tenant with his horsewhip for no reason.

'You have work to do?' echoed Clinton with a laugh that emerged as a snort. 'That makes a change, Quenton! I hear you spend most of your time in the village tavern – especially with the innkeeper's daughter!' He lashed out with his riding crop, but James moved quickly back. Clinton scowled when the whip slashed at empty air.

James glared back at him. Clinton's reference to the innkeeper's daughter told him what had prompted the visit, for Bennett had warned him of the youth's advances towards Lydia. The thought of the brutish landlord's son with gentle and petite Lydia curled his anger into a tight knot within his stomach.

'What I do with my own time is my concern,' he called out, stepping back as the horse turned and brushed past him.

Clinton laughed harshly. 'Not any longer, peasant – not if it involves Lydia, do you hear? Stay away from her from now on!'

James knew he should remain silent and let Clinton think he had scared him off, yet he could not stop himself. 'I think I'll wait till Lydia tells me that herself,' he replied. 'She knows a gentleman is not born, but bred – you and I are proof of that.'

There was a narrowing of Clinton's eyes an instant before the big man leaped from the saddle and struck out with his riding crop. The blow caught James on his forearm, but stepping back he was off balance and fell to the ground as the older and bigger man's fist smashed into the side of his head.

He lay stunned, shaking his head to clear the loud buzzing in his ears. With eyes watering from the force of the blow, he was barely conscious enough to see Clinton advancing towards him as he struggled to his feet, trying to ready himself for the next attack. Whatever happened now, Clinton would make sure the Quentons were evicted from the farm; there was no reason to endure the beating which he obviously planned on meting out.

Although James weighed considerably less than his opponent, he had had more than his share of fights. He shook his head again and hoped he would be able to withstand the next onslaught.

'I'm going to cut your peasant cock off!' snarled Clinton as the setting sun glinted on the knife in his hand. He lashed out, but James stepped back nimbly. When he lunged forward again, it was obvious he had little experience with the blade. James waited for the next wild thrust.

As it came he stepped aside, clamped his hand around Clinton's wrist and kicked him savagely in the crotch. The young man grunted as he sank down on to his knees. James slammed his knee up into Clinton's face, but it seemed to have little effect apart from bloodying his nose.

The next moment, Clinton pulled his knife hand free with such force that James was jerked forward to fall against his opponent. A huge hand gripped his throat; meaty fingers closed on him with awesome strength, crushing muscles and sinews and cutting off his breath.

James struggled desperately, using both hands to keep the knife at bay. A rising panic gripped him as he felt the overwhelming strength of the other man. It was as if the fingers clamped around his throat were tearing through the skin. One moment he was lifted off his feet and the next flung to the ground, pinioned there by Clinton's great mass.

His head spun from lack of air. Powerless to fight the big man off him, he knew he had only seconds in which to act before he lost consciousness and the knife was plunged into him. He released one hand from Clinton's wrist and struck out at the bloody face above him, jabbing his fingers into his opponent's eyes.

The young man jerked back with an agonised cry. James used the momentary respite to wriggle his body out from under him, but was too weak to pull entirely free. He clung desperately to Clinton's wrist when the other man fell back across his chest.

There was a loud grunt from above him. At the same time, he felt the warm stickiness of blood spill out across his hand. The fingers around his throat started to relax, and a long gasping sigh escaped from the man sprawled across him.

James lay still, trying to regain his breath. The bright red bloodstain, which had spread up to his wrist, made him grimace as he pushed the inert body from him. The knife was still clutched in the dead youth's hand, and his lips were pulled back in a sneer of death. A thin trickle of blood ran from the corner of one eye where James's fingers had pierced it.

A nearby willow tree provided support as James leaned against it, his legs trembling from the effect of the fight. He looked out across the fields, but there was no one in sight. Not that it would make any difference if there was a witness to what had happened: when Morgan Amersforth discovered his son's body in that area he would automatically accuse James. No one would believe Clinton's death was an accident; the murderer of Morgan Amersforth's son would be hanged without trial.

It was a while before his strength returned. There was not much time to act as he knew a search would be mounted when Clinton failed to reappear at the manor house by nightfall. The corpse would have to be hidden before he could place sufficient distance between himself and the farm.

He dragged the heavy body some distance along the river bank before concealing it in a clump of reeds. Realising that the appearance of the riderless horse would only accelerate the call for a search, he tied its reins to a branch of the willow to prevent the animal returning home.

Although the rapidly approaching night had cooled the air, a layer of sweat coated his skin as he started the long run home. A prickle of loneliness struck him when he spotted the thin plume of smoke rising from the little hovel. It might be the last time he saw the place where he was born – that, as well as his family.

His mother walked out of the cottage just as he came to a breathless halt. 'Son?' she cried as she saw the blood on his shirt.

'It's Clinton Amersforth,' he said quickly. 'He's dead – I killed him. We had a fight . . . he fell on to his own knife – it was an accident, Mother!'

'Clinton's dead? Oh, James . . . They'll hang you for sure!' The frail woman flung her arms about his neck and held him tightly. He felt her body tremble before she pulled away and stared up at him with eyes filled with frightened tears. 'You must run – go now!'

'I can't! What about you . . . the children . . . ?'

Her voice, shrill with panic, was a frantic shout. 'It'll be you Lord Amersforth wants punished,' she said, crying hysterically now. 'We'll be all right, son. Run, James – you'll be as good as dead if Morgan Amersforth catches you!'

She pushed him into the hut, glancing over her shoulder as if fearing the avengers of Clinton's death were already upon them. The children watched with anxious eyes as she helped him fling a few essentials into a cloth bag.

He hugged each of them in turn. 'Timmy . . . Rosie,' he whispered, then took the bag from his mother and moved outside. There were dark, threatening clouds sweeping in across the moors as he turned back to her and took her into his arms.

She gave a moan of anguish. 'Run as far as you can, James,' she said. 'Even England won't be big enough to hide you.'

She pushed him away from her in the direction of the moors, but her fingers still clutched his shirt, as if she could not bear their parting. 'Go!' she pleaded. 'Go now!'

He pulled her back into his arms. 'Goodbye, Mother – forgive me!' He saw the smaller children peer fearfully out of the door. Giving his mother one last look, he turned and ran into the approaching night.

It was two hours before he stopped to rest for the first time, falling in exhaustion to the ground. His lungs burned in his chest. Even his ears throbbed from the strain of listening for the sounds of the men, horses and dogs who would inevitably pursue him. Wearily he forced himself to his feet and stumbled on again.

Although the uneven ground and the moonless night slowed his progress, James knew the moors well enough to keep direction, but it was still another hour before he reached the tiny farmhouse he had been heading for. A dog barked as he approached the house. 'Be still, Patch,' he whispered, and the dog's threatening growl changed to a low whimper of greeting as the animal recognised the familiar scent. The mongrel sheepdog dashed ahead as he stepped closer.

The door swung open, revealing a slim man framed against the dim light spilling out through the doorway. 'Who's there?'

'It's James,' came the whispered reply. 'Bennett . . . come here.' His friend frowned, then stepped out and shut the door behind him. 'I need help . . . I'm in trouble, Bennett.'

The other youth laughed. 'Which girl is it now?'

'It's much worse than that. Much worse.' James quickly related the events of that afternoon.

Bennett said, 'They'll hang you for this, James. Where'll you go? What'll you do?'

'London. I can hide out there for a short while. Then on to America, perhaps.' His mother was right; England would be too small for him. Morgan Amersforth was a powerful man and his vengeance would be strong and relentless. 'I need rest, Bennett,' he added, 'Can I use your shed?'

There was a moment's hesitation before the other replied, 'Of course, but—'

'I'll be gone long before daybreak. Just a few hours' sleep, that's all. You can tell your father I'm on my way to the Patterson farm to buy a cow.'

Bennett reached out and touched James's shoulder. 'Go on ahead,' he said. 'I'll bring a lantern.'

When Bennett entered the shed, James used the dim light to inspect the contents of his bag. It contained a few slices of dry bread, a single change of clothing and his only jacket. The garment's elbows were all but worn through. The only other item was a small cloth purse which clinked as he tossed it to the ground. James's eyes filled with tears of shame, realising that his mother had given him most of their meagre savings, money which in a week or two should have been spent on the purchase of a milk cow. He swallowed, placed a few of the coins in the inside of his coat pocket, then dropped the balance back into the purse. He handed it to Bennett, who was watching him curiously. 'I need another favour, my friend,' he said, the words sticking in his throat.

Bennett nodded. 'If I can do it, I will.'

'Your father is what – a senior tenant on this farm?'

'A foreman, so to speak.'

'Tomorrow, after I've gone, tell him the truth about my coming here. He'll hear about it soon enough, anyway.'

'He'd agree to my hiding you even if he knew right now.'

'I know,' said James and briefly touched his friend's arm. 'That's why I want you to give him that money . . . He's to try to use his influence to get my mother and the children placed on your farm. She can work in the landlord's house perhaps, or in the fields if she has to. Young Timmy can help too. Is the old Drake cottage still empty?' he asked, thinking of the small house which had been vacated by another tenant farmer some months ago.

'It is. I'm sure my father can arrange it. He's always been close to your kin.'

They talked a while longer, two old friends who knew they would probably not see each other again. 'I envy you in a way,' Bennett said. 'At least you're your own man now, starting life afresh.'

'Yes.' For James, though, there was little joy in the moment, as the oppressive guilt at abandoning his family sank in.

After a while, as James's eyes started to close, Bennett stood up and covered him with his coat. 'Farewell, my friend,' he said softly. 'God be with you.'

But James was already asleep.

It was the first time James had been to London, and the size and bustling activity of the city simultaneously scared and excited him. The glances of strangers constantly unnerved him as he imagined them to be Morgan Amersforth's men.

He managed to find cheap lodgings with relative ease, using most of his small supply of coins to pay for a few days' rent in advance. The next day he plied the harbour area, seeking work on a ship which would take him from England. He had no idea where he wanted to go or what he would do except that he favoured America. When he stumbled homewards after dark on his third day in London, he'd been unsuccessful long enough to accept anything that came his way.

Instead of going straight back to the tiny room which provided temporary refuge, James was drawn by the noise and laughter emanating from a nearby tavern. He dug inside his pocket, fingered the few remaining coins and, with a shrug of his shoulders, pushed open the doors and was immediately enveloped by the throng of humanity inside.

His first ale did little to dispel the mood of despair which had settled on him. He ordered another, ignoring the feeling of guilt at this extravagance. A huge man in seaman's dress standing beside him gave him a gap-toothed grin and said, 'You'll need quite a bit of this weak swill if you want to get that grim expression off your face – you look like you're drinking cat's piss!' He laughed loudly, a harsh bellow in keeping with his bulk.

James looked up. 'The ale's fine,' he replied, mistrusting the big man's interest in him. Like everyone else in the pub, he looked rough and ready, someone who would think nothing of parting a young man from his money. He tried to shift away but bumped into an equally tough-looking character behind him. The man flashed him a sidelong glance before concentrating on his drink again.

The seaman seemed unaware of James's discomfort as he squinted against the smoke from his pipe and said, 'You've worries then, have you?'

9

'Some.' Sensing that the big man meant him no harm, James told about his search for work, adding that he had to leave England. He did not give reasons for this, nor did the man ask for any.

'You look like a strong one,' the seaman said. 'So, for the price of an ale, I'll take you to my captain. He's over there, at that table.'

James stared through the blue haze of smoke at a group of half-drunk men hunched around a table laden with jugs and empty bottles. 'Is there a position aboard your ship?' he asked.

'Aye. A few of the men came down sick and we had to leave them at the Cape. You could get work till we get there, but after that you'd be on your own.'

'The Cape?'

The seaman laughed. 'Aye, the Cape Colony. Otherwise known as the Cape of Good Hope.'

James rubbed his jaw. 'Lord knows,' he said, 'I need some hope right now!'

The sailor laughed and held up two fingers at the bartender. He waited till James paid for the drinks, raised his jug and said, 'To the Cape of Good Hope.'

James raised his own ale. The Cape – it was as welcome a destination as any other.

CHAPTER TWO

Far below the mountain guardian of Cape Town, the city streets, which had bustled with Cape carts, hansom cabs and loaded wagons pulled by spans of oxen, were already wreathed in shade. A solitary double-decker tram, drawn by two horses, made its way up Adderley Street.

James Quenton sat on the edge of an upturned crate and stared up at Table Mountain, watching the late afternoon sunlight cling to the craggy cliffs, tickling the shadowed crevices as it turned relentlessly westwards.

The harbour too was tranquil. Earlier that day there had been a flurry of activity, belying the shadow of a trade recession under which Cape Town laboured that autumn. Now, only a few workers criss-crossed the water-front expanse, their elongated shadows jerking in short sharp movements beside them.

Coaches, which had milled about in the docks collecting passengers from the newly arrived ships, were gone now. Only the ships remained, tightly packed rows of scraggy rigging stripped of canvas, their tall masts scratching at a blue sky tinged with indigo. The sea seemed to reach right into the city itself: boats were moored within a few yards of the three-storeyed custom house.

The changing day softened the harshness of the white-washed buildings, cushioning the shrill cries of seagulls mingling with the calls of street vendors on the motionless air. From further along the docks came the strident clamour of metal striking metal, breaking the soporific spell that

11

enveloped James. He shivered as the autumn sun retreated around the face of the mountain. The advancing shadows heightened his sense of loneliness, and he looked out to sea as if he could gain comfort from the knowledge that England lay somewhere beyond the misty horizon.

He shifted on the crate and told himself he had to put England from his mind. The Cape Colony was his home now, his future; there was precious little from his past to help him build a new life.

When he stood up, he almost bumped into an old man standing close behind him, watching him with interested eyes. 'Didn't mean to startle you,' the stranger said. 'Just arrived in the Colony, have you?'

James nodded. 'The English ship that came in this afternoon. I worked my way here.'

The old man smiled at him with eyes that were a dark, piercing blue. 'It's a terrible feeling, isn't it, suddenly realising you're on your own in a strange land?'

The accuracy with which the stranger had summed up his misgivings startled James. 'You've been in the same situation yourself, have you?'

'Most people out here have, lad,' the old man replied. 'This is a new land, remember.' He stepped back, moving with an awkward limp.

'Do you work on the docks?'

'You could say that.' He tapped his thigh and added, 'Was a time when I unloaded ships like the one you sailed in on. But . . .' He touched his leg again. 'Now I take care of a warehouse, that one over there.' He pointed to a massive barn-like structure with a corrugated iron roof. 'The name's Pat Stanton,' he said and pushed out a gnarled hand.

James took it in his own. 'James Quenton.'

A light smile played on Pat Stanton's lips. 'James,' he repeated, as if trying the name on his tongue. 'A grand name for a seaman, I must say. Not Jim?' The twinkle in his eye dispelled James's fear that he was being mocked.

'My mother hoped the name would symbolise a better life for me,' he explained, smiling back at the old man. 'I'm inclined to like the thought – as well as the name.'

'Ah, so it's ambition you're having then! Nought wrong with that, lad.' He laughed softly, a chortle which pulled his eyes into tiny slits. 'So, you'll be looking for a place to sleep?'

'I'd better be getting a move on. My crewmates gave me the names of some inns.'

'But you've been cooped up with your fellow Jacks long enough, I'd dare say.' Pat's eyes twinkled with amusement.

'You're right about that! I was thinking I'd take a look around . . . try to find some place where there's little chance of meeting up with any of them.' He glanced at the lights which had started to glow in the city and added, 'I might have left it too late, though.'

'There'll be time for that tomorrow. I can offer you a bunk for the night. It's no inn, but at least the old place is dry and not too cold.'

James glanced at the warehouse. 'I couldn't just—'

'Of course you could! I put together a fair meal, and I'd welcome the company. Grab hold of your bag, lad.' Before James could object any further, Pat moved off in his ungainly shuffle.

The interior of the warehouse was dark with a stale, cloying smell, reminding James of a ship's hold. Pat struggled with an oil lamp, and at last it glowed dully, revealing a cosy corner which he had arranged for himself.

'When I said I could give you a bunk for the night, I was perhaps stretching things a bit.' He waved his arm at the humble quarters. There was a crude wooden cot which looked as though it had been constructed from scrap pieces of timber; next to the bed an empty crate served as a table for the oil lamp, a tin plate and a book yellowed with age. James leaned closer and saw it was a Bible.

Pat Stanton noticed the look, and smiled. 'Don't look so concerned – I'm no religious fanatic. It brings me a bit of comfort, that's all.' He stood with his hands on his hips and thoughtfully surveyed his domain. 'As for your bunk, there're plenty of soft goods around that will serve just fine. But first we'll fix something to eat.'

By the time their simple meal was ready, five mangy-looking cats had appeared on the scene. James was amused to see

Pat care for the animals first, talking in a gentle tone while he dished up food for the two of them.

He was relieved when Pat showed no inclination to pry into his reasons for leaving England, asking only how he came to end up in the Colony. 'A chance meeting in London,' he explained. 'The Cape seemed like an interesting place to get to.'

Pat kicked gently at one of the cats, which rolled on to its back before his feet. 'You haven't jumped ship, have you, lad?' he asked softly.

James shook his head. 'They offered me a position to here. After that I would be on my own.'

'It's as good a destination as any, James. Who knows – it might be your destiny as well!'

Later, after they had washed and dried their plates, they sipped a brew of strong coffee, talking about the Colony and the chances of work. 'You picked a bad time to arrive,' Pat said. 'There's not much going for a young man of your calibre.'

'Calibre? Right now my only ambition is to stay alive. But farming is the only thing I know.'

They sat in silence for a while, the only sound the light slurps as they sipped the steaming brew. Then Pat said, 'You could try to get work on one of the wine estates, although they're more inclined to hire Hottentots. They pay them less.'

'I thought I'd try for something here in the city.'

'Why bother? You said it yourself – all you know is farming. It'd be a waste of time. I take it you don't have much money to keep you going?'

'Only my seaman's wages and that's not much. I have to find work in the next day or two.'

Pat was lost in thought for a moment. 'There is something, but—'

'But what? I'll take anything!'

'It'll be hard, backbreaking work,' Pat said. 'And the money won't be much – especially in your case.'

James gave him a curious look. 'What do you mean, in *my* case?'

'You're young, and it'll take time for your muscles to

14

CHAPTER THREE

The air was laden with the salt smell of the sea when James left the warehouse the next morning. Pat Stanton had given him a rough handwritten note vouching for their acquaintance. 'The man you have to see,' he said, 'is Gert Denker, a Dutchman, who's not to be trifled with. Don't even hold his eyes for too long, and don't answer back – not if you want the work.'

The place James sought was not far from the gates of Alfred Dock, on the slopes of Green Point. It was a cluster of rough wooden huts, identified by a crudely made sign announcing that it belonged to Kenrick Construction.

He headed for the biggest of the huts, linked to a smaller one by a broad plank cat-walk a few feet above the muddy ground. The inside was dark and smelled of damp wood. There was no furniture apart from a tiny desk tucked in a corner. His heavy boots thudded dully on the plank floor, and he felt the boards move beneath his feet.

The man seated behind the desk matched the small size of the unit, making James suspect that it could not be Denker. The clerk looked up, annoyed at the interruption. 'What do you want?'

James stepped closer and removed his cloth cap. 'I was told to ask for Mr Denker,' he said. 'About work. I—'

'You from England?' the clerk interrupted. He was in his late fifties, almost completely bald, his brow creased in what seemed to be a permanent scowl.

'Yes,' replied James, deciding to treat the dour individual

in the same manner as Pat had prescribed for Denker.

The clerk looked him up and down with obvious disapproval. 'Won't last two days out there,' he said with a sneer. 'You want to think again about seeing Denker?'

James decided it was best not to reply. He stayed in front of the desk, twirling his cap between his fingers.

The other man sighed and started scrawling on one of the papers on his desk. He looked up sharply, as if surprised to find the young man still there. He glared at him before jerking his thumb at the door behind him. It looked as though it had been cut into the wall as an afterthought.

The cat-walk sagged dangerously as James made his way across. The door to the other hut was open, and just inside someone was rummaging through a duffel bag. James tapped on the wall, coughed lightly, and waited for the man to become aware of his presence.

'Mr Denker?' he said as the other man continued to search the contents of the bag, piled high with clothes. There was a clink of glass from deep inside.

Denker turned and glanced over his shoulder, then fiddled inside the bag again. James stared down at the broad and powerful shoulders which strained at the fabric of the man's shirt. 'Mr Denker?' he repeated when the other man continued to ignore him.

This time the Dutchman swung around to face him, while remaining on his knees in front of the bag. 'Say what you want to say,' he growled. 'I'm busy.'

'I'm told you have openings for men. On the road works.'

Denker gave him an appraising look, then laughed harshly. 'For men, yes – not boys.'

His response made James flush with anger, but he managed to bite back the retort which sprang to his lips. 'I've worked on a farm all my life,' he said calmly. 'I'm not afraid of hard work.'

'This is not England, farm boy. You just arrived?' He spoke English without the guttural accent James had heard in other Dutchmen, but his speech somehow sounded harsher to the ear.

James nodded and fumbled in his pocket for the note Pat

18

had given him. 'Pat Stanton told me to give you this,' he said, proffering the wrinkled slip of paper.

Denker rose to his feet, causing James to take an involuntary step backwards in amazement at the sheer size of the man. His short neck rested on huge, hulking shoulders, while his barrel chest fell away to a hard, flat stomach. His trousers were tight-fitting, revealing massive thighs. He's like a bull, thought James, wondering how many men had been broken by those huge, powerful hands.

The note was plucked roughly from his hand. When Denker stepped away to study it, the floorboards trembled dangerously. 'You read it,' he snapped, thrusting the note back. A sneer tugged at the corner of his thin lips.

James reddened as he stared angrily down at the paper. Despite Pat's warning, he was unable to keep his anger and shame from showing on his face when he raised his eyes to Denker's. 'I can't read,' he said in a low voice. The note trembled in his fingers. He wondered how Denker had guessed.

'You English,' came the scornful growl. 'And you think you can rule the world!' He snatched the note back and let it flutter to the mud-stained floor. 'You come here thinking this country will make you rich. You think it will open its arms to you, yet you can't even read what another man writes of you.' He turned his back contemptuously, and for one wild moment James was tempted to jerk him around and smash his fist into the smirking face. Damn him! Denker was conveniently forgetting he was himself an immigrant.

He managed to control his rage and stood seething in silence, letting the Dutchman enjoy the power he had over him.

'The only reason I'd take you on,' said Denker, without looking at him, 'is because we're short of men and I don't have the time to find anyone better. But understand one thing,' he added ominously as he swung round. 'The first sign of trouble from you – any kind of trouble or laziness – and I'll break you in two. Don't think I can't do it.'

Pat's warning flashed through James's mind again, making him lower his eyes. 'I'm a hard worker,' was all he said.

Denker gave him a sudden shove. It was a mere flick of his hand, but it sent him reeling backwards. He grabbed at the door-jamb to stop himself from falling. Glancing quickly at Denker in a mixture of fear and surprise, he realised the rough gesture was nothing more than the foreman's indication that he should cross the cat-walk again. 'Sign the contract in the other office,' said Denker. 'We leave at first light tomorrow.'

The big man followed him back across the flimsy structure, making the cat-walk sway precariously under their combined weight. 'What time should I report?' James asked across his shoulder. There was no protective rail along the cat-walk, so he spread out his arms to help maintain his balance.

'You'd better see you're here by nightfall. You'll sleep in the yard along with the other men. And don't bring any liquor with you,' Denker warned. 'If I so much as smell the stuff on your breath, I'll throw you back on the streets. You understand?'

'I understand,' James replied softly.

Denker mumbled some instructions to the surly clerk, then turned and said, 'You tell Pat Stanton I don't need him as a recruiting officer. Especially not for young boys.' He turned on his heel and stomped from the hut. The trembling of the cat-walk could be felt through the floor even after the door had swung shut.

'Sign here,' the clerk said, shaking his head as if doubting Denker's judgement in hiring the youth.

James stood with the pen in his hand and felt the blood creep into his cheeks again. But the clerk made no comment when he reached for the contract to scribble across the space he had indicated. The fact that he had signed something he could not read disturbed James, and he vowed that too would change in the future.

The doubts about his commitment flooded through him as he strolled back to the harbour. Yet it was too late now; somehow he would have to make it through the days and months that lay ahead. Then he could decide on his future.

Moments later, when it started to rain, he hoped it was not symbolic of what lay in store for him.

An icy wind rushed in from the sea when James returned to the Kenrick offices just before nightfall. He pulled up the collar of his short seaman's coat, relieved it was no longer raining.

He hesitated when he reached the hut he had entered that morning, and turned to stare back at the docks. His farewell to Pat Stanton had been brief but warm, and he knew he would miss the old man despite the brevity of their acquaintance.

'No good delaying it any longer,' he said aloud and, taking a deep breath, walked up the few steps to the door of the hut. It was locked. Standing forlornly as the wind tugged at his collar, he heard voices coming from behind the hut and stepped down to go around the side.

The downpour earlier that afternoon had turned the ground into a squelching mess which sucked at his boots as he ducked under the cat-walk and entered the circular yard formed by the huts. Two wagons were parked there, loaded with supplies for the construction site in the Karoo. At the far side of the yard a man tended the teams of mules. Fifteen men crowded around the warmth of a large fire glowing brightly in the gathering dusk. They glanced at James as he came closer, then resumed their various conversations. They were all considerably older than him, and now he realised why Denker had passed so many scathing remarks about his youthfulness. It was obvious that most of the men had worked on the roads before.

He looked around for the big foreman, expecting to find him there and checking that all the men had reported for work. There was no sign of him.

'Try to find a place out of the wind and under cover,' the man tending the mules said. 'There's more rain on the way.'

James smiled his thanks and studied the encampment. The best spots had already been taken. The space beneath the two wagons was filled with the men's gear, leaving him few choices of suitable sleeping places. He opted for a spot near one of the huts, silently cursing Denker for not allowing them to sleep inside.

Propping his gear against the wall, he stepped over to the

fire. The men let him move in, although no one introduced himself or made any effort to include him in conversation. He sensed they were not being deliberately rude; it was just that they had been there before and he had no right as yet to share their common experience. It suited him in a way, for he often found he was less alone by himself than in the company of strangers.

As the muleteer had predicted, it started to rain again a few minutes later, a soft drizzle which quickly soaked through the men's clothing. They scrambled for the shelter of the wagons, clambering in between the wheels where their gear was stacked. James stared at the exposed spot where his own bag lay; it provided no shelter at all. He decided he might as well stay near the fire for as long as it lasted.

'Hey,' one of the men called out from beneath a wagon, 'there's a little space left over here. At least you'll get your head out of the rain.'

James smiled into the dark, ran for his bag and crawled under the wagon. As the man had said, there was precious little space for him. He felt the fresh mud form around his legs as the rain increased in intensity.

Someone cursed when a trickle of water broke through the floorboards of the wagon and ran down the neck of his shirt.

'It's good to be home again,' someone else remarked wryly. 'Denker's darlings,' added another, and the men laughed at the discomfort, which was once more a familiar thing.

His own silent smile spread, till at last he laughed along with them, feeling the first form of acceptance Pat had said he would sorely need in the times ahead.

Pitifully few words were exchanged before the wagons reached the parched expanses of the Little Karoo. Once they had crossed the Cogmans Kloof pass leading through the Langeberg Mountains, a range jealously protecting the watered regions of the coast, the men fell silent as the sun flashed angrily from early morning till its retreat at night.

Although the slow journey was as arduous as Pat had

warned, when they stopped at night James seemed to have more energy left than the others. He knew Denker sensed this, so he purposely avoided the foreman, not letting his remarks provoke him. To his relief Denker rode ahead of them each day, sometimes leaving the creaking wagons far behind as he spurred his horse across the plains.

The landscape mesmerised James: flat-topped hills dotted the prairie, their dolerite sills proclaiming the remains of a geological system of far greater eminence. He could sense the age of the earth, its timelessness matched only by the complete silence which enveloped the veld.

The days and nights dragged on, weakening the men with extremes of heat and cold. When the sun sank over the hills, the chill of approaching winter streaked in vengefully, grasping the tired men till the next dawn.

They passed herds of springbok which fled with stiff-legged jumps as the wagons rolled closer. By day flocks of wild ostriches watched curiously, by night, grunting and roaring like lions calling, while the jackals sang their melancholy tunes to the moon. Yet nothing could disturb the silence, the stillness, the peace. It brought a measure of relief to James's fears of what awaited him.

At last they saw the camp for the first time, four rows of dust-streaked tents set in a haphazard line cleared through the Karoo scrub. The sight was as dismal as the veld surrounding it, even though the faraway mountain ranges shimmered hazily with illusory softness. 'Home, sweet home,' someone muttered, but the remark drew no response from the others.

They climbed wearily down from the wagons, Denker immediately shouting at them to unload the supplies. 'You're lucky,' he said as they started to drag the heavy boxes from the wagons, 'it's too late to get you lot out to the construction point. Use the afternoon to get your breath back, 'cause tomorrow you pitch in with the other men.' He strode off after warning them to stay out of the tents till the labourers returned to camp.

'Where *are* the others?' James asked a man with a dirty white apron strung around his ample waist. The cook turned his bleary eyes on him after checking that the other new arrivals were stacking the supplies where he wanted them.

'They're working on the road about six miles away,' he said, scratching idly at his nose. 'We only shift camp when it gets to around ten.'

James glanced at the two wagons. 'Will there be enough room for all the men? Or are there more wagons?'

The cook gave a loud guffaw and slapped his hips. 'You don't ride on any wagon, you young fool!' he said through peals of loud laughter. 'You walk to work – and back!'

'What about lunch?'

'That gets taken out by wagon. You eat breakfast before you leave in the morning.' He laughed again and added, 'Before you ask about supper, let me tell you that by the time you get back, you won't be interested in anything but sleep. For the first few weeks at least. Not food, not liquor – not even women!' He laughed harshly.

'Seems to be little chance of the latter around here,' replied James.

The cook wiped his eyes. 'Sure as hell not,' he said. 'It's Mother fist and her Five Daughters from now on. After three months you get to ride to Cape Town on the supply wagon. One week off to slake your thirst and have the real thing, then it's back to Mother for another three months.'

James was about to comment, thought better of it, and said instead, 'Are we at least allowed water while we work?'

'There's water. But take my advice . . . don't stop for too many drinks or make your breaks too long, else Denker will have your hide.'

'Seems he enjoys that kind of thing.'

'Don't you ever forget that, boy. There are some tough men in this gang, but none who can handle Denker. If he so much as suspects you think you could take him on, he'd call you. He enjoys breaking bones.' He wagged a warning finger beneath the young man's nose before he turned away to waddle across to the rows of blackened pots heating on the fires.

James joined the line of men carrying supplies from the wagons. More than once he saw them glance at the enticing shade of the empty tents, but the threat implicit in Denker's order proved an all too effective deterrent.

The sun had ceased its cruel assault when the labourers finally returned to the camp. They came marching in against the fading light, a large cloud of dust trailing them as they dragged their tired feet the last few yards. They looked thin and sunburnt. Despite the weariness that showed on their dust-streaked faces, they shouted their greetings at those they recognised among the newcomers. One by one, James's fellow travellers joined their old comrades and were led to empty berths in the tents. At last he alone remained standing in the dusk.

'Don't worry – you won't spend the night out in the cold,' came a voice from behind him. He spun around to stare at a very tall older-looking man. The stranger rubbed a wet cloth across his naked chest and shoulders in an attempt to remove the worst of the day's dust. He smiled, his teeth white against his dark skin. 'There's a spot in my tent,' he said, 'where the night wind blows in. Care to stop it up for us?'

'Sounds fine to me.' James stuck out his hand. 'James Quenton.'

'Amos.' The other man's grip was firm, his fingers and palm covered in hard calluses. 'Grab your bag and follow me.'

James fell in behind him, relieved to find some sort of welcome to the new life he'd now entered. He noticed the rippling muscles in Amos's back and wondered what his own body would look like after a few months.

Their tent was the last in the fourth row. Amos ducked in first, then quickly introduced the young man to the others lying on their groundsheets, using the brief respite to rest before supper. Apart from a few nods and muttered greetings, they paid little attention to the newcomer.

Amos helped him spread out the groundsheet and blanket he had drawn from the company store on the morning of his departure. 'Try to keep them as clean as you can,' he warned. 'There's little enough water to wash *yourself* in, let alone bedding.'

25

When Amos had made his way to his side of the tent, James felt the thin material which offered scant protection from the heat and cold. A pinch of fear twitched his stomach when he thought of the day to come. He glanced at Amos and, as though the older man sensed what was going through his mind, he gave a reassuring nod before closing his eyes and lying back against his bedroll.

'You're going to make it,' James whispered to himself as he followed suit, resting his head against his bag. 'You've got to – there's no other choice.'

He fell in with the group of men when they scrambled from the tent a few moments later, summoned to supper by means of a small-sized slave bell standing beside the cook's tent. There was a rush for the queue already forming outside the kitchen.

James relaxed with them, as an easy banter flowed along the line of waiting men, wanting to, having to belong.

CHAPTER FOUR

With dry dust spiralling up the funnel of wind, the miniature tornado swept the arid earth, dragging with it any loose brush and small pebbles as it screeched on angrily. It hissed and hummed its way towards the group of men sweating in the afternoon heat, as though intent upon adding its fury to the already trying circumstances of their labour.

'Another one,' muttered James. He stopped digging and turned his back on the advancing dust devil, the sharp rays of the sun striking his face as he waited.

His skin was as bronzed as any of the men's now, almost impervious to the stinging heat. But still the sweat poured from him and dripped to the desiccated ground, darkening the loose dirt for an instant before the specks of moisture were sucked away by the torrid air.

A wild whine signified the whirlwind's approach. By now the others had seen it too, and the stained cloths they wore around their necks were already lifted into position. James followed suit, tugging the bandanna tightly across his mouth and nose, shutting his eyes just as the dust tower flailed the air around them, increasing the sweltering heat as it spat out its wrath at the cowering men.

Specks of dust struck the exposed parts of his body, worming their way into every hollow, clinging to the sweat in his armpits, his hair and eyes.

The funnel seemed to hover over them before it passed on, with the ensuing silence broken only by the coughing and cursing of men as they slowly returned to their work.

'You should be used to it by now,' said Amos. He rubbed his hand vigorously through his thinning hair in an effort to dislodge the worst of the dust.

'I doubt whether I ever will be,' replied James, already digging again. Three months had passed quickly: as his body grew stronger the pain on rising in the early morning light had lessened. He could work as hard as any of the men now, and he knew they respected him for it.

The stark memory of those first days and weeks when he stumbled back to camp, his hands raw and bleeding, his skin an angry red flush from the sun, still haunted him. It had been Amos who had nursed his wounds and helped him to his feet on those mornings when his strained muscles threatened to snap. When they had trudged the long cold miles to the construction point, it was Amos who had stayed beside him, comforting him with his presence and an occasional smile. At last the ache had left his muscles, and dry calluses covered the distressed skin of his palms.

Remembering, he turned and smiled at Amos, preoccupied as he swung his pick at the unyielding earth. 'I'm going for a drink of water,' James said, and made his way to where three barrels stood exposed to the blistering heat.

There, as well, the whirlwind had made its presence felt. The water was covered with a layer of fine dust. He gently scooped it up with a mug and threw it to the ground.

'Hey!' Even without looking up, he knew Denker's gravelly voice. The big man came striding over to him. 'What you think you're doing, puppy?' He pushed the young man roughly aside. 'Wasting water, are you?' He stared down at the rapidly evaporating specks of moisture, then struck out in a lightning-fast movement. It was a backhand blow which caught James on the shoulder. He staggered back, his entire arm numb from the force of it, realising the futility of retaliation.

'I was scooping off the dust,' he explained, fighting the impulse to hold his arm which had started to throb now.

'Shut up, puppy. You're off to Cape Town tomorrow, so now you don't give a damn about the others, do you?' Denker swung around, hands on hips, and called out to the men. 'You see what the puppy's done? He's thrown sand in your water!' He grinned maliciously, then kicked the barrel over. The water spread only a few inches before it seeped into the parched ground. 'Now there's less for all of you,' he shouted. 'Take it up with the pup if you want to.' He gave James a hard look before sauntering off.

James felt the men's eyes on him, but knew their glances were not accusing. They had seen how Denker taunted him from the start, trying to break his spirit, anger him into a fight. If they accused him of anything, it was for not standing up to the big man. Yet that, too, they could understand and accept.

He watched the foreman swagger past the lines of men, knowing the time would come eventually when he would be forced to give the Dutchman the satisfaction of fighting him.

Their work had reached a point almost four miles from the camp, and as the men walked back that evening they could feel the first hint of approaching spring in the August air. As they walked, their boots collected dust, which constantly drifted across the red veld and was tinged by the lazy rays of the sun, an immense blob on the horizon. The veld itself was soft now, its menace gone with the retiring day. The silence which enveloped it was broken only by the crunching tread of marching men.

'It'll be windy in Cape Town this time of year,' Amos said, 'but that'll make no difference to what a man and a woman can get up to.' The men walking close to them laughed at James's obvious embarrassment.

'I can give you the name of a whore who'll keep you inside all week,' someone said. 'The only problem is it'll take another week to get you back on your feet. You'd be useless to Denker when she's through with you!' Their laughter rang out on the still air.

'Let the boy alone,' said Amos, giving James's shoulder an affectionate slap. 'I'm sure the ladies will line up for his favours.'

James smiled to himself. He had turned twenty that June, yet they still called him a boy. It did not rankle with him, for he knew he had earned their respect through his hard work and lack of complaint. It was only when Denker spoke to him as though he were a child that he felt a hot flush of resentment.

For once their supper was ready when they arrived at the camp. It allowed the men some time to spend together instead of crawling into bed as usual. They built a huge fire and sat around talking of what the lucky few leaving for Cape Town the next day would do during their stay there.

'A hot bath,' one of them said excitedly. 'That's the first thing I'll do – even if it takes half my pay!'

'To hell with the bath,' someone else cried. 'Those whores like a bit of earth on a man. A bath would be a waste!' There was a general nodding of heads at this.

Their laughter echoed across the scrubland, but they fell silent when Denker suddenly appeared in their midst. He sneered at them, enjoying the effect he had on them. Glancing around the circle of men, he said, 'So, everyone's all excited about Cape Town, huh? One would swear all of you were going!' He laughed at his own remark, but the men did not respond. Their eyes remained fixed on the fire, each of them hoping he would not be the one Denker singled out for special treatment.

They had no need to feel threatened; the foreman had already selected his victim. His mouth was a tight line as he stepped around the fire to stand in front of James. He kicked the ground at the young man's feet, sending a spray of soil against his trousers. James raised his head and held Denker's taunting gaze.

'The pup reckons it's his time for visiting the ladies,' Denker said to the group without taking his eyes from James's face. 'It will be a waste, puppy, if you fuck the way you work . . . Do you also stop every five minutes for a drink of water?'

He bellowed with laughter. Some of the men, those who feared him the most, laughed with him. 'Or have you never had it before, pup?' he continued, his huge hands resting on his hips.

James managed to smile up at the big man, but his eyes were cold and hard. 'Oh, I've had it before,' he said calmly, 'and I didn't have to pay for it either. Have you ever had that, Denker?'

There was a sudden hush around the fire. The only sound was the crackling of the flames leaping high into the air, their shadows creating movement where there was none. Amos laid a restraining hand on his friend's arm. 'Leave it there, lad,' he whispered, but James could tell from the flush on Denker's face that he had already gone too far.

The foreman's fists were clenched with rage. 'You hear that?' he said to the men. 'You hear the pup call me?' His thick neck pulled tightly into his shoulders and he glared down at James.

He stepped back quickly to scoop a burning log from the fire with the toe of his boot. He kicked it straight at James, sending a shower of sparks flying on to him and the men seated near by. They scattered when he reeled away, falling on his back. The surprise was still in his eyes when Denker stepped forward to haul him roughly to his feet.

The Dutchman held him easily with one hand while he sent his balled fist smashing into his face. Even through the sudden blinding pain, James felt a tooth crack under the impact. Hot blood gushed from his broken mouth. A moment later, there was a merciless blow to his stomach. He grunted as the breath left his body, and his legs twitched up from the ground while Denker still held him in his grip.

The foreman released him at that moment. He fell down in a crumpled heap, writhing in agony while he tried to regain his breath and focus on what was happening to him.

He heard Denker's voice as if from a distance, taunting him again. Pain racked his bruised ribs, but he turned slowly and pushed himself to his feet. At least one blow, he told himself – something that would hurt the big bastard!

He never got the chance. All he saw was the shift of Denker's boots before a searing pain leaped from his groin to the pit of his stomach as a vicious kick struck his crotch. The sound of the blow was like a fleshy slap on the still night air. The watching men cringed in sympathy when James screamed and fell back in the dust.

'Go to Cape Town, pup,' said Denker, although James could not hear him above the pain roaring through him. 'Go and see how much you're worth with swollen balls!' He spat down on the fallen man.

James rolled over on to his back, his legs curled tightly against his chest. He saw Amos move towards Denker, his face a tight ball of anger. 'No,' he croaked, but Amos did not hear.

Someone else stopped Amos, pulling the lean figure back before he could grab hold of Denker. It was Thomas, one of those who had come from Cape Town with James. 'Leave him to me,' he said softly. 'I've been wanting the bastard for some time now.'

The men stirred with anticipation, for Thomas had the reputation of being a skilled fighter. They watched as he called out to Denker, challenging him. Quickly they formed themselves into a large circle within which the two men could fight. All except Amos had forgotten the injured James who still lay inert on the ground.

Thomas was as tall as Denker, although the foreman was older and outweighed his challenger by more than twenty pounds. Yet Thomas's body was hard and sinewy, and he was tough and fit. His eyes held no fear when Denker turned to wait for him.

The two men leaped at each other as if reacting to some unspoken command. They exchanged a brief flurry of blows before they drew apart to circle each other more warily.

Thomas moved in again. He was very fast, so that even though Denker shifted away his fist shot out twice in rapid succession, piercing through the Dutchman's guard. The blows did not carry Thomas's full weight and strength, but they contained enough force to split Denker's lips.

The fact that Thomas had struck first did more damage than his fist. The circle of men cheered, the sound making Denker's eyes blaze angrily. 'That the best you can do?' he sneered, although he approached Thomas with greater caution now.

The continued shouts of support for Thomas goaded Denker into sudden action. His opponent was still positioned close to him, making it easy for Denker to stomp down with his foot, trapping the younger man's with his own. He lunged up, clamped his hands around Thomas's neck, and jerked the challenger's head forward to meet his own forehead.

The thump of the head butt was sickening, the blow smashing Thomas's nose under the impact. Denker butted again, his own face filled with the other man's blood. Thomas went down heavily as Denker suddenly released his hold on him.

Denker smiled as he wiped the blood from his face. It smeared across his skin, giving him a grotesque appearance in the flickering firelight. 'Get up!' he snarled.

James watched from across the fire, the pain still spurting through his groin. 'Stop them, Amos,' he groaned. 'Denker will kill him.'

Amos shook his head. 'No, Denker won't let it go that far. And this has nothing to do with you or me. It's between the two of them. It's been coming for a long time.'

Thomas pushed himself to his feet, his breath rasping through the shattered remains of his nose. His legs were wobbly when he finally stood upright, but there was plenty of fight left in his eyes. He resumed his stance and circled Denker again, keeping a wary distance from the destructive power of the foreman's hands.

Denker threw out an exploratory blow, but Thomas had recovered sufficiently to avoid it with relative ease. He retaliated with a fast jab of his own, rocking Denker's head back on his shoulders. There was a loud guffaw from the men, the sound of it enraging Denker.

They watched as Denker swayed, then stepped back to regain his balance. 'Finish him, Thomas!' they cried. 'Go in now!'

Thomas moved in hungrily – as Denker knew he would. The foreman staggered back as if he was about to go down, then spread his legs firmly on the ground. As Thomas swung his fist, Denker lunged forward and flung both arms around his torso, pulling him close in a bone-crushing hug.

They stood locked for a brief moment in an eerie embrace, their sweat-covered bodies glistening in the firelight, mated from head to toe in a gruesome illusion of a lovers' dance.

An animal-like cry broke from Denker's shattered lips as he

drew back his head to butt down with all the force he could muster. Thomas's own cry of pain was drowned by the sound of the next butt. And the next.

Denker broke the embrace suddenly. Thomas started to fall like a broken, lifeless doll. Just before he slumped to the ground, Denker reached out and pulled him up by the hair. His fist sank into the unconscious man's ribs, striking again and again, till the watching men could stand it no longer and pulled him away from Thomas.

'Go with the puppy!' shouted Denker, although the unconscious man could not hear him. 'Go back to the city – you're of no use to me here!' He shrugged off the restraining hands and stumbled off towards his tent, wiping his hand across the wounds on his face as he pushed through the circle of stunned men. They waited till the tent flap swung down behind him before they rushed to Thomas's side.

'One day,' James said softly, his voice shaking with anger and hatred as he stared at Denker's tent, 'someone will kill him. I hope I get the chance.'

'Don't even think of it,' said Amos as he helped him to his feet. 'Just stay out of his way from now on.' He placed his arm about James's shoulders and led him slowly to their tent. He laid him gently on his bedroll, then went to the supply tent for an oil lamp which the men were not permitted to keep in their own tents. It was already alight when he returned, and he studied James's broken mouth in the dim light.

'You got off a lot lighter than Thomas,' he said. 'Crushed lips and a broken tooth. Plus some bruised ribs and swollen balls!' He smiled and said, 'Use the time in Cape Town to recover. You and Thomas can look after each other.'

James tried to smile, but the effort sent a fresh stab of pain up the side of his face. 'At least,' he said thickly, 'I won't feel as bad as Thomas when he comes around. Is he badly hurt?'

Amos gave a brief smile. 'I think Thomas has been hurt before. He's a tough lad – he'll pull through. I reckon he'll be a mite uncomfortable on the trip, though.' He reached across to his own bed and unrolled his blanket, then spread it across James. 'Try and get some sleep. The wagon leaves at midday only, so Denker will expect to see you on the job tomorrow morning.'

James reached down and gingerly touched his swollen testicles. They felt twice their normal size. He withdrew his hand, promising himself that one day he would take revenge on Denker.

When at last he fell asleep, it was amidst a haze of pain and hatred.

Thomas never reached Cape Town.

He died on the second day of their journey to Cape Town, his lungs filling with blood from a puncture caused by his shattered ribs and the jolting of the wagon.

His could have been a lonely grave on the desolate veld, dug barely deep enough to escape the keen sense of smell of predators, for there were things to be done in Cape Town and the men were anxious to be on their way. They would have been satisfied with a hurried prayer and a moment of respectful silence.

'We will bury Thomas properly,' James said firmly. He glanced around the bleak terrain before pointing to a narrow ravine formed by the base of two irregularly shaped hills. 'Over there,' he said, 'in the shade. A man can rest there.' No one argued with him, for they saw the bitter anger on the young man's face.

'Don't blame yourself,' one of them said. 'Thomas didn't die fighting for you. Fighting was his way and I don't think he'd have been too surprised to know that it was the end of him.'

'I know, but it's a waste.' The men nodded, not comprehending the full meaning of his words. He spoke not only of the unnecessary death, but also of the unaccomplished life of the young man. Thomas was one of the many trapped into the soul-destroying labour from which men dreamed of escape, yet to which they returned each time to grapple with the earth once again. It was a sordid living to which too many men became too easily accustomed, their senses and ambitions dulled by time and the false comradeship shared by those others facing a desolate future. It was a path to despair, and it was *that* waste which angered James. The broken body of Thomas would at least be spared that discovery.

The men walked beside the wagon as the driver led the mules to the ravine. They found it preferable to stagger across the uneven veld than to witness the sight of the rumpled corpse bouncing along on its final journey. James was the first to grab a shovel when they arrived at the designated spot.

'Who'll say a prayer?' he asked when the grave was dug deep enough to his satisfaction.

The men glanced uneasily at each other. 'Bayley will,' someone said. 'He's buried people before. His own wife and children.'

They studied the heavy-set man with new eyes. 'On the eastern border,' he said in answer to the unspoken question. He had no need to say more, for each man there knew of the on-going conflict between the settlers and the black tribes.

James smiled sadly. After all this time, they still knew so little about each other. 'We'd appreciate it, Bayley.'

They placed Thomas gently in the grave, covering his face with his sweat-stained felt hat. The loose soil thudded dully on to his body. When they were done, they formed a low mound of tightly packed soil on top of the grave and stacked a small pile of stones at its head. The men stood back, removed their hats and formed a circle. A sudden gust of wind drove through the ravine, stirring up dust which blew across them and causing tears which otherwise they would not have shown.

Bayley squinted at the intense blue sky peeking beyond the rim of the hills. 'O Lord,' he started, cleared his throat, and fell silent. The men watched him, then lowered their gaze to the grave.

'O Lord,' continued Bayley, 'we bring You Thomas the fighter . . . I know him by no other name, Lord.'

'Southey,' someone whispered, 'I think.'

The remark did not unsettle Bayley. His voice gained strength when he said, 'Thomas was a young man, Lord, and it is not right that we should bring him here, to seek entry into Your home so early in his life.' He stopped, stared at the grave, then again raised his eyes to the sky.

'But Your ways are strange, Lord, and I think Thomas would have understood, for he lived by the rules of a fighting man.'

'A good fighter was Thomas,' someone muttered.

'Yes, Lord,' said Bayley, 'and Thomas now seeks to fight in Your army. Grant him entry, we beg of You . . . forgive him whatever sins he has . . . I cannot now recall any which strike me.' The men nodded in agreement.

Bayley cleared his throat before continuing. 'Look after this man, Lord, for he was not a spiteful person. Thomas fought with a smile on his face, not with the wish to destroy others. And forgive the man who—'

'No!'

The men stared at James. 'No forgiveness for Denker,' he repeated. 'End your prayer, Bayley.'

The stocky man seemed disturbed by the request, but he nodded and said, 'You heard that, Lord. We leave it to You to decide. We give You Thomas . . .'

'Amen,' said James and put his hat back on his head. 'Let's get going.'

The men seemed relieved it was over. 'Good words, Bayley,' someone said, as they followed James back to the wagon.

He was about to clamber aboard when he spotted two wild ostriches a little distance away. They seemed to be performing a dance, an intricate waltz of majestic beauty on the silent veld. 'Mating dance,' explained Bayley. 'The drab one is the female.'

James watched a while longer, remembering the soft, full feathers which had been his bed on his first night in the country. 'When they dance like that,' he said, 'they cease to be ugly.' The scene was a stark contrast to the repugnance of death they had just witnessed.

'Get a move on, James,' the men complained. 'Cape Town is waiting!'

He jumped on to the back of the wagon. It was time for the living, he thought as he stared at the forlorn mound which marked Thomas's grave. 'And live I shall,' he muttered, hearing the men around him talk of what they would do with their week in Cape Town. They had already pushed Thomas from their minds, yet James clung to the sight of the grave long after the wagon had rolled around the next hill. He would keep the vision with him as a reminder of the trap from which he had to escape.

CHAPTER FIVE

The August wind curled in from the Atlantic ocean to sweep across the bay, slashing at the city and its inhabitants before beating furiously against the slopes of Table Mountain. The air was filled with dust, reminding James and the others of the open Karoo plains.

Their wagon rolled into the yard between the huts of Kenrick Construction. The men grabbed their sling bags and jumped down thankfully, eager to shed the shackles of their hated life.

The clerk whom James had seen on his first visit to the offices stepped out of the main hut to scowl at the men, his hands on his hips in pathetic emulation of his boss. 'You be sure to be back here on Saturday,' he warned them, 'else Mr Denker will take care of you.' He stepped hurriedly back when one of the men spat at his feet.

James went up to him, enjoying the flicker of fear he saw in the clerk's eyes as he climbed the few short steps leading to the hut. He threw a brown cotton bag at the man's feet and said, 'There'll be one less man reporting on Saturday – your boss saw to that.' He nudged the bag closer. 'That belonged to Thomas. Denker beat him so badly he died on the way here.'

The clerk stared down at the bag, appearing to draw back from the dismal reminder of a man who had once stood proud and tall. 'Pick it up,' James growled and kicked the bag towards him.

'What must I do with it?' the clerk whined, yet he did as

he was told, holding the bag gingerly between his ink-stained fingers.

'Find out if Thomas had any family. Everything he owned is in that bag.' The clerk seemed about to argue, then shut his mouth, went inside and placed the bag beside his desk. James followed him.

'When you find someone,' he said, 'and I'll check with you before we go back,' he added in a threatening tone, 'don't tell them how Thomas died. Say he got sick or something.' The clerk nodded.

It was James who bullied the clerk into paying the men their accumulated wages without further delay, waiting till they were all satisfied before he took his turn. No one queried his assumption of leadership; since they had buried Thomas on the lonely plains, he had stood slightly apart from them, lost in his own thoughts, distancing himself from their increasing excitement as the wagon rolled ever closer to Cape Town.

What had occupied James's thoughts for most of the journey was not Thomas and what had happened, but the emptiness the young man had left behind. Would the others still remember him after a few weeks? Perhaps, but then it would be fleetingly, when the men spoke of the great fight. In between, they would be too busy with their own kind of survival, fighting the depression which always threatened to overwhelm one as the seemingly endless struggle with the earth went on day after day. They would carve at the ground, hating the dust and the heat and the sting of the sun. The nights, too, would become a hated thing, a too short respite for tired, tortured bodies, a brief interlude before facing their labour again. And always the sun, the blasted sun.

After only three months, he knew the men well enough to recognise the trap they had woven for themselves. They all spoke of the day they would be free from people like Denker, the day they would become their own men with a farm and family to care for. The talk would go on night after night, till a man was due for his week's break in Cape Town. Then the excitement of pending freedom would oust all other thoughts from his mind, shifting his dreams to some future spot. The long days would somehow become less punishing, with the short nights being counted off in impatient anticipation. At the end of it all, they returned to take up their tools once again, to renew their ties with the family of men which was their harsh reality. It was only the older ones, men like Amos, who had ceased their dreaming and surrendered to their own kind of acceptance. It was a fate which James was now determined to avoid.

The men in the hut were chatting excitedly, their pockets filled with money which should have been destined for the attainment of their dreams, but which would now be greedily wasted on alluring freedom. One of them watched James count his wages, then said, 'You going to report the fight to the authorities?'

He shook his head as they fled the hut and stepped eagerly into the street. He declined the invitation to accompany them when someone suggested a visit to a house known for its friendly and talented ladies.

'I have to see an old friend,' he explained, smiling as the men jostled and teased him. There was no need to add that his plans did not include women.

Their excited chatter faded into the distance as he headed in the direction of the harbour.

Pat Stanton was at the back of the warehouse when James entered it. An African labourer led him between rows of goods stacked almost to the roof.

The old man was perched at the top of a rickety ladder as he stared down at his visitor in the dim light. Sudden recognition brought a wide grin to his face. 'Will you look at him?' he exclaimed. 'I meet a boy, and he visits me a man. James Quenton – I had a feeling I'd be seeing more of you!' He stepped down gingerly and shook his hand. 'Come,' he said, placing an arm around his shoulders, 'let's get into the sunlight so I can take a proper look at you.' Pat gave his bulging biceps a hard squeeze. 'Well, it seems you've become accustomed to the work.'

'I hate it, Pat, as you said I would. I've seen what it does to the souls of men, and I won't let it do the same to me. That's why I came to you. I want your help.'

Pat's eyes were thoughtful when he turned away to study the heaving ocean. 'No ships today,' he said softly, his words whipped away by the wind. 'They're out there in the bay, hoping the gale will abate. I think they'll have a long wait.' He led James back inside the shelter of the warehouse.

'What help can I give you, lad?' he asked after he had shut the door behind them. His short laugh was harsh when he added, 'I helped you into work you hate – hope I can do better this time.'

'When I spent that night here, you spoke to me about ostriches, Pat. You said—'

'You see any out your way?' the old man interrupted. 'The price of feathers just went up again. More and more farmers are turning to ostriches now. Their plumes will be worth their weight in gold one day, mark my words.'

'I hope you're right, Pat, because I want my share of that gold. That's why I need your help.'

The old man studied the floor as a fresh smile tugged at the corners of his eyes. 'You want me to introduce you to the feather buyers I told you about, is that it?'

James nodded. 'I want to learn all there is to know, so I think they'd be a good place to start. There're plenty of ostrich farms out where we're working. I want to visit them as well.'

'I'm sure one of the buyers could give you a letter of introduction, but you'll need more than that in the end.'

'I know. One has to have capital to get started, but I'll get that. Somehow I'll get that.'

'I'm sure you will, lad. With your looks, you could even marry it!'

James laughed with him. 'I might just do that,' he said. 'You'll introduce me, then? To one of the buyers?'

'Aye, that I can do. But where'll you find the time to visit the farmers?'

'We don't work nights. And the only good thing about that bastard Dutchman is he doesn't allow any work on Sundays. It's probably the only thing in the Bible that Denker lives up to.'

Pat eased himself to his feet. 'You're going back at the end of the week?'

'I have to. My contract doesn't expire until the end of December.'

'And then?'

'I won't be signing up again. I'll not let Denker hold sway over any more time in my life.'

Pat reached out and lightly touched his arm. 'There'll always be Denkers in this world, James – or are you planning to escape them all?'

'With the help of ostriches I might. I intend to be my own man, and I want to do it now, before someone like Denker breaks me. With money and power behind me, the likes of him will never get close enough.'

The old man smiled. 'You'll stay the night?'

'I'd be grateful.'

'Good. Now go get cleaned up. You'll have to look respectable when we meet the feather buyers tomorrow. Most of them are Jewish gentlemen, and they won't take kindly to a money-hungry young man with dirt behind his ears!'

James rubbed a finger across the grime of the journey. 'When I'm clean, will you let me sleep on those ostrich feathers again?'

'It's the least I can do for a future feather baron,' replied Pat as he started for the back of the warehouse.

The feather buyers were amused by the young man's ambition, yet that did not stop them from sharing their knowledge with him. Theirs was a new industry, one in which they regarded themselves as much pioneers as the farmers who bred the source of the wealth now flowing into the colony.

As such they were proud to flaunt the depth of their knowledge, but after a while they came to appreciate the keen insight James displayed. His incisive questions soon changed their amusement to respect and their informal discussions to serious lectures. Most of them operated from Grahamstown, travelling the vast distance to the ostrich farms of the Little Karoo to gather their wares for export. However, Cape Town was still the place they visited at regular intervals, being the gateway to the international markets which kept their activities thriving.

One of them, an elderly man named Morris Sivrosky, took a particular interest in the apprentice, as they all referred to James. He visited Sivrosky three times, lured back by the promise of an introduction to a farmer in the Karoo, not far from where he worked on the road.

He returned to the old man's office on his last day in Cape Town. 'Jan Steenkamp,' said Sivrosky, 'is the only person I can think of with the patience to answer all your questions – you're worse than a young child!' He handed James a brief note he had written for the farmer. 'Give Steenkamp my compliments, and tell him to make a note of your name.'

'Why?' James stared blankly at the letter, once again regretting his lack of education.

'Because, my young friend, I've seen your kind before, and you usually get what you want. I've a feeling we'll do business one day.'

James smiled at him. 'We no doubt shall.' He thanked Sivrosky and hastened back to the docks to take his leave of Pat Stanton before reporting at the offices of Kenrick Construction.

Morris Sivrosky was thoughtful when the door closed behind the young man. He recalled what he had said to the youngster about seeing his kind before. The only problem, thought Sivrosky, was that they were not always *good* men. Time would tell, he decided, time would tell.

James was at Jan Steenkamp's farm almost every night, sometimes creeping back to his tent in the early hours of the morning. Amos was amazed at how he managed to keep going during the day, kept on his feet by the burning desire to escape the constraints of the drudgery which the others had come to accept. It was as though his goal helped him to cope with the arduous conditions.

Jan Steenkamp, a burly man in his forties, welcomed James and his enthusiasm. In a fledgeling industry with almost unlimited potential, there was no need to guard against newcomers and their thirst for knowledge or desire to share in the growing wealth. Steenkamp opened his home and his mind to the youngster, filling him with facts till at last he found James asking questions even he could not answer.

At last the road construction moved so far ahead as to make it impossible for James to continue with his nocturnal missions, limiting his visits to Sundays. It no longer mattered; he had acquired most of the knowledge he needed, so that now Steenkamp could take him into the fields by day to teach him the practical implementation of his lessons.

On one such Sunday late in November, he appeared at the farm before first light, as instructed. The farmer gave neither a reason nor an explanation for the request. When James knocked on the farmhouse door, he was handed a mug of steaming coffee. 'Come,' was all that Steenkamp said as James finished the hot brew.

The farmer led him past a small paddock with high stone walls where some of the young ostrich chicks were being kept, through a fenced-off field where a hen, anxious about the safety of her offspring, advanced in a rapid, shuffling movement, hissing her anger as she gave a menacing flutter of her wings. James was relieved that Steenkamp carried a branch of thorn bush with him; he had learned that an ostrich, ever mindful of its eyes, would retreat when the thorns were thrust towards its face. It was about the only suitable defence a man had.

He was even more relieved that the more aggressive cock was still positioned atop the eggs in its nest, using its darker colours for camouflage while the remaining night still clung to the land. The hen would relieve him soon, her dull brown feathers harmonising with the bleakness of the daytime surroundings. And so they would rotate duty during the incubation period of the eggs.

The hen had stoped some distance away from them, although she still hissed and fluttered her wings. Steenkamp glanced at the bird. 'I'm sure the males are pleased the hens can make no other sound but hiss. Imagine if our women were the same!' James smiled with him, thinking of the stout Mrs Steenkamp who seemed to be very much in command of her Jan.

'Where are you taking me, Jan?' he asked as he followed the big man over a stone wall into another field which he knew stretched as far as the eye could see.

'Why do you English ask so many questions?' replied Steenkamp. 'Wait, and you'll see.'

Steenkamp kept close to the wall as he led them into the field. After a few minutes, he halted beneath a clump of thorn bush and sat down. He indicated that James should do the same.

The two men sat in silence in the growing Karoo morning, the farmer smug with his secret as he stoked a foul-smelling pipe, the younger man amused and impatient at what awaited him. The only sounds were the occasional booming grunts of the ostriches: two short bellows, followed by a third, longer roar.

'Am I allowed to talk?' asked James after a while.

'Talk? You mean you want to ask questions, don't you?' He chuckled and sucked at his obstinate pipe. '*Ja*, you can talk if you want to.'

'This field . . .' James started, waving his hand at the empty expanse. 'Aren't you worried your ostriches will wander off and never come back?' He knew that a twenty-mile walk was a mere stroll for a full-grown ostrich, especially when feeding. They would peck as they moved onwards, never stopping for long.

'They'll come back,' Steenkamp replied confidently. 'They get used to the bone meal I feed them. Besides, there are the nests and the chicks to return to.'

'But I've seen chicks with the older birds when they go out in the fields. Don't they get lost?'

Steenkamp shook his head. 'The males take them with them in a sort of nursery school. They look after them. I've even seen the entire flock return along with my sheep in the evenings. Good herders, those birds.'

The farmer reached out and gripped his arm. 'What is it?' whispered James.

Steenkamp grinned in the gathering light. 'Won't be long now,' he said. 'I can hear Klaas and the others.'

James cocked his head to one side and heard it too, the voices of the coloured labourers as they started to prepare for the day. 'Just what have you got planned for me, Jan?'

The farmer chuckled as he stuffed the still-glowing pipe into his shirt pocket. 'It's time for your final lesson, my impatient young friend.'

'My *final* lesson? There's so much I still have to learn!'

'Yes,' said Steenkamp, 'but there's not much more I can teach you. The rest you will learn when you start your own farm. It is the only way.'

'And this final lesson, then? What is that going to be?'

Steenkamp gave a strange smile before he laid a hand gently on James's shoulder. 'It is one the ostriches themselves will give you,' he said, his expression serious now. 'It is perhaps the one thing your many questions never touched upon.'

James stared at the growing ring of light as the sun, still gentle in its touch, reached out across the expanse of the field. He said nothing as he waited for Steenkamp to continue.

'You have learned fast,' the farmer said, 'very fast. Because you're young and eager to start off on your own. But not once, James, not once did you ever ask about the birds themselves. It was always about how you could use them to your own end, what you needed to know about them in order to make the money you so desperately seek. You must learn to love them, for they'll become your family which will grow with you. We'll all continue to learn about them and from them, so that further prosperity will come. But the ostrich himself has a right to share in that prosperity. Love them, James, for what they will still give you.'

James stared at Steenkamp's earnest face, thinking that he had never seen the good-natured farmer as serious. For the first time he wondered whether he was capable of love. When last had he given any thought to his mother and what had become of her? Perhaps he was so anxious to escape the kind of life his father had been trapped into that he was incapable of loving anything but his own dreams.

Steenkamp's hand on his arm brought him back to the noises coming from the adjoining paddock. 'Soon,' the farmer said. They could hear the voices of the labourers clearly now, and James knew they were herding the group of ostrich chicks towards the field. Steenkamp kept birds of more or less the same age in separate paddocks, each year selecting special males and females for breeding purposes. Those pairs were then penned in smaller camps.

'The dance of the fallen angels,' muttered Steenkamp.

'The what?'

'The fallen angels. It's a name given by those who believe the ostrich is a degenerate, a running bird that lost the art of flying by using its legs rather than its wings.' He reached for his pipe and stuck it, unlit, into his mouth. 'Now you'll see them dance, a magnificent dance of pure ecstasy. Love them for this, James, if for nothing else.'

James knelt down, his body filled with a sense of anticipation. He had already seen the beautiful ballet of mature birds in courtship, as well as the wild antics of young chicks, scarcely able to stand, yet instinctively emulating their elders. It was obvious Steenkamp regarded what was about to happen as something special.

They heard the scraping of the gate linking the paddock to the field. The next moment there was a flurry of movement and a swishing sound as a hundred or more young ostriches fled through the aperture to head for the open field. They moved in a tight pack, yet spreading all the while like an impi of Zulu whose movement was one of cohesive tactic. There was no leadership in the case of the chicks, merely a mass of light brown, mottled colour moving at a great pace out of captivity, running towards what only they knew they were after.

They stopped suddenly after a few hundred yards, as though some mass instinct had decided they could no longer postpone their moment of celebration. There was still a flutter of brown movement towards the back of the pack as they formed into their tight concentration again.

James held his breath, his heart thumping within his chest.

He watched, his eyes stretched for fear he would miss something. As if by some unspoken command, the young birds raised their wings. There was a moment's hesitation, slight and insignificant in the scheme of the day, before the dance of the fallen angels began.

The gathering of birds started to move, a motion so erratic it could only be called hysterical. Or ecstatic. They whirled with their young wings aloft, spinning madly, dizzily, till some started to fall to the ground from giddiness.

My God, thought James, they're worshipping the new day! Or was it life itself? On and on the dancing went, birds falling, struggling upright to continue their frenzy, only to fall down again. The two men watched the mêlée amid a growing cloud of dust; James with a new insight, Steenkamp as one who would never tire of the sight.

Some adult birds had also roamed closer now, and they too joined in, albeit with a greater measure of dignity. Theirs was a synchronised waltzing movement, an impressive display of mature, dazzling plumage.

'Damn!' said Steenkamp suddenly, jumping swiftly to his feet. James felt the magic slip from the moment. He followed the farmer as he ran out towards the flock.

The birds scattered at the approach of the men. They moved a short distance away, where they seemed to settle into a semblance of normality. The dance of the fallen angels was done for the day.

'What is it?' cried James as he watched Steenkamp stoop into the dust which still floated above the ground. Then he saw it: a young bird lay struggling in the dirt.

'Broken leg,' the farmer explained, and James saw the bird's agony reflected on Steenkamp's face. 'Damn! This is the third one this week.' He picked the chick up in his arms and handed it over to one of the labourers who had run closer.

'Can it be mended?'

The farmer shook his head. 'Most of the birds I've lost have been through accidents. Usually broken legs. You saw the crazy things fall to the ground when they get dizzy. Sometimes they break their legs on the fences or something. I've only lost five or so through natural causes.'

It was clear that Steenkamp was upset at the loss of another ostrich. For a moment James wondered whether it was the potential loss of profit which disturbed him, or whether it was the love he had spoken of earlier. The answer came when Steenkamp turned to him and said, 'That chick will not have died in vain, James, if you felt something of what I spoke of earlier. To love life so much that you will risk injury and death, just to dance, deserves love in return.' He placed a heavy hand on the young man's shoulder and started to lead him back to the house.

'The bird will not die in vain, Jan,' he replied, feeling the hand tighten on his shoulder.

CHAPTER SIX

It was a day like any other.

Overhead the gathering clouds cajoled the cruel December afternoon with a vague promise of relief as the men fought with the dry, clinging dust. They glanced expectantly at the darkening sky, praying anxiously for the moisture to crack from the heavens. They knew it would not come; too many days of promise had fallen prey to the powerful spite of the sun. Yet they watched, seeing the clouds flee to a distant horizon where other men waited, watching too, at once hopeful and doubting.

James slammed the tip of his pick into the defiant earth and felt the tool grip there, challenging his tortured muscles to a further bout in the fight for supremacy.

'Your contract comes up next month.' Amos's voice was as welcome a relief as the brief shade provided by the desperate clouds. 'You going to sign up again?'

James let the pick fall to the ground and wiped a grimy arm across his forehead. 'No,' he replied, blinking his eyes against the sting of his sweat, 'I'll be leaving with the next wagon.'

'What'll you do, lad? You need more time before starting your plans.'

James's laugh was bitter. 'Time? I've seen what too much time does to men. That's truer here than most places.' He gripped the shaft of the pick, then let it fall to the ground again. 'It's not just idle talk, Amos – I'll find the money I need in Cape Town. Somehow I'll find it. I'll have no more of Denker lording it over me.'

51

Amos studied his friend, impressed as always by the determination in his voice. He recalled the night, almost four months ago, when James had returned from Cape Town, his face flushed with excitement after meeting the feather buyers.

The young man's goal had not come as much of a surprise to Amos, for he had known of his fascination with the ostriches. All of them had spoken of the new industry, of the riches to be gained from what had been once a wild creature of the plains. Yet it was a wealth which belonged to others, a richness far beyond the means and dreams of road workers. 'I wish you luck, lad, but think about it one last time. If you go, Denker will never have you back.'

'Denker will never see me again, Amos – that's all I need to think about.' He saw Amos suddenly grab his shovel and knew without turning that Denker stood behind them.

'Less talk, pup,' the big man growled. 'I don't know why I haven't booted you out of here before now.'

'Perhaps you've grown fond of me, Denker.'

The foreman threw back his head and let out a loud laugh which quickly changed into a spiteful grin when he kicked James harshly on the ankle. 'You've a short memory, pup,' he snarled. 'The only reason you're not spitting blood right now is 'cause I like a fight to be worth while.'

Even though he knew he was risking a beating, Amos could not stop himself saying, 'Like Thomas?'

For a moment it seemed Denker would do just that, then he shrugged his massive shoulders and spat on the sand. 'And you're too old to be any fun,' he said, turning back to James. 'My man in the office sent me a note . . . Said you didn't want the fight reported. Trying to curry favour with me, Quenton?'

It was the first time they had heard Denker make any reference to Thomas's death. When he was told the news on the return of the wagon from Cape Town, he shrugged and said, 'You bring a replacement with?'

James glared at him now and said, 'The only reason there was no reporting of Thomas's death was because someone else, not the authorities, should have the pleasure of taking care of you one day.'

Denker lashed out and kicked him again, on the shin this time. 'It'll never be you, pup.'

'Pups grow up to be dogs, Denker,' he said through gritted teeth.

'There are ways of taming dogs,' came the menacing reply, although there was a flicker – of what, James could not tell – in the foreman's eyes before he turned and walked off.

'Take care,' whispered Amos as he stooped to his task. 'He'll try to take you once he learns you're not renewing your contract.'

James nodded but did not reply. He had already said everything there was to say about Denker. He looked up quickly when Amos touched his arm, expecting to see Denker heading for them again. But Amos's gaze was fixed on the horizon, where a thin plume of dust tickled the empty blue sky. 'Another dust storm?'

'No, it's company. No sluggish wagon either.'

The other men had also ceased working. Company was rare, usually limited to the occasional farmer passing by, but they would drive at a modest pace, accustomed to the heat and the endless landscape.

The dust cloud moved steadily closer, although Amos judged it to be a good half-hour's ride away. The men resumed their work, stopping every now and then to check on the travellers' progress. There was no longer any doubt that the wagon was heading in their direction.

After a while, a smaller column of dust pulled away from the bigger cloud. It was not long before a loaded wagon, drawn by four horses, drew to a halt near the labourers. Two men jumped down from the driver's bench.

Denker moved rapidly closer and shook their hands briefly, his broad forehead creased with concern.

'I should have guessed,' muttered Amos and spat into the dust. 'The old man's come to check on progress for himself.'

James's glance was quizzical. 'What are you going on about?'

'Sir Anthony Kenrick, the bastard who owns this company . . . the man who grows rich on our labour. He's probably on his way to Grahamstown.'

The new arrivals stood talking with Denker, youngish men clad in ordinary working clothes. 'No, not one of them,' said Amos when James looked their way. 'They're the old man's advance party, probably checking with Denker as to where they should set up camp.'

Denker spun round just then. 'Bring your tools,' he shouted. 'You as well,' he added, pointing to three other men standing near by.

They were sent to a spot about a half-mile from their own camp, where for a while there was frantic activity as they cleared the ground of scrub and large stones. It was some time before the rest of Sir Anthony's convoy arrived, the first a small buggy, drawn by two of the most beautiful horses James had ever seen, and the other a light wagon carrying further supplies. The buggy's canvas top had once been white but was now streaked brown by layers of dust. The driver sat high up, partly protected by a canvas strip which extended over his seat. Behind him, comfortably ensconced in leather seats, sat Sir Anthony Kenrick. James had no chance to get a good look at him before he and the others were ordered to unload the second wagon.

He helped lift the large canvas roll of Sir Anthony's tent, staring in disbelief at its size as it was spread out on the ground. It was bigger than the one that he shared with his fellow workers.

Together with Amos he dragged the roll of canvas to the appointed space beneath the thorn trees. They had to pass the buggy where Sir Anthony sat, as though he preferred the stifling heat beneath the canvas canopy to the direct sunlight beyond it. James could not stop himself from staring; he wanted to get a good look at this man of wealth and power, the kind of man he intended to become one day. Sir Anthony returned his gaze, a mild curiosity in his eyes as if amused by the young labourer's open interest in him.

While the rest of the men busied themselves with getting the tent erected, James and Amos dug a trench for a toilet. They sited it at a respectable distance from the tent, behind a natural rise in the ground.

'What else can you tell me about him?' asked James as he loosened the earth with his pick.

Amos shrugged. 'I can only tell you what I've heard.'

'Tell.'

'He's in his fifties. Owns this construction company and a few other ventures besides. Lives in a big mansion in Cape Town.'

'How did he make his money?'

'So that's what interests you!' said Amos and laughed. 'I've no idea how he made his money, James. He probably inherited it, but he's used it wisely. I'm told he's a shrewd investor, that he's not afraid to take chances. Perhaps he's just one of those bastards who seem to make money easily.'

James stared at the tent where Sir Anthony was making himself comfortable. 'And like all men with money,' he said softly, 'he always wants more of it.'

They worked on in silence, although James's eyes kept returning to the white tent where Sir Anthony rested.

There were few men seated around the fire that night. The harsh December heat had sapped their energy, and most had crawled into their tents after an inadequate supper.

James lingered beside the leaping flames, occasionally joining in the conversation of the others, although his thoughts lay elsewhere. He stood up after a while, bade the men good-night, and headed for the last row of tents. Before reaching his own tent, he veered off into the dark veld, as though he was going to relieve himself. In case anyone was watching, he went through the necessary motions and scrutinised the camp till he was satisfied that things had settled down for the night.

There was little moonlight as he made his way cautiously across the uneven veld, moving in a wide circle around the camp. Every now and then he stopped to listen and watch Denker's tent for signs of activity.

He stopped for the last time when he was a hundred yards from the group of three tents that made up the camp of Sir Anthony and his entourage. Three men sat huddled around a fire between the two smaller tents, the low drone of their voices carrying dully to him. He sank on to his haunches to wait.

A lamp glowed dimly inside Sir Anthony's tent, and once or twice James saw a flicker of movement as someone passed between the lamp and the canvas. There was a constant trembling within his stomach now, for he was risking everything by being there. Yet tonight was his only chance: he had learned that Sir Anthony would be leaving for Grahamstown the next day.

Another movement, in the veld this time, made him lower himself to the ground. A figure appeared beside the fire. Even at that distance there was no mistaking the burly form of Denker. The skin on James's neck prickled with fear, till he saw the firelight gleam on the bottle in the foreman's hand. He knew then that Denker was not searching for him.

The men stood up in welcome, Denker's gravelly voice carrying clearly on the Karoo night air. They stood talking for a few moments before they all trooped off towards one of the tents. James stayed where he was till he heard the clink of glass and the sound of their laughter, signs that they were settling down to enjoy Denker's offering.

He smiled into the night; it was the first time he had reason to thank the foreman for anything.

Sir Anthony yawned and glanced at the pocket watch lying on the camp table beside his stretcher. He told himself he was getting too old for these long journeys. As well as too fat, he thought, studying his massive girth as he settled down on to the stretcher. He closed the large accounts book he had been scrutinising and placed it inside a trunk containing other business documents.

His annual journey to the frontiers of the expanding country had always been an enjoyable experience for him. It was a chance to escape the confines of Cape Town's social life, the irritations caused by his wife and daughter, and the clamour for attention by the young men jockeying for position in his companies. Apart from that, his travels allowed him to check for himself his many business ventures, to establish new ones as the country opened up, and to satisfy a lust for adventure that still thrived within him.

Sir Anthony had great faith in the new country. He liked to think his vision – and his money – played a role in shaping it. It saddened him, therefore, to realise that this year's journey might be his last, that soon he would have to depend on his sycophantic young men to undertake them on his behalf.

He sighed as he recalled earlier years when he had ventured out on horseback alone, his saddle-bags filled with ready cash for the many opportunities he discovered on his way, relying on his wits and brute strength to protect and advance himself. Nowadays, he took his protection and comforts with him; lawyers to administer the purchase of land and property were summoned when needed. Sir Anthony thought ruefully that his young men would no doubt be taking the lawyers with them in years to come.

He reached for a cigar, then changed his mind; he needed rest more than a good smoke. A long and tiring journey lay ahead the next day before they reached Oudtshoorn, *en route* to Grahamstown. It was his first visit to the town. He hoped that Abraham Isaacs, the lawyer he had summoned from George, the closest town of reasonable size, would already be there, and that he had performed the necessary investigations. Sir Anthony was convinced that the ostrich industry would continue to flourish and Oudtshoorn develop along with it. That would mean rocketing land values – as well as a tidy profit for those who bought at present prices. He had instructed Isaacs to search for the best properties and gauge the owners' willingness to sell.

The sudden rustle of the tent flap startled him. His fright quickly changed to annoyance when he saw the young man's head pop through the opening. 'What do you think you're doing here?' he growled, heaving himself to his feet. What were his retainers up to? They should never have allowed one of the labourers to get into the camp! 'How dare you!' he snapped in angry defiance, deciding he would take care of the intruder himself.

James was right inside now. He held out his palms in a

plea. 'I don't mean you any harm, Sir Anthony,' he started. 'Please . . . I need to talk to you – don't alert your men! Just a few minutes . . . please.'

Sir Anthony stopped. Something in the youngster's voice quelled the outrage he felt at the disturbance. He had been approached by labourers before, usually to complain about wages or their treatment, yet no one had ever risked dismissal by sneaking into his tent at night. 'You're the young one,' he said, remembering the way James had stared at him on his arrival that afternoon. There had been a gleam in the young man's eyes – not the usual flame of resentment – which told him this was no ordinary labourer. He felt a sense of curiosity replace his earlier indignation, so that he was quite relaxed as he settled back on to the stretcher. 'What is it you wish to discuss with me? It must be important if you're prepared to risk Denker's wrath to come here. It'd better be no tale of woe!'

'I have a business proposition for you,' James blurted out. 'One that'll make us both rich men.'

Sir Anthony's vast stomach started to shake with laughter. 'Rich? I am already rich, you young fool!'

'One can never be rich enough,' countered James.

'Go on.' Sir Anthony listened in silence while James spoke of the ostrich industry and the money-making opportunity it offered. Sir Anthony let him talk without interruption, comparing what was being said to what he himself knew about the farming activities. He could not help being impressed when James told of how he had spent his leave in Cape Town, and of his further education on Steenkamp's farm. Nor could he deny that the young man had acquired a wealth of knowledge.

'The demand is steadily growing,' continued James, 'but so are the number of breeders. The ones who get in now will be the ones who make the most of the boom when it comes.'

'The boom? You think prices will continue to rise?'

'I do. More and more markets are being opened up throughout the world. Prices will double within ten years.'

Sir Anthony stroked his greying whiskers and studied his uninvited guest. 'This is all very interesting,' he said slowly, 'but you haven't spelled out your proposition. Where do you fit into all this – more importantly, where do I?'

'You provide the capital for a farming venture.'

'Ah! And you?'

'The knowledge and the labour. I'll work day and night if I have to, but I must have the capital to get started.'

'Hmm. How much?'

James took a deep breath. 'We'd need around ten hectares of land to start off with – we can lease that – at least three pairs of breeding birds, some outhouses and sundry equipment. Plus some capital to keep the venture going till we show a profit. Around five thousand pounds in total, I'd say.' He swallowed loudly and waited.

Sir Anthony did not bat an eyelid. 'Around five thousand, you'd say?'

'That should be enough to start off with.'

'Bloody hell – your propositions don't come cheap, do they, boy?'

'Wealth seldom does,' James replied softly, sounding as though he knew all about such things. 'It'll take about a year before we show any return, so the bigger we start, the bigger the rewards will be.'

'You're mighty free with your "we", aren't you? It's *my* money you're talking about.'

'It means nothing without my labour.'

His response made the older man raise one eyebrow. 'And just how do you propose to divide these returns you so confidently predict?'

'Sixty per cent for you, forty for me.'

The older man's snort reverberated round the tent. 'You're a brash young man – why should I risk my money with you? There're many experienced farmers I could invest in.'

James gave a slow smile. 'Because I would work harder than any of them. They've already made their money – I still hunger for mine.'

Sir Anthony's mind raced. Invest in ostriches? He had already decided on buying up land, so why not take it a step further? He juggled the risks in his mind, for he did not part easily with his money – especially to strange young men with ideas beyond their station. Yet he had gambled before and always come out ahead. Very often it had involved a great deal more than five thousand pounds. Besides, there was something about the youngster which intrigued him.

'The division is ninety per cent for me, ten for you,' he said at last, 'and don't even try to argue with me. I'll be keeping you alive for a full year while you look after my investment.' He did not miss the satisfied gleam that sprang into James's eyes. He'll do, thought Sir Anthony, satisfied he had made the right decision.

James eagerly thrust out his hand. 'We're partners then?'

Sir Anthony kept his own tightly behind his back. 'I don't *have* partners, young man,' he said stiffly. 'And before you get any further ideas about my money, let me assure you I'll have a very capable lawyer looking after my affairs. He'll take care of any financial transactions that need to be made. You understand?'

'Of course, Sir Anthony. There's one other thing, though.'

'And what would that be?'

'We have to situate our venture in Oudtshoorn. The soil is rich and loamy – ideal for ostriches – with the right kind of pebbles for them to swallow. Irrigation is—'

'Young man, if I suspected you were thinking of any place but Oudtshoorn, we wouldn't have this . . . partnership, as you call it. Don't for one moment think I'd have let you talk me into this if I wasn't already well informed on the breeding of ostriches.'

James smiled disarmingly. 'When do you want me to start?'

'You already have. Your first task is to get to sleep right away, and to let me have mine. We leave for Oudtshoorn at dawn.'

'I'll be ready.'

'You'll ride on one of the supply wagons. Good-night, young – what the devil is your name?'

'Quenton. James Quenton.'

'Very well, James Quenton, consider yourself in business. Now let me get my rest.' He started to rise, eager to strip off his clothes, then realised that James had made no move to leave. 'Was there something else?' he asked gruffly. 'Perhaps another thousand pounds you failed to mention?'

'No, I was thinking about Denker. When shall I tell him about this new . . . arrangement?'

Sir Anthony sighed. 'I'll inform him in the morning. Now go!'

James reached for the entrance flap. 'Good-night, Sir Anthony.'

'Good-night, Quenton,' the other replied, relieved the youngster had not called him 'partner'.

The dawn was accompanied by a warm berg wind which bode ill for the workers that day. They had all taken their farewell of James before hurrying off, eager to get their march to the work point over before the summer sun added its torment to the wind. Few knew the reason for his leaving, only that he was escaping their lot.

Amos stayed at his side, at once sad and happy for his friend. 'Make your dream come true,' he said softly. 'Do it for us all, lad.'

James stared back, recalling his first days at the camp when Amos had been there to care for him. 'I won't forget you, Amos,' he said thickly. 'When I'm settled and things are going well, I'll send for you.'

Amos smiled sadly. 'There are times when I think I was born on this god-forsaken road, that I've never known any other life. I'm content to die here, lad. Your future is your own, not to be shared with people from the past.'

'I'll come for you – I swear!'

There was a gentle shake of the other man's head. The urgent wind tugged at his hair as he smiled again before turning to make his way towards the men readying themselves for the long walk.

James watched him go, a tall, gentle man who had overcome the ugly battle of bitterness. He wanted to run after him, to beg him to come away with him, but a heavy hand fell on his shoulder and spun him round.

'So, the pup is skulking off with the master, is he?' There was a mad rage on Denker's face.

James shook off his hand and stepped away from the big man. 'You've no say over me any more, so leave me be.'

'Leave you be? You think you've escaped me now, pup, but you'd better keep looking over your shoulder, 'cause I'll be there again some day.' He stepped closer, crowding his bulk against the smaller man. 'You came here with your pretty face and your woman's hands, and now you think you're a man? Just because you've fancy ideas about yourself?' The spittle of his bitter rage stung James's face.

'Quenton!' The sound of Sir Anthony's voice stopped Denker. 'Your master calls, puppy,' he said, spitting on the ground before he turned away.

James started for the wagons, then stopped and faced Denker again. 'I'll see to it that you're finished here,' he said softly. 'Very soon, Denker – that's a promise.'

'You'll *never* be finished with me, Quenton. That's a promise too.' They stared at each other with a hatred that struck through the wind.

'I was about to leave without you, boy,' muttered Sir Anthony as James passed by his buggy on his way to the nearest of the two supply wagons. 'Saying farewell to Denker?'

'Just talking about the future.'

The small convoy rolled out of the camp a few moments later, passing the rows of tents which had been James's home for the past eight months. He did not turn to look, nor did he glance back.

They went past the men, who had already progressed half a mile from the camp. There were a few raised hands, a silent farewell as they faced their own new day. It was only Amos who smiled and gave a slow nod of encouragement.

James raised his own hand, but the column of men was already swallowed up by the dust of the wagons as they moved on towards Oudtshoorn and the future.

CHAPTER SEVEN

The river rolled and bubbled through the green lushness of the Cango valley, the light sound of its flow muted by the afternoon breeze idly stirring the branches of the old willow trees.

James sat in the shade and watched a glorious spectacle of courtship play its timeless role. The previous day he had seen the ostrich male make his selection from the available females, driving at the herd in a magnificent display of plumage, his proud roar booming out time and again as he flapped his wings to lure prospective mates from the rest of the troop.

He knew the cock well; it was one of the first ostriches he had purchased, an enormous creature with a dense, even crop of feathers – his prime breeding bird. He called the male Ratitãe, the Latin for ostrich.

The April afternoon seemed to hold its breath as the two birds, the cock and its chosen hen, grazed in the secluded spot. They moved in unison, their bodies swaying lightly as if in rhythm with the weeping willows, their long necks reaching for the ground in synchronous feeding, as though that were the only thing on their minds.

James held his breath for fear the slightest sound would cause the birds to sense his presence only yards away from their foreplay. He need not have been concerned; the two lovers were oblivious to all but the ever-increasing precision of their movements. There was little feeding, but that was of no consequence; what mattered most was that they achieve an absolute synchronisation of movement. If they failed in that, the preliminaries to love would be abandoned.

On this occasion, love flourished. The ballet of sexual tension reached a peak when the cock demonstrated the power of his desire by flapping each wing in turn. Moments later he flung himself to the ground to stir up the dust with mighty beats of his wings, his neck twisting with clicking sounds from side to side in rapid spiral movements while the hen circled him. Her own response was one of appeasement, head lowered, beak opening and shutting, tail pointing downwards to the watching earth.

James's pulse increased as the moment reached its zenith of tension. The dull roar of the cock filled his ears and he smelled the dust raised by their dance of passion. At any moment now the courtship would make way for consummation.

It happened seconds later. The cock rose to his feet, the final signal for procreation to commence. The hen reacted instantly, sinking to the ground, ready to play her part as the cock mounted her with a last roar of triumph, his wings still flapping in disciplined precision.

James moved stealthily away, granting the ostriches their moment of passion in privacy while they planted the first true seeds of his future, leaving the willows and the restless river as the only witnesses to its making.

The crude wooden hut which served as his dwelling seemed suddenly a stark contrast to the refined beauty he had observed at the river. He stared at the roughly hewn logs, longing for the day when the birds' feathers brought in enough profit to lift him from his humble status. It would take more than one crop before there was any worthwhile money, but he consoled himself with the thought that the hut was better than one of Denker's tents.

The memory of the Dutch foreman brought a familiar tightness to his chest. It was more than three months since he had left the camp on Sir Anthony's supply wagon, yet ugly visions of his time under Denker's rule still haunted him in his sleep.

He moved to the paddock fence only a few yards from the door of the hut, which he had purposely built close to the enclosure in order to be near his birds. There were eight of them, two cocks and six hens. James remembered Steenkamp's warning that the ostrich would opt for polygamy if the cocks were outnumbered, and that it could lead to chaos on the nests. Although the principal hen would allow others to share the nest, there would be too many eggs, so that the male would be unable to cope with them all. The father-to-be would be incapable of leaving a portion of the clutch to die to care better for the rest, so perhaps none of the eggs might hatch.

James had nevertheless opted for more hens, especially as two of them had not yet reached sexual maturity. Studying them now, he wished he could fill the paddocks with birds in preparation for the higher feather prices he knew would come. Despite Sir Anthony's agreement to sponsor the scheme, the old man had insisted on a wary start, forcing James to curb his impatience.

Finding the right land for their venture had been relatively easy – at least as far as he was concerned. The depression and the drought had ruined many farmers, making large patches of once-fertile land available at reasonable prices. He had rejected the first few Sir Anthony and his lawyer, Abraham Isaacs, suggested. 'I want to be alongside the river,' he insisted. 'There may come a time when we will need easy irrigation.'

The site he finally decided on was almost ten miles outside Oudtshoorn itself at the start of the Cango valley. It lay cupped in the gently sloping valley and was bordered by the Grobbelaars River. Beyond the river the landscape underwent a violent change, pushing upwards to form a series of steep and jagged cliffs. To the north, the Swartberg Mountains loomed large and majestic.

Sir Anthony had disagreed with his choice. 'We should be buying land,' he argued. 'What you want is not for sale.'

'Then we lease it,' James countered, knowing that the old man would buy up other parcels anyway. 'This is where we start farming.'

At least Sir Anthony had not interfered in his choice of ostriches. His benefactor left town two days later, with a final reminder that his lawyer, Abraham Isaacs, was now establishing himself in Oudtshoorn and would maintain a wary eye on developments. 'And on the money,' he had added before commencing the next stage of his journey to Grahamstown.

James had spent less on setting up their enterprise than originally envisaged, and now the thought of the sum saved turned his gaze back to the ostriches in the field. He needed more birds – especially now that the breeding season was under way.

A burst of laughter drew his attention. The three Xhosa who worked for him came strolling from the river bank. Thousands of famished Xhosa had streamed into the Colony as a result of the cattle-killing in 1857, wanting nothing more than to trade their labour for food. Believing a visionary who prophesied that after killing all their herds a new prosperity and freedom from the hated English would follow, the Xhosa nation had systematically gone about destroying what had always been their symbol of individual wealth. They were still paying the price years later.

James sighed, pushed himself from the fence and started for the hut. Glancing once more at the river where the two mating birds now grazed contentedly, he went inside.

In 1866 there were just over eighty birds spread throughout the Cape Colony, with Oudtshoorn possessing less than other towns such as Riversdale at the fringe of the semi-arid region called the Little Karoo. Yet it was Oudtshoorn's potential as a breeding area that drew James and Sir Anthony to choose it as the site for their venture.

Situated at the base of the mighty Swartberg Mountains range, it was watered by both the Olifants and Grobbelaars Rivers, although the long drought of the preceding years had reduced their flow to little more than a trickle. The soil was rich and loamy, with an abundance of suitable pebbles to aid the ostriches' digestion. A warm, dry climate offered an almost ideal environment for raising birds with quality feathers.

It was a rural town that James entered on an April morning, a place buffeted by years of drought and depression. It was a town known primarily for its brandy, fruit, wheat and tobacco, although the advent of the domesticated ostrich was rapidly changing that.

Abraham Isaacs, the lawyer, had a tiny office on High Street, a far cry from the much larger premises he had occupied with his partners in George, the established town at the foot of the Outeniqua Mountains some forty miles from Oudtshoorn.

Isaacs had known Sir Anthony long enough to realise the spry old man had a good nose for business, so he had not hesitated in committing his time to investigate the opportunities Oudtshoorn offered. He had even put some of his own money into the ostrich venture, although he had not yet informed James of this. Isaacs was not a man to leave things to others, so he had sold his shares in the George office to his partners and established himself in Oudtshoorn.

He was not too surprised when James entered his office that morning. 'Mr Quenton,' he said with a smile, 'come in, come in!'

When James had seated himself in the single chair across the desk, Isaacs removed his glasses and rubbed his tired eyes. 'It's more money you want, I take it?' he said abruptly, leaning his elbows on the desk. He was a small man, but he'd dealt with all types during his career, and the frustration he saw on the muscular man's face did not unsettle him. 'A young man in so much of a hurry for things to happen,' he went on. 'Always a pitiful sight.'

'I need more birds,' James replied, as though he had not heard the lawyer.

'Of course! More birds, then more labour, and finally more land. When will you stop wanting, James Quenton?'

'When I possess my own ostrich venture, when I'm no longer obliged to consult you on anything.' Isaacs smiled down at the desk top.

'The land is lying idle,' continued James. 'The birds are starting to breed, and there's space for at least four more fenced fields.'

'And the labour to fence these fields and look after the additional birds?'

'One extra man is all we need. I've saved on the original

estimate,' he added. 'We could use some of that for purchasing breeding birds and materials. The additional investment would amount to little.'

Isaacs was thoughtful. 'I can only convey your request to Sir Anthony Kenrick,' he said at last. 'It will be up to him to decide.'

'It'll be too late – it'll take weeks for the message to reach Cape Town! *You* have to make the decision.'

'I?'

'Yes! You're Sir Anthony's adviser – he left you in charge of his investments. If not, then why the hell am I coming to you for every penny?' He lowered his voice and said, 'Why don't you come out to the farm, see for yourself what I've got planned? I've marked out the areas where the other paddocks should be.'

'The farm has changed since I last saw it?'

'No, but—'

'Then there is no need for a personal visit, is there?'

'You'll trust my judgement?'

'I'll think about it.'

James jumped to his feet. 'I have ostriches to tend to,' he snapped. He turned when he reached the door. 'When you make your decision,' he said, 'bear in mind that any additional investment right now will hasten the healthy return on all investments made so far. That would put money into your pocket a lot sooner than you'd hoped for.'

Isaacs slammed his spectacles down on the desk, glanced quickly at them to see whether they were still in one piece and then glared up at James. 'How did you know?'

'About your share? Mr Isaacs, I find it interesting that you should pay so much attention to another man's money – even if Sir Anthony is a major client of yours. That can mean only one thing.'

The sudden smirk seemed out of place on Isaacs's face. 'Most of us have a touch of the gambler in us, young Quenton. Now why don't you go look after our ostriches while I think some more, huh?'

James raised a hand in mock salute. 'Good-day, Mr Isaacs.'

'Good-day – oh, by the way, I've sent someone out to

the farm to see you. Perhaps you should talk to him.'

'Who?'

'Just a labourer. He says he's good at fencing paddocks.'

The door closed on James's satisfied grin.

When he rode up to the hut there was a tall African standing beside the fence, his arms folded sternly while he ignored the acrimonious glances of the Xhosa labouring in the paddock.

James let him wait while he tethered his horse – an unplanned expense to which Sir Anthony had agreed – and washed the worst of the dust from his face and hair. Then he strolled slowly over to the fence.

The African raised his arm, palm outwards, then let it fall back to his side. James gave a brief nod. 'You speak English?'

'Indeed. The missionaries spent time with me.'

Not the other way round, thought James, but managed to bite back his smile. 'Are you the man Mr Isaacs sent to see me?' He studied the African, admiring his muscled body and spread of shoulder. He was about thirty, James decided, thinking that Denker would have been pleased to have such a powerful body labour for him.

'Indeed. I know this ostrich business.'

'Which is more than I can say for your friends over there.' He indicated the labourers in the paddock.

For a moment it seemed as though the black man would strike him. He stiffened, glanced with enraged eyes at the Xhosa, then spat in their direction. 'I am Zulu!' he cried, thumping his muscled chest. 'Those are Xhosa dogs – cattle-killers! Their women have such small buttocks one must raise them up to enter their tiny mounds. The penis of the men is as small as a piccaninny's toy assegai. Their—'

'You're a Zulu?' asked James to stem the flow of insults, wondering at the same time where the missionaries had gone wrong.

'Indeed.' He had folded his arms again.

'You're a long way from home, aren't you?' Even as he spoke, he realised the African would be affronted again, for the Zulu nation had long since made their influence felt beyond their native region of Natal. It was the first time, though, that he had seen one as far west as the Karoo.

'The Zulu's home is anywhere he wants it to be,' came the even reply.

'Indeed,' quipped James and smiled.

They studied each other for a few moments. 'You say you know about ostriches?'

'Indeed. The Zulu has hunted them for centuries. Their feathers adorn the head-dress of the impi warriors. Then, too, I have worked on the farms. The birds and I are both creatures of God.'

A Christian Zulu, mused James, wondering how much he could trust the big African's claim to experience. Yet he knew the man could not be worse than the Xhosa, who seemed to lack a natural aptitude for dealing with the large birds. 'You have a name?' he asked.

'Indeed. I am known as Mthembeni.'

'What?'

The Zulu rolled his eyes heavenwards. 'You may call me whatever is easy on your tongue. Anything but Kaffir.'

James smiled, knowing how the Africans hated the term. Another word sprang into his mind, one he had heard some Dutch children use to describe African men. The word was used affectionately, almost the way one referred to a nanny. 'I will call you Outa,' he announced.

The Zulu shrugged his broad shoulders. 'A name is a name in the eyes of God,' he said. 'You may call me Outa.'

'When can you start?' He hoped he was not about to employ a self-ordained preacher.

'I already have,' came the reply. 'I am about to build the shelters over there.' He pointed to a spot near the fence.

'Shelters? What shelters?'

Outa shook his head, as if despairing at James's lack of knowledge. 'You have seen the birds rutting?'

'Breeding, yes.'

'Then it is the will of God that there will be eggs. The eggs will need protection, so we will need to build shelters. So high.' He indicated a height of about eight feet.

'I will gather reeds for the roof.' Without waiting for James's response, he bounded over the fence, heading with loping strides for the river.

James knew then that the African had not lied about his experience with ostriches. The V-shaped shelters were the one thing he had forgotten to erect.

'Outa!' he called out to the departing figure.

The tall Zulu turned slowly, a small smile playing on his thick lips at the sound of his new name.

'I don't want to hear about God all day long, do you understand? You can keep what He has planned to yourself.'

'You are a heathen?'

'No, I'm not a bloody heathen, damn you! I just don't want Him thrust down my throat all the time.'

The Zulu grinned broadly, his white teeth almost as dazzling a display as an ostrich's plumage. 'I am just a little bitty Christian,' he called back, 'but one can never be too careful when choosing a master. No more talk of God!' The two men smiled at each other.

James asked, 'What does it mean, whatever you said your name was?'

Outa's smile widened, yet there was a seriousness in his eyes when he replied, 'Mthembeni . . . One you can trust.' He smiled again before turning away.

The Xhosa were watching the newcomer with hate-filled eyes, making James wonder if he had bought himself a parcel of trouble. Still, Outa promised to be an entertaining addendum to his lonely life.

Mthembeni . . . one you can trust. Time would tell, he decided.

The Xhosa were gone by the end of April, one of them carried off by his comrades after suffering a fearful beating at the hands of Outa.

'What do we do now?' demanded James, trying hard to disguise the pleasure he felt at their leaving.

Outa seemed unconcerned. 'What were they,' he asked,

'but three jackals eating our food? We will do the work ourselves.' James shook his head at the tribal disdain the proud Zulu displayed for the Xhosa.

Two weeks later the fences of the new paddocks were in position so that they were able to take delivery of a further ten ostriches. 'You see?' said Outa with obvious satisfaction. 'We have no need of the Xhosa.'

The late autumn air was alive with the sounds and sights of mating. Noting this, Outa discussed his concern with his employer beside their fire one night. 'The birds rut,' he started, 'and at night I sneak to the Xhosa women to plunge my fleshy assegai deep inside their flesh. But you – you stay by your birds at all times. You do not like rutting?'

James glared at him across the flames. 'It seems you have found some use for the Xhosa after all,' he snapped. 'Someone must stay here to look after the farm.'

'I can stay. I do not have to rut every night. I have the will – praise God – but I do not have to every night.'

'You're not my caretaker,' said James, smiling gently at the black man. There were available women in town, of course, many who had displayed more than a passing interest in him. Perhaps Outa was right; it was more than a year, anyway, since he had pushed one of the women passengers aboard ship up against the hard wood of a cabin wall, taking his brief moment of relief before her husband returned from visiting the ship's officers. Their time together was nothing more than snatched intervals of hurried passion, always filled with the fear of discovery and punishment. She had left the ship in Cape Town without even a farewell glance at him.

'Tell me a story,' he said suddenly, gruffly, feeling his body stir at the fading memory. Night after night he and Outa had shared the fire, telling each other tales from their past, sometimes talking about their beloved ostriches.

'Indeed,' came the stock reply. 'What kind of story?'

'One about ostriches.'

Outa was lost in thought for a while. Then he looked up with a smirk on his lips. 'You know of the Bushmen?' he asked, shifting closer to the flames.

'Of course.' The little brown men who had roamed and been chased from most parts of Africa had ruled the Karoo as well. The coming of the white man had ended that, so that only their paintings adorned the caves which had once been their homes.

'The Bushmen tell the tale,' Outa started, 'of the ostrich when it moved down from the northern parts. They saw the birds for the first time when they reached a land of great water, the place they call Okavango, many miles north of here.'

'I have heard of it,' said James, settling back to hear what Outa had to say that night.

'They watched the ostriches for many days and nights, till someone asked, "Why does this great bird not fly?" It was many months before they thought up an answer for this.'

'The ostrich has never flown!'

The inter;ection made Outa glare. 'It is *my* story.'

'Sorry.'

'Indeed.' He let the silence demonstrate his annoyance at the interruption before he went on. 'The Bushmen decided,' he said slowly, enjoying James's frustration at the time it took him to get to the point of the tale, 'that the ostrich was the only animal to possess the secret of fire.'

'Fire?'

'Yes! The secret of fire!'

'And that's the tale?'

Outa shut his eyes. Again there was a lengthy silence. 'So,' he started, flashing James a warning look, 'the ostrich feared that other creatures would steal the secret from him. And so he hid the secret under his wing, where they would not think to look for it.'

'And that is why he dare not fly?' James chipped in. 'Because the secret would drop from beneath his wings?'

'Indeed!' The Zulu was beaming with the successful telling of his tale.

'Is this true, Outa?'

'It is what the Bushmen tell,' he replied. 'But who can believe what brown men say?'

James pushed himself to his feet. 'Outa,' he said, 'I'm going to take your advice and go into town tomorrow night. I've had enough of your stories.'

'Indeed. Indeed.'

James was rudely awakened on a mild and sunny May morning by Outa's hysterical banging on the hut's door. He leaped from his bunk, thinking that some tragedy had befallen them during the night. His fears were allayed by the smiling face that greeted him as he stumbled from the hut.

'We have eggs!' bellowed Outa. 'Come see!' He led the way to the paddocks where an egg, its shell glossy and pitted, showed beneath a protective hen. James was relieved Outa had displayed the foresight to herd the males into an adjoining paddock before waking him. The agitated birds fluttered their rage from across the fence.

'There lies our future,' he said, hugging Outa in his excitement. 'I wonder how many other hens have started laying.' The birds should lay an egg every other day till their clutch of about fifteen was complete. James did a quick calculation based on the incubation period of forty-two days. 'We'll have our first chicks in the middle of July,' he said. 'It won't be too long before the paddocks are filled with baby ostriches. Then we're on our way!'

The Zulu's brow was creased in concern.

'What's wrong?'

'There will be too many eggs, too few cocks,' Outa replied as he searched through the other nests. 'We shall have to watch closely.'

'That we shall, but not tonight. Tonight I go to town, and you can bury your fleshy assegai as many times as you wish!'

Outa still looked unhappy. 'Why go to town,' he asked, 'when the women come to you?'

James ignored him and started back for the hut. He had met a number of women in Oudtshoorn, and most of them were intrigued by the good-looking Englishman who was rumoured to be more interested in ostriches than women.

74

They were determined to change that, and consequently he soon had a supply of willing ladies. Some of them were married, although that in no way deterred him. It amused him how prepared they were to meet him, sometimes riding out to the farm in the afternoons, going with him to the river bank, to the spot where his ostriches had held their dance of passion. He had even been with them in their own homes, where they risked everything while their husbands were in the fields or in town.

James was not attached to any of them. They were merely a convenience, a fun-filled diversion from his daily chores. When he was done with them, he hurried back to this true loves. Outa often warned him that sooner or later some irate husband would deal him a punch more lethal than the kick of an ostrich.

During that afternoon he had gone into the paddocks, wanting to gaze at the freshly laid eggs once more. Afterwards, he cursed Outa for not warning him the cocks had been released back into the field in preparation for their turn on the nests that night. He did not go to town that night after all.

The first he knew of their presence was the booming roar of rage as a cock, his prize specimen, rushed at him with awesome speed, its wings fluttering with menace.

James ran. He heard the cloven feet behind him pound ever closer in a deathly rush of aggression. Through his blurred vision he saw Outa making for the fence, a branch of thorn bush in his hand. 'Down!' called Outa. 'Get down – oh, sweet Jesus!'

James dived for the earth and lay there with his arms protecting his head. The cock was upon him, trampling on his exposed back. He felt his shirt tear and the blood flow warmly across his skin.

'Shoo, you sinner, shoo!' Outa was there, fighting with his thorn bush thrust out at the bird's eyes. James felt the weight lift from him as the cock retreated, the threat of damage to its eyes overcoming its need to kill the menace to its unborn chicks.

'Get up!' Outa hissed. 'Run for the fence.' James raised his bruised and battered body and limped to safety. Outa followed closely, keeping a wary eye on the big bird, for he knew they were clever enough to find ways around the thorn and repeat their attack.

'You are lucky,' he said when he had James spread out on the ground beside the hut, 'that I was at hand to save you.'

James was in too much agony to blame him for what had happened. 'When an ostrich attacks,' Outa continued his lecture, 'one must always lie flat. He can only kick forwards, and when he does that, he will tear you apart with that long toenail of his. On the ground he can only hurt you, but that is better than being dead.' He let James suffer a little longer before he started dressing his wounds, continuing to tell him about the ostrich's evil temper. It was the last thing James wanted to hear.

'That cantankerous old bird,' he muttered when Outa was unnecessarily rough. 'Once his chicks are born, I will personally pluck all his feathers and make stew of him!'

'Indeed! Whatever you decide to do with him, he has done enough to keep you at home tonight. Your little white spear will stay in its sheath.'

James glared at him.

CHAPTER EIGHT

'Keep that thorn branch ready,' James warned Outa as they managed to get an enraged hen off her nest. She stood near by, hissing angrily at them.

He knelt down to place his ear against the clutch of eggs. 'All of these,' he said, hearing the sound of movement within the thick shells. They scooped them into their arms and carried the six-inch-long eggs to the hut. James stared down at the layer of eggs lying on his bed. 'You must take the rest,' he told Outa.

The Zulu nodded before leading the way back to the paddocks where they checked on the other clutches. Their worst fears had been realised; the cocks, unable to cope with the large numbers of eggs, were abandoning the nests through sheer boredom. The chicks would not hatch unless the eggs were protected both day and night so the men had taken the only course open to them: by removing the eggs from the nests, they had placed them in their beds and slept cautiously with them at night, acting as human incubators.

'It can't go on like this,' James said when he appeared some mornings later at the smaller hut Outa had built for himself. 'I'm too scared to move at night in case I break the damn things. I'm not getting any sleep!'

Outa muttered in agreement, staring dismally at the crisply cold June morning. He slapped his side suddenly and said, 'Is breeding not women's work?'

'It is.'

'Then why not let women do it?'

James frowned. 'What are you talking about?'

'Women! The Xhosa women! We shall hire them to sit on the eggs during the day. They have nothing else to do!'

At first James scoffed at the idea, but a few days later his fields were filled with chattering women squatting in the shade, their billowing skirts spread across their unusual brood. It became the talk of the district, with many farmers coming to witness the strange sight for themselves. Most of them laughed and shook their heads in disbelief.

Some weeks later, however, when the eggs were replaced by rampant ostrich chicks, James was gratified to learn that Xhosa women were suddenly very much in demand.

'God bless you, Outa,' he said.

The eggs, when hatched, produced an abundance of cocks that would one day sport the large, curled white plumes on which the industry was based.

James surveyed his vastly increased flock with pride. Another week, then he could separate the chicks from the adult birds. He smiled as he remembered the first days after their birth. The chicks, although the size of a full-grown fowl when born, were quite helpless and unable to stand on the first day.

They overcame this minor impediment rapidly, and were now making up for it by wild emulation of their elders. They copied their dances and crouched down when danger threatened, letting their zest for life fill the fields with the constant movement of their speckled bodies. At this stage their spiky feathers were of no value, but within a few months they would be clipped in preparation for a far more lustrous crop.

He watched the birds for a while longer, till the sound of an approaching cart drew his attention. It was Abraham Isaacs. Since the birth of the chicks, the lawyer had visited the farm at least three times a week, taking an almost paternal pride in their development.

'Morning,' he called out as the cart drew to a halt. 'Everything still under control?'

'Perfectly!' James helped the older man down. 'The only

problem we have is trying to control the little blighters. They're quite wild!'

The two men stood side by side and watched the antics of the young birds. 'Outa is a wonder with them,' James said after a while. 'At times I think the birds can understand his chatter.'

'Is he still trying to make converts of them?'

'He never stops! But the birds know a sinner when they see one. I don't think he'll have much success.'

'I think we should inform Sir Anthony about progress, don't you?'

James nodded. He did not miss the lawyer's use of the word 'we'. His arrival in Oudtshoorn with Sir Anthony Kenrick had been received with suspicion on the part of Isaacs, but that had gradually changed to respect as the lawyer discovered he was a hard worker as well as a knowledgeable one. James sensed that the older man had grown quite fond of him. It was the birds, he thought. They shared a mutual love.

'Before he left,' Isaacs was saying, 'Sir Anthony expressed the wish to be present when you pluck the first chicks. You have a date yet?'

James thought for a while. 'I want to clip the chicks at four months,' he said, 'to force their crop to develop evenly in later life. In early October, let's say.'

'Hmm. I think that will be too soon for him.'

'We'll clip the first feathers in January next year, leaving in the quills for another two months to protect the birds. The real crop will be ready six months after that.'

'It'll take as long as that?'

'At least. Why not arrange for Sir Anthony to be here when he does his yearly tour of inspection in January? Then he can watch the first proper feathers being pulled.'

'That will probably have to be it,' the lawyer agreed. 'Now,' he added, placing a hand on James's shoulder, 'what would you like to put in your report?'

James gazed at the field with a sad smile. 'Mr Isaacs—' he started, but the lawyer interrupted him, saying, 'Isn't it time you called me Abraham?'

'Abraham . . . I can't read or write – I thought you knew that.'

The lawyer scratched his beard thoughtfully. 'Then I will write it for you,' he said. 'This year at least. By the time Sir Anthony arrives, you will write your own.'

'You'll teach me?'

'As much as a simple man like me knows,' replied Isaacs with a mischievous smile. 'But in return you must teach me all you know about ostriches. Do you agree?'

They shook hands for the first time.

Ten days later they moved the chicks to separate paddocks. Outa became their keeper, the hand that fed them their meals as well as supplying the pebbles they required for trituration of their food.

The farming expenses suddenly rocketed, for supplies of crushed barley and bone-meal had to be procured for the feathered siblings. The lessons Steenkamp had taught James were soon implemented. On more than one occasion both he and Outa had to act rapidly to slit a bird's neck when a piece of bone lodged itself deep inside, an operation from which the ostrich soon recovered with few side-effects.

The two men were exhausted by the time night fell, although they took turns to rise during the hours of darkness. They placed fresh wood on the fire and listened carefully for sounds which did not belong in the paddocks, then crawled thankfully back into their warm beds.

The cold winter nights lay heavily on the valley now, forcing them to forgo their fireside chats, instead retiring early to their huts. Dawn found them lingering within the warmth of their blankets.

Perhaps it was that which caused James to miss the first indications that something was wrong in the paddocks early one July morning. Or perhaps the men who executed their foul deed did so with practised stealth.

The first sign he had was the booming of one of the ostrich cocks. He was alert instantly, listening for sounds to indicate a jackal or some other intruder in the fields. When he heard the hens add their raging hiss to the roars of the cocks, he clamberd quickly from his bunk and swung open the door. It was dark outside, but he sensed the dawn was near.

The fire was still glowing as he bent down to scatter kindling on to the coals. It took quickly, and he thrust one of the torches, which always stood by in readiness, into the fresh flames, shouting at the same time in the hope that the sound would scare off whatever animal was in the paddocks.

It seemed to take ages for the torch to burst into flame. His heart pounded in his throat as he leaped across the fence of the closest paddock, then stopped to try to identify the source and direction of the disturbance.

A cock boomed again. James ran towards the sound. The male was venting his rage on the fence dividing the adult camp from those of the chicks. He was kicking furiously, so that James was able to slip through before the bird noticed him. 'Outa!' he called out, for now he knew that something had happened in the paddock containing the ostrich chicks. From the corner of his eye he saw Outa running closer with a burning torch held high in his hand.

James almost stumbled over the first of the dead chicks. There were eight of them lying in a row, warm blood still oozing from their slit stomachs. He knelt down and placed his hand on one of the carcasses. This was no animal come for food, he realised as he studied the neat knife cut in the flickering torchlight.

Outa appeared beside him. 'Get more torches,' said James, his voice thick with anger. He glanced around at the dark perimeters of the camp where the killers might still be lurking. Why would someone do this?

'Bastards!' he shouted into the dark. 'I'll kill you for this!' He watched for a sign of movement that would betray their presence. There was a sob in his throat when he thought about the other camps and what he would find there.

He turned and saw Outa struggling to set the other torches alight. 'Hurry!' he shouted.

A spiteful laugh echoed from some distance away. James spun round and strained his eyes against the night. They were at the river! He started forward, the torch flickering as he moved.

There was a shout, from near by the huts this time, making him change direction. 'Quenton!' the voice called. 'Do you see what happens when you mess with other men's wives? Next time it'll be *your* stomach that's slit, you English bastard!'

James gave a roar of rage as he rushed towards the sound of the voice. There was another laugh from the bush, followed by the sound of a horse's hoofs. The horseman appeared suddenly from behind the hut. Outa dropped the torches and leaped at the animal, only to be knocked backwards by the momentum of the horse. He fell close to the fire but immediately sprang back to his feet. The flickering flames cast shadows of the horse and rider against the hut, making them appear huge and sinister. James caught sight of a sjambok raised high in the horseman's hand before he brought the whip crashing across Outa's shoulders. The crack of the sjambok and the sickening slap of impact carried to his ears moments after Outa was flung back to the ground. The Zulu covered his face with his arms as the whip was raised again.

James ran. He hurtled across the fence with a low, savage growl deep in his throat. The horseman saw him coming and veered away, stooping low in his saddle to scoop up one of the flaming torches lying beside the fire. He threw it on to the dry thatched roof of the hut before galloping off.

James reached Outa, placed his hands on the black man's shoulders and tried to get him to his feet. His fingers slipped on the wet blood flowing from a long cut opened up by the deadly sjambok. Suddenly he caught sight of another rider dashing through the fields. The horse leaped easily over the fence and disappeared into the lingering night. At least two of them, thought James – but who?

Outa was whimpering with pain as he struggled to his knees and crawled towards the hut which was rapidly being devoured by hungry flames. James pulled him back. 'It's too late! Let it burn – we can build another!'

They clung to each other while they watched. The fierce light reflected on their faces showed the anger, pain and despair etched there. Soon there was little left but glowing embers and smoking ash. James got wearily to his feet.

'I'll go and see how many they've killed,' he said, his voice heavy. 'The cowardly bastards!'

Outa grabbed his arm. 'Let us wait till it is light,' he said through gritted teeth, more concerned for the cold anger he saw on his master's face than with the pain throbbing across the broken skin of his shoulders. 'The sun will be here soon,' he added, pointing to the first glimmer of dawn on the nearby hills.

James stayed stiffly on his feet, but the Zulu's hand remained firmly clamped around his arm. He sighed loudly before sinking down beside Outa. 'He hurt you badly?'

Outa shrugged, the movement making him flinch. 'It is not the first time I have tasted the white man's sjambok,' he said. 'It is nothing.'

'What is the pain of the sjambok,' said James, placing a hand gently on his shoulder, 'to a little bitty Christian?' He drew Outa's head on to his shoulder as both men started to laugh, a racking sound which mingled with their tears of loss.

They sat side by side, the Englishman and the Zulu, waiting for the ugly day to break.

They found nineteen slaughtered chicks, nineteen birds whose feathers would never adorn the shoulders of fashion-conscious ladies.

They picked the dead birds up one by one and carried them to the side of the paddocks. The adult ostriches let them work undisturbed, as though sensing the men felt the loss as deeply as they did. Outa turned away from the look on James's face, for he feared what the mixture of anger and sorrow might bring.

'I will bury our children,' he said when they had collected all the carcasses. 'You start building a new hut.' He was relieved when James nodded numbly; the labour would keep the bitter thoughts of revenge from his mind.

Abraham Isaacs arrived shortly before noon. He climbed

slowly from his cart and silently surveyed the ruins of the hut. He spotted James leaning against the wire fence, his face turned away. Isaacs took a deep breath and went to stand beside him. 'Are there enough birds left,' he asked after a while, 'for Sir Anthony's visit?'

James stared at him with bloodshot eyes. 'How did you know about this?' he asked hoarsely.

Isaacs ignored him. 'I asked you a question?'

'They killed nineteen,' he said so softly that Isaacs was forced to lean closer. 'But there will be enough birds for the plucking.'

The lawyer let his breath out slowly. 'Then there is no need for him to hear of this,' he said. 'I have arranged for some timber to be delivered from town . . . Use it to rebuild your home, then carry on with our venture. This is no time for self-pity.'

James spun around and gripped the lapels of Isaacs's coat. 'Who did it, Abraham? If you knew about this, then you must know who was responsible. Tell me – I want that bastard, Abraham!'

Isaacs pushed him away with surprising strength. 'Forget your childish desires for revenge!' he snapped. 'You've done enough harm, but it's over now, do you understand? Continue to build what you started – forget this talk of revenge.' He lowered his voice and added, 'James, this was a terrible, cowardly thing they did. I'm as angry as you, but it is done now. Nothing will be gained by further violence.' He smiled, patted the young man's shoulder and said, 'Perhaps you should be a bit more careful about your choice of women in future, huh?'

His words did little to reassure James, who lowered his head into his hands. 'This is all my fault.'

'Yes,' replied Isaacs gently, 'that it is. But feeling sorry for yourself will not change things. Perhaps what happened will have taught you something.'

James gave a shame-faced nod. Isaacs patted his shoulder again before heading for his cart.

'Will you take Outa with you?' James called out. 'His shoulder is badly cut. It needs attention.'

Isaacs nodded. 'He can get a lift back with the supply wagon when it brings your wood.' Isaacs waited till James had spoken to the Zulu. He heard him say, 'Do exactly as Mr Isaacs tells you, you hear?'

Outa climbed up stiffly beside the lawyer. He flinched when Isaacs cracked his whip across the horse's back.

They trundled over the dirt track, leaving the scene of bitter carnage behind them. Isaacs realised they must present a strange sight – the black man sitting solemnly next to the white man in a black suit.

After they had travelled a few miles, Outa spoke up suddenly, saying, 'My master is hurting very bad. In his heart and in his head. It is good you stopped him.'

Isaacs glanced at him. 'And you, Outa, do you not hurt also?'

It was a while before Outa replied, saying, 'We Zulu have learned it is not always wise to seek revenge when the anger is upon one. It is also not a Christian thing to do.'

Isaacs bit back his smile. 'I see. And what would be the Christian way of extracting revenge?'

Outa gave him a smug look but did not reply.

They were but a few miles from the village when Isaacs said, 'I hear a certain Mrs Fouche has bruises on her face this morning. They say her husband learned she was lying with another man. Do you know this Mrs Fouche?'

Outa nodded but kept looking straight ahead. 'I have seen her often,' he replied after a while, thinking of the many times the small plump woman had ridden out to the farm. He had always suspected her greedy ways would cause them trouble.

'And do you remember,' continued Isaacs, 'that your master told you to obey me?'

Outa nodded again, although now he watched the lawyer carefully. 'Then I am telling you,' said Isaacs, 'that your master must not learn about Fouche. What you as a Christian do with the information is your own business.'

A mischievous gleam showed in the Zulu's eyes. 'It will be as you say. But this Christian will need a wagon.'

'You can borrow mine.'

'It is not big enough.'

Isaacs sighed loudly. 'I shall arrange a larger one.'

'And socks.'

'What?'

'Socks. I will need socks.'

Isaacs gave him a baffled look. He thought it best not to ask questions; he'd acted irresponsibly enough as it was. 'I shall get them,' was all he said.

He laughed when Outa told him how many socks he needed. 'You'll get them,' he said again, laughing with real pleasure as they rode into Oudtshoorn.

The wagon bringing the wood Isaacs had arranged came and went. But there was no Outa.

James was not unduly concerned, guessing it had probably taken longer than Isaacs thought to find someone to tend to Outa. He knew the lawyer would look after the Zulu; if he could not get him back to the farm that day, he would find a place for him to spend the night.

He lit the fire early and made his bed beside it, using the blankets Isaacs had sent along with the wood. Even if the hut had not been burned down, he would still have spent the night on guard in case a second attack was mounted.

The anger still lingered inside him, but he had lost his mad rage of that morning. He'd been a fool; he'd allowed his body to rule his mind, and that had cost him nineteen beautiful birds which would now play no part in his future. He cursed softly; there was no place for set-backs in his plans.

He dozed off from time to time, often waking with a start when a sound broke the stillness of the night. Usually it was only a restless hen feeding or urinating close to the fence.

When he woke again, it was because of a wagon approaching from across the fields. He rolled out from under the blankets and gripped the sturdy branch he had cut and shaped into a club that afternoon. I'm ready for you bastards, he thought, wondering why they would risk the noise of a wagon.

He relaxed as it came steadily closer. These were no early-morning marauders; the wagon moved openly, its driver obviously having no fear of discovery.

At last it rolled into sight near the paddock fences. 'Outa!' he cried out when it stopped near him and he saw the tall Zulu perched atop the driver's seat. 'What the – where have you been? And that?' He pointed at the wagon.

Outa smiled smugly. 'Just doing my Christian duty,' he said. James moved closer when he spotted movement in the back.

Nineteen chicks were tethered to the sides of the wagon, each with a sock pulled over its head to quieten and render it docile, in just the same way as adult birds were handled during plucking. James swung around to face his servant.

'Christian duty be damned!' he cried. 'You've stolen these chicks!'

Outa shrugged. 'Just easing the burden of labour on my fellow man.'

James touched the nearest bird. The chick pulled away from his touch, its down coarse and spiky. 'Where did you get them?'

'Do not force a little bitty Christian to tell a lie.'

'It is Fouche,' said James. He had thought about it during the day and, although Elsa Fouche was not the only married woman with whom he had dabbled, he had taken the greatest risks with her. Outa's face remained impassive. James knew he would not reveal the truth, even if beaten.

He started to laugh, a laugh so filled with relief, pleasure and affection for the Zulu that he started to double up.

'It is not funny,' said Outa haughtily. 'We are lucky that ostriches do not carry brand marks like cattle.'

'You're right,' said James once he'd controlled his mirth. He straightened up and placed his hands on the Zulu's shoulders. 'You know something, Outa? That's the next thing we'll do – brand our ostriches!'

Outa was busy untying the ostrich chicks. 'That Mr Isaacs,' he said across his shoulder, 'he is no Christian, but he's a good man!'

James stood with his hands on his hips. A Jewish lawyer and a Christian Zulu . . . How could he go wrong?

CHAPTER NINE

Katherine Kenrick found the Karoo heat almost unbearable, and was terrified the sun would blemish her creamy white complexion. She told herself she was fortunate – imagine if they'd arrived during the summer as Sir Anthony had originally planned!

The hostile countryside into which her father had led them unnerved her, while the tiring, dusty journey and the uncouth people they met along the way made her long for the dances she would miss during her absence from Cape Town.

It was dreadfully hot even inside Abraham Isaacs's office where the two men discussed business matters. Katherine toyed with a twist of blonde hair which had strayed loose and glanced at her mother sitting demurely in one corner, studying her gloved hands. She knew that Lady Kenrick resented being forced to accompany Sir Anthony on his journey, although her mother would never reveal her true feelings in front of her daughter – especially not with Isaacs present.

She studied her father's face as he listened to Isaacs reporting on the progress of the farm, his eyes bright with excitement at being where things were happening.

When the men finished, Isaacs led them to a large open carriage he had borrowed for the occasion. Katherine and Lady Kenrick raised their parasols to ward off the direct sunlight.

It seemed to take an age before they reached the farm. Katherine looked away as they passed a hen urinating beside a paddock fence. Lady Kenrick flapped a silk handkerchief before her nose.

'Ah, there he is!' bellowed Sir Anthony when the carriage drew to a halt and James moved forward to greet them. 'You've become a regular farmer, Quenton,' he added, enthusiastically shaking James's hand.

Katherine stared at the man her father had spoken about so often. He looked quite crude, yet she found her gaze settling on the dark chest hairs revealed by his open-necked shirt. He glanced at her just then, making her jerk away her gaze. She pretended to study a group of ostriches with great interest.

Sir Anthony introduced Lady Kenrick. When he said, 'This is my daughter, Katherine,' she was obliged to face James again. 'She's waited anxiously to see our lovely birds,' added Sir Anthony with a mischievous gleam in his eye.

She glared at him, gave James a fleeting glance and a brief nod, then studied the paddocks again. His hand was suddenly on hers, a touch of warmth as he raised it to his lips.

'I can see that, Sir Anthony,' James said. 'She can't keep her eyes off them.'

She pulled her hand away, tucking it protectively against her breast. He continued to stare at her with what seemed an amused smile – no, it was arrogance! – which seemed to grow as she glared frostily back at him.

'Outa,' he shouted suddenly, as though he had grown bored with her, 'bring the chicks!' He moved off with the Kenricks and Isaacs in tow.

Katherine first stood as if rooted to the spot, then quickly caught up with them, still clutching her hand to her chest. It seemed to glow where his lips had touched the skin, and she wiped it against her dress. Had the man no respect for a lady?

'Is that your Zulu?' asked Sir Anthony, pointing to where Outa waited in readiness, dressed in his newest clothes which had been specially washed for the occasion.

'That's him,' replied James with a smile. 'There are four

other labourers now, but Outa is in charge. Sometimes I think he governs me as well!'

Katherine stared at the big African. A Zulu! It made sense of course; a wild, rough man living in close proximity to a savage.

It was as if he could read her mind. 'Outa is a Christian,' he said, 'and he's really quite civilised.'

He's mocking me, she thought, feeling her face glow hotly. 'And,' continued James, 'he's saved me a number of times.'

She could not stop herself from exclaiming, 'Saved your life?'

James laughed. Despite her earlier resentment she thought it was a nice sound. 'He's done that, too,' he said, 'but I was talking about my . . . our venture here. Outa knows everything there is to know about ostriches. I'd have been lost without him.'

'Perhaps we should give him your share,' grunted Sir Anthony, his smile showing he was teasing.

James helped Outa and the labourers drive the young ostriches into a small enclosure which had been specially built alongside the paddocks. Each of the men held a hooked stick which they used to select individual birds, catching them around the neck with the crook to lead them into the kraal.

He pointed to a triangular box in a corner of the kraal and said, 'We'll pluck them in there.' One of the thirteen-month-old birds was led into the box where Outa quickly slipped a sock over its head. The distraught ostrich, denied a view of what was happening to it, became immediately docile. Isaacs smiled at the memory the sight of the socks evoked.

'We'll be clipping the wing feathers and the largest blacks,' explained James. 'Only the males will be clipped.'

'But they're still so young,' said Lady Kenrick, standing a safe distance away from the fence.

'They are, but we have to get the feathers before they're damaged. We'll leave the quills in though, so the birds won't injure themselves.'

'And the next plucking?' Sir Anthony asked, as he joined the men inside the kraal.

'We'll leave the quills in for another two months. There'll be a further crop six months after they're pulled out – a total of three plumages over two years.'

Sir Anthony gave a satisfied grunt. 'Thirty-five feathers in each wing, am I right?'

James nodded, then jumped forward to help with a young male who was clearly in no mood to have his proud plumage removed. 'Just over a pound's weight of feathers,' he said once order was restored in the box.

Katherine had been standing in silence beside her mother, but now she stepped to the fence and rested her arms on the top strands of wire. He moves like an animal, she thought, watching James stand spread-legged before he nimbly prepared the next bird. A light sheen of sweat coated the dark hairs of his bare arms.

She started to speak and was shocked to hear the hoarseness in her voice. She cleared her throat before she said, 'How many times can they be plucked?' She'd forgotten her earlier reaction to the smells which assailed her; what she sensed now was the dust of the action, the male sweat of the man directing it.

James did not respond to her question. He was battling with an arrogant young cock, the largest of the brood. Two of the labourers had to help him before the bird was subdued. Only then did he turn to her with a light smile on his lips. 'How many what?' he asked, yet Katherine felt sure he had heard her correctly the first time.

She flicked her gaze from his when she felt herself blush. 'I . . . I wanted to know how many times you can pluck them. How many plumages, I think you'd call it?' When she looked up again he was standing in front of her with only the wire fence separating them.

His voice was low when he said, 'The feathers deteriorate after the fifth plumage. Like humans, the birds lose their beauty with the passage of time.' He smiled at her, their bodies almost touching. She felt the heat rush through her to touch her eyes.

She turned away with a curt, 'Thank you,' and walked back to her mother on trembling legs. What on earth was wrong with her, responding to a brute in such a way? Yet she could not deny the excitement throbbing through her. She moved away from her mother, as if everybody there could sense her shameful reaction.

It was even worse once the plucking was over, when they passed by James's hut on their way back to the buggy. Her quick glance took in the sparse furnishings, the bunk which held his body at night. When she turned, she was sure she'd catch him watching her, a knowing smirk on his lips. Disappointment stabbed at her; he was not even looking her way. Her emotion of mere moments ago was replaced by embarrassment. It did not help telling herself she had momentarily fallen prey to an instinctive physical attraction, that she was merely responding to a man who had an animal sensuality. That kind of thing happened from time to time; it would pass once she left the farm and he was out of her sight. But what a feeling!

She was surprised to find herself smile at James as they left, secure now in her mental defences. As Isaacs set the buggy in motion, she heard her mother tell Sir Anthony, 'My dear, you really ought to have a decent cottage built for that young man. He'll become a savage if he carries on living like that.'

Her father laughed. 'Don't concern yourself about James Quenton,' he replied, 'he'll look after himself. He'll build his own cottage one day – more than that, I'm sure!' Isaacs nodded in agreement.

'I think you're quite right, Father,' Katherine piped up. 'I think you chose the right man for your venture. I found it all very interesting.' She ignored their looks of surprise, turning instead to study the tobacco fields of the neighbouring farm as they passed.

James and Outa watched the dust of the buggy disappear down the road sweeping past the large willows. 'We did well,' he said. 'Sir Anthony was pleased.'

Outa beamed. 'I shall get water,' he said, glancing at the day's dust which coated them both. He collected two wooden buckets standing beside the hut and headed for the river.

James sank on to his haunches. He'd found it satisfying to be greeted so warmly by Sir Anthony; the old man had been genuinely pleased to see him again. It had not been the same with Lady Kenrick. Or Katherine.

Despite the air of nonchalance he'd worn around her, he was painfully aware of his social shortcomings. He was nothing but a labourer to them, and his ten per cent share meant little. That would change, though, once the ostriches started producing real money for them. He had to be patient while he gradually increased his shareholding from his takings of the profit. Surely Sir Anthony would let him buy in to the business at a later stage? There'd come a day when he would be the richest man in the district – in the Colony perhaps! No woman would ever look down on him again. Money and power would buy him all the acceptance he needed.

He smiled suddenly, realising how tense he'd allowed himself to become. It had been foolish to let a little slip of a girl upset him, yet a picture of Katherine's fairness remained in his mind, a cruel reminder of his present station in life.

Outa gave him a strange look as he struggled towards him with the buckets. 'It is hard being a kaffir,' he panted, lowering the buckets thankfully to the ground. His muscular arms gleamed with sweat.

'We shall dig a furrow from the river,' replied James, playing along with Outa's griping. 'Then the poor kaffir will not have to walk so far.'

Outa doused his head with water. 'You should help me, not sit around like a cock whose shins grow red with lust. Oh yes, I saw the mating dance today!'

James rose quickly to his feet and dipped his hands into the nearest bucket. 'She is but a girl,' he replied angrily, splashing his face with water to hide his embarrassment.

Outa had not yet finished teasing him. 'Girls do not move so stiffly around men,' he said, 'and men do not play with girls the way you did.'

'You are a rumourmonger – like an old Zulu woman with nothing else to do.'

'Even an old Zulu bitch has eyes to see,' Outa shot back.

As he washed in sulky silence, James wondered who else had seen – Sir Anthony? What of it; he'd done nothing but respond playfully to the masked voluptuousness he'd sensed in Katherine.

He slowly lowered his hands, letting them rest in the cool water inside the bucket, shocked by his silent admission that Katherine was more than just a girl.

Sir Anthony was back on the farm early the next morning, alone and on horseback this time. He appeared even more relaxed without his wife and daughter around.

'I've discussed the matter with Abraham Isaacs,' he said without preamble, 'and we've agreed you should get a twenty per cent share of the profits.'

James stared back at him. 'I—'

'Don't thank me – you've earned it! But don't think it will happen again . . . You'll have to pay your own way from now on.'

Were they being generous, wondered James, or merely making an investment? Sir Anthony was too shrewd to give money away for no reason. He no doubt argued that once James had raised some capital, he would be tempted to leave and start his own ostrich venture. With a twenty per cent share, however, leaving would not be that easy.

'I'll thank Abraham when I see him,' he said, in no way resentful of the logic he was convinced the two men had followed. Twenty per cent would make the waiting easier, as long as they didn't intend blocking him when the time came to increase his share with his own money. Twenty per cent would not keep him satisfied for ever, as he intended to have it all.

He smiled at Sir Anthony again. 'When are you returning to Cape Town?' he asked, thinking of Katherine.

There was a long, loud sigh before Sir Anthony replied. 'I planned to go on to Grahamstown from here, but I think I'd go stark-raving mad if I had to spend any more time than necessary with my darling women.' His sigh was even louder than the first. 'We're leaving Oudtshoorn tomorrow,' he continued. 'Why not return with us? The break will do you good – how long has it been now . . . eighteen months?'

'Since I started on the farm, yes. More than two years since I arrived in the Colony.'

'As I was saying, the break will do you good. And give you the opportunity of meeting . . . ah . . . shall we say, ladies of good breeding?'

'I . . . I don't know. There's so much to be done here.' The truth was that he was not yet ready for Cape Town. Or Katherine.

'Nonsense! Outa is perfectly capable of carrying on with the farm'.

'Perhaps next year,' James said warily.

'Don't wait too long,' Sir Anthony replied with a twinkle in his eye. 'Eligible ladies have a way of being snapped up.'

'I'll come as soon as I can.'

'Good! That's settled then. You can let me know via Abraham.'

'I'll write my own letter, Sir Anthony,' he said proudly, enjoying the look of respect on the other man's face. 'Abraham is teaching me. He says I'm a good pupil.'

'I'm sure you are, young Quenton, I'm bloody sure you are!'

They arranged to meet in Oudtshoorn early that afternoon, from where James would take Sir Anthony on a tour of some other ostrich farms. 'Looking forward to it,' the old man said. He slapped James's shoulder, saddled up and rode off in a cloud of dust, leaving the young man to wonder whether he'd get to see Katherine before she left for Cape Town.

There was another visitor to the farm that same morning.

James was washing himself in preparation for his visits with Sir Anthony when a small cart approached. A black-coated figure sat hunched upon the driver's seat, a black hat pulled tightly down over his brow. At first he thought it might be Isaacs, but the visitor was much smaller than the lawyer.

He pulled on a clean shirt and waited beside the hut. The little man eased himself to the ground when the cart drew to a halt. The low hat precluded any form of identification, and he gave no greeting as he moved to the paddock fence to study the ostriches. Giving a satisfied nod, he made his way back to the hut.

'So,' he said, his tinny voice striking a chord in James's memory. 'So,' the visitor repeated, 'the inquisitive young man found the answers to his many questions. Not that I had much doubt on that score.'

'I'm sorry . . . I don't . . .' The little man raised his face, giving James a proper look at him. It all came rushing back: the tiny, dark office overlooking the docks in Cape Town, the high-pitched voice going on and on, spitting out facts and answers as fast as the questions were coming. 'Morris Sivrosky!' he shouted and gripped the old man's bony shoulders. 'What are you doing here?'

'Such a question you should ask a feather buyer? You think I come to look at camel droppings?'

James laughed at the serious expression on his face. 'Forgive me, Mr Sivrosky. It's been a long time.'

'*You* should worry about time!' He turned to study the farm again, giving another approving nod. 'I hear good things about you, boy. I think I'll buy your feathers.'

'If I'd known where to find you, I'd have asked for you a long time ago. We plucked yesterday.'

Sivrosky sighed. 'A feather agent wouldn't know such news, the boy thinks. I'll give you a fair price.'

'They're top-quality feathers, Mr Sivrosky.'

'From a second plucking? A fair price, I tell you, not a penny more. Sentimentality has no weight and therefore no value.'

James shook his head in resignation. 'A fair price will be fine. When will you look at them?'

'Tomorrow. I am busy now.' He climbed back aboard the cart and rode off without a farewell.

It had been an interesting day.

He did not see Katherine. Finishing his tour of the farms with Sir Anthony as darkness fell, he took his leave of the old man before galloping back to the farm.

It was only when he saw the light of Outa's fire that he realised he had never asked about Amos. He doubted whether Sir Anthony would have known of his old friend's existence, but he should have asked.

How soon we forget, he thought, and hurried forward to the warmth of the fire.

CHAPTER TEN

February 1868 held little promise of an end to the long drought. The heat, implacable in its demand for total submission, scarred the already defeated earth.

On his journey towards Cape Town, James rode slowly across farms ravaged by the sun, past homes where hopes lay smothered amid dust and ruins. He wondered where their owners had retreated to. Some, he knew, had pulled up stakes to head east or north; others had seen a glimmer of hope in the news of diamonds being discovered up-country. But the drought was everywhere; their wagons could never roll beyond the power of its reach.

He spent a night in an abandoned house which possessed nothing but memories, a once proud home that time and the drought had reduced to little more than neglected strips of clapboard and corrugated iron creaking and clanging in tune with the mournful wind.

He made no effort to trace Sir Anthony's road workers. The long road to Cape Town lay ahead, and he had no desire to see the dirty tents and surroundings which had once held him captive. He spurred his horse onwards, thinking he would meet Amos again some other place, in another time.

Sentiment tugged at him again when he reached Cape Town and passed by thinly settled Camps Bay. He stopped and looked down at the gates of Alfred Dock. It was already midday and he should have headed straight for Sir Anthony's home, but instead he spurred his horse in the direction of the harbour.

The great warehouse looked the same, a rusting, awkward shell hiding its many treasures. James dismounted and glanced at the few ships rising idly on the Atlantic swell. How many newcomers with fresh hopes and best-forgotten pasts had they disgorged on to the shores of the Colony?

The warehouse door was open. The smells, too, were unchanged, a familiar odour which would always spell a welcome to him. Yet when he entered the building he saw there had indeed been changes. In place of the crude cot on which Pat snored the nights away, there was now a comfortable bed. There was no tin plate holding scraps of food for the warehouse cats, and no Bible.

'What do you want?'. James turned to face the source of the gruff voice. A burly man about Pat's age watched him with suspicious eyes.

'What happened to Pat?' He had no need to ask if his friend was there; he'd already seen the answer to that.

The other man shrugged his shoulders. 'Who knows? Just went missing one day.'

'Missing?'

'It's thought he fell off the jetty one night. The old fool took to walking his darn cats.' He stopped, laughed, then said, 'Claimed it cleared his mind. What with his game leg and all . . .' His face hardened again as he added, 'What's your business here, anyway?'

James left the dark building without replying. Even the February sunshine was unable to relieve the raw numbness he felt inside him. Dear old Pat – not even the cats remained as a reminder of his existence.

He rode through the harbour at a fast trot, eager to escape the place which had cradled his entry to the country, thinking that, one by one, the traces of his shaky past were being erased from his grasp.

There was nothing now but the future.

Dinner was an awkward affair, with James at a loss for words in the luxurious surroundings of the Kenrick mansion.

Sir Anthony himself had greeted him when he arrived,

coming down the steps leading to a wide vine-covered verandah. 'Looks like you had a hard ride,' he said, making James intensely aware of the state of his clothes. He was glad when Sir Anthony offered him a bath, and even more relieved that Katherine did not spot him before he had the chance to wash and change. He saw her for the first time at dinner.

Now he studied her across the table, but she kept her eyes averted. Her greeting had been cordial yet reserved, and he found himself wondering why he'd expected more.

Lady Kenrick, on the other hand, was frostily polite. It was clear she did not approve of her husband's invitation to his farm-hand, as James was sure she regarded him.

He watched them all closely, following their example when it came to reaching for the correct eating utensils. Sir Anthony kept the conversation flowing, asking questions about their ostrich venture, a subject on which he knew his guest could speak with authority. James was thankful, yet resented his own social shortcomings. She probably thinks me a simpleton, he thought, glancing at Katherine again. She still did not look his way.

'Is it true you're a ruffian?' There was a sudden shocked silence as everyone stopped eating to stare at the little girl seated beside Katherine.

'Marianne!' Sir Anthony glared at the girl, then glanced at his wife's flushed face, confirming his suspicion that she had been the one to refer to their guest in that fashion. 'Apologise to Mr Quenton immediately!'

'She calls everyone she doesn't know a ruffian,' said Katherine quickly, laying a protective hand on the girl's shoulder. 'She didn't mean any harm.' Her warm smile dispelled the quick anger which had flashed through James.

'I was one . . . once,' he managed to say, smiling as he turned to the girl. 'But I'm trying to change. Don't you like ruffians, Marianne?'

She flashed her teeth at him. 'I think you're a nice ruffian. So does Katherine.' The nine-year-old seemed to enjoy the consternation that the latter part of her statement had caused. James decided he liked her.

While everyone else tried to steer the conversation on

to safer topics, Marianne flashed him a quick wink before concentrating on her food again. She's going to break men's hearts when she's older, he thought as he watched the complete innocence of the auburn-haired beauty as she immersed herself once again in her supper. He'd been surprised at her presence when she arrived at the table, till he learned she was the Kenricks' niece. Sir Anthony explained that his brother and Marianne's mother had been killed in England when their carriage overturned. The girl had been in his care for the last year.

'So you've built a cottage on the farm,' he said, trying now to draw James back into the conversation.

'It's no mansion, Sir Anthony, but it's a great deal more comfortable than the hut. I didn't want to go to great expense on land that's leased.'

'Hmmn. The damn bugger still doesn't want to sell?'

'Father!' cried Katherine. 'Your language!'

'Sorry.' He didn't look it. 'What's his name again?' he asked James.

'Jooste. Says he might decide to farm again when the drought breaks.'

Sir Anthony gave a loud snort. 'He'll probably increase the lease when the contract is due. We should find other land. I bought up a parcel near—'

'No,' interrupted James, more sharply than he'd intended. 'I mean, I'm going to work on Jooste again. He'll sell in the end.'

'So,' asked Sir Anthony, changing the subject with a dismissive shrug, 'how are you enjoying being a twenty per cent partner? Happy with the arrangement?'

'Yes . . . yes, of course. You've been very generous.' He wondered why his host had raised the subject – surely Abraham Isaacs kept him informed of his progress as well as his attitude? Then he smiled, realising Sir Anthony was impressing upon his wife and Katherine his true status in the venture.

When dinner was over at last, James gratefully accepted Sir Anthony's invitation to have a glass of brandy in his study. He bade Katherine and the mischievous Marianne

101

good-night, thanked Lady Kenrick for her hospitality, for which he received a cool nod and a fresh appraisal of his dress, and then fled thankfully after his host as he led the way down a long corridor.

'Nothing like a glass of good brandy to wash away the tension caused by women,' said Sir Anthony as they entered the study. 'I love them dearly,' he added, 'but in small doses.' He poured the drinks into elegant glasses the like of which James had never seen before, offered him a cigar and then slumped into a large leather chair. James settled for a smaller chair facing his benefactor.

They raised their glasses, smiled briefly at each other, and leaned back in silence while they sipped the brandy and toyed with their cigars. Sir Anthony sighed contentedly. He studied James closely, grunted and said, 'Are you uncomfortable here? With my wife and Katherine, I mean? Do you feel you don't belong, that you're too much of a ruffian, as young Marianne so tactlessly put it?'

'No,' James replied quickly, blushing at the lie. 'I . . . Yes,' he confessed with a sigh, 'that's exactly how I feel.' His short laugh had a sad ring to it. 'I really am not much more than a farm-hand, am I? I may be achieving a measure of success with our venture, yet I'm still not much more than the crude young labourer who came to your tent that night.'

Sir Anthony started to rise, then sank back in his seat. He stabbed his cigar at his guest and said, 'I want to tell you something.' The cigar made a few more empty stabs before he went on: 'I was born into the nobility, surrounded by riches and high society from the time I was released from my mother's womb. But, this . . .' He gave a sweep of his arms, the gesture encompassing the entire house. 'None of this,' he continued, his voice gaining strength, 'is a result of that money. What you see is what Anthony Kenrick earned for himself.' He thumped a thick forefinger against his chest.

'I ran away from home when I was a few years younger than you, away from spineless young men living off the reputation and achievements of their fathers or ancestors. Away from idle-brained women who measure a man according to the size of his inheritance and the length of his ancestry.' The flow of words seemed to bring an old anger along with them.

James sat perched on the edge of his chair, intrigued by the revelations of the man who evaluated him on terms most others would never have applied.

Sir Anthony smiled, the anger gone from his face as quickly as it had appeared. 'I was immediately disinherited, of course – I think my father hoped that would bring me running home. But it was fifteen years before I returned to England, just in time to save the family estate from financial ruin.' He gave a short laugh and there was a faraway look in his eyes. 'Oh, you should have seen them . . . I was the prodigal son returned! They took my money with no questions as to how I'd earned it. If they only knew!'

James remained silent, sensing the other man had not yet made his point.

'Everything was fine then – all was forgiven. I even inherited my father's title!' He crushed out his cigar with slow, circling movements, as if playing for time while he ordered his thoughts. 'Like you,' he said gently and reached for his brandy, 'I wanted to see for myself what I was worth. I possessed a sharp mind when it came to making the most of opportunities, and I knew when to fight and when to use people. Again, just like you.'

'Sir Anthony, I—' The older man held up his hand to silence him.

'You're a guest in my home, visiting here by my invitation. You're in my house, which my wife and daughter – and now Marianne as well – adorn with considerable grace and beauty. None of them could ever understand what it was like at the start or what was required of me. I shall never tell them, and I don't think they wish to know. The point I want to make, James, is that they are as much my guests as you are. I hope your realising this will help make your stay here an enjoyable one, for that is what it is intended to be.'

'I abandoned my family,' James said, suddenly realising Sir Anthony knew virtually nothing of his past. 'My mother, my little sister and brother – I don't even know what's become of them.'

'We all abandon people,' came the gentle reply, 'in some

103

way or another. Does it trouble you? Haunt you at night?'

'Not any longer. What troubles me more is how seldom I think of them.'

'You are at that time of life when memories hold little value for you. Don't be too hard on yourself, James.' Sir Anthony smiled. 'The long miles of your journey show in your eyes. Perhaps you should go to bed.'

'Yes.' James downed the last of his brandy, stood up, then turned to Sir Anthony again. 'I saw a man kill another,' he said, 'in a fight which should have ended with nothing more than bruises, or at worst broken bones. It was murder.'

'And that troubles you, does it? More than the other . . . your family?'

'Yes. The murderer works for you. Gert Denker.'

There was little reaction on Sir Anthony's face. 'That is a serious charge, James,' he said after a while.

'It's a true one. The labourers will verify it.' He told of the fight and about Denker's treatment of the men. When he had finished, Sir Anthony let out a long sigh.

'I'd always known Denker was a hard man,' he said, 'and a hard man is what is needed out there. But to take pleasure in beating a young man to death!'

'It should never have come to that,' James insisted. 'To Thomas it was nothing more than another fight, another test of his skills.'

'You say it was never reported?'

'I wanted to believe there were better ways for Denker to pay for his crime.'

Sir Anthony was lost in thought for a moment, then seemed to make up his mind. 'I'll see to it he's replaced as soon as I can get somebody out to the work site,' he said firmly. 'I'll not have a killer on my payroll.'

'There's a man there,' James said quickly, 'by the name of Amos. He's worked on the road for years. The men respect him. He'd do a good job for you.'

'Amos, you say? I'll look into it.'

'Well, I'll say good-night then.' He started for the door.

'Good-night,' Sir Anthony called out. His voice stopped James just before he left the study. 'Remember what I've said to you tonight, James Quenton. The only difference between the two of us is the kind of world we ran from. Be patient, for it's not as easy to return to yours as it was to mine.' He gave a salute with his glass as James slipped through the door.

The bed was warm and inviting as he stripped off his clothes. He thought about the request he had made on Amos's behalf. Had he done that, he wondered, for Amos – or to salve his own conscience?

The thought lasted no longer than a few fleeting seconds before much-needed sleep overwhelmed him.

Katherine shifted the soft pillows beneath her head and studied the ceiling. Sleep continued to elude her no matter how hard she tried to force the image of James Quenton from her mind.

She knew she should feel shame at her reaction to his presence in the house, yet every thought of him brought a fresh wave of sensual excitement flooding deliciously down through her stomach. It seemed to reach her toes before it washed back over her.

It didn't help to remind herself he was uneducated, that he lacked the sophistication she so greatly admired in men. She sensed he would appear awkward in conversation with her friends, yet she could not deny that he was more of a man than any two of them put together. She was quite wanton, she thought with a smile as heat flushed delightfully through her. Had she inherited it from her father? She giggled at the thought of the frosty Lady Kenrick reacting to a man in such a way.

She wondered how much time they would be allowed together. None at all, if it was left up to Lady Kenrick. Perhaps after a few days, when her father had finished showing their visitor around his various business enterprises, James would be free to spend some time around the house. Perhaps then they could talk.

The creaking of the bedroom door made her grab at the bedclothes and pull them up around her throat, so that only her face and frightened eyes showed. Was he coming to her?

Had her first impressions about him been correct after all? A wild, primitive man?

It was a tousled mass of auburn hair which peered through the opening. 'Kath?' came the whisper. 'You still awake?'

'Marianne – you little wretch – you should be asleep!'

The girl slipped into the room, closing the door quietly behind her. 'It's too hot,' she said as she planted herself on the bed. 'Besides, I wanted to talk to you.'

Katherine sighed. She had come to love her cousin as a sister. 'All right, Pumpkin, let's talk.'

Marianne toyed with the edge of the blanket. 'Come on,' prompted Katherine, 'speak up!'

'I'm sorry, Kath, for making you blush at dinner. About what I said . . . you know, about your thinking James is nice.'

'So you should be, you little brat! I'll never trust you again.'

'Oh no, Kath, please! I was just being jealous.'

'Jealous? But I thought you loved George?' She smiled, recalling how Marianne played up to George Laboulaye, a young Frenchman her father had befriended some years ago and who was now a regular visitor to the Kenrick mansion. George always played along with the little girl, flirting with her in his magnificent fashion. Marianne was determined they would marry some day, and George, who was twenty-six years old, had sworn he would be true till then. Dear George, thought Katherine – she should have fallen in love with him.

A new thought struck her. George would be arriving at the Cape in a few days – how would he and James get along? They were not unlike, although George was more . . . well, smoother. Still, George was a special kind of man who would accept James for what he was, instead of evaluating him according to social standards.

'I do love George,' Marianne was saying, 'but he's so far away, and James is awfully dashing.'

'You can't love two men at the same time, my sweet. Don't forget, George will be here by the end of the week.'

The youngster thought about this for a while, her expression indicating she could not quite comprehend the problem. 'I suppose you're right,' she said with a sigh. 'I'll stay true to George. At least I know where I stand with him.'

Katherine laughed and hugged her cousin. 'I'm so glad, Pumpkin – now I have James all to myself.'

The little girl seemed relieved she had not ruined their friendship. She saw Katherine's gesture as an invitation to join her in bed. 'I'll wake up early,' she promised, 'before your mother finds me sleeping here. You don't mind, do you?'

'Of course not, Pumpkin. Hmm – you smell of flowers. George would like that.'

She wriggled closer. 'Is George a ruffian, Kath?'

'Oh yes! Underneath that French charm and old-style courtesy, George is the biggest ruffian of all.'

'I'm glad. I like ruffians.'

'So do I, Pumpkin, so do I. Now go to sleep.'

After a while, Marianne's light snore added its own distraction to the thoughts which kept Katherine from her rest.

CHAPTER ELEVEN

James and Sir Anthony were in the city by nine o'clock to start their tour of Sir Anthony's business ventures. There was a milling company, a timber-yard, then a stop at what Sir Anthony termed his headquarters in Newmarket Street. The place was staffed by a bevy of young clerks and aspirant managers pathetically eager to cater to their employer's every whim. James saw more than one pair of sweating palms being wrung together.

He felt relieved when they were out in the fresh air again, and he could tell Sir Anthony felt much the same. 'Damn sycophants,' muttered the older man. He hauled out his pocket watch, glanced at it, and suggested they have some tea before returning home for lunch. 'There's time, of course,' he added, 'for us to pay a visit to my construction company, although I tend to think you'd prefer to give it a miss.' He glanced at James with raised eyebrows.

James thought of the huts, the sour-faced clerk, and of Denker. 'Tea sounds like a marvellous idea,' he said.

The days slipped by in a whirlwind of visits as far afield as Stellenbosch, where Sir Anthony owned a vineyard. With each call, James grew more impressed with his benefactor.

He sat beside Sir Anthony at a number of meetings, where he learned for the first time just how astute the old man was as a businessman.

There were many who approached Sir Anthony with

propositions. He always listened patiently, as he had with James. Some of the requests seemed to bear merit, but then James would watch Sir Anthony tear holes in them with calm yet harsh logic, finding flaws where there appeared to be none. 'Playing devil's advocate,' the old man said and winked as one shame-faced hopeful packed his documents and departed in gloom. 'It could work,' continued Sir Anthony, 'but the stupid bugger should have had his answers ready. I'll find somebody else to develop the idea.' It merely served to impress upon James how little he himself knew about business and how fortunate he had been to gain knowledge of ostrich breeding before approaching Sir Anthony with his own scheme.

The most interesting meeting of all took place at the Kenrick home, when James was introduced to George Laboulaye.

He was in his room when the Frenchman arrived, so he was able to study him from behind the privacy of lace curtains. 'George has a sharp mind,' Sir Anthony had said. 'He seldom misses an opportunity.' From the way in which he spoke, James could tell he was very fond of the Frenchman.

'Just what kind of business is he in?' he had asked.

'I tend to think he's the only one who really knows! One could call him an agent of sorts, I suppose. Very well connected – old French family. He could be useful to you.'

James raised his eyebrows in question. 'Oh, yes,' continued Sir Anthony without explaining himself. 'Oh yes, indeed! Very useful. In fact, I took the liberty of writing to him about our ostrich venture.'

James had waited, but no further details were forthcoming. He tried to hide his resentment at Sir Anthony's having discussed their venture with an outsider without first consulting him. Just what was this Laboulaye to Sir Anthony? And to Katherine?

Now, he stepped back into the shadows of his room as Sir Anthony's brougham, sent to the docks to collect the Frenchman, come to a halt in the driveway. The man who climbed down was very tall and slim. James knew he was just three years older than himself. He was not really handsome, yet one could not miss the zest for life which radiated from his wide smile as he greeted Sir Anthony.

The next moment, James felt a renewed flash of resentment when Katherine rushed towards George Laboulaye, hurtling into his arms.

'Kath! My darling Katherine!' His voice, deep and without any noticeable accent, floated clearly to where James stood. So, he had been right after all – there was something between Katherine and this Laboulaye fellow. Damn the man!

George placed the laughing young woman back on her feet and turned to Marianne who stood a few feet away, trying but failing to keep a look of total adoration from showing on her face. He knelt before her and drew the little girl into his arms, whispering something which only she could hear. Marianne's squeals of delight and excitement were quite clear, however. A ladies' man, James thought miserably, deciding he definitely did not like Mr George Laboulaye. But he was duty bound to put in an appearance and feign a courteous greeting.

'Your visitor,' George was saying as James came out the front door, 'he is here?'

'He's here,' replied Sir Anthony.

'Good! I have followed this ostrich business with great interest. I've watched its growth in Europe, and have some thoughts on the matter.'

'I thought you would. Ah, there he is now. James, I'd like you to meet—'

'James Quenton? Sir Anthony wrote me about you. When was it? Last year I think. I lose track of the time . . . I have been looking forward to this meeting!' The flow of words stopped abruptly when he stuck out both hands, gripping an overwhelmed James's palm firmly between them. 'There is much I wish to talk to you about.' George pumped his hand furiously, his eyes crinkling at the corners as he smiled down at the shorter man.

James was quite taken aback by George's open friendliness. Despite his earlier feelings, he found it hard not to warm to the Frenchman. 'Yes – I – I'd be interested to hear about the European markets.'

George gave a series of rapid nods and seemed about to tackle the subject right away, but Sir Anthony saw what was coming and gripped his arm, saying, 'There'll be plenty of time for talking. First we'll get you freshened up. I'll open a bottle of red wine, let it air in the meantime. Both you and the wine should be ready by lunch-time.' George allowed himself to be led away. Lady Kenrick followed quickly, her expression one of a mother who had just welcomed home her long-lost son.

It was then that James noticed Katherine had remained near the doorway. She smiled demurely before lowering her gaze. 'Have you enjoyed your stay so far?' she asked softly.

He stared at her, realising again how little he had seen of her since his arrival. They seemed to meet only at meal-times, when there was no chance to talk beyond general topics. 'Yes, thank you. Your father has been very generous with his time.'

They stood awkwardly, shifting position and searching for something to say. 'I—' James laughed when they both started to speak at the same time. Her own face creased in amusement.

'You first,' Katherine said.

'I was going to say that George seems a fine man. Any plans for a wedding?'

Her eyes widened in surprise before she began to laugh. 'George—?' she started. 'You mean . . . ? Oh no, it's not like that at all!'

He hoped his relief did not show. 'I thought—'

'Goodness, no! George is almost family, like a brother to me! Heavens, Marianne would kill me if what you thought was true. She's the one who loves him, you see.'

'I'm sorry, I—'

'Are you? Sorry, I mean?' There was a teasing look in her eyes.

'No! I mean, I just thought . . .' He heard his voice trail off, finding himself unsettled by this new side to Katherine. Was she flirting with him? Was that possible?

'Katherine!' The sound of Lady Kenrick's voice made them step apart from each other.

Katherine smiled again, her gaze holding his this time. 'I'd better go. I hope we can talk some more before you leave.'

'Yes, so do I.' He wondered whether she heard him as she rushed off, her long skirts swishing as she hastened to respond to her mother's summons.

Sir Anthony's brougham rolled through the mountain suburbs of Newlands and Kirstenbosch. Two white horses pulled in perfect unison, tossing their manes as the load increased uphill.

Katherine sat beside James, a white parasol raised protectively above her head. She smiled as she recalled how shocked her mother had been when Sir Anthony suggested Katherine might accompany their guest on a tour of Cape Town on his last day there. She could have hugged her father, yet managed to keep her face impassive while she pretended to agree reluctantly to his suggestion. She had to bite back her smile when Lady Kenrick insisted on acting as chaperone. Sir Anthony had stood firm on that as well, arguing that the coachman would be enough of a presence to ensure their orderly conduct.

She glanced sideways at James, but he was staring straight ahead. Did he feel uncomfortable with her? She was sure he had been pleased when her father made his suggestion. 'You look as though you were born to be driven about in a carriage,' she said.

He returned her smile. 'I might not have been born to it, but I have no doubt I'll quickly get used to it.'

'Would you like a carriage of your own?' She lowered the parasol as they passed under the shade of ancient oak trees.

'I'm *going* to have one,' he replied with determination. 'Before long.'

'Is money very important to you?'

He looked at her in surprise. 'Yes,' he said, 'it is. It's what most people seem to judge others by. It gives one security. And power.'

'Power to do what?' Their bodies touched as the carriage jolted over an uneven section of track.

James shrugged. 'Power to release the hold others have on one. Power to act on things as they arise, to meet challenges.' He was pleased at her interest in him.

'Will my father's ostriches make you rich? Rich enough to give you such power?'

'They're *my* ostriches, too, Katherine. I now own twenty per cent of the venture.'

'Of course. I forgot.'

'They'll make me rich,' he continued. 'I'm already thinking of buying a townhouse in Oudtshoorn. Unless I can get to buy the land we're farming on, of course. I'd prefer to build there.'

'A mansion?' she asked with a smile.

He laughed. 'I think that will have to wait a few years, but yes – one day there will be a mansion.'

She laughed with him, a pleasant sound, light and rare, reminding him of the first time they had been alone together, the day George Laboulaye had arrived.

Thinking of the Frenchman made him say, 'You know that George is going back to Oudtshoorn with me?'

She nodded. 'I'm glad you two get along so well.'

James gave a secret smile. It was true he had warmed to George after learning he was no threat to gaining Katherine's affection. He had been impressed, too, with the Frenchman's suggestion that he act on his behalf to establish direct marketing links with European distributors.

There were too many middlemen involved in the marketing of ostrich feathers, George had argued. Why not cut them out and retain a greater profit? James was quick to agree, although he warned himself to ensure his new friend's role remained only that of marketing agent. He could not afford another person sharing in the venture's profits.

Sir Anthony, who had presided as informal chairman over their discussion, was more excited than either of them. The only condition, he insisted, was that George should acquire more knowledge about the industry before he commenced his marketing activities. That was easy enough to arrange; it was agreed he would accompany James to Oudtshoorn and spend a few months on the farm.

It was midday when James and Katherine finally reached the beach. They unpacked their picnic basket while the coachman removed himself to a spot a discreet distance away from them. It had taken them longer than planned to get there, so that already a soft haze had spread across the

113

bay, raising the leper colony of Robben Island from its watery foundations to create high cliffs where there were none.

'It's good to smell the sea again,' said James when they had finished lunch and were strolling along the beach. He had to raise his voice to be heard above the crash of the waves and the crunch of their feet on the sand. Katherine still held her parasol, although the day spent outdoors had touched her fair skin and added a warm glow to her face.

'Marianne confessed to me she'd fallen in love with you,' she said. 'I managed to talk her out of it.'

'I'm flattered! What did you say to her – that ruffians make bad company?' He reached out to touch her arm when he saw that he had embarrassed her. 'I'm sorry – I didn't mean that to sound the way it did.'

'No, I'm the one who's sorry. Marianne heard that from my mother. You must forgive her . . . I think she's terrified Father's whims will destroy her security.'

'So I'm a whim, am I?' he said, smiling to soften the words.

'I must confess I thought of you in much the same way as Mother,' she replied blushingly. 'I'd more or less convinced myself you were after my father's money – up to no good.'

'And now?'

'To quote Marianne,' she said, amazed at her boldness, 'I think you're rather nice.'

'I'm glad. I thought of you as a spoilt brat when I saw you at the paddocks.'

'And now?'

'Rather nice!'

They laughed together, touching as their bodies moved with their mirth and the sudden release of tension. James slowed his walk to touch her arm lightly. The sea haze moved closer as if wanting to cloak them in its muted touch as they kissed. Their embrace was in keeping with their discovery of each other – probing yet gentle, warm and slow.

'I think we should go back,' Katherine whispered as they drew slowly apart. 'It's a long ride.'

'Yes.' He gazed down at her half-closed eyes. In that instant, he knew she would one day be his; one day when he was ready for her.

They kissed each other again, quickly, feverishly. Katherine clung to him as if he was about to depart on his long journey back to the Karoo. 'I don't want you to go,' she whispered into his neck. 'We've had so little time together.'

'There's a great deal to be done on the farm,' he replied gently, stroking her hair.

She pulled away from him. 'You mean you miss those birds of yours,' she said with a sulky smile. 'I should be jealous. And insulted,'

'When I'm with them, I'll miss you, Katherine.'

'Then come back to me!'

'I shall.'

'When?'

He sighed and drew her to him again. 'I don't know . . . When I feel I'm ready, when I possess some of that power we spoke of earlier. When I have that, and wealth.'

'I'll wait.'

They kissed again, breaking their embrace only when Katherine glimpsed the coachman peering at them from beneath the trees where he rested.

The sky above Oudtshoorn was a clear, blinding blue. The air was hot and dry, denied the relieving moisture by the awesome Outeniqua Mountains which impeded its progress from the Indian Ocean. The town of George, lying on the ocean side of the mountain, had a lush green landscape.

'The town has a proud name,' mocked George Laboulaye when the diverse climate was explained. 'I think I must visit it before I return to Cape Town.'

'When are you planning on leaving?' asked James. The four months George had spent on the farm had passed quickly.

'Soon. I think I've learned enough to be able to talk with some measure of authority. Do you agree?'

James smiled and nodded. 'You'll go back to Europe as soon as you can?'

'On the first ship. I'm anxious to put our plans into operation.'

'Let's hope they work,' James muttered. 'Have you enjoyed

your stay here?' he added in a more friendly tone. They were lying beside the river, its flow reduced by the drought to little more than a trickle. A bottle of brandy rested between them.

George squinted at the sky. 'It's been quite an experience. An enjoyable one, yes.' It was true; it had been a long time since he had dirtied his hands and smelled sweat on his body, for he had laboured as hard as Outa or any of the other workers. There was something about the ostriches which fascinated him, so that he often risked life and limb to get close enough to study their habits.

Aside from the work and his learning, he had enjoyed being with James. He was not quite sure whether what he felt for the other man was liking, or nothing more than an admiration for his ambition and dedication to his goals. He sensed that James was capable of immense selfishness, a man who would ride roughshod over others if they proved useful to him. He was prepared to concede that such traits were necessary to someone with James's background.

He also enjoyed the change from his normal circle of acquaintances. James provided a fascinating contrast to the self-indulgent set with whom George felt he spent too much of his time.

George Laboulaye was from an old French family, and his name guaranteed him entrance into the great homes of Europe. It seemed to make little difference to his hosts that he was devoid of any significant wealth, it having been close to a century since a Laboulaye had last occupied the grand vineyards of Bordeaux. That right was denied his family because of the financial follies of his grandfather, as well as the old man's propensity for wine, women and song – in that order. George was convinced he had inherited similar traits from his forebear, although he argued that the sequence of preferences was different.

He considered himself a financial survivor. Unlike the rest of his family, who spent their time decrying the unfairness of their lot, he could not recall a day when he had gone hungry or lonely. He had fled their indignation while still in his teens and moved to Paris where he started making the most of his opportunities, moving constantly to where they seemed to offer reasonable profit as well as a measure of stimulation. Now it happened to be Africa.

He glanced at the man lying beside him. In a way they were both opportunists, perhaps it was that which attracted them to each other. 'You'll arrange for the export from this side?' he asked.

'Yes. Sir Anthony will assist with that. All you have to do is find wholesalers interested in buying direct from me.'

'I'll find them. They won't say no to extra profit.'

They each took a sip from the brandy bottle. George wiped his lips and said, 'You think Sir Anthony would be prepared to sell you all his shares, assuming you could pay for them?'

'I don't know,' came the cautious reply. 'Abraham Isaacs owns twenty per cent as well.'

'Marrying Katherine could change things.'

It was a while before James answered him, saying, 'By next year I shall own this land, or a house in Oudtshoorn. Then I shall be ready. If she wants me, I shall marry her. But it will be for love, not for shares.'

'Of course,' said George hastily. 'I didn't mean to imply—'

'But you're right – things could change dramatically.' He reached for the bottle and passed it on with a smile.

George Laboulaye rode out of Oudtshoorn a week later, carrying with him a letter from James to Katherine. The day after his departure, a sweeping cold scurried in across the Karoo veld bringing dark rain clouds with it.

The downpour washed away roads and bridges, broke the long drought, and ushered in a new era for Oudtshoorn.

It was an era for which James was more prepared than most.

CHAPTER TWELVE

James saw George Laboulaye again only in March of 1869, nine months after he had left the farm to sail for Europe. It was the day before James's wedding to Katherine, a calm, balmy morning of the kind that Cape Town delivers so well at that time of year.

'How did you do it?' asked George as the two men shook hands when he arrived at the Kenrick estate. 'Was it that letter I delivered to Katherine on your behalf? But that's almost a year ago!' he finished, remembering the young woman's expression of delight when he had handed her the letter.

James laughed. 'No, I visited the Kenricks on two occasions since then. I proposed in January.'

'Sir Anthony's approval I can understand – he liked you – but how did you get around Lady Kenrick? I'd have thought she'd fight tooth and nail to prevent you even forming a relationship with Katherine – let alone marrying her!'

'She did! But you know Sir Anthony . . . she had to bend to his will in the end. She's given in with good grace though.'

The two men laughed and started for the house as a servant hurried forward to collect George's luggage. 'You look more prosperous than ever,' George said, brushing an imaginary speck of dust from the shoulder of James's jacket.

'Most of it is due to your efforts in Europe.' Four shipments of feathers had already passed directly from the warehouse Sir Anthony had arranged in Cape Town, *en route* to distributors in Europe. Profits had improved substantially.

'So, what is it to be for the beautiful Katherine – a house on your own land, or one in Oudtshoorn?'

A dark look flashed across James's face. 'That bastard, Jooste, still doesn't want to sell,' he muttered. 'He's been even more stubborn since the drought broke. He'll probably want to move back when our lease expires.'

'What'll you do, then? Why wait till he acts, why not find alternative land now?'

'I'm not giving up on him – he'll sell to me yet.'

'Where'll you live in the meantime?'

'I bought a townhouse in Oudtshoorn. It's modern and comfortable, although it's a long ride to the farm and back each day.'

George arched his eyebrows. 'A townhouse! Profits must really be good, then!'

'Feather prices have risen once again,' said James, leading them to a small vine-covered verandah at the side of the house, 'and you're aware of the shortage in supply. I've purchased more birds, even though Sir Anthony and Abraham Isaacs opposed me . . . They said I was moving too fast. I've proved them wrong.'

'I think we'll need the extra production, James. For the foreseeable future, at least. America is becoming a valuable market as well. Tons of feathers are being diverted from the docks at London, with everyone getting their share of the profits.'

'Another direct channel, you mean?'

'If possible. I want to go to America to investigate things.'

'You realise, of course, that we've antagonised the feather buyers? They hate what we're doing.'

He had thought Morris Sivrosky would have a heart attack when he informed the old man he would no longer be selling his feathers to him. 'For me,' the feather buyer had said, 'it makes little difference. But there'll be many you rob of their living. If others follow you, it could mean their ruin. Beware, for they will not accept this as easily as I do.'

George was busy with his own thoughts. He looked up suddenly and said, 'I have had first-hand experience of that antagonism.'

'What do you mean?'

'Twice in the last month there were attacks on me, although I think they were more interested in scaring me than killing me. They succeeded!'

'They attacked you? Did you report it?'

'There was no proof, my friend.' He laughed and added, 'So, your wedding invitation came at a good time. It takes me away from Europe and allows time for passions to cool. Even better if I go straight to America from here. I've never seen New York.'

James laughed with him. 'Enjoy America,' he said. 'The first positive word on progress I get from you, I'll buy even more birds.'

Their discussion was interrupted by the arrival of Marianne. She leaned against the wall in emulation of a womanly sulk and said, 'You greet your friends first, then me?'

George jumped to his feet and held out his arms. 'Marianne, my only true love! It's James who arrested me on my way to you.' He winked at him as the girl hesitated before moving into the circle of his arms.

James watched the charade. It was only George who was playing a game, he thought; Marianne would be a woman long before her friends and family noticed it.

He left George talking earnestly to his young admirer and went inside the house. Sir Anthony met him near the entrance, and listened carefully while James explained George's intention of visiting America.

Sir Anthony did not seem surprised. 'A good idea,' he said. 'The sooner we get in there and satisfy their demands, the better for us.'

'You make that sound almost sinister.'

'I meant it to. The Americans have the climate to breed ostriches, so sooner or later some enterprising fellow will try it. Their transport costs would be a lot lower than ours – both on their domestic market and on exports. They'd cut our throats on price.' Someone called and Sir Anthony bustled off.

James stayed where he was, shocked by the truth of what Sir Anthony had said. He decided there and then to purchase additional birds on his return to Oudtshoorn.

There was no sense in risking the delay until he heard from George.

It was not the biggest or most glamorous wedding Cape Town had ever seen, although Lady Kenrick ensured that a number of prominent people were in attendance. James found to his pleasant surprise that he was not in awe of them, as if his marriage to Katherine suddenly provided the confidence and social acceptance he had lacked.

From across the room, George Laboulaye watched him, wondering why he felt a trace of anxiety. His two closest friends had been joined in matrimony, so he should he filled with happiness for them. Yet the unease lingered, and he forced a smile when Katherine waved at him. They made a handsome couple, he thought and waved back: James strong and dark beside the petite fairness of his wife.

Shortly afterwards, Sir Anthony silenced the orchestra before stepping up on to the stand. There was a hushed silence when he announced he was granting all his remaining shares in the ostrich farm as a wedding present to Katherine.

George watched the newly wed couple embrace each other with excitement. It was all James's now, he thought, all of it except the shares owned by Abraham Isaacs.

He had a feeling that, too, would change one day.

The townhouse stood on a corner site, its small front garden surrounded by an iron railing of somewhat art nouveau fashion. Its walls were constructed from ochre stone common to the Oudtshoorn district. A circular verandah at the corner of the house was tucked beneath a free-scale, tiled conical tower set in the roof, its base resting on a collar of ironwork with a motif of honeysuckle. The fan of the verandah, which embraced much of the perimeter of the house, was supported by cast-iron pillars with railings, forming an attractive portico over the front steps.

Katherine loved the house, especially the way in which the roof formation and ornate ceilings followed the shapes of the rooms beneath. The house was vastly different from and smaller than Sir Anthony's mansion, but it was more cosy. And it was hers. It was more than a new home; it was the symbol of the new life she had started with her husband. She wondered what it would be like with children in it.

The thought of a family curbed her smile as she put down the *Thumb English Dictionary* she had been using in James's study. They had been married for six months already, but James would not yet agree to their having a baby. 'Our child will be born in our own home,' he had argued.

'*This* is our home, James!' she countered.

He shook his head and said, 'This is our *house*. Our *home* will be on the farm.' The way he had reached out angrily to set the leather-bound globe spinning on top of his desk had told her how deeply he resented the refusal of Jooste to sell him the land. Since that night, almost two months ago now, she had not raised the subject again.

Katherine sighed and left the study. Sunlight filtered through the stained-glass windows at the end of the passage. It touched her face, reminding her of her first Karoo summer, which would start soon. 'Mrs Blake?' she called out. A chubby face peered around the kitchen door.

'Mum?'

She smiled at her housekeeper. 'Any chance of a cup of tea?'

The big woman stepped into the passage. 'Of course, mum. You just make yourself comfortable in the meantime.'

Katherine followed her towards the kitchen. She had insisted James appoint the widowed Mrs Blake. 'She has three children to care for,' she had argued, 'and she'll be good company for me while you're busy with your ostriches.' Mrs Blake had joined them in their first month in the townhouse. James had never taken to the large woman, and Katherine sensed that the hostility was mutual. She could not pinpoint any particular reason for it, and consoled herself with the thought that James, who spent most of his time on the farm anyway, would have little opportunity to clash with the housekeeper. Or vice versa, for Mrs Blake had a domineering and forthright way about her, and had already proved intensely loyal to Katherine.

'It'll be awful hot in the kitchen just now,' the housekeeper said and steered her out of the house and on to the open verandah facing the street. 'I'll serve it out here.' Katherine smiled and allowed herself to be bossed around as usual.

The verandah protected her from the midday sun as she settled herself on the couch against the wall. She could smell the dust and the heat on the street, yet it did not bother her the way it had when she had visited Oudtshoorn the first time with her father. How long ago that seemed, she thought, recalling her meeting James on the farm that day. How primitive he had appeared – how physical! He still was the latter, for on her occasional visits to the farm she had seen him stripped to the waist, working as hard as any of the labourers. Then there was more, too – their lovemaking.

She shut her eyes, blushing at the thought of the previous night. There were times when she sensed that James was somewhat disconcerted by her wild abandon. But she enjoyed it so – it was better than all her girlish fantasies had been! Each time she wished that their loving had a dual purpose: pleasure and procreation.

If only James was not so obsessed with owning the farm! It would be his eventually, she was sure of that, but it might take years and she did not want to wait that long. He was impatient for his farm; well, so was she impatient to start a family. What could he do if she allowed it to happen? He'd be angry at first, but he'd soon come to like the idea. Yes, perhaps that was what she should do – arrange a little 'accident'.

Mrs Blake gave her a curious look when she appeared with a tray of tea and biscuits. 'You seem amused, mum,' the plump housekeeper said.

'I was just wondering, Mrs Blake . . . Tell me, do you think I'd make a good mother?'

The woman smiled as she sugared Katherine's tea and handed her the cup. 'The best,' she replied, 'and the most beautiful.' Katherine flushed with pleasure.

Mrs Blake watched her a few moments longer before she said, 'Have a biscuit, mum – we'll be needing to build up your strength, then, won't we?'

The housekeeper waited till Katherine had taken two of the home-made biscuits from the plate before she went back inside the house.

It was dark when James returned from the farm, smelling of sweat and dust and ostriches. 'You stink,' said Katherine as she embraced him. 'I've already run your bath,' she added, kissing him again. 'Mrs Blake can add some hot water before she goes home.'

He smiled down at her. 'And what,' he asked, 'have I done – or have still to do! – to deserve such a warm welcome?'

'Nothing . . . I just missed you today.'

'And on other days?'

'Oh, don't be silly – of course, I always miss you!'

He kissed her and moved to the bathroom. Mrs Blake, who had been aware of his arrival, had already poured a large pot of boiling water into the bath. 'The old witch is probably hoping I'll scald myself,' he muttered, removing his sweat-stained shirt.

Katherine glanced quickly around to see whether Mrs Blake had heard him, but the housekeeper was busy in the kitchen, readying their dinner before she left for the night. 'Don't be so nasty,' she said, amused at the thought of Mrs Blake plotting to harm him. 'Why do you dislike her so?'

'Because she doesn't like me. Haven't you seen the way she always glares at me? As though she's decided I'm something evil.'

'Really, James – you're imagining things! I think it's merely because she's so protective towards me. She's very kind and sweet – really she is!'

'To you perhaps. She reminds me of your mother . . . *she's* just more direct, that's all.'

Katherine did not respond, for she could understand James's resentment of Lady Kenrick's treatment of him. At the wedding it had taken a stern glance from Sir Anthony before she had, with obvious reluctance, pecked her son-in-law's cheek. She had not yet had a kind word to say about him, and her parting words to Katherine as they left on their honeymoon had been, 'Don't forget you can call on your father when things go wrong.' Not *if*, but *when*. In none of her letters did she ask after James's well-being.

'You going to scrub my back for me?' asked James as he settled into the steaming water. He was smiling again, his disagreeable thoughts of Mrs Blake gone from his mind.

'I can do even more for you,' she replied in a coquettish tone of voice, 'just as soon as Mrs Blake leaves and you've finished your bath.'

'Just what is it you're up to, woman?' He grabbed her wrist with his soapy hand, pulling her towards him. They laughed as he slipped in the water when he tried to kiss her.

She gently pulled free. 'I'm not up to anything – why shouldn't a woman just want to be with her husband? I'm feeling loving, that's all.'

'Then get your caretaker on her way home, my sweet, and show me just how much.' He started to splash frantically, spilling water over the sides of the bath.

Katherine laughed and went to tell Mrs Blake her chores were done for the day.

CHAPTER THIRTEEN

The soft rain trickled down the bedroom window-pane like sad, hesitant tears. Katherine turned away from the sight and the symbolism, thinking it was time she stopped feeling sorry for herself. Still . . . she bit down on her knuckles thrust between her quivering lips.

She knew she was making matters worse by lingering in bed on such a day; it was two months since the violent cramps had come six weeks before her baby was due. The pain had gripped her just after she had sent Mrs Blake out on an errand and there had been no one to hear her shout or witness her fear as she writhed on the wooden floor, unable even to crawl to the front door for help.

Mrs Blake had come back in time to send for Dr Maxwell, but it had been too late for the baby – a little boy. They had not even decided on a name.

A day ago Dr Maxwell had declared her physically fit once again, although his anxious expression indicated he was still concerned about her emotional well-being. As she eased herself from the bed and started to dress, her gaze fell on a finely crocheted child's jacket on the cupboard shelf. Tears welled in her eyes.

She gently lifted the garment and fondled its softness. It had been a gift from Mrs Blake who had made it at night in her own home. The housekeeper had brought along her own brood, two boys and a plump little girl, when she handed over the present. Katherine replaced the jacket on the shelf and wondered what she would have done without the kindly

126

woman over the past few weeks, for Mrs Blake had proved that she was far more than a housekeeper. She had kept the household running with normal efficiency, often staying on till long after dark, when James returned from the farm. But it was the care, the friendship, which Katherine appreciated most. Mrs Blake had become like a warm, loving aunt to her.

Her mind turned to James while she finished dressing. He could have stayed with her today; it was Saturday and far too wet to do much, but he had said they expected some eggs to hatch, and he wanted to be on hand when that happened. The eggs – he was more concerned about his ostrich eggs hatching safely than he'd been about his own child! She immediately suppressed the thought as she recalled his face when he had received word of what had happened and come rushing from the farm to be at her side. There had been fear in his eyes – fear for *her* safety. That night she was sure she had heard sounds of sobbing coming from behind the closed study door. It was wrong of her to think he did not share her pain at the loss. There had been no indication that things would go wrong but she couldn't expect him to be as affected as she still was at this stage. Yet . . . she wished he had stayed at home today.

As she had anticipated, he had at first been angry when she announced she was expecting their child. 'How could you be so careless!' he had snapped, crushing the excitement she felt at breaking the news. 'You know I wanted us to wait.'

'Why? I know how you feel about wanting to own the farm, but I still can't see—'

'No, you can't, can you? Or don't want to, more likely.' He seemed to regret his harsh words, for he reached for her and said more gently, 'My love, it's just . . . well, I want the best for him – that's why I wanted us to wait.' It was always *him*, Katherine had thought then.

'Our child will have the best one day,' she replied softly, 'but I don't share your obsession that he or she be born into it. There's nothing wrong with what we have right now.'

He seemed to show a grudging acceptance of the situation after that, although he was rather remote initially, as if Katherine's slowly increasing bulk was a constant reminder of her betrayal of his wishes. After a few months she had thought he seemed to demonstrate more interest – even excitement – at the prospect of becoming a father. Just the night before she lost the baby, James had helped her into bed and asked, 'Have you decided on a name yet?'

She had smiled shyly before saying, 'I thought that's one decision I should consult you on for a change.' He laughed gaily, kissed her and replied, 'Then go ahead, my love, and draw up a list. I'll cast an eye over it tomorrow night.' But, of course, there had been no time for a list, and no need for it by the following evening.

Now, Katherine told herself she was wrong to think he felt relieved that there would be no child before he was ready for it. James was feigning his high spirits for her sake, she decided; her overwrought state had led her to imagine things.

She sighed, glanced once more at the rain-streaked windows, then stepped into the passage.

Mrs Blake came rushing from the kitchen at the sound of the bedroom door. 'You shouldn't be up and about yet, mum!' She pulled Katherine's shawl more tightly about her shoulders. 'It's a cold and miserable day . . . it's better to be in bed.'

Katherine mustered a smile. 'Dr Maxwell said I'm quite all right now, Mrs Blake. Some activity will do me good.'

'Doctors!' replied the big woman with a derisive snort. 'What do they know about a woman's feelings?'

'I really am all right now – my . . . feelings, too, Mrs Blake. Really!'

The housekeeper seemed unconvinced as she bustled her charge into the drawing-room, made her comfortable in one of the large mahogany easy chairs, covered her legs with a blanket, before rushing back to the kitchen to prepare tea. Katherine smiled; as far as Mrs Blake was concerned, a cup of strong tea could dispel any ailment – physical or emotional.

Abraham Isaacs arrived while she was busy with her tea. She was pleased to have company, and especially glad it was the lawyer's, for she had become fond of the little man. 'It's good to see you up and about, Katherine,' he said after he'd kissed her cheek and taken a seat near her.

'I should have been up days ago, but you know what Mrs Blake is like!'

Isaacs smiled. 'Good for Mrs Blake,' he said. 'These things take time, dear girl. You sure you're feeling better now?'

'Quite well, thank you, Abraham,' she lied. 'If it stops raining by tomorrow, I might take a short walk.'

The lawyer studied her for a moment, and it seemed to Katherine he looked right into her mind. She lowered her gaze and fidgeted with the blanket. 'When did you last visit the farm?' Isaacs asked suddenly.

'The farm? Oh, not since . . . not since before the baby.'

'The place has changed,' Isaacs went on. 'There are two more outbuildings now, and James is—'

'I know, he's told me he's erected a shed for those incubator machines of his. Is he doing the right thing, Abraham?'

The lawyer laughed. 'With the incubators, you mean? Well, they're still very experimental at this stage, but you know our James – he'll play a pioneering role in anything! I wouldn't worry about it if I were you, he's sure to make it succeed.'

'Yes, he's very much like my father in that respect.'

'Speaking of whom,' said Isaacs, 'have you had any news since . . . ?'

'He wanted to come here right away when he heard about the baby. I told him not to – it wouldn't have served any purpose, Abraham, and I know he's very busy right now.'

'Lady Kenrick?'

Katherine's smile was sad. 'She holds James responsible, of course, even though I never mentioned I was alone when it happened. She'd have blamed him in any case.'

Isaacs was silent for a while, then said, 'Have you ever thought about becoming involved with the farm?'

'What do you mean, Abraham?'

'Well, getting to know how it operates, that sort of thing. It might be just what you need right now. James has his hands full as it is, so he might welcome your help.'

She thought about what he had suggested. Help on the farm? Abraham might be right; she needed something to keep her occupied. She had often spoken to James about

129

employing a manager of sorts, so that he could have more time at home, but he had scoffed at the idea. If she was involved, they would have more time together, would share the same challenges and problems. But would he allow it? It seemed he didn't approve of her making her own decisions. 'You know something, Abraham?' she said at last. 'I might just give it a try. As soon as tomorrow, even!'

Isaacs jumped to his feet. 'Good for you,' he said, smiling broadly. 'Let me know how you feel in the morning. I'll get my servant to drive you out there in my buggy. It can be a surprise for James.'

Katherine felt so excited at the prospect of doing something that she stood up and accompanied Isaacs to the door when he left. As she stood on the verandah and watched him make a dash for his buggy, she no longer found the rain depressing. It was now a gentle thing, washing away the dust, the way Isaacs's idea had washed away her melancholy.

She would have stayed there, content to watch the rain, but Mrs Blake would have none of it, and chased her back inside.

'Who's been putting these mad ideas into your head? Mrs Blake? Abraham?' James was leaning with his forearms on a paddock fence, a sneer on his lips as he looked down at his wife.

'No!' cried Katherine. 'It was my own idea. I merely asked Abraham for the loan of his buggy and driver. I thought I would surprise you,' she finished lamely, thinking she would have to remember to warn the lawyer not to mention anything. 'I just thought—'

'You just thought,' interrupted James. Katherine would almost have preferred it if he had shown anger instead of the scorn she saw on his face and heard in his voice. She glanced longingly at Isaacs's buggy, wishing she could flee from the farm and the man who suddenly seemed like a stranger to her.

James pushed himself from the fence and said, 'When you

were thinking, did it ever cross your mind that farming is man's work? Do you think there's something glamorous about working with cantankerous birds, Katherine?'

'No, I . . .' She found herself retreating from the sting of his words. She stopped, her back up against the wire fence. 'I just thought . . . I thought I could help with the bookkeeping, perhaps, or with the incubators.'

His harsh laugh was like a slap in her face. 'No, my dear,' he said, his voice cruel. 'You thought wrong. There's no place for a woman on this farm.'

The wire rung was hard and cold in her hand. 'There was a time when you spoke of our family being on this farm,' she said softly, 'yet now you say there's no place for a woman, not even your wife.' She bit her lip to stop it trembling.

'You know very well what I mean,' replied James with a loud sigh, 'so please don't be so emotional. *Living* on this farm is one thing, but it's vastly different from *working* on it.'

'Are you saying you don't need me?'

'Not for this, Katherine. Go home and rest – forget these silly notions of yours.' He stepped quickly towards her, as if sensing she was about to burst into tears. His voice was gentler when he said, 'I think I understand, my love, that you're feeling a bit depressed right now. Worthless, perhaps . . . I believe women react this way when they lose a child, as if it's their fault. But you'll soon be your old self again. Don't feel the need to prove anything to me.' He smiled and kissed her forehead. The touch of his lips was cold.

She wished she could say something – anything! – which would tell him how much she needed his support and love. She wanted him to know how much courage it had taken to ride out there, how her anxieties had changed to excitement the closer she came to the farm and thought about the prospect of working closely with him. Now all she could do was stand and stare at her husband in disbelief. With a few words and a smirk of male superiority, he had dismissed her need to be close to him as some womanly whim. Or was he right?

'Why don't you say hello to Outa before you go home?' James was saying. 'He's always asking after you.' He was already staring out at the paddocks, her suggestion a matter which was closed as far as he was concerned.

'Where is he?' she asked hoarsely.

He jerked a thumb in the direction of his old hut. 'At the back over there, somewhere. I told him to clear out some of the orchards to make place for the small camp we need for the chicks.' He moved off without a word of parting.

Katherine moved stiffly towards the orchards, her eyes misty with tears of rejection, making it difficult for her to focus on the peach trees Outa was digging up with obvious reluctance. She managed to regain a measure of control before she called out to him.

The Zulu straightened up, his face creasing with delight at the sight of her. He bowed in rapid succession as he shuffled closer. 'The madam is well?' he asked, concern springing into his eyes.

She smiled. 'Yes, thank you, Outa.'

'This little bitty Christian prayed for the madam,' he said, his eyes downcast, 'but God's will . . .' He gave a little shrug.

'Thank you for your thoughts, Outa. I'm sure your prayers helped make me strong again.'

The Zulu smiled, pleased at her words. 'I have something to show the madam,' he said proudly and dug into his trouser pocket. He handed her a small, porous stone.

She looked down at the flat stone lying in her hand. She knew it had to be something special, so she chose her words carefully when she said, 'It's very beautiful . . . You must be very proud to have it.'

Outa's chest swelled. 'It is a snake stone,' he said.

'Ah, yes, a snake stone.' She had heard of them. A snake stone was rumoured to possess special qualities and if applied to the bite marks of a snake, was supposed to saturate itself with the poison. They were said to have originated from the Dutch East Indies. She knew it was more than just some native superstition, for she had heard of many white farmers who paid high prices to possess one, passing it on from one generation to the next. In the Karoo, which was filled with puff-adders, it was a much sought-after possession.

132

She pretended to scrutinise the stone before handing it back. He dropped it back into his pocket, then curled his fingers protectively around it.

'Where did you get it, Outa?'

He glanced around as if fearing someone would overhear him. 'A witch, madam. I paid her much money for it.'

'A witch?'

'Yes, madam. She is a Xhosa, but still a witch. She lives up there.' He pointed at the Swartberg Mountains, which loomed large and watchful over the farm.

'Is she a powerful witch?' she asked, trying hard not to smile.

'Very powerful, madam! She makes this little bitty Christian shake with fear!'

'Does she cast spells?'

The Zulu grinned sheepishly, suspecting he was being mocked. 'I do not know about spells,' he replied, 'but she has the *muti* to make men well. There is a story of one who would die with the broken blade of a knife inside him. This witch, she took it out and healed the man. But this Christian, he thinks that maybe God did it through her hands.' He shrugged and added, 'It is hard sometimes, being a little bitty Christian as well as a kaffir.'

'Outa! Don't ever talk of yourself that way! It is bad enough that some white men call Africans by that name, but you must never do it. Do you understand?'

'Yes, madam.' He seemed embarrassed, then looked up with confusion in his eyes. 'But, madam,' he said, 'are the Xhosa not kaffirs?'

Katherine sighed; it seemed that Outa would never discard his old tribal hatreds. 'No, Outa,' she replied patiently, 'it is just an ancient Arab word meaning non-believer, and you're a Christian, aren't you? Even the Xhosa are children of God. The same as you are.'

'I see, madam. Then I have sinned.' He looked genuinely contrite.

She thought it best to change the subject by referring to the snake stone again. 'What does Master James say about your stone?'

The Zulu scowled. 'He says I am a heathen to believe

133

in things like witches and magic stones. He says it is just an ordinary stone. But I have tested it against my palate,' he added. 'It stuck there by itself, which is the test of such a stone.' He patted his pocket. 'This is indeed a snake stone. Perhaps one day, the puff-adder will bite the master and I will save him with it!'

'No, Outa – don't say such things!' But she almost wished something would happen to bring James down from his pedestal. She was ashamed of her thoughts and quickly said, 'The master tells me he is making space for a paddock . . . but there are so few of the orchards left! It is sad to see them go.'

'Yes, madam, my heart, too, it is saddened by it, for I love the beauty of the trees.' He added, 'But tending them is woman's work. I just like to look at them, of course.'

'Of course. And to pick the occasional peach, I suspect.' From his comment she thought it wise not to ask his opinion about a woman wanting to become involved with ostrich farming.

'Indeed!' His face went serious again when he said, 'The madam, she will come to visit more often?'

'I'll try, Outa. And perhaps soon, I hope, to live.'

'This little bitty Christian will pray for that day.'

Katherine laughed as she moved away, thankful to the big Zulu for having raised her spirits. As he helped her into the buggy, she glanced around to see whether James was anywhere near by. There was no sign of him.

'Tell Master James I said goodbye,' she said, seeing from Outa's frown that he sensed her dejection.

'Goodbye, madam,' he said gently. 'God be with you.'

'And you, Outa.' The buggy lurched forward, taking her away from the farm, away from the man who did not need her there.

CHAPTER FOURTEEN

It was already ten in the morning when James left Oudtshoorn to start the long ride to the farm. His head throbbed thickly from the effects of too much brandy the night before and his mouth tasted sour and dry from too many Old Boy cigars.

His need for the solace of brandy had been brought about by news of Amos's death. Pneumonia, the letter from Sir Anthony had stated. A poor state of health caused by too many wearying years of a hard life had taken their toll, and Amos's mind and body had put up little resistance. Mingling with James's genuine sense of loss were traces of guilt, even though he kept telling himself he could not in any way accept blame for Amos's death. And yet . . . perhaps, if he'd thought of Amos just once in a while, had sent for him to join him on the farm as he'd promised, he might still be alive.

He pulled his soft felt hat lower over his forehead to ward off the morning sun. It provided little comfort; his head throbbed angrily by the time he reached the farm. Outa came over to take the horse's reins from him. He took one glance at his master's bloodshot eyes and said, 'I shall make coffee.' James nodded curtly and climbed carefully from the saddle.

Outa brought them each a mug of steaming brew. They moved to the paddock fence, leaning their elbows on the wire strands while they drank. Before them lay fields planted with lucerne, introduced into the country for the specific purpose of providing feed for the ostriches. James had planted every spare patch of the farm, so that he was able to keep three grown birds to an irrigated acre, thereby justifying his insistence that Sir Anthony should lease such expensive land beside the river all those years ago. 'Did you inspect the incubators this morning?' he asked when he had drained his mug.

Outa nodded and turned away so that James would not see his resentment at the uncalled-for check. It happened more and more these days, the proud Zulu thought, as if his master no longer trusted him. Even though he had no particular love for the incubators, how could there ever be the slightest doubt that he would neglect his beautiful ostriches? He did not quite trust the machines, and was therefore twice as vigilant as James required.

There had been a number of problems when they first started using the machines. If the temperature was not right, the moisture within the eggs evaporated too fast. Even when that problem was rectified, a human presence was still required when the time for birth was near, mainly to help free those chicks that stuck to the gluey substance inside the shell, a task normally performed by their natural parents.

Eventually, even Outa had to concede that the incubators did wonders for production. The eggs were removed from the nests as they were laid, with a few dummies being left behind to fool the ostriches. That way they laid double and sometimes treble the number of eggs they normally would.

The birds were still allowed to hatch some eggs of their own, especially when poor rainfall caused the number of fertile eggs to be low. After birth, the adult ostriches were given several incubator chicks to rear, with up to forty of them being accepted by a single bird. The only danger arose when the incubator-bred fledgelings were bigger than the hen's own brood. When that happened, she killed the newcomers. The majority of the incubator brood were cared for by labourers, however, who acted as foster parents, providing the chicks with feed and water – even the stones they needed to triturate their food.

*

Much later that day, Outa approached James and asked, 'We go again tonight?'

'We go.'

The Zulu sighed. For a few nights in a row now, James had dragged him into what Outa considered to be white man's affairs. It had started a week ago, when James wanted to dismiss a sulking Xhosa. Outa, who since his chat with Katherine had tried to curb his years of inbred hatred towards all other tribes, took his master to one side and said, 'Do not be hasty. The young man suffers the sickness of the heart – worse, it is his pride, his fleshy assegai which has been insulted. The woman of his heart no longer desires his feeble prodding.'

James snorted. 'So another man has taken his woman. What of it? I won't have the bastard being surly when I give him orders.'

'You do not understand,' Outa replied patiently. 'He has lost her to a white man, her own master.'

James had laughed, although he was curious, too. It was not uncommon for a white man to bed a coloured woman, although it was frowned upon in rural areas such as Oudtshoorn. But an African woman! 'You know who he is?'

'I know,' replied Outa. He regretted having revealed the farmer's identity when James insisted he accompany him to the man's farm, to see whether they could spot the couple together.

The labourers had already retired to their makeshift shacks when Outa and James sat hunched around the fire that night. James studied the hut in which he had first lived, and which Outa had since claimed for himself. The cottage he had occupied before his marriage to Katherine stood empty, although he stayed there whenever he spent the night on the farm.

He stared at the dark outlines of the buildings he had erected: a small warehouse, a store and a hut containing the incubators. They were all constructed from wood, lacking permanence because of the possibility of being forced to move to other land. Damn that Jooste, he thought; the land should have been his by now, with permanent structures and foundations for the future. He knew it was only lack of capital which prevented Jooste from taking it back for his own use.

137

The lease had twice been extended, but at vastly increased rates in keeping with the rocketing value of land as the price of ostrich feathers kept rising.

The moon was high before he stood up and said, 'Let's go.' Outa sighed loudly, mounted his horse and followed.

They left their horses a mile from their destination, clambered through a fence and made their way towards the faint glow of light showing in the farmhouse. When they were fifty yards away, they veered in the direction of the cluster of shacks housing the labourers. They settled down among a group of pepper trees from where they had watched and waited in vain the previous few nights.

James knew that most of the huts stood empty; it was a small farm where mainly tobacco was cultivated, and it still suffered the effects of the long drought which had ended more than six years ago.

'Do we stay till midnight again?' whispered Outa.

'Longer, if we have to. He probably waits till his whole family is asleep before he goes visiting. He'll come tonight – I feel it!'

Outa lowered his head on to his knees, wishing he could stop shivering. They should be in their beds or beside the fire, he thought angrily, not spying on some white man who had developed a taste for black flesh. He had no idea what James was after or why his presence was required. He only hoped it would be over soon. He thought, too, of earlier days on the farm, when he and James had worked side by side in close harmony. It was a pity that had ended. He could understand and accept his employer's changed role, for wasn't that what they had been striving for? Building a thriving venture from almost nothing? A successful farm over which James ruled as lord and master? That was what they had worked for – it was what they had wanted. Even he, Outa, had shared in that success, for he was now foreman with the grandest house of any farm worker – he was sure of that! But . . . it was sad. It was sad that his master seemed to have lost his love for the ostriches, seeing them only as a means to increase his wealth. And it was sad that more and more often, harsh words were used when before, a smile, a joke, or a quiet fireside chat was all that was needed to ensure his servant's support in building for the future. Ah, it was sad that the master's heart had turned as hard as a snake stone!

The sudden grip of James's hand on his arm jerked Outa from his reverie. 'There! I knew it!'

Outa saw a shadowy movement at the side of the farmhouse. 'It might not be him,' he said, but he hoped it was; the sooner James was satisfied the better.

'It's him.' They shrank back silently against the base of the tree as the sound of the man's footsteps passed not far from them. James smiled into the night as he recognised the farmer. 'Let's give him a few minutes to get firmly in the saddle.'

'You're going to go in there?' the Zulu asked in surprise, glancing at the shack into which the farmer had disappeared.

'Both of us are. I want you as a witness.'

Outa groaned, yet he had no option but to get to his feet and follow when James slapped his shoulder a few minutes later, saying, 'Let's go!'

There was a single curtainless window at the side of the shack. A candle stub flickered in its tin stand on the floor. James peered carefully around the edge of the window, even though the sounds of copulation assured him the couple would not be paying attention to possible intruders. He realised that the other workers had to be aware of their master's comings-and-goings; they would not dare to be around the shack at night.

The man and woman were lying on a narrow cot, both of them noisily enthusiastic in their coupling. 'He grunts like a pig,' whispered James as he stepped back.

'Perhaps, but he has an assegai like a horse!' Outa wondered what James planned on doing next. 'A little bitty Christian should not listen to the joy of others like this,' he grumbled.

'Come,' whispered James. He moved quickly past the window. The door crashed open under the force of his boot. It slammed back against the wall. The candle flickered in the sudden draught and cast moving shadows across the naked, sweating bodies.

'Liewe Heer!' The man rolled off the woman and sprang

139

against the wall in fright. His hands automatically reached down to cover his sex. He stared up at the intruders in fear and embarrassment.

'You can go now, Outa,' James said loudly. 'I'll meet you back at the horses.'

The farmer groaned as he recognised James's voice. His head sank on to his chest, and he seemed to shrink in size as he slid down the wall, coming to rest with his naked buttocks on the clay floor. 'Quenton,' he sobbed. 'You!'

'Yes, Jooste. I came to see how a deacon of the precious Dutch Church, a distinguished man with a wife and four children, conducts himself with his black whore.'

Jooste was crying with shame and frustration. James glanced at the woman. She lay on the cot with her back to him, her arms covering her face. She was surprisingly slim for an African, with long, slender legs and small, tight buttocks. He pitied her – and the man sobbing on the floor – but the emotion passed. 'Get dressed,' he told Jooste. 'There is no need for anyone ever to hear of this.'

Jooste nodded in a mixture of relief and defeat, for he knew the price he would pay for James's silence.

'I'll be waiting outside,' said James. 'There's no better time than now to discuss terms for the sale of your land.'

He closed the door. It shut out the sobs of the broken man inside, but the malevolence of his devious machinations went with James, clinging to him like a ponderous mantle.

It was almost midnight when the hoofs of James's horse echoed down the silent Oudtshoorn streets. The ride from the farm had helped to dispel the sombreness of his conscience, replacing it instead with an almost euphoric sense of victory. The land was his, or would be once Jooste signed the documents the next day. God help him if he changed his mind overnight!

Excitement coursed through him, spread to his groin, so that a sudden sexual desire gripped him and made him hard. He brought his horse to an abrupt halt and stared back at the street he had passed only a moment ago. Maggie . . . yes, she was what he needed now, sweet Maggie who demanded nothing of him. Perhaps that was why he kept returning to her. That – and because she was discreet.

They had been seeing each other for over a year now, never with any prior arrangement. Yet they shared nothing but mutual affection and sexual desire. Maggie was the attractive widow of an English sergeant who had taken a fatal fall from his horse in British Kaffraria. James suspected he was not the only one granted her favours, yet it made no difference; she always made him feel special.

He stared into the blackness a moment longer, then made up his mind and slowly turned his horse. The animal snorted, eager to end its own long night.

The quiet, tree-lined street James entered led down to the Grobbelaars River. There were only a few small houses, their entrances hardly visible through the trees. The street ended at the start of a narrow lane leading to the river and a solitary cottage hidden well back in the bush. It was a convenient approach, especially at night, for there was little chance of being spotted.

He urged his horse silently forward. The cottage was in darkness. He tied the animal's reins to the porch railing after checking there were no other visitors.

He did not knock on the front door but at the bedroom window. There was no response. He knocked louder and said, 'It's James.' This time the curtains were drawn slightly apart before they fell back into place. He moved to the front door and waited. Light footfalls sounded from inside before there was the turn of a key in the lock. The faint glimmer of a hand-held lamp glowed through the crack above the door.

'James Quenton – a fine time of night to come visiting!' The woman wore a nightdress of thin white cotton. It did little to hide the voluptuousness of her full, firm body. Her dark brown hair hung in tangled curls across her shoulders.

'Hello, Maggie. May I come in?'

She smiled up at him. 'Well, I should think so! I mean, after waking me and all.' She stepped aside, and her woman smell, heightened by the warmth of her bed, embraced him.

His reaction was instantaneous. 'Wait!' she said, giggling as he gripped her buttocks fiercely with both hands to draw her roughly against his protruding hardness. 'Let me at least close the door, you randy bastard!' He smothered her complaints under his kiss as she shoved the door closed with her foot.

'Ah, Maggie, Maggie!' he mumbled into the sweetness of her neck. 'It's so cold and you're so warm . . . Let me share it, Maggie! Let me inside you.' He pulled up her nightdress. Her skin shone like ivory in the weak light, and her heat and smell assailed his senses.

'What are you—? No, James, not here. The lamp, damn you! Ahh!' He took the lamp from her, holding her easily in one arm as he lowered their united bodies to the hard floor. 'You're a bloody animal,' she murmured as her legs moved up and tightened around his hips, drawing him deeply into her.

Their writhing lasted less than a minute. All the elation of his victory, his sense of power, the stimulation of seeing Jooste's coupling – all came bubbling up in an intense climax stirred on by the moist heat of the human receptacle beneath him. Even his long groan was one of conquest.

It was as if the woman sensed his need, for she held him to her despite his selfish gratification. After a while she relaxed her body, although he remained hard inside her. 'My darling James,' she said, smiling as she took his head in her hands, 'I don't see you for weeks, now you wake me in the middle of the night and rape me on the passage floor.' She giggled. 'Not much of a rape, I'm sorry to say.'

'Then take me to your warm bed, Maggie my dear, and we'll try again. Or here, if you prefer.' She managed to wriggle free and led him to her bedroom.

Afterwards, he lay beside her and stared up at the dark ceiling, his hand resting on her flat stomach. 'You should be home with your wife,' she whispered as she moved closer.

'I had things to do on the farm.'

'But you came to me.'

'I needed you.'

She smiled. 'You should have gone to her,' she said. 'She's so beautiful and—'

'And what? A lady?' He rolled over and laid his leg between hers. 'So are you, dear Maggie. A lady and, above all, a woman.'

142

'Am I? Do you caress your wife like you're touching me now?'

He stopped and sighed, rolling on to his back. 'Ah, Maggie, I've told you before! It's not that I don't love her . . . I don't know, I just need you, that's all!' He shifted back against her. 'It's as though I'm truly myself with you. It's so different with you.' He nuzzled his lips against her ear.

'The other woman is always different,' she replied, but there was no bitterness in her voice.

'There you go, being moralistic again. You're always trying to save a man, to restore him for his wife. You're a good woman, Maggie Lawrence.' He nibbled her ear again and added, 'Once more, Maggie, then I'll go home.'

She sighed, turned to him and opened her arms and her body.

Katherine awoke with a start. She had fallen asleep in front of the drawing-room fire. All that remained of it were glowing embers. What had woken her? Was it James? The striking of the old clock in the hallway dispelled her confusion. She pushed herself stiffly from the chair in which she had fallen asleep. Good heavens! Was it that late already?

The echo of the clock's twelfth chime floated down the hallway as she dragged herself into the bedroom. She was not unduly concerned at James's absence; he often slept on the farm when they worked into the night, though she wished he would not.

The sheets were crisp and cold when she climbed between them. They played their part in fighting off the sleep which had rescued her earlier that night.

A long while later she heard the front door being opened. It squeaked – she would have to tell Mrs Blake about that. Then she heard it click as James closed it. She could picture him resting with his back against it; he always seemed to close a door with a deliberate motion, pausing beside it as if it were a part of life through which he would never return. Why had she suddenly realised that?

She heard him walk down the passage. He came into the room, and the sounds of his undressing filled the once-empty space. The bed moved under his weight when he sat down.

'James?'

'You still awake? It's long after one, Katherine.'

'I *was* sleeping. Then I—'

'I've got the land, Kath,' he interjected and leaned across to touch her in the dark. 'It's mine – Jooste agreed to sell. I'll build that home for us at last.'

She should have been happy for him, happy for them both. Yet what she felt instead was fear – James was ready for his son now. Dr Maxwell had warned her having a baby would be risky. She shut the memory of the pain from her mind, and told herself she was being selfish. She tried to concentrate on James's ramblings about the mansion he would build.

'It'll be the biggest and the finest house in all the district,' he was saying. 'Everyone will talk about it.' He laughed and rolled back the bedcovers, 'You know what I'll call it? Ratitāe: the ostrich!'

She remained silent when he moved in behind her back. As he settled himself, Katherine smelled the woman and their loving on him. It was not new to her.

A baby will change that, she thought, a child will change everything. She turned her face into the comforting embrace of her pillow.

Abraham Isaacs studied the silent rage on Jooste's face. 'You sure about this?' he asked.

Jooste nodded. 'Show me where I sign,' he mumbled.

Isaacs pushed the contract across to him. The price was too low, he thought; the land was worth at least four thousand pounds more. What had James done to the man?

Jooste scrawled his name, rose to his feet and left the office without another word. The closed door could not shut out the anger which remained in the room. Isaacs did not look at James as he placed the contract into a file. 'I'll make the necessary arrangements for the bank transfer,' he said, regretting the journey he would have to make to George. Crossing the Outeniqua Mountains was no pleasure during winter.

'It's about time we had our own bank,' said James. 'We'll need it with the money the industry is generating.'

'In a year or two, that's what I hear.'

'Good.' James leaned forward and tapped a second pile of documents on the desk. 'You had a look at those yet?'

'Yes. They're in order.' The lawyer spread out the contracts, one with a new distributor in Vienna, the other with an outlet in New York. 'George Laboulaye has not been idle,' he said.

'He gets his share of it,' came the curt reply as James signed the documents. He handed them back to Isaacs. 'One other thing,' he said, turning back to the lawyer.

'Yes?'

'I want the farm to be mine. All of it.'

Isaacs smiled down at the desk. 'I was waiting for this,' he said slowly and raised his eyes. 'You want me to sell you my shares.'

'We can come to an arrangement, Abraham. With the expansion I have in mind, the farm might not be big enough. I was thinking of starting a second venture – on a smaller scale, of course. We could transfer your capital to that. The farm must be mine.'

'And Katherine's,' Isaacs reminded him.

'Of course.'

The lawyer sighed and leaned back in his chair. 'Start your second venture by all means, but it won't involve me or my capital.'

There was a dark look on James's face. 'Don't be awkward about this, Abraham. I'll offer you more than a fair price for the shares.'

Isaacs leaned forward. 'You know, James, there was a time when I admired your courage and ambition. Now—' He stopped and leaned back again with a sad look in his eyes. 'What I see now is greed,' he went on, 'nothing but pure greed. I don't know what you did to Jooste – I don't want to know! – but you practically stole that land from him.'

'I didn't come here for—'

'Let me finish. Please.' The strained silence hung like an invisible curtain between the two men. 'I don't want any part of your farm,' continued Isaacs, 'I don't want the magnificent riches you so recklessly claw your way towards. I never wanted it. When I invested in your and Sir Anthony's scheme almost ten years ago, it was for the pure fun of it. I wanted to share in the excitement of having a dream. It was not for the money, James.'

'Don't be a hypocrite, Abraham. You never refused your share of the profits.'

The lawyer gave a short laugh. 'No, I didn't, did I? And I'm grateful to you, James. Together with the income from my practice, I can retire with a reasonable amount of security. But it wasn't just the money.'

'Get to the point, Abraham. I've a lot to do on the farm.'

'The point is that I've already discussed the sale of my shares with Sir Anthony.'

'And his advice to you was?'

'To dispose of it as I see fit. Of course, he'd prefer not to see it go to outsiders.'

James smiled for the first time, although it seemed to Isaacs more like a triumphant smirk. 'You'll sell to me then?'

'Ten per cent. On condition.'

'What condition? And the other ten per cent?'

'To Katherine.'

James threw back his head and laughed. 'What difference does it make? It's all one and the same!'

'It does make a difference . . . because that's the condition of my selling to you.'

'What are you talking about, Abraham?'

Isaacs stared steadily at him. 'I'll sell to you on the following proviso: from now on, all investments and their income are divided according to your and Katherine's individual shareholding. Separate accounts, with Katherine countersigning any purchases or expenses. Her seventy per cent must be controlled separately.'

'You're mad! Katherine has no interest in the farm, you damn fool!'

'Then perhaps it's time she developed one,' came the even reply.

'She won't do it. I'll talk to her and—'

'I'll talk to her, too, James. About Maggie.'

A vein pulsed thickly on the side of James's head. 'You fucking Jew bastard!' he hissed. 'Damn you!'

Isaacs stared coldly back at him.

'Why? Why are you doing this to me? Why are you fighting me?'

'I'm not fighting *you*, James, merely fighting for Katherine. I sense in you that which destroys things – and people. It is something which seems to be growing along with your success, and I fear it will ruin those around you. Remember, I am a Kenrick man first and foremost.'

James slammed his palm down on the desk and sprang to his feet. 'I'm finished with you! I'll bring in my own lawyer to conduct my business.'

'Katherine's seventy per cent will remain under my care,' snapped Isaacs, 'or with whoever I appoint to take over from me.'

'You'd better find someone fast, Abraham, because I'll ruin you for this!' He slammed his chair back against the desk.

Isaacs smiled sadly. 'Take this with you,' he said, holding out a brown envelope. 'It's the contract for the sale. Take a look at it when you've calmed down. You'll find I'm asking a reasonable price.'

James hesitated, then snatched the envelope from his hands. He started for the door.

'You needn't worry about the other ten per cent,' Isaacs called after him. 'I'll talk to Katherine about it myself.'

'I'll make you pay for this,' came the angry whisper. The door slammed shut behind him.

Isaacs leaned back and rubbed his eyes. 'I only hope,' he said aloud, 'that others don't pay along with me.'

He started clearing his desk, stacking the documents and contracts into their correct covers. He had had enough of business for the day.

CHAPTER FIFTEEN

Dr Maxwell shifted his glasses on to the bridge of his nose before he sat down opposite Katherine. 'Everything is still fine, Mrs Quenton.'

She shut her eyes. A small smile played on her lips.

The doctor reached out to take her hand in his. 'Now,' he said gently, 'you know I warned you the last time. There will obviously be risks again – for you and the child.'

'I know.' Her voice sounded light and brittle in spite of her smile. '*This* child will be fine. James's son will be born this time.'

Dr Maxwell nodded and stood up. 'Let me not mislead you, Mrs Quenton,' he said, swinging round to face her. 'It will not be an easy birth.' He started gathering his things. 'Make sure James lets you get plenty of rest.'

'I shall.'

'Good.' He smiled down at her. 'And you'll be seeing plenty of me from now on.'

After he had left the townhouse, she drew aside the bedroom curtains and stood at the window. The flower-bed Mrs Blake had planted was in full bloom, yet Katherine was unable to appreciate the array of colour. 'Oh, God, I'm scared!' she said aloud. Even now she still woke in the middle of the night, sure that she could feel the tearing pains in her body.

It had taken her a year from the time James bought the farm to fall pregnant, adding a further strain to their relationship.

There was a soft knock on the bedroom door. 'Yes?'

Mrs Blake came in. 'Tea, mum?'

Katherine managed a smile. 'A lovely idea, Mrs Blake. I'll have it out on the verandah.'

She walked out into the afternoon sun. The usual sounds of the town – the roll of wagon wheels, a child's excited shout, the thudding of a spade in some nearby garden – washed over her. The town had changed so much since her first visit to Oudtshoorn. Why, they even had their own telegraph office now! And there was Grannie Patterson's Canteen, of course, their first hotel – even if it was attached to a dwelling-house. She was certain things would change even more rapidly with the ever-increasing demand for feathers. She remembered James telling her that there were little more than eighty ostriches in the Colony when he arrived; now, in 1875, there were over thirty-two thousand, with almost 37,000 pounds' weight of feathers exported the previous year. Although other places had greater quantities of birds than Oudtshoorn, the town's feathers proved to be of superior quality and fetched the best prices.

'You shouldn't be in the direct sunlight,' fussed Mrs Blake when she reappeared with tea and a plate of biscuits still warm from the oven. 'You'll get wrinkles,' she went on. 'Look at me – fifty years young and as puckered as a dried prune!' Her fingers pulled and tucked at the folds in Katherine's dress while she spoke.

'You're worse than my mother, Mrs Blake! Now pour the tea and join me!'

The plump woman settled Katherine on to the couch on the verandah, then sank down beside her with a sigh. 'Now what would Dr Maxwell be wanting with you, mum? Everything all right, then?'

'Of course.'

Mrs Blake clamped her jaw tightly. She, too, remembered the previous time.

'Dr Maxwell said it will be fine. And I'll have you with me – so what can go wrong?' She laughed gaily, but there was a nervous ring to the sound. 'James will be so proud,' she continued. 'He needs a son to take over from him, to perpetuate his feather empire, he says.' The fear had abated now that she sat in the sun with Mrs Blake at her side.

'Will Master James be home in time for supper for a change, you think?'

'Now, Mrs Blake, he's very busy. There are all the new chicks to be tended to.'

'With all them fancy incubators he's got? And hordes of labourers to mind them? He's supposed to be with you at night! Especially in your state.'

'He likes being personally involved with the farm, that's all.' Mrs Blake sipped her tea in silence.

Things would change once the child was there, thought Katherine – especially if it were a boy. James would want to be with him as much as possible. They'd all be together a great deal more once the building of the house on the farm was complete and they moved in.

'I'd best be looking in on your dinner,' said Mrs Blake, 'and you should come inside – these winter afternoons are treacherous.'

'It's so nice, I'll stay a while longer.'

She was still there when the last bastions of light tiptoed across the roof-tops. Mrs Blake's heavy tread sounded along the passage. 'Get in with you, child,' she scolded. 'Waiting out here won't bring him home any earlier!' She tucked a shawl around Katherine's shoulders. 'I've lit the fire in the drawing-room, so make yourself comfortable there.'

Katherine followed her to the kitchen. 'I think it's time you went home to bully your own family,' she said, reaching for the woman's thick coat hanging behind the door. 'Come on! I'll even help you on your way!'

'But, mum – your dinner—'

'It's in the oven, isn't it?'

'Yes, but—'

'Then I'll eat it when James gets home. Or when I'm hungry. Now go on home.'

The older woman hesitated, but Katherine shook the coat and said, 'I promise I'll go and sit beside the fire as soon as you've left.' She helped her shrug into the heavy garment.

She shut the front door behind the protesting woman. It closed with a thin click, shutting out the evening chill, yet at the same time fencing in the silence within the house. She told herself she should be used to it, but Mrs Blake was right; James had no real need to be at the farm for so much of the time.

She sighed and moved to the drawing room where the fire tried valiantly to introduce more than just its warmth to the room.

The field of lucerne stretched lush and green down to the river. James leaned his elbows on the paddock fence, and gave a grunt of satisfaction. 'Tomorrow,' he told Outa, 'I want you to pull up the remaining orchard.' He jerked his thumb in the direction of the last few fruit trees standing behind the huts.

'For lucerne?'

James nodded and added, 'Make sure you leave a border between the new field and the house.' He turned to study the labourers digging the foundations of his mansion. Ratitāe: another year and his home would be complete, the symbol of his achievement, there for all to see and envy. It would be his – and his son's, of course. The thought of the unborn baby brought a smile to his lips. It had to be a boy!

'The madam wants to keep the orchard,' said Outa quietly. 'She says she will enjoy looking at it from the door of her kitchen. It will not be the same with lucerne.'

'You work for me,' James snapped, 'not the madam. Now get going!' He scowled as Outa moved silently off. Ratitāe was his, not Katherine's, and there would be more than enough servants to attend to kitchen duties. Her function would be to care for their son till the boy was old enough to appreciate the attentions of his father.

There was a tight smile on his face when he thought how easy it had been to thwart Abraham Isaacs's plan of getting Katherine involved in the farming venture. Had Isaacs really thought she had the courage for that? Or the nerve to stand up to him?

He had been unable to stop Isaacs from drawing up separate accounts, yet so far Katherine had willingly countersigned all of his expenses, and there had been many of those. The thought of Isaacs brought with it a familiar flush of guilt. He quickly pushed the ugly memories from his mind, turning his attention instead back to the construction of the house. The labourers were laughing now, ready to end their day and start the long trek homewards.

Most of the fittings James wanted were being imported from Europe, arranged with the assistance of George Laboulaye. The floors of the fifteen-room mansion would be of marble; there would be French wallpaper and costly teak panelling. A master builder would soon arrive from England, ready to take over supervision of construction once the foundations were laid. When the walls of Ratitāe started to rise, construction of the outbuildings would also commence. There would be no more temporary wooden structures on his farm.

Other expenses had been the on-going purchase of breeding birds, as well as the lease of additional land further along the Cango Valley. Some of his ostriches had been moved there, and a shack had been built for the two labourers who cared for them.

He wondered whether he should try to find more land, although the prices farmers were demanding for their strips of arid earth were getting quite out of hand. All the best properties had already been taken, with even the small yards behind the tiny homes in Oudtshoorn now being planted with lucerne. It seemed as if every inhabitant possessed a bird or two. Farms once filled with tobacco, fruit trees and wheat, were being stripped and replanted with lucerne. The last caution was being thrown to the winds.

James sneered at the small ambitions of ordinary people; there was no longer any risk, so they clambered for petty riches made possible by the courage of others. No matter. Ratitāe was already one of the biggest and most successful ostrich ventures. It would grow bigger still.

He shrugged off his impatience, and headed for the orchard where Outa seemed to be taking an unnecessarily long time in studying the task which awaited him the next day. The Zulu saw him coming, reached out and picked a golden peach from the nearest branch. He held it out to his master.

James could not resist laughing. He took the peach from his hand. 'All right, you sly bugger, we'll leave the orchard as it is for the time being. I'll ask the builder's advice when he gets here.' The peach was sweet and soft, as life at Ratitāe promised to be.

As he bit into the fruit again, he recalled the words Pat Stanton had spoken on his first night in the country. The Cape of Good Hope: his destination and now his destiny as well.

The sun had already set when James rode into Oudtshoorn. He went along High Street, glancing at the spot designated for the construction of the Standard Bank the next year. He smiled in satisfaction; theirs was becoming a proper town now, as befitted the status of its feather industry.

He studied the townhouse before he went inside. Should he keep it, he wondered, once Ratitāe was finished? He decided he would; it could be used for overnight visits to the town.

Katherine was in the drawing-room, trying to accommodate her vastly increased bulk in a comfortable chair. There was a glow to her skin, reminding James of the first time they had met. He felt a sudden rush of affection towards her, and reached out to touch her face. She looked up in surprise. 'You're home early,' she said. 'I'm glad.'

'How are you feeling?' He settled himself on the armrest of her chair.

'Fine. Dr Maxwell came to see me today. He says—'

'Did he say whether it'll be a boy?'

'Don't be silly – doctors aren't that clever!'

'Everything's going as it should?'

'Everything's fine. We'll have our child by the middle of February.'

James patted her hand and stood up. 'I'll go and wash for dinner.'

Katherine smiled contentedly as he left the room. She had been right; the baby would bring them closer to each other. They would become a proper husband and wife once again. It seemed as if James was trying; it was months since she had sensed another woman on him. And she appreciated the way he'd admitted he'd been wrong to ignore her interest in the farm. She recalled her surprise that day when he had arrived home from Abraham Isaacs's office in the middle of the morning, immediately after acquiring the land he had wanted for so long. He had been unusually tender towards her, saying, 'Now that Ratitāe is ours, I think it's only right that you share in its future. It was cruel of me to have ignored your wishes.'

Staring at him in disbelief, she said, 'No, James, it was silly of me. I can see that now.'

He shook his head and smiled at her. 'There are limits to what you can do, of course, but I think I should keep you informed of developments, let you countersign expenses, that sort of thing. Don't you agree? That way, you'll be a part of the venture.'

'James, I . . . I don't know—'

He laughed lightly and said, 'It's already been taken care of, my love. When I signed the purchase papers this morning, I instructed Abraham to draw up a legal document to that effect. It separates our income according to our individual shareholding.' He added, 'Of course, it also means you'll have to pay for most of the building of the house! You don't mind, do you?'

'Of course not! But is this really necessary?'

'It's for your own protection, my love – it's *your* inheritance, after all. Abraham will explain it all to you in the next day or two.'

Abraham Isaacs had arrived mere minutes after James had left. 'Goodness!' exclaimed Katherine. 'I couldn't be blamed for thinking you and James have some clever scheme cooking!'

Isaacs gave her a quizzical look. 'What do you mean?'

'Don't look so alarmed, Abraham. I'm only teasing!' She explained James's conversation. Isaacs's laugh was a bitter sound. 'Yes, Katherine,' he'd said, 'your husband is certainly concerned with protection.'

After he had left, she pondered the unspoken messages his words contained. It was almost as if the lawyer was warning her against James. But why? He and Isaacs were business partners. Friends. She had shrugged off her nagging doubts and concentrated instead on a happy future.

The memory made her realise again how much she missed Abraham. Even after all this time, she could still not believe what had happened. There had to be some mistake; Abraham was not the kind of person those evil people had made him out to be – he wouldn't molest a young girl! Not Abraham! And where had that horrid Venter family suddenly got the money to buy a farm near Riversdale? There were rumours about that, too, that they had been paid to claim their ten-year-old daughter was enticed into Abraham's office with the promise of sweets, and that the lawyer had then lifted her dress and touched her. But who would pay to destroy the harmless Isaacs in such a way?

It no longer mattered; the harm had been done. Isaacs was a Jew, and the Afrikaner community of Oudtshoorn had believed the word of one of their own. The lawyer had to flee the town before he was lynched. The Venters had moved away soon afterwards, saying they wanted to give their little girl a fresh start in life. It was only later, when it was learned the once-poor family had suddenly acquired enough wealth to buy their own farm, that the rumours started. By then it was too late to help the wronged Isaacs or even to clear his name; he had shot himself a month after moving to Grahamstown, a sad and broken man. Sir Anthony still blamed her for not letting him know in time to find Abraham and uncover the truth.

The young man who took over Abraham Isaacs's practice in Oudtshoorn was nice enough, but he was not Abraham. And he seemed terrified of James.

Katherine forced the morbid memories from her mind. She picked up the letter lying on the table beside her, reading the surprising news for the third time since its arrival. Marianne and George Laboulaye!

James entered the room just then. 'Why are you shaking your head like that?'

'It's a letter from Marianne. She's just returned from her tour of Europe – you remember me telling you about it? She

155

wants to visit us. She'd like to be here when the baby's born, she says.'

'I'd have thought you'd be pleased to see your cousin again. You're always complaining of how lonely you are during the day.'

'Of course I'm pleased! I was shaking my head because—'

'She must be quite a young lady by now,' James interrupted while he poured himself a large tot of brandy.

'That's just it, I'd forgotten she's already sixteen. It's just that George is so much older than her.'

'George? You mean George Laboulaye? Are you telling me that—'

Katherine nodded. 'A romantic liaison, Marianne calls it.'

James snorted loudly. 'I'd like to hear what George calls it! My God, she's only a child, and George is—'

'—only a few years older than you,' Katherine said. 'Marianne is a woman now, James.' She laughed nervously when she saw his annoyed expression. 'Besides, you know she's always had this . . . feeling for George. She's probably exaggerating the whole situation.'

James was not convinced. 'I'll talk to her when she arrives here,' he said, swallowing his brandy in a quick, angry gulp. 'Then I'll take it up with Mr Laboulaye.'

. She folded the letter with trembling fingers and wished she had not mentioned it. But Marianne would have anyway; there was very little that was private with her. 'Please don't upset her right at the start of her visit,' she said softly. 'Marianne is very independent. She doesn't like being dictated to.'

'Perhaps it's time she changed her ways. You always were too soft on her – all of you were. Even your father let her get away with too much.'

Katherine bit back the defence which sprang to her lips. James had seen Marianne on only two occasions since their marriage; he could not possibly know of the fiery spirit which everyone who came into contact with her both admired and enjoyed. In some ways, she considered Marianne was more like Sir Anthony than she herself was. Yet she did not resent it. 'You'll let her come to visit me?' she asked.

'Of course. She'll be good company for you, and perhaps

156

she'll come to her senses while she's here. When is she arriving?'

'Unless she hears otherwise from me, she'll be here early next February.' She forced herself to smile and added, 'I think you'll – we'll be surprised at how much she's grown. I'm sure she's quite beautiful!'

James's answer was to grunt that he was ready for dinner.

He did not help Katherine as she struggled up from her chair.

CHAPTER SIXTEEN

The Karoo veld was hot and silent. Animals rested in their burrows or in the scant shade of thorn trees, reptiles slithered beneath the protection of rocks and crevices; even the noisy cicadas seemed to recoil from the harsh spread of the midday sun.

Then they heard it, a deep rumbling tremor conducted by the earth itself. Small antelope leaped to their feet, frightened hares bolted deeper into their sandy shelters. There were other sounds, too: a shrill yapping which set the antelope running off at speed.

The source of their terror crested the hill moments later. There were twelve riders, their horses cantering easily across the uneven veld. Beside them a pack of fifty dogs ran in the dust, panting loudly in the stifling heat. Most of them were bitches, for the work they were expected to do often required that sex.

Marianne rubbed the sweat from her brow and wished the men would call a halt. She had never ridden side-saddle for this far or for so long. The terrain, too, was very unlike England, the atmosphere and method of the hunt vastly different from those in which she had participated during her stay there.

Even if she disregarded the disparate terrain, the dry dust, scant vegetation and rugged kopjes versus the green grass and gently rolling meadows of England, there was little to this hunting party which she could compare to the other. There were no red coats, no blaring of bugles of the chase, no master of the hunt. Instead, the men on their large farm horses wore every-day working clothes. In place of riding crops they carried an assortment of rifles and shotguns. The most important difference, she decided, was the grim determination on their faces.

This was no fun outing. These men had started their day with early morning coffee; if their hunt was successful, there would be no celebration afterwards, only laughs and comments of relief before they returned to their farms and their daily chores. They were in pursuit of a killer who threatened their livelihood, and that was serious work.

The jackal they hunted was old and cunning. Together with his pack, he had destroyed countless numbers of sheep, killing and maiming more than hunger called for, biting the noses and lips off the farmers' stock. Now, a new dish had been added to his menu: ostrich eggs and ostrich chicks. The forces seeking his destruction multiplied in number and determination. His hunting pack had been ruthlessly slaughtered over the past two months, till only he, their leader, remained. To the farmers he was a criminal of the veld.

Marianne was the only woman among the group of eleven men. They had stared at her with polite but curious eyes when she and James arrived at the gathering place just as the sun was rising that morning. 'My wife's cousin,' James had explained as he introduced her to the other farmers. 'She insisted on coming along.'

The men seemed uneasy at first. Not only did it seem improper for a young lady – or any woman for that matter – to participate in men's affairs, but also that such a pretty girl should go along on a chase which might mean spending the night on the open veld! 'I've been on fox-hunts in England,' she said forcefully when she saw them glance at each other.

'I've told her this will be very different from an English hunt,' James said, 'but I can't deny she's a good rider!' He assured them he would return with her by nightfall if they were unsuccessful. 'Just don't make any comment about how it's done in England,' he warned her as they mounted up. She glared at him.

She felt their eyes on her for the first half-hour, studying her riding, yet at the same time scrutinising her body. She was used to the latter, so concentrated on showing off her riding skills. She soon saw they no longer had doubts on that score, yet she was relieved when they slowed the pace once she'd passed the test.

The group comprised a mixed bag: six of the men were sheep farmers, with three ostrich breeders apart from James. The eleventh man rode ahead of the group. He was a grey-haired coloured man who spoke very little, yet who seemed to get their full attention when he did.

They finally stopped to boil coffee in the shade of some thorn trees. The farmers were reticent in Marianne's presence at first, then seemed to acquire more confidence once holding the familiar handles of their coffee mugs.

One of them, a tall sheep farmer named Slabbert, came to sit beside her. She held back an amused smile when she saw the others glance enviously at him. 'So, Miss Marianne,' he started. 'Are you from England, then?'

She flashed him a smile that made him swallow loudly. 'From Cape Town, although I've just spent six months in Europe, including England.' She held his gaze till he glanced quickly down at his mug, a flush spreading rapidly up his cheeks. She let him off the hook and lowered her gaze to her own coffee.

The other men's eyes were on her, studying every dimple, each loose strand of hair. She knew how they felt; although they wished they had beaten Slabbert in making the first move, it was safer to watch her from a distance. That way they could think secret thoughts without being forced to undergo the treatment of her deep brown eyes.

Marianne smiled again, to herself this time, although her thoughts about the way she always acted with men were not complimentary. She always loved the way they looked at her; she enjoyed letting them know that she was aware of what they were thinking. It didn't matter who or what they were – educated, refined, debonair or simple like these farmers – she enjoyed exercising her power over them all.

Slabbert cleared his throat. 'You say you hunted foxes?' He slurped his brew noisily.

'Yes. They're very similar to the jackal.'

James stood up. 'The local species is in fact a fox,' he said, lowering himself to his haunches. Slabbert seemed relieved by his presence. 'It's the same size and shape and reveals the same behaviour patterns. Only its colouring is different. Its back carries a dark stripe tinged with silver . . . and the effect of its killing is far greater.'

Slabbert was trying very hard. 'I have killed many jackal,' he said and coloured again. 'But many more have got away from me.' He laughed stupidly, even though the other men nodded their heads in agreement with his statement.

'Is it difficult to corner them?' asked Marianne, looking directly at Slabbert. She sensed James's annoyance at the way she ignored him.

'Oh yes! This one we're after now, old Sock, is the cleverest of all.'

'Sock?'

Slabbert smiled, and Marianne thought he was quite handsome. 'That's what we call him,' he explained. 'He has white fur on his right front leg, just like a sock. Everyone knows of him. He's been in these parts for years now.'

Slabbert warmed to his subject, even to the point of shifting closer to Marianne. 'This Sock,' he continued, 'is very clever. He won't even take the poisoned bait we put out for him. The old man said he was there, but he moved on.'

'Perhaps he smelt the human scent,' Marianne ventured.

Slabbert shook his head. 'The old man has killed many jackals – he knows how to hide the scent. But Sock is different from other jackals. If he still had his female with him, he would have let her taste the meat. Female jackals throw up poisoned food before it kills them, you see.'

'How do you know she's not running with him?'

'We killed her two days ago,' replied Slabbert. 'We dynamited her burrow, but that didn't get her. The bitches were waiting for her when she fled, though.'

Marianne glanced at the panting dogs. She knew the farmers had learned that the males hesitated when facing a female jackal, as if reluctant to kill her. They had trained bitches to do this work once it became evident the female species did not share such an emotion when it came to

161

their own sex. That explained the predominance of them in this pack, she realised, although all the farmers seemed convinced that Sock was a male.

'I explained most of that to Marianne last night,' said James. 'She's playing dumb for your benefit.' He ignored her angry look, and threw out the coffee grounds from his cup. 'Jacob!' he called. The coloured man looked up. 'Did you see any sign at the water-hole?' He stomped off to go and talk to the tracker.

Marianne watched him with narrowed eyes, disappointed to discover he was no different from most other men. Like those she had known before, he could not stand someone else enjoying her attention. He was her cousin's husband, yet he thought he could lay more claim to her than anyone else. She felt a sudden stab of guilt when she thought of Katherine, although she argued that she could not blame herself for James's reaction. But was that true? Perhaps her insistence on coming along on the hunt had made him think she wanted to be alone with him.

Slabbert was talking again, telling her in great detail about jackals and how many times he had caught and killed them. She pretended to listen, but her thoughts turned inwards.

What was it about her that made men act the way they did? It had been like that for some time now. Not boys her own age or older, but men. Men like James, even those old enough to be her father.

It had amused her at first, when she suddenly became aware of their furtive glances when they thought their wives weren't watching, the way they let their bodies touch hers, laughing all the while to disguise their lust as friendliness.

Her amusement had turned to enjoyment when she learned how she could play with them, how a smile and a certain look could bring a false victory flashing into their eyes.

Yet play was all Marianne did. She had kissed and clung passionately to men, but when the rules of the game threatened to change, she quickly hid behind the convenient innocence of her youth, turning men's lust into frustrated embarrassment. She rather enjoyed knowing that they thought her a bitch

– a sixteen-year-old virgin bitch! She wondered when the description would change.

At least she knew who the man to change her status should be. George Laboulaye. But George – damn him! – was wise to her ways. She had spent three months with him in France, three long months in which she availed herself of all her young womanly wiles to ensnare him. All she had received for her trouble was one warm embrace and a wet kiss, which, admittedly, she had initiated. Still, she had felt his reaction to her, and she knew that all was not lost. Her time would come.

Dear George. He'd not even let that change their relationship. He'd held her hand as he'd held it before, laughed with her and flirted over dinners in the cosy inns they visited on their travels. But he'd granted her no second chance at seduction. Damn him – he didn't know how honoured he'd be! It would be his fault if her virtue fell prey to someone with similar charm but less scruple.

She jerked when Slabbert touched her shoulder. 'It's time to get going again,' he said, holding out his hand to help her up. She saw James watching them. 'Old Jacob will go ahead,' Slabbert told her. 'He says he has an idea how Sock will run.'

James was beside her when she reached her horse. He helped her into the saddle, and it seemed his hand fell unnecessarily across her rump before brushing her leg. She was reminded of the way in which he had stared at her when she arrived in Oudtshoorn three days ago. It had not been the kind of look one expected from someone who was family.

He was studying her now with a strange expression. 'Be careful of young Slabbert,' he said. 'He's not as innocent as he appears.'

'Why, James!' she mocked him, her eyes hard. 'You're being protective towards me!'

His smile was more of a sneer when he lightly gripped her arm and said, 'Despite what you may think, Marianne, you're still a very young woman. Six months in Europe can't teach you everything – not even six months with good old Uncle George.'

So that was it! Katherine had tried in her timid way to warn her that James disapproved of what he believed was her affair with George. Marianne had laughed and confessed that she had exaggerated their relationship. Unfortunately so, she had added. It was a shock now to learn that James's so-called disapproval was nothing but thinly disguised jealousy. But why? Until just three days ago, he had not seen her for years! Or had seeing her changed his attitude so?

Marianne was very astute in spite of her youth and playful outlook. It had not taken her long to see that her cousin's love was unrequited. Katherine was a wife to James, not a partner in life. She was someone who granted him social acceptability and who now owed him, as far as he was concerned, a son and heir. And once that had been fulfilled?

She forced a smile as she pulled her arm slowly from James's grip. 'Uncle George,' she said deliberately, 'merely removed the need for self-protection. He's one of the few people I can trust.'

'Are you sure you have the measure of that trust?' His voice was hard and cold, belying the smile which seemed fixed on his face.

'Quite sure. And now, we have a jackal to hunt.' She dug her heels into the horse's flank, causing the animal to knock James aside as it reared forward.

· She heard him laugh as she rode off behind the others.

They came across the jackal's trail two hours later, beside a small stream flowing with surprising strength through the Karoo veld. The tracker dismounted and pointed to a small piece of wood trapped in some weeds at the edge of the water. He picked it up, laughed, then made a scratching motion down his flank.

'What's he found?' asked Marianne.

'The jackal's fleas were worrying him,' explained Slabbert, 'so he gripped a piece of wood in his teeth and swam into the river. Then he sinks down till only his jaws show, letting the fleas in his coat jump on to the wood to save themselves

164

from the rising water. When they're all on, the jackal lets the wood drift away.'

'And he's relieved of his problem,' she finished for him. 'Goodness, he really is clever!'

The tracker's shout spurred them into movement again. Marianne held her mount back as the dogs leaped forward in a frantic charge, their angry baying a death knell for the elusive jackal. She thought she saw a brief flash of brown on top of the nearest hill – had the terrified animal been watching them?

She let the men ride off, feeling a sudden reluctance to watch their prey meet its end. Slabbert had made the jackal seem almost a noble creature of the veld, on its own now, using its skills to try to outwit its pursuers. But the wily old tracker's abilities were superior.

She heard the dogs' barking become even more frantic, signalling that it would soon be over. By the time she crested the hill across which the hunting party had disappeared, James had turned back to look for her.

He was smiling as she rode up to him. 'You missed the kill,' he said, pulling in his horse to ride alongside her. 'No stomach for it, Marianne?'

She gave him a sidelong glance before she dug in her heels and rode ahead of him, past the group of excited farmers stooping over the bloody, torn bundle of flesh and fur lying on the ground, to where the open plains beckoned.

When at last she reined in her horse, she was thankful there were still a few hours of daylight remaining. Now, at least, she would undertake the return journey with the entire hunting party. She was not sure she could have done it alone with James.

Marianne dipped the cloth into the basin beside the bed, wrung out most of the water, then gently wiped Katherine's forehead. 'Are you sure there are no pains?'

Katherine shook her head and gave a small smile. 'Quite sure,' she said. 'I just feel tired, that's all.'

'And so you should be, what with carrying all that weight around! Do you think it'll be twins?'

'Heaven forbid. Can you see James trying to divide his empire in two?' She managed a laugh, thinking it strange how less frightening James was with Marianne there. Less frightening? Surely that was not right? James was awesome, perhaps, but surely not frightening. She had to admit she always acted and spoke in a manner to satisfy him. Even the discomfort of pregnancy was being endured to please him; otherwise there would have been no child. Katherine grew more terrified the closer the time of birth approached. Never again, she promised herself.

'When you're back on your feet,' Marianne was saying, 'I think you should make an effort to get involved in the farm. Half the time James doesn't even bother to explain what he asks you to sign. Find out more – I would!'

Katherine reached out to touch her arm. The young woman's skin was cool and soft. It was as though the sun – which Marianne adored – had no effect upon it apart from lending a deep golden glow. It set off her auburn hair, leaving tiny white lines beside her eyes which added an attractive maturity to her youthful features. 'I'm sure you would,' she said. 'In fact, you'd probably do a better job than James! You'd spend less money, for one thing!'

They laughed together, their heads almost touching, one woman pale and gaunt from her pregnancy, the other young and dark and bursting with promise and vitality. Marianne pulled back suddenly. 'You know, that's a very good idea! You can appoint me to manage your share. That man of yours needs some control.'

Katherine smiled at the vision of Marianne and James in competition with each other. In a way, her cousin's words were a sharp reminder of Abraham Isaacs's warning. 'I'm sure James knows what's best for us both,' she said defensively, whether on behalf of herself or James she was not sure. 'I'm sure he'll ease off once the baby is here and the house is completed.'

Marianne snorted loudly. 'Not James. Once he's achieved

status, he'll want power. And he hopes to get that through money.'

Katherine made no attempt at defending him this time. Her lack of reaction was due partly to her private admission that Marianne was right, and partly because she found it difficult to take offence at whatever her cousin said – she found her too refreshingly honest and outspoken for that. Also, she recalled how her cousin had not been in the least bit daunted by James's attempt to dominate her when she first arrived. Katherine wondered whether things might have been different between James and herself if she had had that kind of spirit. But she could never be like her cousin; they were complete opposites to whom James would react in different ways. He would have responded better to someone like Marianne, she decided; perhaps her strength would have softened the harshest of his ways. But it was no good thinking along those lines; he was married to her, and soon she would bear his child.

The sudden pain was a harsh reminder of that. She could not stop the scream that escaped her. 'Sorry,' she whispered when the worst had passed, but Marianne had already run from the room.

She was back a moment later, preceded by the reassuring bulk of Mrs Blake. 'A little pain then, mum?' the woman asked and smiled, although the gesture could not hide the worried crease of her forehead. 'You want I should call Dr Maxwell?'

Katherine shook her head, although she knew that Mrs Blake's had been a rhetorical question. The big housekeeper would decide for herself.

'Perhaps you should,' whispered Marianne.

Mrs Blake said, 'No, you go. I'll stay with her.'

Marianne did not argue. Ever since her arrival, she and Mrs Blake had been testing each other's will. So far they were evenly matched, but Marianne knew this situation did not call for a renewed bout. She dashed from the room, her skirts lifted high.

She bumped into James as she hurtled down the passage. 'Whoa!' he called out, catching her in his arms. 'That eager to greet me, are you?' He laughed at the anger in her eyes when he kept her held tightly to him.

'Let go! It's Katherine, she—'

He released her so fast she almost lost her balance. 'The baby? Is it the baby?' He started to push past her but she held him back.

'Quick! The doctor! Your horse—'

'Is the baby—'

'Too hell with your bloody baby! Start thinking about your wife!'

For a moment she thought he would slap her. Then he turned and ran down the passage. She followed him.

'It's only the pains that've started,' Mrs Blake said when they both burst into the room. 'Now will one of you go for the doctor?' she added, glaring at Marianne.

James stared down at Katherine's white face for a few moments before he turned and ran for his horse.

It was dark inside the house. A lamp glowed dully in the corner of James's study. He clutched a full glass of brandy in his hand.

'I'll have one of those if you don't mind,' said Marianne, appearing beside the desk.

He wordlessly filled a glass and handed it to her. She took a large sip, shuddering at the harshness of the liquor. 'Terrible stuff,' she muttered, 'but it does help.'

He remained silent. The clock ticked loudly from across the room. Almost eight. Still there was silence from the room at the end of the passage. The last scream had come almost an hour ago. They had both run for the door, where Mrs Blake's bulk stood in anticipation of their anxiety, effectively blocking their entrance and a view into the room. 'Just pain,' she announced calmly. 'There are enough hands in here to help.' With that she had shut the door in their faces. Marianne had retreated to her room till the four walls held in too much tension.

She gently touched James's shoulder and said, 'I'm sorry.'

'Sorry?'

'About what I said this afternoon. I was frightened and—'

She was surprised to see him smile. 'About my being more concerned with the health of the baby than Katherine?'

She nodded and took another sip of brandy. This time she did not wince.

'I can't blame you,' he said in an uncharacteristically gentle tone. 'You were quite right.' He smiled again, yet there was a sadness in his eyes that halted her angry response.

'Try and understand,' he went on, 'how it was the last time. At first I was against her having the baby, but then—'

Marianne could not stop herself. She reached out to touch him again. 'Oh, James,' she said, 'I should have realised. I'm sorry.' His hand squeezed hers.

She continued to stand beside him, silently, till he said, 'You don't like me much, do you?'

She gave a small smile of embarrassment.

'I . . . James, I don't know. I really don't. I'm a very defensive person. Aggressive, as well, I suppose. It often brings out a similar reaction in others, and we end up disliking each other for no other reason than that.'

'Was that the case with me?'

She looked down at him, studying the gentleness on his face, wishing he could be like that more often. It made him much more attractive.

'No answer?'

She laughed. When she gently removed her hand from his, she felt the calluses on his skin, the scars from what he had once been. 'I suppose,' she started, seating herself awkwardly on the edge of the desk, 'I wanted you to remain a romantic ruffian, the one I met in Cape Town that first time.'

'But you were just a slip of a girl then,' he said and laughed. 'You can't expect your impressions to remain the same.'

'I'm still a girl, remember? You told me so the other day on the hunt, when you warned me against Slabbert and the likes.'

'I was wrong. You're a very beautiful and desirable woman. But you haven't answered my question.'

'First, answer one of mine. Do you want me? As that beautiful and desirable woman you just described?'

169

He swivelled back in his chair to look up at her. 'My God,' he said breathlessly. 'You *are* direct, aren't you?'

'It helps to avoid misunderstandings.'

He shook his head slowly. 'You're a strange one, Marianne. How can you ask that? I'm your cousin's husband!'

Her smile was knowing. 'I'm asking you as a man, James.'

Their eyes held each other's. At last he nodded and said softly, 'Yes, I do want you. Any man would. Are you satisfied?'

'Is that why you're jealous of George?'

'Jealous? No, envious perhaps. But—'

'That's what made me dislike you. You tried to treat me like a little girl who's been led astray by a lust-filled man. Yet you've just admitted you feel the same. I resent that, and that's why I dislike you.'

To her surprise he threw back his head and laughed. 'Bloody hell,' he said, 'you really are something!' He leaned forward and grabbed both her hands. 'I apologise, Marianne Kenrick, for being a hypocrite. Am I forgiven?'

Her smile remained on her lips when she withdrew her hands from his. 'For that, yes. But for being ruthless and self-centred, no. The other thing I don't like about you is the way you treat Katherine.'

His pleasant humour was gone. 'There is nothing wrong with the way I treat my wife. Perhaps if she had more—'

'Don't let's start an argument, James,' she interrupted. 'I've probably been too personal as it is. Please, let's try again at being friends.' She slipped from the desk and started for the door. 'I'll see whether I can pry any news from the formidable Mrs Blake.'

'Marianne!' The strength in his voice stopped her, made her turn to face him. 'I wonder,' he said, 'how it would have been if it was you and I—'

'Don't say it – don't ever, ever say or think that!' She fled from the room.

Oh God, she thought as she hastened down the passage – this was no longer a game but something which threatened to turn ugly and hurtful. She had to get away from here. As soon as Katherine was over the birth, she had to get back to

Cape Town. How could James compare her and Katherine? As individuals, yes, but as wives?

Even so, when she knocked at Katherine's bedroom door, she shivered at the realisation of how rapidly scorn and amusement towards James had changed to an ominous mixture of attraction and revulsion.

The sudden scream from behind the door stopped her from dwelling on that unsettling fact.

Much later, when it was all over and Katherine lay in an exhausted sleep, Marianne took coffee to the doctor. 'I appreciate your staying overnight,' she said. 'Mrs Blake is preparing your room.'

He took the coffee from her with a smile. 'She's very weak.' He glanced at the closed door of Katherine's room. 'It was a near thing. I warned her . . .' He shrugged and added, 'I'll rest more easily if I'm here.'

'Do you think there might be any complications?'

Dr Maxwell patted her shoulder. 'Shouldn't be, but it's best not to take any chances.'

After the doctor had retired, Marianne went to the study where James had settled down with a fresh bottle of brandy. He smiled when she walked in, but there were tears in his eyes.

'Why tears?' she asked. 'There should be joy! You have a fine, healthy son and your wife is well. Weak, but well.'

'The tears are relief,' he said thickly. He raised his glass and said, 'To Ralph. To my son.'

She raised her own empty hand. 'To Ralph,' she replied, 'and to a brave Katherine who bore him for you.' She turned and headed for her own bedroom.

Relief, she wondered, but for who? Ralph, or Katherine, or them both?

CHAPTER SEVENTEEN

Leading the infamous rankings of world prisons were Dartmoor and Devil's Island. Then there was the Breakwater.

Its high walls closeted despair, and housed white, native and coloured prisoners who laboured at the construction of a breakwater for the Prince Alfred Docks in Table Bay.

Among them were murderers, seamen who had abandoned ship, petty thieves and smugglers of diamonds. Of the latter group, most were men who could not be regarded as common criminals. They were men to whom penal servitude and hard labour were foreign concepts with which their personalities were not adequately equipped to deal. But the Breakwater knew no class distinctions.

Each man wore the broad-arrow prison outfit with his number stamped on the back of his jacket. There were no individual cells, only long grey wards with concrete floors. The prisoners slept on a bed board with a mat, a pillow and three blankets. Between each white prisoner slept a native, to reduce communication as well as the risk of escape.

Many of the warders were no better than the men they guarded. They came from almost every walk of life, often applying for the position with doubtful references. They carried rifles, yet were not trusted to keep them loaded. The warders' bayonets were at hand though, for they were often called upon to use them.

Their days were as long and monotonous as those of the men they guarded, and at night they trudged through the lighted wards, checking on each prisoner. At dawn it was the guards who rose first, in preparation for the convicts' march to the quarry site. Their day ended long after the last man was safely back inside the Breakwater walls.

They administered punishment when necessary, sometimes dishing it out for no other reason than to relieve their own frustration. The daily drudgery of their lives was soul-destroying; prisoners and warders alike were all captives of the Breakwater.

That morning the bell sounded at five o'clock, as it did every day. The clatter of the ward doors being unlocked came a half-hour later, the signal for the prisoners to begin moving out.

A day the same as those that had gone before awaited them. Breakfast was stale porridge, after which they trudged out through the main gates to be in the quarry by six. Lunch was served at midday, and work continued till they were herded back to the gaol at five o'clock. After being granted the freedom of the yard till eight, they were locked away for the night. And so another day would pass by – another day marked off with a mental cross in each prisoner's mind. Yet it was hard not to think of the terrible similarity of the day that lay ahead.

Gert Denker was not among the men when they headed out of the gates that morning. With another man, he was led instead into the main prison building, to the room where the dreaded treadmill was housed. The second convict glanced at him, but the Dutchman was staring straight ahead, trying to ignore the machinery. It was not his first visit to this room.

The treadmill was the favourite punishment among the more sadistic warders, preferred even to the normal twelve lashes with the cat-o'-nine-tails stiffened in brine. It was designed to hold two men, a sort of moving staircase which had to be kept revolving once the process was started. If those being punished slackened their pace, the plank stairs lacerated their shins. The brake was controlled by the warder and, when Denker saw who would administer the punishment that day, he knew the brake would not be used very often.

The warder's name was Kruger, a small round man with a pink, hairless face. Both his ears were deformed, clinging to the sides of his face like shrivelled, flesh-coloured prunes. 'So,' he said, prodding Denker with the point of his bayonet, 'you still remember this place?'

Denker ignored him, even though the memory of his previous session on the treadmill tugged icily at his stomach. His punishment had lasted a full day that time, with only five minutes' rest every half-hour or so.

It had been a different warder then, less cruel than Kruger. Even so, Denker had tried to break away after three hours of punishment. They handcuffed him, then, to a bar above the treadmill. There he had hung while the revolving planks slashed at his legs. He did not know how long the punishment would last this time.

'Seems you bastards have too much energy,' Kruger was saying, referring to the fight between Denker and the other convict in the yard the previous evening. 'Let's see you get rid of some.' He pointed at the treadmill.

Denker stepped forward. The man with him was sweating with fear now, but after a moment's hesitation he, too, stepped towards the planks. 'How long?' growled Denker as he readied himself.

Kruger's thin lips curled into a sneer. 'Three days for you – seeing as it's your second time. One for your fighting friend.'

Three days! Denker gave a nonchalant shrug, trying to disguise the fear tightening his stomach. The treadmill started moving beneath him.

His feet and legs moved mechanically and, even when the machine increased speed, Kruger just stood near the brake, his hand tapping the lever ineffectually. He smirked at Denker. 'Your friend still needs some practice,' he shouted and laughed when the convict beside Denker lost his stride, breaking the rhythm for both men. The planks bruised their legs.

'Don't concentrate too hard,' Denker told him. 'Think about other things.' Though they had tried to kill each other the night before, they now needed to co-operate, needed harmony of movement to prevent the machine from battering their shins.

His own thoughts were focused on the future, on the

day he would finish his ten-year sentence and be a free man once again. On that day he would start out after James Quenton. His revenge would be long overdue by then, yet doubly satisfying for what he, Denker, had suffered because of that sanctimonious bastard!

It must have been Quenton, of course, who had told Sir Anthony Kenrick about the fight with Thomas – it had to be him! Denker had left the road-construction site in a thick rage, his mind filled with thoughts of violent revenge. He had tempered this by the time he reached Cape Town, for he realised the time was not yet right to get even with James Quenton; he still enjoyed Sir Anthony's protection. But one day . . .

Denker had instead headed north-west, joining the rush of hopeful diggers to the diamond fields around Kimberley. Things had gone well at first, when he worked a claim with an Australian he had met on the long and dusty journey. The partnership fell apart after two months, however, when the Australian discovered Denker was holding out on some of his finds. He met his physical match for the first time in many years and was thrown off the claim with nothing to show for his efforts.

He stayed along the sidelines after that, not able to begin again once word of his dishonesty had reached the ears of others. Somehow he managed to survive, doing odd jobs in areas where he was safely separated from the actual claims. Occasionally he held down a foreman's position for a week or two, usually with groups of newcomers with enough capital to employ teams of labourers. That, too, ended once they came to know of Denker's reputation.

It was inevitable that he would drift into illicit diamond buying, paying the natives to bring him diamonds from the claims they worked for others. Again, it was his foul temper which landed him in trouble. When he suspected one of them of cheating on him, he beat the young African almost to death. The youth recovered and laid charges.

There were many other illicit dealers, often intelligent and cultured men who ran their operations with skill. Their numbers swelled so rapidly that savage sentences were passed in an effort to stamp out the malpractice. Most of them received from five to ten years depending on the scale of their operation.

Denker should have received perhaps six months for the assault, with a further three years for his attempt at illicit dealing. But other traits of his behaviour on the diamond fields were raised during the trial: his cheating his partner, the rumoured rape of a black woman, a further attempt at fraud. The magistrate handed down a ten-year sentence and Denker found himself on his way to the Breakwater prison.

There was no reason for him to blame James Quenton for his continued misfortune, yet he did. To Denker's way of thinking, he would not have gone to the diamond fields if it were not for James, and he would therefore not have been forced to give up ten years of his life in a stinking prison. His hatred and lust for revenge were all that he had to cling on to in the years which still lay ahead.

The sudden thought of that dismal future slashed into his thoughts, bringing a fresh rage bubbling through him. Eight merciless years left! God, how Quenton would pay! He'd ruin him – somehow he'd see him destroyed.

Even above the rage spinning madly through him, Denker realised he did not have the ability to destroy what James had – not in a business sense at least. Perhaps he could cause the farm to be burned down . . . or kill his damn ostriches. But, no, he owed Quenton much more than that.

He would have to take from him what every man valued most of all: his own life. He would kill him with his bare hands, feel the life being squashed out between his fingers. Only that would satisfy him.

It was as if he could see James's face before him, eyes bulging, mouth open in a silent plea for mercy. His own eyes closed tightly with the vision of his satisfaction. In that instant he felt himself lose rhythm, stamping down faster than the turn of the treadmill. The planks came up, striking him cruelly on the shins. Denker's eyes flew open. Sweat dripped from his brow as he tried to get the spinning machine under control again. The man beside him cursed.

Kruger was laughing now, his face shining with excitement as he watched the two men struggle with each other and the revolving planks. He waited till they seemed to re-establish their rhythm, then slammed down on the brake. The men lurched forward as it ground to a halt. Kruger laughed again.

'Like two old women,' he said, wiping his face. 'Your first bloody half-hour, and already you're all done in!' His stomach jerked with twisted amusement as he pulled Denker from the treadmill. 'Five minutes, then on you go again.'

He jerked up his bayonet when he saw the glazed look in Denker's eyes. 'You want to hit me? You that angry?' He prodded the big Dutchman, taunting him with laughter in his pig-like eyes. 'Go ahead, go ahead and try – I'd love to put the cuffs on you, you bastard!' He was surprised when Denker laughed into his face.

He could not know that the Dutchman laughed at the absurdity of hating the warder – did the fool really think he was worth that?

Denker turned away, bending over to take in deep breaths of air. His hatred was a special thing, not meant for sadistic warders. It was to be nurtured for a further eight years, for a very special person, someone who was worth the wait.

On Ratitāe, four hundred miles away from the Breakwater, it was a special day for Ralph Quenton. He was one year old, a handsome child, slender like Katherine, yet with James's dark complexion. It was a day filled with busy excitement, for he and his mother were about to depart on a journey to Cape Town. He could not fully comprehend this, yet sensed the change in pace around him from where he sat on the kitchen floor of the large mansion. Near him, Mrs Blake fussed at the servants preparing food for the long journey.

'I've packed in some nice cold meats,' the housekeeper told Katherine.

'Really, Mrs Blake – it's not as though we won't find any food along the way!'

'Even so,' Mrs Blake persisted, 'it's a long journey – the coach could break down between farms or something. Better to be prepared.'

Katherine decided to let the woman carry on; looking

after her employer made her happy. She knelt down in front of Ralph. 'A birthday boy,' she said, lifting him into her arms. 'We should be having a party instead of starting a journey!' She kissed his forehead.

'I agree.' The sound of James's voice made her spin around.

She smiled nervously and handed him the little boy when he held out his arms to take him. 'You could have postponed your departure for a few days,' James went on, cradling Ralph in his arms. 'I can't see the need for this sudden rush.'

'James, it's only because—'

'I know, I know! But just because your father is ill needn't mean you have to rush off with my son.'

'Marianne's letter said it was more than a mere illness. He's in a bad way, James.'

'You know how Marianne tends to exaggerate. Sir Anthony's a tough old man – he'll get over whatever ails him.'

'It's been years since I've seen him,' she said lamely.

'But why take my son with you? My God, Katherine – he's still a baby – far too small for such a journey!'

She stepped away from his anger. From the corner of her eye she saw Mrs Blake's jaw tighten. The servants pretended not to watch them, yet Katherine knew they were listening to every word. 'Let's talk outside, please,' she told James, leading the way from the kitchen.

The leather soles of her shoes echoed on the marble floor of the passage as she headed for the drawing-room. The sudden silence caused by the Persian carpets beneath her feet seemed almost daunting. It had always been her favourite room, but now the six-foot-high wood panelling, the French wallpaper and silk drapes provided no comfort.

James had stopped close behind her when she turned to him. She said, 'The effect of the journey on Ralph concerns me, too, but I can't leave him here.'

'Why not? Your precious Mrs Blake can take care of him while I'm at work.' He clutched Ralph to his chest, both arms encircling the boy as if fearful that Katherine would try to snatch the child from him.

'James, you said it yourself – he's still a baby! He needs to be with his mother. I can't leave him behind.'

178

'He already spends too much time with his mother,' he snapped back. 'Too much time with females, in fact – you, Mrs Blake, the servant girls – you're trying to turn him into a girl, damn you!'

His sudden curse drained the remaining colour from her face. She swallowed loudly, as if the sound would help curb the impulse to flee the room. Her voice shook when she said, 'I don't want to argue with you, James.' She wrapped her arms about her shoulders to control their trembling. 'I . . . I understand your need to have Ralph with you, how impatient you are to have him grow up and help build Ratitāe with you. But he's still a baby – neither boy nor girl right now. Some day he'll be the feather baron you so badly want. Right now he's nothing but a baby.' A slow anger was building inside her, threatening to oust the feelings suppressed for too long. It sounded to her as if a stranger was speaking when she said, 'It might've been better if you'd shown more interest in your son before now – his childhood won't last for ever.'

James was breathing heavily. 'I shall raise him in my own manner, in my own good time,' he replied, his voice a low growl.

'I'm sure you will . . . but, James – he's not a part of your business, not some investment lying idle till it's mature enough to realise a profit for you. He needs his father *now*, while he's still a child.'

'Then why take him from me?'

'I'm not taking him from you,' she managed to answer calmly. 'I was speaking of your being a father to him instead of some business associate. You'll have enough years to turn him into a replica of yourself.'

James stared at her as if seeing her for the first time. She wondered whether it was because of her small display of defiance; perhaps she should have done it long ago.

She stood her ground when he stepped closer to her. 'All right,' he said hoarsely, 'take Ralph with you. But if anything happens to him . . .'

He continued to glare down at her, the unspoken threat glowing in his eyes. Then he turned away, taking Ralph with him.

Katherine slowly let out her breath, shivered, then walked back to the kitchen on trembling legs.

James strode past the sweeping marble staircase on his way to his study at the side of the house. It was a large yet dark room that overlooked the southern side of the farm. He perched Ralph on the desk and jerked back the curtains. The lucerne fields were filled with young ostriches feeding among the green lushness. As he turned away from the window, his gaze fell on the large clock hanging against the wall. Even the visual reminder that it was still early morning did not stop him from opening the bar cabinet built into one corner of the room.

He filled a glass with brandy, twirling it in his hand while he watched Ralph investigate a fountain pen on the desk top. 'No, Ralph,' he said, stepping forward to remove the pen from the child's grasp as Ralph started banging it down on the desk. Taking a pencil and note pad from the drawer, he gave that to him instead. Only when he was satisfied that the little boy would do no damage did he move back to the window.

He drank slowly, thinking of Katherine, the Katherine who had suddenly faced up to him, angry and unafraid. He realised – not without a degree of shock – that he had actually admired her. For the first time in many years of marriage, he had felt some respect for his wife.

James seldom gave any real thought to their changing relationship. He knew subconsciously that whatever feelings he had once possessed towards her had been connected with what marriage to Katherine might grant him. Once he had got what he wanted from her, she played a diminished role in his life.

There was little physical attraction left, yet there were times when he acted tenderly towards her, a sudden unfamiliar rush of affection which was little more than a sense of loyalty. Or guilt? Katherine, like her father, had helped pave the way for his present success.

The silence behind him made him turn to check on Ralph. The boy was lying stretched out across the desk, the pencil stuck in his mouth. The note pad lay on the floor. 'Don't eat the thing, son,' James said, gently removing the pencil. The child smiled up at him when James gently scooped him into his arms. 'I'll miss you,' he whispered.

Ralph pointed through the open window with an excited little sound. 'That's right,' James said, 'ostriches – our ostriches. Yours and mine.'

He heard Katherine's voice from somewhere near the kitchen. She sounded slightly breathless, making him wonder whether she was as surprised as he had been at her display of anger. He told himself it was an evanescent emotion, one that would not be hastily repeated. She would, no doubt, apologise to him for her words. He sipped his brandy, unable to admit that he was trying to reassure himself on that score; the last thing he needed was a wife who suddenly discovered she had a personality of her own.

Unlike Marianne, he thought. She was already a young woman with her own mind and he could not imagine her in any other way. He would be able to accept her and would welcome the combative nature of a relationship with her. She could be almost an equal in life, love and in business. Yes, even the latter. There were times when he wanted – even needed – someone at his side, someone who could appreciate the scope of his activities, as well as understand the decisions required of him. The thought that he had never wanted Katherine to be involved brought with it the bitter memory of Abraham Isaacs's attempts to force that on him.

A familiar tightness filled his chest as he quickly swallowed the rest of his brandy. Even after all this time, Abraham could still haunt him. It no longer helped to tell himself he had no need to feel guilty; the old fool had tried to interfere, to curtail his vision and he had paid dearly for his arrogance. Yet, the means of his angry revenge plagued him from time to time. It was done, though, and there was no use dwelling on the deed. The family of the little girl he had used to implicate Abraham in the scandal was far away, content with their new lives and unaccustomed wealth. James hoped he would never see or hear from them again. He started to reach for the bottle, then withdrew his hand. No, he thought, ghosts and brandy do not mix well.

Ralph was pulling at his hair. He prised the boy's little fingers loose, saying, 'Let's go look at our birds.'

Keeping Ralph in his arms, he went outside, deciding as he walked that he would soon have to remove the boy from Katherine's attention. It was time his son learned the ways of a man. Just a few more years, then the training could start.

He wished Ralph was already at an age where he could be taught about the operation of the farm. Right now he was as useless as a baby daughter, with no comprehension of what his father had built for him. 'All this will be yours,' he whispered, turning to look back at the house. It was an immense place, far too large for their needs. But it was what he had wanted, a visible symbol of his wealth and a worthy home for his son.

It was a double-storey building, a unique blend of Cape-Dutch and Victorian-style architecture: slate roof complete with gables, white columns, shutters. A wide verandah, both upstairs and downstairs, surrounded the front and sides of the house. The upper balcony boasted an encirclement of intricate filigree cast iron. 'It will be yours,' he whispered again.

A thundering noise of wagon wheels heralded the approach of the coach to collect Katherine and Ralph. James waited till he saw it hurtle round the last bend in the road. It came to a halt in a cloud of dust, the coachman raising his hat when he saw James.

Katherine appeared at the front door, followed by Mrs Blake and two maids with her luggage. She and James stared at each other for a long moment before he moved closer, kissed Ralph, then handed the boy to her. 'Goodbye, James,' she whispered.

'Goodbye.' He did not smile as he leaned forward to kiss her cheek.

She let the coachman help her inside. When she turned to look out of the open door, only Mrs Blake and the maids were there.

James had already entered the house without any further word or gesture of farewell. Neither had he waited for the apology which died on her lips when he turned away from her.

CHAPTER EIGHTEEN

Katherine sat with Marianne in the small courtyard at the back of Sir Anthony Kenrick's home. She wiped away a tear.

'He's aged so,' she said in a thin voice. 'He used to be so strong, so . . . so indestructible. It's hard to imagine that same man lying a cripple in bed.'

Marianne glanced at her. 'I'm sorry. I should have prepared you. I suppose one doesn't notice the change when you see a person day after day.'

Katherine touched her arm. 'It's all right,' she said. 'Even Mother seems to have lost her strength.'

'I know. She lived her life on the basis of his strength, remember. Now she's lost.'

'Perhaps all of us lived off his strength. Except you.' There was no accusation in the words, and she was glad to see that Marianne sensed none.

She studied her cousin, marvelling again at the added beauty which the past year had brought. Marianne's face was fuller, softening her features and highlighting the classic bone structure. Her mother must have been a spectacular beauty, Katherine thought, with a will as strong as her daughter's.

'I meant to ask,' she said and lowered her gaze. 'Have you heard from George? He's due to arrive around now, isn't he? His last letter said he would pay us a visit at Ratitāe.'

Marianne smiled self-consciously. 'I was going to tell you – he's arriving sometime this week. But – it's been almost two years!'

'You think he'd forget you? Dear Marianne – how could any man ever do that!'

'Oh, I don't know . . . I was such a child . . . a spoilt brat on her first visit to Europe. I'm sure he was just being kind for the sake of his friendship with our family.'

'Nonsense!'

'I don't want to build up false hopes, that's all – oh, what's the use! I can't wait to see him again. And for him to see me!'

'You'll take his breath away, Pumpkin,' Katherine said, as if they were both children again. 'I remember that night,' she went on, 'when we lay in my room discussing our two ruffians. I got mine, and I know you'll get yours. He won't stand a chance against your beauty.'

'How is James?' asked Marianne. 'Why didn't he come with you?' At least, she thought with relief, whatever she'd felt towards him had not dwelled on her mind since leaving Oudtshoorn. Then she saw her cousin's expression and quickly said, 'What is it, Kath? Is something wrong? Is it James – the two of you?'

'I – I don't know. It's as if . . . as if he doesn't love me any more – I wonder whether he's *ever* loved me!' She buried her face in her hands.

Marianne shifted closer, expecting to see tears, surprised to find there were none. 'How can you say that, Kath? Of course James loves you! Perhaps—'

'I'm sorry . . . it's probably just the long journey that's depressed me. I'm tired, that's all.' She tried to smile, but failed.

'Is it something he said . . . something he did?'

'I don't know! He's so distant. I just can't seem to reach him!'

'Hah! Sounds very much like the James you married. That's the way he is, dear cousin. Isn't this a case of your wanting him to be something he's not?'

'He couldn't even say a proper goodbye to me!' Her high-pitched voice was more like a shout. 'He pecked me on the cheek, Marianne – like he would a sister! He hardly ever touches me these days.' The tears were there now, threatening to spill down her pale cheeks.

184

Marianne moved back. 'I'm not in a position to tell,' she said gently, 'but hasn't all the sudden change had an effect on you both? The baby, the house? Perhaps things will settle down after a while.'

Katherine sniffed. 'If only he'd come with me. Perhaps here, away from the farm, we might have talked about things. About us.'

'Why didn't he?'

Her cousin's laugh was thin and harsh. 'He couldn't afford to take time off for a visit, of course. You see, he no longer has any need of my father. Or any of us for that matter.'

'Now, Kath – there you go again!'

'You think I'm being unfair? He has Ratitāe, and now he has Ralph. There's nothing more I can give him. Nothing except love, even if he has no need for it.'

'I'm sure you're wrong! He's probably one of those men who don't know how to show their feelings, that's all.'

'No, Pumpkin,' came the soft reply, 'that's not the problem. I don't think James is capable of loving anyone but himself. He doesn't mean to hurt – not always, at least – but he can't love and neither can he respond to love. I used to think that having a child would change him. Then I hoped it would be Ratitāe. I know better now.'

'But you carry on loving him?'

Katherine looked directly at her. 'Yes, as foolish as that may sound. I can't stop loving him.'

Marianne smiled brightly. 'All right,' she said, leaning forward to kiss her cousin's forehead, 'that's enough misery for now. I'll fix you a nice cup of tea, shall I?'

Her efforts were rewarded when Katherine said, 'You know, you're beginning to sound just like Mrs Blake!'

It rained the day George Laboulaye arrived in Cape Town. He sent a message about the ship's arrival to the Kenrick estate, then waited in the shelter provided by the overhang of a warehouse roof.

George was thirty-five that year, a tall, handsome man with

light streaks of grey already showing in his thick hair. His visits to Cape Town were always a pleasant event, accompanied by a knot of excitement within his stomach. This time, however, it was anxiety that gathered there.

He thought it ironic that in his many dealings with a variety of people over the years, he had never once felt nervous about seeing any of them again – whatever the circumstances of their last meeting. Yet now he stood watching the rain, back in his favourite city, petrified at the prospect of seeing a wisp of a girl again. He was fully aware that there was no longer anything girlish about Marianne Kenrick; the time he had spent with her during her visit to Europe had made that abundantly clear.

George had looked forward to her coming to Paris, for he visualised fulfilling an avuncular role towards the girl who had been a special person in his life ever since they first met. He wanted to show her the sights, buy her gifts, impress her by treating her as an adult – perhaps even arrange for her to be taken out by one or two of the young men he knew at their distributors. He was determined that Marianne would return to the Cape and boast proudly to her girl-friends about her dashing 'uncle' in Europe.

He had waited at the railway station in Paris for the group of young students, accompanied on the tour by four lecturers. Sir Anthony and Lady Kenrick had given permission that their niece should be allowed to break away from the tour to spend some time with him. George straightened his coat, smiling broadly as the train pulled into the station.

For some reason – foolishly so, he thought afterwards – he had visualised a girl, not much changed from the Marianne he remembered, who would hurtle from the group into his outstretched arms. The last thing he expected was the beautiful young woman who walked with slow confidence towards him, thick auburn hair swinging in time with the provocative movement of her hips, a knowing smile denting her cheeks with deep dimples. It was the start of a nightmare time for him.

During her stay with him, he had constantly to remind himself of his responsibilities – towards Marianne as well as Sir Anthony. To himself as well. This was Marianne, damn it – she was the little girl he'd watched grow up! Despite appearances, she was still a young adult, prone to her emotions, and very, very vulnerable. She was seventeen years younger than him – she was Sir Anthony's niece! But one night, when she moved quickly up to him, all soft curves and womanly smell, he realised that he had not succeeded in disguising his reactions to her. It had been even more difficult for him after that.

After her departure, it had taken a while for George to stop being affected by even the mere thought of her. Brigette had helped, though; he thought she'd come along at just the right time. Brigette was very much like him in many ways. She was an individualist, yet easy-going, not too concerned about what the next day would bring. He had been rather surprised when she started hinting at marriage. Still, she was a mature woman who knew what life was all about, she loved him, and he loved her. Or did he? He enjoyed being with her, they were well matched sexually – but did he really love her? It was rather late now for second thoughts, though – they had been married for three months already.

Brigette had not opted to accompany him to the Cape; a colony in primitive Africa was not quite her idea of having fun. George found it difficult to conceal his relief; it was going to be awkward enough breaking the news of his marriage to Marianne without a wife in tow. He wondered why he had never written to her about it. There was no reason not to; he had made no promises, given no intimation of a future relationship between them. In any case, he was sure the news would have made no difference to Marianne – she had made up her mind about him the very first time she told him she loved him. She'd been eight then, he recalled. No, he was doing the right thing by telling her in person. But, God – how it terrified him!

A woman's voice broke into his reverie. 'Bloody gloomy,' she said. She was standing beside him, staring at the rain. George smiled, recognising her as one of the entertainment troupe which had joined the ship at Le Havre, headed for the culture-starved diamond fields of Kimberley. Like him, they had gathered in the lee of the building to wait for the rain to subside.

. She was quite pretty, and had made it obvious from the start that she was interested in and available to him. He'd refused her with a gentle politeness which had not offended or embarrassed her. In different circumstances, at another time in his life, he would have reacted to her.

'Even the fairest Cape,' he said now, 'at times shows a different face to the world. The way we all do.'

The woman sighed, thinking again that the romantic man beside her would have been an interesting lover. A pity. 'Any chance of your coming up Kimberley way?'

He laughed. 'No, unless they start farming with ostriches! I think they have eyes for only one sort of wealth at the moment.' There had been plenty of hopeful prospectors on board ship.

'Well,' she replied, sighing again, 'if you do, you know where to find me.'

'I most certainly shall.' He peered out, relieved to see the rain ease up a little. 'I'd better wait at the gate for my people.'

'Someone special?'

'Old family friends.' He turned, held out his hand, clasped hers within it, and said, 'I wish you luck. Take care in Kimberley – I'm told it's as rough as they come.'

She smiled and was almost beautiful. 'I've been in rough towns before. I'm no angel myself.'

'With your looks, dear lady, and that pleasant disposition, you could well be. Don't let life change you.'

She bit her lip. 'You're a true bloody gentleman, you know? About the only one I've ever met. A pity you didn't let this angel show you heaven one night. God bless you, George Laboulaye.'

'And you.' He raised her hand to his lips, picked up his bags, then walked out into the soft rain.

Marianne saw him just as the covered carriage was about to enter the Alfred Docks. 'Stop!' she called out to the driver.

The carriage was still moving as she opened the door, ready to jump out.

She saw the look on George's face even before she embraced him, and she knew. Her bounding heart seemed to stop beating. It changed instead into a lifeless, heavy object that dropped down inside her, the weight of its despair threatening to plunge through the cold skin of her body. Yet she was up against him, her arms reaching for him even though her racing mind told her she'd lost him.

His body was stiff, although he held her tightly to him. 'Marianne,' he said into her hair. She heard the guilt in his voice and wondered why it was there. He owed her nothing; there was no commitment between them save friendship – something which she herself had attempted to change.

She found the strength to pull away gently. 'Hello, George,' she said in a voice that was achingly thin. 'You're looking well.'

The sadness she saw in his eyes changed her anguish to anger. Damn him! He'd not even had the courage to act out a charade until the timing was right. She wondered who the woman was. How could he have chosen anyone over her?

'Marianne . . . you're wet. Let's get in the carriage.'

'No!' She felt her hair grow heavy with rain, but she did not care. 'George – we've known each other too long for silly games. Get to the point – your face is as long as that of a sick dog.'

His attempt at a smile didn't work. 'I never could hide things from you—' he started, then gripped her shoulders fiercely and said, 'Marianne. I . . . I'm sorry . . . I'm married now . . . three months ago. In Paris.'

Oh God, she was too late! There was no chance for her to fight back! He was hers, damn it – not some little French whore's! With time she could have shown him his mistake – given him more than he'd ever dreamed a woman could give! But now it was too late.

She heard herself say, 'Married, and you look so glum about it? Why, George, an old bachelor like you should be happy to be rescued while you still have your looks!' Moments ago she

189

had accused him of playing games, yet here she was playing out her own vicious charade.

He was staring strangely at her. 'It's just that I thought—' His arms fell back to his sides. They stared at each other through the rain.

'Thought what – that I still had a childhood crush on you? Oh, I see – because I flirted so heavily with you while I was in Europe?'

She laughed. It sounded empty and false and cruel, but she could not stop it. 'Really, George – I was a silly little girl testing her newly discovered womanhood on every man she came across. I had no idea you took it so seriously!'

It was his turn to show anger, but his was a silent rage. Marianne could tell he knew she was lying. It did not matter to her – nothing mattered any more.

The ride back to the Kenrick estate was an awkward one of long, strained silences between their attempts at casual conversation. The rain started falling more steadily again, dripping down from the carriage roof.

Marianne watched its sad trickle. Never again, she promised herself, would she allow a man the slightest chance of hurting her.

George made the return journey to Oudtshoorn with Katherine. It was almost a relief to escape Cape Town and the emotional barrier Marianne had erected between them. It was a barrier he could not broach, a solid wall warding off his attempts at explaining his mixed feelings towards her.

He had wanted to tell her of his confusion at the sudden discovery of her being a woman when she visited him in Europe. He needed to explain how he had struggled to find an equilibrium between his responsibility towards her and her family, how much he desired her when she was at his side. It was essential she understood the decision he had finally made and how the new woman in his life came along at that exact time when he was most disturbed and confused. But she would not let him talk of how the timing of life had cheated them.

It was not as though Marianne ignored him; she was friendly enough when he was around, but not once did she allow him to engineer the opportunity for them to be alone. The wall of scorned womanhood was up and he was powerless to scale it.

'She hates me,' he said to Katherine on the journey to Oudtshoorn. 'I feel so much for her, but now I've turned her against me.'

She squeezed his arm. 'She's hurting, that's all. Our Marianne is a proud and determined young woman. You've bruised her pride, so give her time. She'll get over it.'

George had his doubts.

The sight of Ratitāe managed to drive thoughts of Marianne from his mind. From the time they drove beneath a gigantic signboard proclaiming their entrance to the great expanse of Ratitāe, he had felt a tug of excitement as he thought back to the farm's humble beginnings. He had to hand it to James; the man had vision, as well as the determination to turn his dreams into reality. How long had it been since they had last seen each other? Five years? Longer? 'How long have you been married?' he asked Katherine.

'Eight years.'

'That's the last time James and I saw each other.' He gave a short laugh and added, 'Too long.' Time enough for them both to change, he thought wryly.

He was not prepared, however, for the cool reception he received from his business associate. After giving Katherine a peremptory peck on the lips, and twirling the exhausted Ralph quickly in the air, James extended his hand to George. There was no welcoming smile when he said, 'It's been a while.'

'Too long,' George repeated, thinking back to the youngster he had met so long ago in Cape Town. He realised suddenly how much Katherine, too, had changed. There was little left of the happy, excited girl. More than once along the journey he had sensed her misery.

'Quite an empire you've built for yourself,' he said. The statement received little more than a nodded response.

'I'm glad you're here,' James said, letting Ralph slip to the ground. 'We have lots to talk about – especially America.' He started for the broad steps leading up to the house.

At James's insistence, George had spent a great deal of time in the United States, arranging for distribution of Ratitāe's ever-increasing feather crop; yet now he resented the tone James used with him, like an employer demanding a full report from a junior.

After a strained dinner during which James hardly spoke, just nodding instead every now and then while Katherine told of her visit and Sir Anthony's ailing health, George was shown into the study. The door was closed firmly behind them. Without asking, James poured a large glass of brandy for each of them. 'Local variety,' he said gruffly, 'but good stuff.' George was surprised to see him down the contents in one swallow before quickly refilling the glass.

'You've put on weight,' George said and smiled. 'Too much of the good stuff?'

James ignored him. George raised his own glass and said, 'To Ratitāe.' He took a small sip, sighed, and added, 'You're right, it *is* quite good. Well, about America, I—'

'I don't want to hear about America just yet – I first want to talk about your scandalous behaviour.'

'My what?'

'Don't act the innocent with me. I'm talking about Marianne and you know it.'

'My God! You, too!' How had James known? Katherine had made no mention of his marriage at dinner.

'I find it sickening that a man of your age should try to seduce a young girl in strange surroundings, at a time when she's scared and lonely, missing her family – Good God, man, you're practically part of the family!'

George stared at him in amazement. So this had nothing to do with what effect his marriage had had on Marianne. 'You're mad,' he said slowly, glaring at James. 'You don't know what you're talking about.'

'Don't tell me I'm mad! No employee of mine—'

'Employee? I'm no employee of yours! I never was! I'm a free agent, damn you!'

'You made your money out of it,' snapped James. His face was ugly in the dim light.

'Of course I did – you think I'd work for nothing?' He shook his head in disbelief. 'I don't understand you, James. There's never been any confusion about the marketing role I play for you. But I'm more interested in hearing what you've to say about me and Marianne.'

'I've already said it. The poor child came back to this country confused – infatuated with you. Does she know how many women you've had, how you play with them? Damn you – she's still a child!'

George was unable to stop the harsh laugh which escaped him. 'Marianne hasn't been a child for years – but then you know that, don't you?' He saw the sudden flush on James's face and knew he had guessed correctly. 'That's it,' he said softly, 'you want her yourself, you double-faced bastard! You can't stand the thought of my having been with her.' He couldn't believe what was taking place between them. There was no intimacy, no hint of the beginnings of dreams they had once shared. He slammed down his half-full glass and stood up.

'Just for the record,' he said, 'I never laid a hand on her. And I'm married now, to a woman in Paris. Marianne knows about it.'

There was a trace of embarrassment on James's face. 'I was just trying to protect her,' he said gruffly. 'She's an impulsive girl and—'

'Don't turn into a liar as well as a lecher, James,' he said as he reached for the door. 'I'll fill you in on America tomorrow. After that, I think it'll be better if you find someone else to look after your overseas interests.'

'There's no need to act that way,' James called out.

George spun around. 'It's no act, James – I don't agree with your fanciful schemes about America. You'll hurt your own industry, even destroy it. I don't want any part of that.'

James's mouth was a tight sneer now. 'How noble,' he said, virtually spitting the words out. 'Go ahead, go wallow in your new-found respectability! I'll do as I please, and do it better without you.'

'Goodbye, James. Just don't forget your own respectability. Especially as regards Katherine.'

'Get out!' It was an angry hiss.

George closed the door softly behind him, saddened at how it had ended.

CHAPTER NINETEEN

Marianne stared at the fluttering curtains, wishing she was at home. The hotel was quaint enough, nestling gently among the trees of Constantia Kloof, with a magnificent view all the way to the Atlantic Ocean. It was the room, as well as its laden atmosphere of waste which made her gloomy.

She did not move when the man beside her stirred. Her eyes remained fixed on the curtains even when his hand moved to her bare shoulder. 'I thought you would be asleep,' he said, squeezing her flesh between his fingers. She shrugged off his grip.

He was lying on his back, his head tucked into the crook of his arm. A silly, sleepy smirk of vanquish clung to his full lips. Marianne studied him, yet her eyes gave no inkling of what she was thinking.

His satisfied grin widened as he reached for her hair, gripped a tendril, and slowly pulled her face closer to his. Her eyes were open when he raised his lips to hers. His tongue started to probe, seeking the same heated response he had found when they had fallen on to the bed earlier that afternoon. There was none. His tongue stopped moving.

'You're a weird one,' he said, letting his head drop back on to the pillow. 'This afternoon, Marianne, you could hardly wait! Now you're as cold as a dead fish.' His smile had changed into a sulk.

'Perhaps that's because I'm not in my natural element.'

The young man misconstrued her meaning. He reached beneath the blanket, forced his hand between her legs and held her so hard that she flinched. 'Let's put you back in it, shall we?' His finger moved roughly inside her.

'Aubrey,' she said softly, 'I don't ever want you to touch me again – not anywhere! Do you understand?'

The smug smile slipped from his face. His hand was suddenly gone from her, and he started to slip out from beneath the cover of the blankets. His mouth was a tight, bitter line when he said, 'The only difference between you and a whore is that a whore's a better actress. At least she would see it through to the final curtain.' He reached for his clothes.

His skin was pale in the dim light. Marianne smiled for the first time when she studied the flaccid reticence of his penis as it waggled when he tried to slide his foot into the leg of his trouser. A silly little organ, she thought idly, useful only for brief moments when it fooled seducer and the seduced with its temporary state of power. Even then, it could not tell and did not care who played which role.

Aubrey was almost fully dressed now. He tucked the folds of his shirt into his trouser waistline while he glared down at her. The cover of clothes brought back a measure of confidence which her earlier rejection had destroyed. It demonstrated itself in hurtful sarcasm when he said, 'Shall I leave the money on the table?'

She did not reply, unable and unwilling to be drawn into an angry response. She understood his resentment, but did not care. 'Goodbye, Aubrey,' she said as he stalked to the door. He gave her a last withering look before closing it with a loud slam.

She lay back against the pillows and studied the ceiling, thinking how easy it was to destroy a friendship. But, then, had she and Aubrey ever had that? They had known each other long enough, although time and a similar circle of acquaintances did not constitute friendship. She was aware that Aubrey, like most of the young men in that circle, desired her. At that stage, though, she had had George Laboulaye in mind as the man who would claim her, so she had enjoyed but remained unaffected by their attention, as well as their not-so-subtle advances. It had been George himself who had

196

changed the parameters of her needs and reactions, almost a year ago now.

Aubrey was not the first to whom she had turned. There had been no conscious choice in that respect, for an alternative was not what Marianne had in mind. Her needs were selfish ones or possibly for self-punishment, although she would and could not admit to the latter. It was as though she was determined to prove her own strength through what she regarded as the vulnerability of men; Aubrey was but one link in that process. She found him handsome enough, with an attractive physique which clothes seemed to cover in an attempt to tease, and in this he had not failed her.

It had been a simple task getting him to take her to lunch; he had asked her often enough. The seduction was simpler still. How gullible men were, she thought as he flailed the horses of his carriage in his rush to get to the hotel. It amused her how they always assumed that they were the ones with power over her, that it was she who had the desire. For a while, as he lay firm and swollen inside her, his hard, muscular body covering hers, she had abandoned herself to just that. Her whimpers and moans were those of genuine pleasure, as it was for this, too, that she was using him. 'Am I the best?' he had demanded as his control broke and the tide of his pleasure flowed deep inside her.

'Yes! Oh, yes!' she groaned, knowing that at that moment, in the final clutches of intimacy, every man was the best. She realised also that her attempt to feign discomfort and pain when he entered her had not fooled him as it had some of the others.

It was afterwards that her depression had set in, when the wine they'd had at lunch took over from the priority of lust and Aubrey promptly fell asleep. She did not mind; there was nothing she wished to converse about, and her physical needs had been satisfied for the moment. Yet she knew there should have been an afterglow; when a man and woman had joined their bodies to give and receive pleasure, it deserved that something remain of the union. There should have been some inner satisfaction far beyond the physical. With Aubrey, as with the others before him, there was none. All she felt was a hollow emptiness; not bitterness, not regret, just emptiness.

She realised what was missing, and could not stop herself from thinking of George. Was that why she reacted as she had when Aubrey awoke and touched her so possessively?

She rose from the bed, thinking that perhaps Aubrey had been right in what he'd said to her – perhaps she was worse than a whore. A whore at least had the satisfaction of the money she earned, while she had nothing.

While she washed in the tiny bathroom, she pondered the problem of finding transport home. Or would Aubrey overcome his hurt pride and return for her? She almost hoped not, then wondered if he would talk to others about that afternoon. It was unlikely, she decided; the tale would not flatter him, and she was sure that once his ego was restored, he would come back for more. Then, at least, he would accept the situation on her terms, as the others had.

The innkeeper had a knowing leer on his face when he offered her his Cape cart and a driver to take her home. She made the man stop outside the gates of Sir Anthony Kenrick's house to avoid questions about her arrival. If asked, she would say she had insisted that Aubrey let her walk from the gates; it was a pleasant enough afternoon for the excuse to be accepted.

There was no need for any excuses, for the circumstances of Marianne's arrival would in any event have gone unnoticed that day. She was but a few yards up the long driveway when a servant spotted her. The woman came running towards her, her skirts held high. 'Madam! Madam!' she shouted.

Marianne stopped in her tracks upon seeing the consternation on her face. A cold fear flowed through her. She looked over to where an unfamiliar buggy was parked in front of the steps leading up to the house.

'Madam, it's the old master, Master Anthony!' The flow of words halted suddenly, as if Marianne's expression told her that she already knew what was to follow.

'He's dead,' Marianne finished for her. She was surprised at the steadiness of her voice.

The woman nodded grimly. 'The doctor is with the old missus.' Her eyes were swollen from crying.

Marianne placed her hand on the woman's shoulder. It was hard and bony, and she realised with a shock that it was the first time she had ever touched her. 'It's all right, Doreen,' she said. 'Go inside and make tea for us all.'

The servant stared at her, as if waiting for the expected tears to come. 'Go, Doreen. I'll come inside in a little while.'

She waited till the maid turned and ran back to the house. Only then did a small cry escape her, but she bit her lip to suppress her tears. She told herself there would be time for those later, when the memories came. Tears then would have been sorrow tinged with guilt for not having been there when he died.

She stared at the sprawling garden as if seeing it for the first time. The large eucalyptus tree beckoned to her, a favourite place of her childhood. In its full, sturdy branches she had let her mind escape to foreign scenes and places. High above the ground, hidden from the eyes of others, she had felt safe and secure. The tree was her sanctuary, her confidant, for it told no one of her secret dreams. At times it played its part in them, acting as her ship that ploughed across the mighty oceans, its branches the rigging, carrying full white sails that moved in the wind. And she was the queen who set its course. Sometimes the tree became her house or a palace from which she reigned supreme. It was many things to her, always her friend, a safe place to which to run. Just as Sir Anthony had been.

When she looked up at the window of the room in which he lay she could not form a mental picture of him dead. He was too strong, too vital to be visualised that way. Even his long illness had not changed the image she always carried of him. Marianne realised then that she had spent so little time with him since his illness, but consoled herself with the knowledge that Sir Anthony would have understood the reasons. They'd never had a need to explain things; he was like her tree, a strong, sturdy friend.

She lowered her gaze, trying to think instead of him sitting in his study. That was where he belonged – not lying in a bed where his body slowly betrayed his mind and will. The study was his sanctuary, although he had always been prepared to share it with her.

The memories came flooding back now, old sights and smells and sounds. It was as if she could hear the creak of the leather chair as he shifted back to read a document or light a cigar, welcoming her silent presence with an occasional wink and a smile, yet always putting aside his pen when he sensed she wanted to talk. It was a place for sharing love, for learning and friendship, or for nothing more than a quiet togetherness while she watched him work, breathing deeply the smell of his cigars.

A sob broke from deep within her. 'Oh God,' she cried as her tears fell. She spun round and started to venture deeper into the garden, away from the tree which had broken her strength with its reminder of times gone by.

She cried openly now, stricken by the sudden realisation of her loss, as well as by the feeling that she had disappointed him by not being there when he had needed her most.

They buried Sir Anthony on a Friday, two days after Marianne turned nineteen. The harsh February heat burned into the heavy black clothes of the crowd of mourners.

Marianne stood beside her aunt, her arm linked through that of the older woman. She strengthened her grip on her when she felt her start shaking as the coffin was lowered into the grave. On the other side of Lady Kenrick, James supported a heartbroken Katherine. Marianne shed no tears; her crying had already been done.

There were almost two hundred people who afterwards came to the mansion to pay their respects once the funeral proceedings were over. Most of them had been friends or business acquaintances of Sir Anthony. Among the latter group, some had liked and admired him, while others felt envy, some of them even a touch of hatred. Yet everyone there had respected him.

Marianne watched them stroll through the large house and garden, nibbling at the generous spread that had been arranged for them. They stood in small groups, chatting and laughing in suitably subdued tones. Of Katherine and Lady Kenrick there was no sign. She caught sight of James standing in conversation with an elderly man, his head bent attentively forward listening. She wondered how he felt about Sir Anthony's death; it was difficult to tell with him.

He spotted her watching him and smiled. It was more than an acknowledgement; it told her he found the large gathering as farcical as she did, that he understood her withdrawal. She willed him to come to her, and it was as though he saw and understood the signal in her eyes, for he excused himself from the man to whom he'd been talking.

She watched him make his way through the crowd, his gaze holding hers all the while. Then he was beside her, a presence that for a few moments needed no words. Without any discussion, they started down the long drive, out of sight of the guests.

'I don't think he would have approved of this,' James said as they turned the corner.

'The guests, you mean? Probably not. He'd probably have preferred a small, intimate funeral. Just a few close friends sitting around, talking of old times.'

He smiled. 'Yes, you're right, they'd have had a great deal to talk about.'

They carried on walking till they came to the gates. 'Have you ever been along the mountain path?' she asked.

'Once, when I came here to be married. Shall we?'

'If you want to. I need to be away from the house and all those people.'

'Yet not alone?' They moved beneath the old oak trees leading the way to the winding path along the border of the estate.

'No, not alone. I've had enough time to review my private memories of my uncle – isn't it strange how sadness often brings back one's childhood? Now I think I'd like to talk about the man he was. The way *you* knew him.'

James was silent for a while, then said, 'I hardly knew him at all, now that I think about it.'

'Not in terms of time spent together,' she agreed, 'but he always spoke of you in a . . . I don't know . . . a certain way, that's all. As if you two knew and understood each other very well.' She laughed suddenly, a fragile sound. 'I remember being jealous of you!'

'Jealous?'

'Yes! I was still a child, remember, but I thought I alone had the right to gain his understanding. I hated it when he spoke of you as though you were his son. He was very proud of you.'

There was a sound to his soft laugh of a deep sadness she had not thought him capable of feeling. He said, 'Sir Anthony once told me . . . he said the only difference between the two of us was our beginnings.'

'Did you love him?'

'Love? No, I don't think so. His power intrigued me, and I came to respect him. I was grateful to him. I knew I was using him, yet it never bothered me. He was using me, too, you see.' He stopped, forcing her to turn towards him.

'I don't understand. Why would he have used you? You're wrong, you know, he—'

His laugh interrupted her. 'Don't look so angry – your uncle knew damn well that all I wanted was his capital to get started. Sooner or later I would have made everything mine.'

'How can you say that? He helped you still further by giving those shares to Katherine!'

'Of course, but he no longer had need of them, and he knew there was no sense in delaying my gaining control. You see, Marianne, Sir Anthony was not interested in the money. What he wanted was the adventure, the risks of starting the business. His situation no longer permitted him to do it himself, and that's what I mean by his using me. We used each other, both of us accepted that without ever feeling the need to explain it. We're adventurers – the two of us – that was the understanding we had.'

She thought this over while she started to walk on again, feeling his eyes on her when he followed. 'No marriage plans?' he asked when he was beside her again.

The path had narrowed, forcing them to move closely

together, their bodies touching frequently. 'No plans. I seem to scare my suitors off.'

'Then they're not worthy of you,' James replied and laughed. She did not move away when he placed his arm around her shoulders and drew her to him. It was a harmless enough gesture, a casual touch made easily by two people who knew each other well.

He released her suddenly, but she was off balance and grabbed his shoulder, so that she pressed against him.

'Ooh!' she squealed, laughing like a little girl. Then she looked into his eyes, and the smile slipped from her face. 'No, James,' she pleaded, but his arms had already encircled her, drawing her close. His lips reached for her throat. Their touch was moist and warm and frantic, like the urgent pressing of his rigid maleness.

For brief moments Marianne stood locked to him, neither responding nor fending him off, caught in her own emotional and physical confusion about her status with the man who clung to her.

'Oh, how I've wanted you,' he murmured into her hair. 'For so long now.' His hands gripped her long tresses, pulling her head back as his mouth sought hers, found it and forced it open. His tongue probed roughly. It was as though her breath was being squeezed and sucked from her at the same time.

She opened her eyes, making what was happening appear suddenly ugly. She saw the husband of her cousin, caught in his own manic lust for her. His mouth, tongue, his feverish hands that pounded and pulled, the prodding of his organ as if he was trying to tear through her clothes – all were a vicious infringement of the limits of their relationship. She screamed, 'Stop!', and pulled her mouth from his, slamming her hands against his shoulders. 'Stop it, James!'

It was as if he saw but did not hear. He looked down at her with a haze across his eyes, his hands still upon her shoulders, forcing her slowly to the ground. She tried to tear free, but he was too strong. The ground, hard and uneven, was suddenly beneath her back. He was going to rape her!

Then it was over. James was kneeling over her, his face ruddy, yet with some semblance of control now. He breathed heavily, and his eyes did not meet hers. 'I'm sorry,' he said hoarsely, 'Marianne, I'm sorry . . . I . . .'

She shut her eyes, laying her cheek on the grass. It stung her soft skin. Her breasts heaved from fright and exhaustion. 'You bastard,' she hissed.

She felt him beside her, pulled away when he touched her shoulder. 'Are you hurt?' he asked, his voice sounding normal again. 'I'm sorry . . . it was so sudden . . . I've wanted you so much! You drive me mad, did you know that?'

She looked up at him. 'I've just witnessed that madness,' she said shakily. She was glad of the anger; it reduced the level of shock at his behaviour. Yet she knew he was not entirely to blame; she had hesitated for too long, caught in her own crazy indecision about her feelings for him. She scrambled to her feet, pushing his hands away when he tried to help her brush off the pieces of earth clinging to her outfit.

'I'll still have you,' he said. 'You know that, don't you?'

Marianne stared at him. He was once again the James she had come to know in Oudtshoorn, smiling smugly as if nothing at all had happened a few moments ago. Perhaps it was better that way; it was easier to deal with the James she knew. 'You'll never have me,' she snapped as she headed down the path.

His laugh followed her. 'You can deny it now, Marianne, but you know we're two of a kind. Sooner or later you'll admit that to yourself.'

She spun around, her hands bundled into tight little fists. 'Then I'll come running to you, is that what you think? After you've tried to rape me just to prove your point?'

He stopped in front of her. 'Perhaps I should have,' he said softly. 'It might have saved time.'

He caught her hand when she tried to slap him. 'I've already apologised for my behaviour,' he said, still slightly out of breath, 'but I'm damned if I'll apologise for what I know is the truth.'

'And what is the truth?' she asked, jerking her hand from his grip. 'Is it that I desire you and resisted purely because of Katherine?'

'I don't know what your reasons were,' he said as he

moved past her, leading the way now. 'All I know is that you and I are too much like Sir Anthony to be kept apart. We'll be together some day.'

'Together?' she shouted, not caring if the guests could hear her from the house below. 'You think sex – *rape* is being together? You're madder than I thought!'

When he glanced at her over his shoulder, scornful laughter in his eyes, the gesture was so superior she was tempted to pick up a stone and hurl it at him. 'It'll only be rape the first time,' he said, 'but I doubt it'll come to that.' He turned and walked on again.

Marianne watched him with mixed emotions: anger, confusion, now also apprehension. She had just been subjected to near rape by a man who was practically a relation; she should be shocked, hysterical, outraged. Yet she felt none of those things.

She waited till James had turned the corner before she carried on down the path. As she entered the grounds of the house, she realised that, since George Laboulaye at least, the afternoon's episode had been the first in which she was not the one in control.

CHAPTER TWENTY

The *Oudtshoorn Courant*, the town's first newspaper, came into being in May 1879. A large proportion of its content naturally dealt with the ostrich industry as well as the men who built it. If the newspaper had seen the light of day only two weeks earlier, it would undoubtedly have reported in detail on a tragic event at Ratitāe.

After the catastrophe had taken place, it was tempting to lay the blame on one person, as if that individual's predestined fate had had an influence on what also happened to another. Yet no one could ever say for sure whether or not that was so, or whether fate, in that crucial moment which decides between adversity or advantage, had not opted impetuously to entwine two persons in one single grip of doom. Perhaps the issue had already been decided upon nineteen years ago, when Katie Reinders was born.

Katie was a coloured woman who helped Mrs Blake in the kitchen, and also cared for Ralph during the day when her chores were done. She was a dark-skinned, lissom beauty who had enjoyed the attentions of men from an early age. At times she thought back still to her first, although she mostly managed quickly to shut the ugly memory from her mind.

She was only thirteen, and he was her uncle. The whole family, all seven of her brothers and sisters and their bachelor uncle, had worked and lived on a sheep farm near Ladismith. He had taken her on the hard Karoo soil, his breath and the hand across her mouth reeking of cheap fortified wine.

Katie had known exactly what was happening to her; a

peasant existence surrounded by three older sisters ensured an early introduction into the ways of life. So she lay on the stony ground, crying at the pain and brutality of the act. But, because she understood what was taking place, she was not overly afraid; the only damage she suffered was physical.

When he was done with her, buttoning his fly and walking off into the night without a word, she had crept to a nearby dam and washed herself in its cold, gravelly water. During the night, she whispered about what had happened to her eldest sister. The girl merely laughed, saying that he had taken her when she was just ten. Next time, she told Katie, she must make sure the dirty pig paid for it.

Katie experimented with her body after that, trying youngsters her own age as well as older youths and grown men. She soon found that most of them were willing to pay for her services.

When she turned sixteen, Katie and one of her sisters started working the road gangs in the area. There were white men, who paid handsomely, coloureds and even some Africans, whom the girls normally made pay double.

They sneaked into the crowded tents at night, both of them often catering to the needs of all the men who slept there. They departed when it was still dark, before the foremen discovered them in the tents, although on some gangs they satisfied those men as well. They could charge a foreman a higher price for the pleasure of their company, as well as the promise they would not tire out the working men.

Katie eventually left home to stay with one of the gangs as they built their road through the stark veld. They finished their project at the same time as she discovered she was expecting a child. She took her money and made her way to Oudtshoorn, where she managed to find work on Ratitāe before her new condition showed. At least Mrs Blake had allowed her to stay on once it became obvious, for Katie had proved herself as diligent at housework as she had been at her earlier, though vastly different career.

Now, three months after the birth of the child, with the baby boy being cared for by an elderly couple on one of the neighbouring farms, she was secure in her position as housemaid to the Quentons.

Although her income was nowhere near what she had made through selling her body, she had a place to sleep, food to eat, and the good life on Ratitāe was to her liking. She avoided the attentions of the labourers for fear she would be trapped back into her old ways, even though she found it difficult to fight the rising heat of her natural sensuality. When it was at its worst, Bertus had come along. He was so unlike the others – he cared for her, Katie was sure of that.

She had met Bertus, a tall athletic-looking man who smiled constantly, right at the start of her employment at Ratitāe. The only problem with Bertus was that he was married, yet that had not stopped him from flirting with the other women on the farm. Katie was sure many of the girls had willingly fallen prey to his charms. Her own body was willing, but her mind told her to protect her new place in the sun.

In the end, it had been her mind that trapped him into discovering her body. When her physical need overwhelmed her desire for protection, she had engineered their meeting beneath the willows where she often took little Ralph on walks.

In the shade of the old trees, against the soothing sound of the gently flowing river, Katie concentrated on granting herself the satisfaction that came from honest lust, without the mercenary mechanics of meeting the demands of a paying customer. She was aggressive, hungry, selfish and demanding, using everything she had learned for self-gratification this time. Bertus thought it was all for him. He was enslaved.

It was inevitable in a small community like the Ratitāe labourers, all housed in a long row of cottages on the side of the ridge beyond the main mansion, that others would learn of their relationship.

Everyone, even those who had lain with Bertus, feigned disapproval. He was, after all, a married man, even if his wife was of a sour disposition, spending the hours between work drunk.

What made matters worse was when the woman came off second best after mounting a vicious attack on Katie with fists, elbows and feet. After retreating from the initial force of the attack, Katie had taken advantage of the woman's inebriated state to land a solid right to her eye, cutting the skin and sending her crashing to the ground where she lay in a momentary daze before wailing loudly as she ran for the sanctuary of her cottage.

As far as the labourers were concerned, Katie had shown bad grace in not allowing the wronged wife to beat the hell out of her. She was treated as a pariah after that, yet it did not stop her and Bertus from meeting even more openly.

Her worst fear had always been that someone would complain to James about her behaviour. Now, precisely that had happened. He had already demonstrated that he would not tolerate dissent among his labourers. What would he do – dismiss her? Would she be forced to return to the road gangs?

She knew who had told James – it had to be the one called August, for she had always known he would take his revenge on her one day. August was a short, stocky individual with no front teeth. An old, angry scar ran all the way from his brow to his chin, matching his crabby disposition. Katie shuddered as she remembered the time he had caught her on her way to the labourers' cottages.

It had been after dark, on a night when the Quentons had entertained guests. When Katie had completed her duties in the main house, she started the long walk back. August was waiting in her path, whether on purpose or by chance, she did not know.

He guffawed as he threw her to the ground, spreading her legs as he knelt over her with his pants half-way down his buttocks, his penis already exposed. 'Lie still, you whore bitch!' he snarled at her when she struggled. He was not much bigger than her, and was having great difficulty in keeping her pinned down.

She struggled on till he struck her with his fist. Her head snapped back against the hard ground, dazing her for moments during which August shifted his weight till he was sitting across her chest. Katie opened her eyes and saw his toothless gums gleam in the moonlight when he laughed at her, forcing his erect penis down towards her face. 'Open your mouth, woman,' he commanded. She did as she was told, then bit down with all her might just when August thought she had acceded to his demands.

His scream filled the night. He toppled off her to lie moaning in the grass like a wounded animal. She spat down on him as she scrambled to her feet. 'I don't lie still for filthy things,' she said as she wiped her lips and then spat again. 'Especially not small filthy things!' August's only response was to whimper with pain.

Although he never molested her again, Katie feared what she saw in his eyes, knowing it would be just a matter of time. She guessed that his life had been full of rejection; because he had wanted her more than most things, her refusal to let him have his way with her had created an intense bitterness which she knew he would neither forget nor forgive.

She felt desperately sorry for herself when Mrs Blake told her that James knew of her affair with Bertus. Men had always caused her problems; men, and the heat between her legs.

She sat alone in her tiny room as night fell, still ignorant of what action her masters would decide to take. She wondered if she should pray. All she could remember of prayers were a few snatches of words from her childhood. Instead, she started to weep.

Through the open door of his study, James heard Katherine speaking to Mrs Blake in the passage. He capped his fountain pen, stood up and moved outside. He caught a brief glimpse of her dress as his wife went up the wide staircase. She was going to her room, he thought; perhaps it would be best to talk to her there, away from Mrs Blake's hearing. The housekeeper would only infuriate him with her support for Katherine.

James and Katherine had had separate rooms for some years now, ostensibly because he often returned from the lands late at night and rose early in the mornings. He was pleased she had not made any effort to resist the suggestion.

Her room was on the same side of the passage as his,

two doors away, almost directly opposite Ralph's. He heard her soft, 'Come in,' when he knocked.

She was seated at her dressing table, watching him in the mirror, a small, worried smile on her lips. 'Come inside, James,' she repeated, turning to face him. He closed the door and sat stiffly in a chair in a corner of the room, wishing he had a cigar in his restless hands.

'I suppose Mrs Blake has told you about Katie?' he started.

Katherine was silent. She studied her long fingernails, then fidgeted with a hairbrush. 'She'll have to go, of course,' James continued. 'I'm not passing judgement,' he added, 'but I won't tolerate this kind of thing with our workers.'

'One should always tolerate love,' came the gentle reply.

'Love? Really, Katherine, you can't go about equating the life of a labourer with romance! Katie's liaison with Bertus was purely carnal – and where could it have led? He's a married man – for what that's worth to them!'

'I think you're sounding very arrogant, James. They're human beings with hopes and dreams like the rest of us.'

He jumped to his feet. 'What do you know of them?' he snarled. 'They plot their own destiny! Katie leaves and that's that! She can stay till the end of the week – no longer.'

'But little Ralph adores her! Katie takes—'

'We'll find another maid for him. He'll have forgotten all about her within a day or two.'

'But—'

'I didn't come here to argue with you – merely to tell you of what I plan to do.' He saw anger flash in her eyes, like the day they'd argued about her taking Ralph to Cape Town.

Her voice stopped him as he reached to open the door. 'I don't wish to argue either,' she said softly, 'but I've been meaning to ask you about George.'

James turned slowly. 'What about George?'

'I . . . I had a letter. Why didn't you tell me he was no longer working with you?'

'Why didn't he tell you himself, while he was still here? We parted ways the last time he visited Ratitāe.'

'Perhaps he didn't want to upset me right then. But

I would have thought you'd inform me. George is—'

'It wasn't important,' he interrupted with an irritable wave of his hand. 'We disagreed about our marketing priorities. It was his own decision to break with me.'

Katherine stared back at him. 'I should have liked to think we could have discussed it. George is an old friend, a family friend.'

'It was George's decision, as I've already told you. What else did he say in the letter?' he asked, wondering if George would have mentioned their conversation about Marianne.

'I still think we should have discussed it,' she persisted, ignoring his question.

'I told you a long time ago,' he snapped, his mouth a tight line, 'to leave business up to me.'

'George is not business.'

'Our survival depends on our ostriches, not on the likes of George Laboulaye. There's no place for families – or hangers-on – in business.' They stared at each other, James with growing irritation, Katherine with quiet determination.

'There was a time,' she said, her voice sounding terribly controlled, 'when the business depended on a family, *my* family – my father, to be more precise.'

'Don't try to make me feel guilty, Katherine – your father had a stake in a business which *I* built. Everything we have today is a result of my efforts. I'm sure that if Sir Anthony was still alive, he'd agree with me. He'd say I owed him nothing.'

He reached for the door handle, turning away from her defiance. Behind him she said, 'You're right, this is not the time for argument. Perhaps we can talk again tomorrow.'

His answer was to close the door behind him.

Katherine lowered her head into her hands, wondering how it was that she could still love him. Yet she knew that despite everything – his manner, his actions, the lack of a proper, warm relationship between them – she would always love him.

She remembered the time when she was certain the arrival of their child would change things, would make them close again, the way it had been for a while after their marriage.

212

Ralph's birth had changed nothing at all. Perhaps with time it would, perhaps as he grew older – as they *all* grew older – his existence would create the family they had never been.

She started brushing her hair. Her eyes were dry, for she had learned it no longer helped to cry.

James's rage brought on the need for solitude – solitude, and brandy. He walked briskly down the passage, heading for his study. He could be alone there.

He hesitated as he passed by Ralph's room, stopped, then went inside.

The three-year-old sat in the middle of the floor, making quiet clip-clop sounds as he played with a toy carriage fashioned from wire by one of the coloured youths on the farm. He smiled at the sight of his father, then concentrated on his toy again.

James studied his son who would one day take over the reins of Ratitāe. 'Ralph,' he said, feeling a flash of annoyance when the boy frowned at the interruption to his play. Ralph looked up with big brown eyes that gave away nothing at all. James knelt beside him. 'Do you like Katie?' he asked.

The little boy nodded enthusiastically. 'Katie kind,' he said and reached tentatively for the carriage, before withdrawing his hand, as if having decided it would be better to humour his father. 'I like Katie.' He glanced longingly at the toy.

'Well,' said James, 'I'm afraid Katie is in a bit of trouble. She'll have to go away. Will you miss her?'

'I don't want Katie to go – Katie my friend.'

'We all lose friends, son,' replied James, thinking that he had been right, that Ralph had been exposed to too much womanly influence. Katherine, Mrs Blake, Katie – it was too much. He would have to change that. He pushed himself to his feet with a frustrated sigh. 'Well,' he said, 'Katie will still be here for a few days. Ask her to take you for a walk, all right?'

Ralph nodded again. He watched James, seemed satisfied that his father had said what he wanted to say, then reached for the carriage. By the time James reached the door, the room was once again filled with the sound of the horses' hoofs.

James went to his room instead of going downstairs to the study – there was a bottle of brandy there as well. While he poured the drink, he thought of Marianne. What kind of son would *she* have given him?

More than a year had passed since Sir Anthony Kenrick's funeral, the last time he had seen her. Yet he thought of her almost daily, and his desire for her had grown even stronger with time. He could remember with absolute clarity their walk along the mountain path, the feel of her body as he had struggled with her, the doubt and confusion he had seen on her face. Even her anger when he managed to contain himself had failed to hide her physical response to his near-violence. She wanted him – he was sure of it!

He glanced down at his empty glass, surprised to see his hand shake when he reached for the bottle again.

CHAPTER TWENTY-ONE

It was a bright hot day, unusual for autumn, but for Ralph Quenton it was a morning of gloom. Katie was going away, his father had said. But why – did she no longer love him? He would ask her, he decided, down by the willows where she always took him on their walks. They could sit there while she sang for him the way she always did, making up songs to suit the game they were playing at that time. Then he would ask her if she still loved him.

It was not even ten in the morning when Katie gave in to his continued plea that she take him for a walk. He smiled at her when she placed a hat on his head to protect him from the harsh sun. 'Smile, Katie,' he shouted, disturbed by the sad look in her eyes. 'Smile!' The young woman did her best, but Ralph's heart sank when she turned away from him so quickly – she didn't love him any more! He tagged unhappily behind her as she started for the path to the river. What had he done wrong to make her want to leave?

Katie made sure she stayed ahead of the child, for she knew she would start crying if she looked at his crestfallen face. She had cried once already that morning, when Katherine herself broke the news of James's decision. Katherine had wept with her.

She knew she would miss Ralph terribly. He was such a fortunate child, and she should hate him for that. Born into the world of the white man, he would have every advantage on his side. Yet she could not hate him; he had not yet learned their ways and she was a friend to him.

She would miss Bertus, too, of course – what would she do without her man? Perhaps they could meet when he came to Oudtshoorn. Her heart started to beat wildly at the prospect. She would let him know where she was as soon as she had found another position. Mrs Blake had promised to help her find a new employer. Katherine also had said she would give her a good reference.

She felt a little better now, knowing that her years on the road, surviving on what her body could provide for her, had not hardened her. What she wanted was her own man, his children, a normal life with her own family. She was finished with Ratitāe, but not with Bertus.

When they reached the willows, Ralph promptly sat down on the grass. 'Sing, Katie, sing!'

She laughed at his earnest expression. Already giving orders, she thought, yet she did not mind. She started to sing, an old song they shared, one she had made up for him under those very same willows. Her voice was light yet strong.

'Sing more, Katie!' shouted Ralph when she stopped suddenly and stared with anxious eyes into the surrounding bushes.

It was a sudden stab of icy fear which had interrupted her. She felt the menace on the air, sensed the cold eyes which watched her from somewhere across the river. Was it August? She could see no movement, so she started singing again. Yet she could not rid herself of the sensation of being watched.

When she studied the opposite river bank again, only the light breeze moved through the bushes.

It was an old male baboon that studied her. He sat safely in the tall grass on the slope of the hill across the river. His brown fur moved lightly above the perpetual frown on his dog-like face, as the wind drifted across the veld.

The baboon was alone, for many years had passed since he had been cast out of his troop, the family of which he had been the leader. Only once in thirteen years of leadership had he failed in his duty, missing the danger signals to which he should have responded with a warning bark to the rest of the troop.

When he reacted it was not only too late, but he had also misjudged the direction of safe retreat, and the signal contained in his warning led the pack directly into the waiting farmers' guns. The troop's numbers had been sadly depleted that day. They had banished him from their midst, forcing him to survive alone, an outlaw, a rogue, desperate, hungry and dangerous.

He missed the troop, for together they had waged what could only be termed a war against man. Their forefathers had fought the forefathers of the men who sought to destroy them; the generations had learned from each other, had become wise to their different ways. But the war between them went on.

The old patriarch felt no bitterness towards those who had expelled him from their society. That was the way of the troop; he would have inflicted the same punishment on any other sentinel who had acted as he did. He felt no resentment, but he missed them dearly.

Together they had gorged themselves on fat, juicy prickly pears, till the farms spread themselves so wide that that delicacy became scarce. Then they turned to the farms that had destroyed their source of food. They gouged the eyes from lambs, tearing open the animals' bodies to get at the curdled milk inside. They discovered new food, too: fields of mealies, carefully cultivated vineyards and vegetable patches.

He missed the excitement of the other males as they rode the farmers' fences, swinging on them till they crashed to the ground. Together they had fought off packs of dogs and learned to avoid the baited cages with which the farmers hoped to capture them. The old leader himself had learned to lift the heavy doors of the traps, escaping with his life and the bait.

He had killed his fair share of the hunting dogs. As fearless as the hounds were, he would fold them in his powerful arms while sinking his two-inch fangs into their necks, at the same time pushing them away from him, tearing their flesh while they cried out in agony.

The baboon missed the sound and sight of the troop as they climbed excitedly up barren rock-strewn hills, making their way to the wild beehives. He missed the organised search of their proclaimed feeding grounds for edible roots, herbs, flowers and berries.

It was different on his own; there were no sentinels to rely on for warning, so that now he was forced to spend the majority of his time studying the terrain before moving in, the hunger throbbing achingly in his stomach.

He still ate scorpions, trembling with fear as he turned over rocks in search of the deadly insects. But it was lonely without the others around him. Herbs and berries were easy enough to find on his own, although now he had to take care to stay away from the feeding grounds of the various troops in the same area.

The years of his isolation had been unkind, making him desperately thin, so that his coat had started to lose some of its fur. His gums were sore, threatening to expel his decaying teeth, a situation which would spell his death. His left eye was practically useless: the brow was pulled into a tight knot of scar tissue from a wound caused by a rock thrown at him by a terrified farmer's wife. An ugly abscess, unable to heal itself because of his continual scratching and erratic diet, oozed a filthy, milky fluid down his cheek.

He was a pitiful creature, hated by humans and rejected by his own.

More and more, the lonely baboon turned to the small plots of the farm labourers. There were always vegetables to be found there – pumpkins, sweet potatoes, beans and mealies. Most of the vineyards and larger fruit orchards had made place for fields of lucerne.

He had studied the farm below him for two days now, watching the men in the lucerne fields as they worked with the ostriches. Behind the big house lay the smaller cottages of the labourers, the ones with the vegetable patches. The baboon watched them patiently, studying the movements of the men, for that was all which concerned him. He had no fear of women; often he and his troop had raided the fields right in front of a farmhouse while the man was absent.

Sometimes the men would try to trick them, dressing up as women in order to lure them closer. But the cunning baboons knew better than that.

Twice before, he had raided the vegetable patches on Ratitāe, both occasions during the day when all the menfolk were at work. Each time he had managed to eat his fill before the screams of the women brought them running.

It would be more difficult from now on, and that was why he had planned his approach from the side of the river. The distance he had to cover was longer, but he could cross over and make his way undetected to the willows, through the lucerne fields, around the back of the big house, then across the hills to approach the cottages from the rear. Once there, he would have to move fast. Only one more raid, then he would find a new area in which to survive.

The only thing holding him back was the presence of the woman with the child. She was likely to scream if she saw him, and he was too hungry to risk that. He listened to the sound of her voice as she sang.

The baboon sat completely still when she stopped and seemed to look directly at him. He waited a while longer after she started up again, although now the pangs of hunger became an urgent pain. He stood up.

The old male was almost five feet in height on his hind legs. He moved carefully through the grass before wading through the river a hundred yards away from where the woman sat. He studied the path he had chosen, turning every now and then to check on her. She had not seen him.

If he could just get through the river without her spotting him, he would be safe.

Katie stopped singing when she noticed that Ralph seemed to have fallen asleep. She leaned back against the tree trunk, but even the thought of Bertus could not dispel the unease she felt. She decided it would be safer if they went back to the house, and called softly to Ralph.

The boy looked up. His smile of surprise suddenly changed

to an expression of absolute terror. Katie swung around and saw the baboon.

It had just left the river. The animal seemed so close, so threatening as it loped across the path in the direction of the field. Then it stopped and turned to face her.

The baboon moved on to its hind legs, so that it was raised to its full, impressive height. His eyes were dark, smouldering with a mixture of scorn and frustration.

Katie scrambled to her feet. Even above her own fright, she thought of the child in her care. Ralph! She had to get him away from there. She looked at the field, hoping there was a labourer about. The camp was deserted.

'Go!' she shouted, hoping to scare the animal off. He continued to stare at her. Beside her, Ralph jumped to his feet. She felt his tiny hand on her arm. 'Go home, Ralph,' she whispered. 'Go!' She would be between the baboon and the path Ralph would take; he would be safe. The child stared at her in confusion and fear.

The old male was undecided. Should he retreat from this damn fool woman? He'd heard her shout, but it was not the hysteria which normally greeted his presence. Still, her reaction increased the risks he faced. He weighed up the aching hunger in his belly against the consequences of discovery.

She shouted again. He turned to look at the field, searching for signs of the men. That was when the rock hit him.

Katie had not thrown it with any great force, yet the stone slammed against his brow, cutting the skin and bringing a sharp instant of pain and fright before he bared his teeth and barked at her. He saw her stoop to pick up another stone. It was far off its mark this time. He started forward in a lumbering movement. She screamed. He opened his mouth, exposing two-inch-long eyeteeth, and barked again.

Katie reached down to pick up the terrified Ralph, deciding it would be faster to run with him. They had to get away from there!

The baboon was on her before she had covered two yards. She smelled his foul breath, felt his rough fur scrape across her arms before she went down headlong into the grass, dropping

Ralph as she fell. The child's cry of terror sounded above her own scream. The animal was sitting on top of her, snarling and clawing at her dress like some mad rapist. Blood ran hotly down her back.

His weight was suddenly gone from her, but she kept her arms clamped firmly across her head for fear he would bite her neck. Ralph's cry came again, forcing her to move despite her fear.

'Ralph! Ralph!' She spun around, keeping her arms to her face. The child was not beside her, nor was there any sign of the baboon. 'Ralph?' she called again, her voice filling with hysteria as she realised what was happening – even before she spotted the baboon splashing through the river with the child clutched securely in his arms. 'Oh, no . . . oh, God, no!'

She scrambled to her feet, tripped and fell down into a crying, moaning heap. Hands pulled her roughly to her feet. Katie screamed, then saw it was one of the labourers. 'What is it with you?' he demanded angrily, shaking her harshly. 'What are you up to with all this wailing?'

She could not speak. She pointed at the river, where the baboon was already making his way into the bush on the opposite bank. The labourer cursed loudly and released her. He started forward then stopped, realising that Katie was too hysterical to report the event with any degree of clarity. 'I'll get help,' he said. 'You follow that damn thing to see where he goes.' He ran off before she could protest.

She turned to face the river. Go after that wild beast? But she had to! Ralph was in her care, he was her responsibility – she had to go. Oh God, why was she being punished so?

The water felt icily cold, matching the fear in her heart as she stumbled through to scramble up the bank. She stopped at the perimeter of bush, fearing the creature lay in ambush. She saw him then, clambering over the lower rim of rocks as he made his way towards the cliffs. Katie shouted, but it had no effect on the baboon.

Ralph seemed pitifully small in its arms. He lay so still that she could not tell whether he was dead or had fainted from fright. Please, God, let him be all right!

She started forward again, running up the slope till she

was forced to go on hands and knees as the angle of ascent increased, oblivious to the burn of the slashes the baboon had inflicted on her back. Even the fresh cuts caused by the thorns and rocks as she scrambled ever upwards went unnoticed. Her torn dress came almost completely apart when a low-hanging branch of a thorn bush struck her, jerking her back. She threw the tattered remains of the dress back across her shoulder to cover a breast which had fallen free. She sobbed constantly now, yet kept her eyes on the baboon as she forced herself to move faster, knowing that once the animal started climbing the face of the rock he would easily outdistance her.

From a long way off came the sound of barking. They were coming! The master and the others were coming! She glanced quickly at the men rushing towards the river, feeling some of her worst fears abate. There were three dogs with them, including James's Great Dane, all of them held tightly on leash. Please, God, let them tear that awful creature's heart out! She felt anger now, fuelled by the promise of support, even though the men were still some way off. She froze at the sight which met her when she turned to face the cliffs again.

The baboon was perched on a slim ledge, dangerously close the the edge of the precipice. He looked down at her, Ralph still held under one arm.

Katie did not move, for fear the animal would react. She and the baboon watched each other, little more than a hundred yards apart. The creature barked at her, then turned and went on, climbing up towards the top of the cliffs. She realised that James would not arrive in time to save his son; it was all up to her now. She bit her lip and started forward.

The baboon was waiting for her when she finally clawed her way over the last of the rocks to find herself on a small plateau overlooking the expanse of Ratitāe. He stood at the very edge, staring at her with his dark eyes.

She lay on the ground, breathless and terrified. Her legs were shaking from fear as well as the exertion of the climb. Somehow she managed to lie quite still, her eyes never leaving those of the baboon. She could see Ralph clearly now. He seemed unharmed, for she could see the rise and fall of his little chest. Had he fainted? She hoped so; at least that would spare him the worst of his ordeal.

The baboon was holding Ralph gently in his arms, the way he would his own offspring, but there was a malicious expression in his eyes which sent a cold tremor of dread coursing through Katie.

The barking of the dogs was closer now. The baboon shifted his gaze from her to glance downwards. He bared his teeth and gave a low growl. When he turned back to face her, his eyes were quite calm, as if wondering what move she would make.

She shifted on to her hands and knees, crawled forward one step. Then another. The baboon let her come. When she was no more than five yards away, he stirred, clutching the child firmly to him.

'Leave the boy,' she whispered, as if the animal could understand her. She shifted another pace closer. 'Let the boy go,' she said again. Katie felt strangely unafraid, although she did not know what to do next.

Slowly she moved to her feet, ignoring the wind which rushed across the plateau to jerk at her dress, tugging the torn shreds from her shoulder. She stood before the animal, one breast exposed as though she was held captive by a man, forced to strip slowly for him. The baboon's eyes were locked into hers. They were mere feet apart now, so that she could see the brown fur stir above his brow. Neither of them moved.

The sound of the men and dogs was terrifyingly close now, just below the edge of the plateau, Katie thought. She saw the baboon's glance shift sideways when there was a frenzied bark from the cliffs behind her.

A further split-second passed, time during which Katie knew there would be no further opportunity for her to make her move. Without a sound, she hurled herself at the baboon. She was taller than the animal, and managed to lock her hands on to his ears to keep his fangs from her throat. She hung on to him with all her might, squashing Ralph between them.

They moved jerkily on the precipice edge, an ugly, silent waltz, their bodies and eyes locked together, two outcasts from their individual societies. Both had known moments of happiness, of belonging, now both lived with loneliness and pain. To the rogue baboon, life was a present he did not want. To Katie the outcast, life still offered some kind of future.

She fought desperately to drag the baboon further away from the cliff, but the animal's angry power was too much for her. He tugged her ever closer to the edge, his own back facing the fatal drop. They teetered at the brink of the precipice.

'Master! Master!' Katie cried as James appeared a few yards away from them. She saw him slip the leash from the Great Dane. 'No!' she screamed, but it was too late.

The huge dog rushed forward, striking them as they swayed on the edge. It was the moment in which fate made its decision.

They tumbled over the edge – woman and child, baboon and dog – their bodies entwined, into the yawning space.

When the labourers scrambled on to the plateau to stand beside James, there was nothing but the wind.

CHAPTER TWENTY-TWO

Katherine stood beside the tiny grave, watching the breeze ruffle the fresh bouquet of flowers she had placed atop it.

As always, her gaze turned to the ornate gravestone, its diminutive size befitting the child corpse it guarded. Ralph Anthony Quenton, the inscription read, Born 18 March 1876, Died 29 May 1879. There was no other legend, for the child's tragic death had seemed to blot out whatever mark he had made on the lives of others. Perhaps later, thought Katherine, when more time had passed, when the enormity of the tragedy had ceased to overwhelm them. Even though close to a year had passed since his death, she still could not think of her Ralph without a vivid picture of the high, jagged cliffs forcing itself into her mind.

When she glanced at them now, they appeared serene, ageless, quite picturesque in the March sun. She knew that James had climbed them more than once, sometimes with flowers he picked along the way. They had never spoken about his sombre pilgrimage to that place of death, or of what seemed to be his need to punish himself. Even of Ralph they had spoken little, for what was there to say?

She had expected rage from James, displays of tortured anger caused by fate's second snatching of a son. He had displayed no emotion at all, as if what he felt was being carefully wrapped up inside, a silent sore which revealed itself only to him. Perhaps she had misjudged him; perhaps he had loved Ralph more than she realised, and felt the loss of a son, not outrage at his once again being cheated of his hopes and dreams for an heir to Ratitāe. Maybe that explained why he could go on with his life as if nothing had changed. Except for the pilgrimages to the rock face.

In a way, Ralph's death had brought about the change in their relationship which his living had not achieved. It was as though James had moved closer to her, seeking from her the strength and solace he could not always find in himself.

Sometimes he came to her room, late at night when the heat from her snuffed-out lamp had long gone. His was a wordless presence in her room, a shadowy figure who sat beside her on her bed, his fingers stroking the living heat of her body. After a while, she would pull back the covers to let him lie with her, till his slow, searching touch transformed itself into an urgent caress. Then she let him take whatever it was he needed from her. For the moment, that was enough for her.

She turned away from the grave, shutting the gate to the fenced-off area behind her. The graveyard, which none of them had foreseen of use so soon at Ratitāe, had been hastily laid out among the trees some two hundred yards behind the house. Katherine wondered who would be next to lie there.

She tried to shrug off her gloom as her hand slid unconsciously to her belly. Just two weeks ago, Dr Maxwell had confirmed she was expecting once again. It was strange, she thought now, how certain she had been it would happen. Even the memories of her first loss, the pain of Ralph's birth, did not awaken the old fears in her. It had been just a deeply rooted certainty, for she had neither a longing for another child, nor a feeling of any particular elation at the prospect.

Dr Maxwell had demonstrated more emotion than she. 'How could you let this happen?' he had asked angrily. 'I warned you the last time, Katherine, and now—'

'It's too late, doctor.'

'Yes, it is, isn't it?'

For a month now, she had carried her child without telling James. It was time for him to know.

She did not glance back at the graveyard as she made her way up the hill towards the labourers' cottages. There was a

226

second bunch of flowers clutched in her hands, for another task remained to be performed.

Katie's grave lay in a large, shoddily maintained lot some distance from the cottages. It was an area scraped clear of Karoo scrub, a dusty patch with no trees to ward off the brutal sun. There were other mounds apart from that of Katie. They were the graves of children who had died of some illness or another. A larger heap of sand covered the body of a Xhosa labourer who had been kicked to death by a broody ostrich. On the other side of the yard, lay the grave of Katie. There were no gravestones.

Katherine noticed that her last bunch of flowers, brought only three days ago, had been shifted on to one of the child graves. She smiled sadly when she placed the fresh flowers on Katie's, covering the stems with a round rock to prevent the wind from scattering them. Even as she stepped back, she knew the flowers would be moved by nightfall; Katie's transgressions had still not been forgiven.

The large house was silent when she stepped inside. She popped her head into the kitchen, searching for Mrs Blake. Probably in her cottage, feeding her children, she thought, giving silent thanks for the big woman's presence on Ratitäe.

It had been Mrs Blake who took charge when Katherine and James were too shattered by Ralph's death to do very much. The housekeeper had had the bodies retrieved and the graveyard prepared. It was she who made the necessary funeral arrangements, who kept Ratitäe running while the parents overcame the worst of their grief. Katherine's only regret was that time and distance had precluded her mother and Marianne's presence at the funeral. She had needed them – especially Marianne.

It was quite dark when James came in from the fields. She heard his dry cough from where she sat in the drawing-room. His heavy tread sounded down the passage, followed by a dull thud when he closed his study door. She smiled, reminded suddenly of her father. Both he and James clung to their studies for sanctuary, although she guessed it was for different reasons.

She waited a while, giving him enough time to pour his

habitual brandy. She knocked once on the study door before stepping inside.

James looked up and frowned, but his expression held surprise more than resentment. The glass of brandy stood before him, otherwise the desk was empty. 'Katherine, what are . . . ? Can I get you a drink?' He seemed confused, put out of his stride by her presence.

'No, thank you. Wait, yes, I think I will have one. A brandy? With water?'

His smile seemed almost shy. 'A brandy? You sure?'

She nodded. 'I think I need one.'

'Is something wrong?' he asked over his shoulder as he poured her drink. She shook her head when he handed her the glass.

'No, nothing's wrong. May I sit down?' God, how formal they were being with each other!

James looked confused again. 'Of course.' He pulled a chair closer, held it while she sat down. He moved stiffly around the desk to sit down opposite her, scratched the side of his neck, then pulled his own glass closer. They stared at each other.

Katherine raised her glass and took a tiny sip. The liquor stung her throat as it went down, but she managed not to cough.

James said, 'That's the first time I've seen you drink anything but wine. A bit strong for your taste?'

'Very! But it helps warm one's stomach.'

'It helps for many things,' he replied slowly, shifting his gaze from hers, as if regretting his statement.

'Yes.'

The grandfather clock in the corner continued its laborious task, a tick-tock countdown of wasted time. Katherine cleared her throat. 'I was at the grave today.' The clock worked on. She took another sip of brandy, and noticed her hand was shaking. 'Do you . . . do you find it difficult to recall . . . moments? Specific moments with Ralph? I do.'

'I don't want to talk about it.' He stood up as if ending their meeting, for so far it could be called nothing else.

'We must!' Katherine surprised herself with the strength

of her voice. James sat slowly down again. 'We must talk about it,' she said more gently, 'because I won't let it happen again.'

He stared blankly at her.

'There must be no more lost moments, time that has floated by, time we waste while our child grows older.'

'We have no child, Katherine.'

She hesitated, then said, 'We shall have.' As she spoke the words, she was reminded of her youthful, romantic dreams of such an announcement, the shared excitement between husband and wife at the thought of the seed of future expectations. Her smile was sad, almost cynical in the dark gloom of the study.

'You're expecting?'

'Yes. A few weeks now. The baby is due in December.'

He stared at her without any change in his expression. Then he said, 'Why, Kath?' using the abbreviation of her name for the first time in years, 'Why take the risk when you know—'

'It was unplanned, James. But I'm not sorry. Are you?'

'No, of course not.' He raised his glass, then lowered it to the desk again. 'Did you allow it because you feel sorry for me? Because of . . . Ralph?'

'Why do you find it so difficult to acknowledge him?' she asked, giving him no chance to answer when she added, 'I told you it was unplanned, but no, it wouldn't have been for any reasons of pity – not for you or for myself. It would have been for both our futures.'

There was a poignancy in his voice when he said, 'I don't love you, Katherine, you know that, don't you?'

'Yes. And I'm wise enough now to know the child won't change anything. But . . . perhaps it will give us something we can share. Let's at least try for that this time.'

'No more wasted moments, is that it?'

'That's right.'

Their gaze held each other's for a long while before he said, 'I owe you that at least. I promise I'll try.'

She stood up, leaving her half-filled glass on the desk. 'Thank you, James – I can't ask more of you than that.' She

229

seemed about to leave, then turned and added, 'I'd like to ask Marianne to visit around that time. Do you mind?'

He looked up, unable to hide the sudden pleasure which sprang into his eyes. 'No,' he said, 'no, of course not. I – it will be good to see her again.'

'And my mother? It's been a long time . . . I worry about her now Father's no longer there.'

To her surprise, James gave a soft laugh. 'Well, I don't suppose I can keep her from Ratitāe for ever! Yes, tell Lady Kenrick she's welcome.'

'Thank you.' She pointed at the brandy. 'That stuff provides a false warmth. Have you ever discovered that?'

'Too often. But it's so damned obliging.'

She gave a slow shake of her head. 'No, James, you're the one who's obliging.' She started for the door, smiling to remove the sting from her words.

'I'm sorry, Kath,' he said as she opened it, 'for everything. You never deserved it.'

She turned and stared down at him. 'To tell the truth,' she said at last, 'I don't know quite what it is I deserve. Perhaps that's why I feel no bitterness towards you or life.' She gave him a small smile and left, closing the door softly behind her.

James stared at the thick oak of the door, its wood grain enhanced by skilled craftsmanship. Despite the truth she had spoken about the brandy, it felt wonderfully warm and comforting when he quickly swallowed it and poured another.

The festival atmosphere of Christmas came to Ratitāe early that December. Each evening, the sounds of high spirits drifted over the ridge from the workers' quarters. There was laughter, dancing, fighting and loving.

'Oh, let them be!' said Katherine from her bed when James threatened to silence them with a warning blast of his shotgun. Marianne agreed with her. 'I think it's quaint,' she said.

'Quaint?' snapped James. 'There are still two weeks to

Christmas. Imagine how drunk they'll be then! They'll be useless on the farm.'

Marianne smiled at her cousin as James stormed off. 'I get the feeling your husband is more tense about this birth than you are.' She studied Katherine's pinched face, fretting silently about Dr Maxwell's words. 'She's risking everything,' he told Marianne when she arrived with Lady Kenrick almost a week ago. 'Last time was bad enough – now it'll be a miracle if she pulls through.'

Katherine's voice interrupted her frightened thoughts. 'Where's my mother?'

'She's retired already. I think she's still trying to recover from the journey – do you have any idea how much persuasion it took to get her here?'

'I'm pleased she did. Is James treating her decently?'

'He's trying, although your mother doesn't really help – she makes no effort to disguise how she feels about him.'

'I wonder whether she'll ever stop disliking him. It's a pity.'

'You'd better get some rest now.'

Katherine reached out, gripped her hand with surprising strength. 'Marianne – we must talk.'

'Talk? You'd better save your breath for the baby, my dear. You're going to be needing it.'

'No . . . listen, please!'

Marianne leaned closer, alarmed by the urgency in her cousin's voice. 'What is it, Kath, what's bothering you?'

'You know about my shares—' Katherine started, 'there are separate accounts for me and James. Most of the farm is in my name.'

'Yes, but—'

'Listen! I want you to have them if . . . if anything should happen. Do you hear? I want you to have them!'

'Oh, Kath, don't be silly! Nothing is going to happen to you!' The edge in Marianne's voice lent little validity to her words. 'I won't hear any more such talk!'

'Marianne, please let me finish. Tomorrow, when James will be in town for most of the day, I want you to get Kenneth Slater to come see me – he's my lawyer, the young man who took over from Abraham. Please don't tell James.'

231

Marianne looked stricken. 'By why, Kath, why – oh, no – you want to make a will, don't you? Oh, Kath, please don't!'

'Don't be silly, Pumpkin. It's better not to take any chances. But you have to promise me—' She stopped talking as a vicious spell of coughing gripped her. Marianne passed her the glass of water standing beside the bed. 'You're talking too much,' she said with feigned anger, hoping it would hide her alarm.

'You must promise me,' Katherine said again when she had her cough under control, 'that you'll take my share of Ratitāe. Will you, Marianne? Promise me you will!'

'I can't! You're going to have your child, and both of you will be fine. It's *his* inheritance—'

'I'm terrified James will destroy that inheritance if he continues with his greedy expansion – more birds, more land – it can't go on for ever, Marianne! You have to protect it . . . for my sake . . . for the sake of my father, your uncle.'

'Oh, Kath, it's terrible to talk this way.'

'Promise me!'

Marianne shut her eyes and nodded. 'If that's what you want,' she said softly. 'I promise.'

'And you'll send for Kenneth tomorrow?'

'Yes.'

Marianne sat silently beside her till she saw Katherine's eyelids begin to droop. 'Get some sleep,' she whispered. 'I'll pop in later to check.'

'You treat me like a baby,' came the drowsy reply. 'You're worse than Mrs Blake.'

'Speaking of whom, you'll be surprised to learn we took a walk together this afternoon. I think we've buried the hatchet.'

'Good. You'll need her friendship.'

Dimming the lamp, Marianne pretended she hadn't heard. She leaned across to kiss Katherine's brow and left the room.

Oh God, she thought as she walked slowly down the corridor, her cousin seemed to have decided she was going to die. It was as though Katherine had no spirit left with which to face the birth. She decided she would talk to Dr Maxwell again in the morning. He might be able to provide Katherine with some reassurance, although she doubted it.

She found James in the drawing-room. 'She's sleeping now,' she said, taking a seat near him.

'Good.' They were still tense around each other although neither had broached the subject of their last meeting. At least he had been friendly enough towards her so far, she thought with relief.

'I'm concerned about Katherine,' she said. 'She seems to think something bad is going to happen to her.'

James looked up sharply. 'The birth?'

She nodded. 'Perhaps that's natural,' she said quickly. 'I mean, this is only the second time I've been around at a birth. Perhaps most women react that way.'

'I think you're both being unduly concerned. She's no doubt still upset about Ralph.' He smiled and closed the book he had been reading.

Marianne wondered whether he was trying to reassure her, or whether he didn't realise how weak his wife was. Surely the doctor would have spoken to him as well? She decided against asking. 'Do you miss him?' she said instead.

He was silent for a while, then said, 'Of course I miss Ralph. Very much. It's as though years of my life have been snatched away.' His smile was too quick, too twitched, as if he hoped it would shrug off whatever else he wanted to say. 'What about you?' he asked. 'When are you going to try childbirth for yourself?'

She laughed gaily, almost a response of relief at the way he seemed determined to avoid referring to what had taken place between them. 'Me? Don't you think I should get married first?'

'That would be a good place to start, yes,' he replied, laughing with her. 'But I would have thought . . . I mean, you're what – twenty already?'

'Twenty-one,' she corrected him. 'And you're sounding rather like my aunt. I'm not an old maid yet, you know.'

'I'd noticed.' The hoarseness in his voice brought a sudden hint of intimacy into their conversation. Even the fixed way in which he stared at her seemed to want to will her into following his lead.

She looked away. They would have to talk about it some time, but not just then. Perhaps after Katherine's child was born, when some of her apprehension had melted. On the other hand, shouldn't she ignore it completely, let time find its own way of dulling the past?

She gave a fleeting smile, pushed herself to her feet, and said, 'I think I need an early night, and I want to check on Katherine before I go to bed.'

'Mrs Blake can take care of that,' he replied. 'Why not stay here a while? We haven't had a proper conversation since you arrived.'

'There'll be lots of time for talking,' she said firmly, 'once the baby is born. We can all sit around and discuss your new family.' She ignored his taunting smile as she started to turn away. 'Good-night, James,' she added over her shoulder.

'You really can let Mrs Blake take care of Katherine, you know. She's very good at that kind of thing.'

Marianne turned to face him. 'So am I,' she replied, 'and I think you depend on Mrs Blake for too many things. After all, she's a housekeeper, not a nursemaid.'

'And *you* are?'

She stared back at him. He wore a smile that was part mocking, part pleading with her to stay. 'Why else would I have come here?' she replied pointedly as she moved out of the door.

She heard his low chortle but did not stop. Yet as she climbed the stairs, she remembered, at one stage of her journey to Oudtshoorn, having asked herself much the same question.

When Marianne had said to James that they were inclined to depend on Mrs Blake for too much, she had no idea they would be doing just that only two days later.

It happened very fast. It was an early hour of the morning when she awoke suddenly, as if something or some noise had disturbed her. She moved quickly from her bed, even when her confused senses had established there was nothing amiss. Her sense of unease continued to dog her, so she slipped on her dressing gown and left the room. The passage was silent when she stopped outside Katherine's room. The she heard dull gasps of pain. The door slammed back on its hinges when she burst into the room. 'Katherine? Is it time?'

Her cousin was unconscious, her breath coming in short sharp rasps, as if a gigantic weight was forcing itself down on her chest. Her face was drained of all colour. 'Katherine! Oh God! Mrs Blake! Mrs Blake!' As she spun away from the bed and ran into the passage, she remembered that the house-keeper was in her own cottage at the rear of the house. She spun around, heading instead for James's room. She entered without knocking. He jerked upright when she screamed at him.

'James – it's Katherine! Something's wrong! Go to her. I'll fetch Mrs Blake!' She hurtled back into the passage without waiting for a reply.

Her nightdress trailed like a thin veil behind her as she ran barefoot across the small patch of grass separating the house from Mrs Blake's cottage. She was shouting even before she started banging furiously on the door. 'Mrs Blake!' she screamed over and over again, feeling the skin on a knuckle split under her frantic blows, 'Hurry, Mrs Blake – please!'

When the door jerked open, the housekeeper took one look at Marianne's face before she started running for the main house. Marianne caught a glimpse of a child's sleepy-eyed face near the door before she raced after the big woman. Despite her size and bulk, Mrs Blake was inside before her.

Lady Kenrick stood in the passage when they reached the top of the stairs. 'What is all this fuss?' she demanded. Marianne did not answer her; she remained close behind Mrs Blake as the big woman shoved Lady Kenrick roughly aside.

James had lit the lamp in the room. Mrs Blake took one glance at Katherine before she said, 'Ride for Dr Maxwell!' She leaned towards Katherine, then swung back when James lingered in the room. 'Go, man, damn you – go!' He fled from the room.

Marianne moved in beside her. Lady Kenrick had followed

them, realising at last that something was seriously wrong with her daughter. 'What is it, Mrs Blake? Is something amiss?'

The housekeeper's voice was a mere whisper. 'I don't know. I don't know. Oh God, let him be in time!'

Fresh fear spurted through Marianne; it was the first time she had seen Mrs Blake unable to take control of a situation. A small cry escaped her, making her bite down on her knuckles. Then she was shaken by Mrs Blake who said, 'Go put on some tea – we'll be needing it by the time the night's over.' She gave Marianne a brief smile of reassurance before pushing her in the direction of the door.

The large kitchen, usually filled with warmth and comforting sounds and smells, was silent and unfriendly as Marianne stoked the coals in the big black oven. The minutes ticked slowly by. Where would James be now? In Oudtshoorn already? It was so far – and he would still have had to saddle up his horse. She tried to occupy her mind with her preparations for tea instead of trying to will the time away, but her thoughts kept returning to the room upstairs. The silence unnerved her even more.

It seemed like hours before she heard the horses thundering up to the house. She rushed out of the kitchen, opening the front door just in time to allow Dr Maxwell to run through. He did not even greet her as he dashed up the stairs. James followed a few moments later, the unspoken question in his eyes. 'I don't know,' she said, 'I've been in the kitchen.' She saw the first faint glimmer of sun on the horizon as he moved past her.

When she turned, he was standing at the foot of the staircase, one hand on the banister, his head lowered almost to his chest. 'James?'

She went to him, laid her hand on his shoulder. 'It will be all right, Dr Maxwell will do what is required.' Was he crying?

When at last he looked at her, his eyes were dry. There was something else to be seen there though, a mixture of terror and bitterness. 'Oh, James,' she whispered, 'it's going to be all right, you'll see.'

'Will it?' His voice was raspy, as if his body was reluctant to release the words. 'Two sons, Marianne, two sons have already been snatched from me. Does God want this one, too? Doesn't He ever get enough?'

'James, no – don't say such things!'

'What else does He want from me? Katherine, too? Will He only be satisfied when He has *me* as well? Damn Him!' He raised a fist and shook it up at the ceiling. 'Damn You!' he shouted. 'Do You hear me? Damn You!'

Marianne turned away from his impotent rage and frustration. The kettle whistled on the kitchen stove. She used the sound as an excuse to hurry away from him. She thought James wrong to turn his back on the source of strength they needed most right then. Yet, in a way, she could understand how he felt.

At last there was nothing more for her to do in the kitchen, nothing to occupy her frightened mind. Should she go upstairs?

The house was silent when she stepped into the passage. She was half-way up the stairs when there came the sound of a baby's cry. She froze. It was all right! Thank God – it was all right!

She rushed forward, lifting her nightdress high as she hurtled up the staircase. Mrs Blake stood in the centre of the passage. Marianne started to laugh with relief, then saw the expression in the woman's eyes. She stopped, her heart leaping into her throat. 'Mrs Blake? It's all right, isn't it? It must be! I—'

The housekeeper took a quick step forward and enveloped her in her strong arms, keeping her upright on legs which threatened to collapse at any moment. 'She's gone, miss. Our lovely Katherine is gone from us.' Tears coursed freely down the big woman's cheeks.

'It can't be! No, it's not true – I heard the baby!'

Mrs Blake pulled her even closer. 'The baby is fine, miss, but your cousin . . . We couldn't save her.' Marianne buried her head into the comfort of Mrs Blake's shoulders. 'She had a son, a beautiful boy,' the housekeeper whispered into her hair.

When at last Marianne looked up, she said, 'May I go to her?'

'Go to Lady Kenrick instead. There's nothing more you

237

and I can do. We must care for those who remain – the baby, his father. We must be strong now, child.' She smiled before slowly releasing her grip on Marianne. 'Go to her. I will take care of . . . things.'

'James, does he—?'

The housekeeper nodded. 'He's in his study. Leave him alone for now.'

Marianne wiped away the worst of her tears before knocking softly on Lady Kenrick's door. The tall, elegant woman stood in front of the window, her back to the door. 'Aunt Eda?'

'Come inside, Marianne,' Lady Kenrick said, continuing to stare through the window. Her voice was firm – almost too strong, thought Marianne. She went to stand behind her aunt.

'Aunt Eda,' she started, her voice breaking into a sob, 'Oh God!'

Lady Kenrick turned. Her narrow mouth was tightly drawn. 'Hush, child, crying will do us no good now.'

'But—'

'I did my crying years ago, after Katherine married that beast. She was doomed even then.'

Marianne stared at her aunt. Did she hate her son-in-law so much? So intensely that even the death of her daughter did not reach her now?

'We shall bury Katherine,' continued Lady Kenrick, 'then you and I shall leave. We shall leave that devil here on his own. He can have the farm – he can have it all – he can die with it!'

'No! We can't!' She had made Katherine a promise; she couldn't just walk away now.

'Yes, we can. He has done enough harm to my family. His evil must not touch you as well.'

'But the baby . . . Katherine's son!'

'The child will go with us,' replied Lady Kenrick calmly.

'James will never allow that.'

'Then we shall fight it in the courts. He has had his last hold on the Kenricks.'

Marianne wondered whether she should tell her aunt about Katherine's request. No. The time was not right for it. Now that

Katherine's fears had become a reality, she still did not know how she was going to live up to her promise. Sorrow bubbled up in her again so that she reached for Lady Kenrick's hand. The older woman's touch was cool, controlled.

'Leave me now, child,' she said gently. 'Go and rest – it's been a long night for us all.' She kissed Marianne's brow and led her to the door.

Alone in her room, Marianne's tired mind grappled with her situation and the mental defence which resisted the reality of Katherine's death. But at last the truth won through, causing her to weep again as the sun swept across the veld to announce a new day that had already long begun on Ratitāe.

CHAPTER TWENTY-THREE

From her bedroom window, Marianne could see the fenced-off area of the graveyard, the graves themselves partially obscured by the tall trees, There, between them, Katherine lay buried beside Ralph.

Apart from Mrs Blake and the labourers of Ratitãe, the only other mourners at the funeral had been the immediate family. Marianne knew she would never forget the sight of Outa as they lowered the coffin into the grave, his proud stature slumped under the weight of his loss as he wept openly before them all.

Afterwards, she had seen him run into the nearest field, mingling with a flock of ostriches, as if willing them to share his burden. She knew he would talk with them, that the birds would allow him among them, letting him move freely with their chicks, sensing he was lost and in need of what was familiar to him. Marianne understood that need, for everything which now surrounded her was strange.

Lady Kenrick had said little when she explained her promise to Katherine. All she had asked was, 'My dear child, do you really think you're the kind of person who could undertake such a task? You, who've known only the good life? Leave it, Marianne – Katherine would understand.'

Marianne was unable to leave it, nor had Lady Kenrick tried again to persuade her. She had boarded the coach for Cape Town a day after the funeral, giving her niece a soft kiss and a glance which said she expected her to meet her end now that she was staying on at Ratitãe.

The question of whether she would have the courage to stay on entered her mind again, as it had many times since the funeral. She wiped the back of her hand slowly across her mouth, thinking of how Katherine's dying had changed her own life. Katherine's full seventy per cent share in Ratitāe was now hers; she was a rich woman in her own right. Although Marianne had never been exactly poor, she had been dependent on an allowance fixed by her uncle's estate. Now her wealth was her own.

She knew she could still walk away, go back to Cape Town and let James carry on as before, drawing only her profit from the operation. It would have been simple if that was the only factor to be considered. But there was Katherine's son.

The sudden bawl from the room next door brought her to her feet with a start. She raced for the door, even though she knew Mrs Blake was with the week-old child.

The housekeeper smiled when she entered the room. 'Just wind,' she said quickly. 'Otherwise he's as good as gold.'

Marianne moved nearer the bed to stare down at James's son. 'I'm not too sure who he takes after,' she said. 'James or Katherine?'

'His mother,' replied Mrs Blake, gently rearranging the bed cover around the child's neck. 'He has her fair skin and slight build.'

'That's true, although time will tell whose personality he's inherited.'

Although Mrs Blake made no reply, the slight tightening of her lips revealed her fears in that direction. She said, 'The boy should be named soon. A child must have his identity from the start.'

'I agree, although we should bear in mind the circumstances. I'll speak to James though.'

They both sat down on the bed, watching the child in his cot. 'Poor mite,' said Mrs Blake, 'to have no mother. God alone knows what life holds for him. I'll do my best, but—'

Marianne took a deep breath. 'That's what I want to talk to you about,' she said. The housekeeper looked up, one eyebrow raised quizzically. 'I can stay on for a while, as long as is necessary in fact.' She laughed and added, 'There's little enough for me to do back in Cape Town.' She thought of her young men, the dances and outings, and knew there was nothing she would miss, for life had held small satisfaction since what she regarded as George's betrayal of her faith.

'That would be grand,' said Mrs Blake, smiling at the younger woman. Marianne could tell that the responsibilities of the past week had placed a strain on the housekeeper. As with Ralph's death, the family had looked to her to keep things going. The care of the baby, too, had fallen mainly on her shoulders.

'There's more to it than that,' she said softly. 'Katherine left me her shares.'

'In Ratitāe?'

'Yes.'

Mrs Blake stared steadily at her for a long while, then gave a brief nod. 'Good. I'm glad she gave it to you, Miss Marianne.'

'You are? Oh, are you really?'

Mrs Blake nodded again. 'Yes,' she said with a short laugh. 'It's no secret that Master James and I don't see eye to eye. He'll probably want me to leave once things are back to normal.'

'Oh no, he won't!' Marianne said firmly. 'I won't let him! Part of the house is mine as well, you know.'

To her surprise, Mrs Blake reached out and squeezed her hand. 'No, miss,' she said, 'don't go starting off on the wrong foot with him because of me. I'll be all right. There're a few farms who'll have me and my brood.'

Marianne quickly covered the woman's hand with her own. 'Anyone would want you, Mrs Blake,' she said earnestly. 'I want you! I'm going to need you to help me!' She let go the woman's hand and moved to the cot. Staring down at the sleeping child, she said, 'You see, if I stay here, it will be for him – not for the farm. Oh, I'm so confused about it all!'

Mrs Blake's voice was so low Marianne could hardly hear what she said. 'Stay for both reasons.'

'What?'

'I said you should stay for both. The farm as well as the child. They'll both need you.'

Marianne shut her eyes as she recalled Katherine's words about the shares. An inheritance James would destroy, she had said. When she opened her eyes again, her gaze rested on the forlorn graveyard. She made her decision at that moment, realising that the fortunes of Katherine's child were tied up with those of Ratitāe. 'I'll stay,' she said softly.

Mrs Blake's laugh was low and comforting when Marianne turned to her. 'I'm glad,' the big woman said. 'I'll stay to help. Together we'll be able to stand up to him.'

A girlish warmth rushed through Marianne when she knelt down and placed her head on the comforting bulk of the woman's knees. 'Oh, thank you, Mrs Blake. I'm so scared, though – of everything!'

The housekeeper's hand gently stroked her hair. 'It's good to be scared. One learns one's lessons more carefully that way.' The hand continued its soft stroking, then suddenly stopped. 'Master James? Does he know yet? Of the inheritance, I mean.'

Marianne shook her head. 'At least, I don't know. Perhaps the lawyers have already informed him . . . he hasn't said anything so far.'

'There's your first challenge then, Miss Marianne. Have it out with him.'

'He'll be outraged. I know it!' The thought of having to face James made her scramble quickly to her feet.

'He'll no doubt be more than outraged, but there's nought he can do about it.' She studied Marianne's face for a moment, then added, 'I wouldn't tell him just now about your wanting to become involved in the running of Ratitāe. Best handle this thing one piece at a time.'

Marianne bit her lip. 'I'd have to, wouldn't I? Get involved, I mean.'

'That you would. It's what your cousin would have wanted.'

'But what do I . . . I mean, I know nothing at all about farming!' Her arms fell limply to her side. 'I haven't done a proper day's work in my life!'

'You'll learn about the farm,' replied Mrs Blake with a reassuring smile. 'You've the mind and the spirit for it, and I've a feeling you've a head for business.' She fell silent, studying

Marianne strangely before saying, 'The other thing you'll need is courage to stand up to Master James. Your decision to stay shows you have that.'

'You make him sound almost sinister. You hate him, don't you?'

'Hate him? No, Miss Marianne – it's not that. He scares me, that's all. Not as a person, but for what his actions can bring. He is a man of tragedy – I feel it.'

Marianne laughed, a fragile sound. 'You're being melodramatic, Mrs Blake.'

'Perhaps. And it's not my place to criticise the man who employs me. Just tread warily, that's all I say.'

'I shall.' Marianne straightened her dress. 'Well,' she said with a tremor in her voice, 'there's no time like the present. I'm sure James is in his study, so I'll talk to him right away.'

'You do that, Miss Marianne. I'll be thinking of you.'

Marianne turned at the door. 'Mrs Blake?'

The bed squeaked when the big woman moved. 'Yes, miss?'

'If we're going to be a team, I can't have you calling me Miss Marianne all the time.'

The housekeeper's expression did not change. 'What would you have me call you?'

Marianne's gaze was drawn to the strips of sunlight filtering through the open curtains as the sun crept on its westward course. They fell across the other woman's face, softening the lines of strength which she had once mistaken for severity. 'Once,' she said softly, 'I heard you call Katherine "luv". No one has ever called me that.' She laughed suddenly, a short, embarrassed sound. 'I'm sorry . . . I've no right to . . . It's something that must be earned.' She started through the door.

Behind her she heard Mrs Blake say, 'You already have. Welcome home, luv.'

The grandfather clock ticked loudly on, an inexorable witness to passing time and changing fates. The light in the study was dim, in keeping with the veil of gloom etched on James's face.

'You look terrible,' said Marianne. She was seated across

the desk from him, in the same chair that Katherine had occupied when she'd told him of her pregnancy.

'How do you expect me to look?' he asked bitterly.

'Like a father,' she retorted, adding, 'I know it's not the same, but Katherine was very dear to me, too.' She reached across the desk to touch his hand. 'You have a son,' she said, 'a little boy who needs you – even if he can't realise that yet. You must carry on with your life.'

'I didn't love her, you know,' he said softly, as if she hadn't spoken. 'I told her so.'

Marianne was silent.

'In this office,' James went on, 'in that very same chair you're sitting in, I told her I didn't love her.' He rubbed his eyes, then placed his hands on either side of his brow, staring at her through the fringe of his fingers. 'She knew it, but I should never have said it to her.'

'Love would not have saved her life,' Marianne replied gently, wondering at the same time whether that was true.

'No, it wouldn't. It might have made me feel less guilty, though.'

'Guilt won't help your son, James. Your feelings are something you'll have to work out for yourself, but you owe more to the living than just moping in this gloomy study all day long.' She stopped and let her gaze rove about the room. 'Just look at it!' she said harshly. 'Cigar stubs, empty bottles – and it smells!' She was pleased to hear him laugh lightly.

'You're right,' he said, 'it *is* a pigsty.'

She smiled with him. 'I came here to talk to you about something else, though.' Her nervousness was gone now, her confidence returned by the sorry state of the man she faced. She was the stronger in their present situation.

'I'm glad,' he said. 'I have something to say to you as well. I want you to stay on and care for my son. Just for a short while, till he's a little older. Would you do that? Please, I need you here.' It was his hand that reached for hers this time, turning it palm upwards so that her knuckles lay on the desk top.

She returned the pressure. 'You stole my words,' she said. 'That's what I came here to tell you. At least, that was part of it.'

245

'Good! And the rest?'

Her previous qualms came rushing back. She felt her chest tighten as she forced herself to speak, saying, 'Are you aware of Katherine's shares? That she left them to me?'

His hand released its grip on hers to disappear into his lap. Her own lay awkwardly on the desk till she slowly withdrew it. 'Yes,' he said warily, 'my lawyer informed me. I decided the time was not right to talk to you about it.'

'Do you resent her doing that?'

He gave a tight smile. 'I've become accustomed to the Kenricks maintaining their slice of the profits. I can live comfortably off my share. I always have.'

'It should have gone to your son.'

'You needn't worry about anything,' he said, making it clear that he did not wish to discuss Katherine's decision. 'I'll continue looking after things. Your lawyer's welcome to check the books, of course. I assume you'll be keeping that Slater fellow Katherine used?'

She nodded, her pulse starting to race. Despite what Mrs Blake had said, she knew she could not avoid spelling out her full intentions regarding Katherine's inheritance. Not any more.

'I can't say I approve of Slater,' James was saying. 'He's too young and inexperienced for my liking. You're quite welcome to use the same people I do.' He laughed and added, 'They're quite honest, I assure you!'

Marianne started to speak, but it turned into a dry cough. 'Sorry.' She swallowed loudly.

'Some water? There's more than just brandy here.'

She held up her hand and took a deep breath. 'James—' she started. 'I . . . about those shares. I—'

'Seventy per cent is yours,' he interrupted. 'I'll check with you regarding the expenditure, of course, although it's best to approve a certain sum in advance. You'll appreciate I can't write to Cape Town every time I need to buy birds or equipment.'

'You won't have to write to Cape Town.'

His query showed on his face. 'I intend to be more than a silent partner,' she continued, then waited for his response.

246

It was slow in coming. He studied the desk top as though seeing it for the first time. He looked up, held her gaze for a long moment, then said, 'I'm not sure I quite understand.'

'I'm saying that I intend to get involved with Ratitāe. With the farm itself.'

There was a lengthy silence broken by James's sigh. 'I don't think you fully appreciate the implications of that.'

'Probably not – not yet, anyway. I'll learn though.'

He gave a slow, almost sad shake of his head. 'You Kenricks just won't let go, will you? This is not some fun thing, Marianne, not some outlet for a bored dilettante's frustration.'

'I resent that.'

'You've no right to. In fact, you've no right to anything.'

'Yes I have. I'm a Kenrick, perhaps more so than Katherine was.'

'You think that's enough?'

'No, but it helps. Are you going to fight me on this?'

They stared at each other like two antagonists who had just exchanged blows and were now taking stock of each other's strength. At last he said, 'No, that would be foolish and short-sighted. If you're determined to go ahead—'

'I am.'

'—then it would slow up progress if I left you ignorant about the operation of the farm.'

'You'll teach me, then?'

He nodded. 'I'll be a hard taskmaster, though. You might come to regret your decision.'

'I might, but not as easily as you think.' His irritation at her stand was obvious from the way in which he seemed to ignore her, as if the subject was now closed as far as he was concerned. 'There's one other thing,' she said.

'Yes?'

'Two, actually,' she corrected herself. 'One, Mrs Blake stays on as housekeeper. We'll be needing her.'

James seemed to think this over for a moment, then said, 'Just keep the woman out of my hair. Most of the house is now yours, anyway, and I'm more than prepared to leave the running of it up to you. You'll be taking Katherine's room, I suppose.'

'Yes.'

'And the second thing?'

'Your son. Have you a name for him?'

'Stanley.' It was said without any hesitation.

'Stanley?'

'It was my father's name. In a way, he was a good man. He might have achieved something if given the chance.'

Marianne smiled and stood up. 'His son did it for him,' she said. 'Who knows? His grandson might even take it a step further.'

His gaze stayed on her as she moved towards the door. 'Marianne,' he said softly when she reached to open it, 'we never talked about us.'

'Us?'

'You know what I mean.'

She hesitated before she said, 'James, you're talking of a one-time occurrence – something which happened a long time ago. It's past and forgotten.'

'Are you sure of that?' There was a smirk on his face which she found unsettling, although not in the way he intended.

'James,' she said in as firm a voice as she could muster right then, 'I don't believe we should even be talking this way. You've hardly buried your wife, in case you've forgotten.'

'I haven't – *you* were the one who said I should get on with living.'

'Yes, I did,' she shot back, 'but for your son, not for yourself.'

Her words had little effect. 'Well,' he said, settling further back in his chair, 'we'll just have to wait and see, won't we? Time will tell.'

Marianne opened the door. 'Yes,' she said, 'it certainly will. In fact, I have a feeling it will tell all kinds of things.'

CHAPTER TWENTY-FOUR

'Aphrodisiac pills?' exclaimed Marianne, studying the brown bottle in her hand. Supplied by Peterson Limited, Cape Town, the label read. 'For the ostriches?'

James laughed at her expression of disbelief. 'We give it to the males during breeding season.'

'Does it work?'

'I don't know . . . I have my doubts. The birds seem to do all right without the aid of pills.'

Marianne turned the bottle in her hand before placing it back on the warehouse shelf. She gave an amused shake of her head as she started after him when he headed through the large shed. 'These,' he said, pointing at a pile of feathers, 'are used almost solely for dusters. The longer ones are taken up for millinery, evening capes – flower arrangements as well.'

'Speaking of dusters,' said Marianne, 'I read in the *Oudtshoorn Courant* that the South American rhea feather is used for that. They kill hundreds of thousands of birds each year, exporting the feathers to Europe and the United States. Why don't they farm them instead of killing them?'

'Not worth the expense,' James replied across his shoulder. 'The feathers are very much like those of an ostrich chick in appearance and quality. They're called Vautour, by the way. You do get half-white rhea feathers, but the majority are dark grey.'

'And they have no other commercial value?'

'Apart from dusters, none at all. We've exported some

ostriches to Buenos Aires, Australia, as well, but there's been little success with their breeding.'

'Let's hope it stays that way,' she murmured, recalling what he had told her about the potential threat from America.

The sunlight was dazzling when they left the warehouse. Marianne was suddenly aware of the state of her clothes. They were filthy from her efforts in the paddocks earlier that afternoon. Along with the labourers, she had chased ostriches with her crooked stick, catching them around the neck, forcing them into the wooden boxes for clipping. Her skin was grimy, her hair covered in dust. If her socialite friends could see her now! And her young men? They would run a mile, she was sure of it!

'Why the secret smile?' asked James.

'Nothing. Just thinking.'

They walked in silence, heading for the largest paddock filled with their breeding ostriches. They passed by hundreds of V-shaped thatched shelters along the way. There is a fortune out there, thought Marianne. Just that morning news had come that ostrich feathers had reached an all-time high price of almost £6 per pound weight. It was rumoured to carry on rising. That year, 1881, there was £8 million tied up in capital in the Cape alone.

It was two months since Marianne had started her training, a time during which James had been ruthless in her initiation into ostrich farming. 'You'll start at the bottom,' he said, 'it's the best way to learn.' She had known that to be true enough, although she suspected that he also hoped to break her will that way.

The thought of what lay ahead had frightened her at first. As time went on, she discovered within herself a physical stamina that she never knew existed. There was no chore she could not do, none too degrading. Marianne had clipped feathers, built shelters, planted lucerne – even slit an ostrich throat or two when the situation arose. She had been chased by an angry cock, urinated on by a hen, yet she felt more alive than at any other stage of her twenty-one years.

'I've been driving you very hard,' James said suddenly, as if he had read her mind.

'I know. Did you hope it would break me? Make me change my mind?'

He laughed. 'I'm not sure. Probably, yes.'

'Well, you haven't succeeded. Or is there worse to come?'

'No, you've shown you can take it. And you've learned enough of the basics. Next we'll teach you about incubation.'

'And marketing?'

He flashed her a sidelong glance. 'You seem to be pretty well informed on that already.'

'I can read.' She pushed aside a wayward strand of hair and said, 'I was thinking . . . perhaps at a later stage, a visit to Europe, you know. America, too. I'll learn a lot that way.'

James's smile slipped from his face. 'Yes,' he said slowly, 'so you would. And no doubt bump into George Laboulaye while you're there. He's still very involved with feather marketing.'

She stopped walking, forcing him to turn to her. 'I wasn't thinking of George,' she said, the beginnings of anger in her voice.

'Do you ever?' he asked, starting them walking again.

'George belongs to the past,' she replied evenly, even though she knew it was a lie; George would always be a part of her. At times, she thought of what might have been; at others, it was more the human need to cling to youthful feelings and sensations. Now James's words made her wonder how she would react if she saw George again.

They passed by an encampment, smaller than the others, which contained only five birds. They were all rarities, four albinos and a hen displaying melanism, its feather tissues showing an abnormal development of dark pigment, making them pitch black instead of the normal drab grey. The hen resembled a male in all respects, except that her beak and the scales on her shins did not turn red during the mating season. She was Marianne's favourite.

The female albinesses appeared totally white from a distance, while the males had traces of white among their body feathers. James was trying special breeding experiments with the birds, as some farmers had achieved considerable financial benefit from the oddities.

They reached the main camp and leaned their arms on the wire strands of the fence, watching the birds in silence. After a while, James said, 'I think we should sell off four or five birds. A good breeder is fetching around £180 at the moment.'

'Why only four or five, when we have so many of them?'

His smile was indulgent. 'Because,' he explained, 'we have to maintain and even increase our production volume. I'd rather the birds were used to breed for our own benefit.'

'There's too high a production already – the crop has trebled in five years!'

'The demand is there.'

'It can't last for ever. The market will be saturated within a few years. And then? Prices will plunge. We'd have nothing to fall back on.'

'That's why we have to produce volume.'

Marianne did not agree with him, yet thought it better not to start an argument. Her view was that they should plant crops instead to carry them through in the eventuality of a market slump, yet she knew James would dismiss her thinking as foolish inexperience. Still, she was determined to give the matter further thought. The next step she had in mind was a complete split of the farm in operational terms: separate paddocks and birds for each of them. Then she could do as she pleased, as well as plant some crops if she wanted.

She was suddenly intensely aware of his nearness, the way it had been that day after her uncle's funeral, she on her back on the mountain path, his hands on her breasts, his knee spreading her legs. She shifted away from the fence to place a few extra inches between them, at the same time warning herself to take care. The attraction she'd always felt for him was a danger now, especially as the physical activity she indulged in these days had sharpened her naturally high sexuality. Marianne found it more and more difficult to keep her mind off sex, while the antics of the randy ostriches did not help much either. It was fine during the day, at work, where her mind was busy with the task at hand. It was only at other times, especially in the long evenings, when sometimes

James would look at her with challenging eyes, forcing her to remember, that the old tension would rise within her. When that happened, she always made her excuses and fled to her room, feeling his knowing eyes on her back.

'I could have taken you then,' he said suddenly as if reading her mind.

'Then why didn't you?' she replied, knowing it would prove nothing to pretend she had no idea what he was talking about. She knew she was wrong to have given him the satisfaction of responding to what he had said, yet she could not go on avoiding the subject. Sooner or later they would have to talk it out. Or bring it to fulfilment.

'You were too young, you—'

'I'd had more than one man by then,' she snapped angrily, immediately regretting the hasty words.

There was a hurt look on his face, an expression of disappointment, like a little boy who had just learned his mother was capable of loving someone else besides himself. 'That's not a very ladylike thing to say,' he muttered, appearing angry now.

'I've never pretended to be a lady.'

'What, then – a whore?'

She slapped him. Hard. Then she ran, lifting her skirts high as she raced along the uneven path.

He called out to her, but she ran on into the house and to her room, slamming the door behind her. She threw herself on to the bed and did not stir from there, even when she heard Stanley start crying from his room. The bawling went on till she heard Mrs Blake's hurried tread along the passage. A door slammed. There was the sound of a muffled voice, that of Mrs Blake.

Marianne was still in her room when darkness fell. She could smell herself now, the smell of stale sweat mixed with dust. A bath was what she needed, but that would mean going downstairs to ask Mrs Blake to have hot water prepared. Or would the housekeeper have done that anyway? The first thing Marianne did on returning from the fields at the end of the day was to call for bath water. It was seldom necessary, for Mrs Blake would already have the pots steaming on the stove. Would she have done the same tonight?

Marianne silently opened her bedroom door and peered down the passage. Then she tiptoed stealthily along till she reached the bathroom. She had guessed right; steam rose from the filled bath. She locked the door, slipped from her soiled clothes, and sank gratefully into the hot water.

It felt good, removing some of her earlier tension and bringing with it a degree of clarity to her mind. Just what was she achieving with her life? she asked herself, casting her mind back across the past few years.

First, she had loved a man who spurned her. But was it really love? What did it matter? She had not been good enough for George in the end. Perhaps James had been partly right; for a while she had been little better than a whore. At least whores did not hurt others.

For a while – a foolish while – she had thought Ratitāe would give her new direction, provide a foundation for a fresh start in life. Under different circumstances it might have, but not now, not while she lived under the same roof with a man she sometimes hated, at times pitied, and who could raise within her an ugly, forbidden sexual hankering. Mrs Blake had been wrong; she did not have the gumption to stand up to James, or to accept the responsibility of Ratitāe.

Doubts still quelled her much later that night, long after Mrs Blake, with customary intuition, had silently served her dinner in her room. Marianne lay with her head propped against the pillows, her long auburn hair, washed and scented now, spread across her shoulder. Despite her fears, she knew she could not just give up and return to Cape Town. Not yet, not in defeat. What else but Ratitāe and her promise to Katherine was there for her to cling to?

The soft knock at the door startled her. 'Who is it?' It was late – surely Mrs Blake had retired to her cottage long ago?

The door opened. James stood there, his silhouette large and bulky in the frame of light coming from the passage. Marianne's bedside lamp was barely glowing. She reached across to turn the flame higher. 'What do you want?' she whispered hoarsely.

He leaned back against the door after he had closed it

behind him. 'I came here to apologise for hurting you. I had no right to say what I did.'

Marianne stared up at him without replying. She drew the bedcover high up around her neck.

He moved further into the room. 'I reacted like a child,' he continued, his voice low, 'a jealous child.'

'Let's forget it.'

'I can't! Marianne . . .' Suddenly he was beside her, so close she could feel the warmth of him. The bed's headboard seemed to cut into the skin of her back beneath the silk of her nightdress as she tried in vain to move away from him. It would be so easy to give in to him then, to grant herself the physical release she needed, to let him take from her what he wanted. But what if he wanted more than she was prepared to give?

The thought cleared her mind. 'James,' she started, 'I think—'

His hand was on her shoulder, his fingers seeking the heat of her skin beneath the flimsy material. 'I want to explain – I want you so much, so very much. It's like an incurable ache within me. Just the thought of others . . .'

Marianne did not breathe.

'You are so lovely . . . so lovely.' The raspy hoarseness of his voice frightened her more than the glazed look in his eyes.

'James, no! Please leave!'

'You want me, Marianne – I know you do! We've waited too long, my darling. Too long!' He leaned closer before she could stop him. His lips were at her throat, his weight crushing her on to the bed so that she was powerless to fight him off.

'James! For God's sake – no!'

He was beyond control now, his breath hot, murmuring over and over: 'Marianne, Marianne!' His lips crushed against hers, licking, biting, tasting.

She struggled in breathless disbelief against his lust, terrified by her own response when his hands wormed their way beneath her nightdress to clutch hard and feverishly at her rising nipples. Her cry was small, containing her fears and

255

confusion. To James it was a signal of her final submission. His groping became frantic.

When he ripped at her nightdress, she tried one last time to break away from beneath him. It was too late; he had jerked away blankets and sheets, exposing her to him, her nightdress rising high around her hips.

His mouth was on hers, a hungry, wet crushing of her lips as he pulled at his own clothing, desperate for their naked skins to touch. She felt him slip his hands beneath her buttocks to raise her.

'No . . . please . . . oh Jesus, James . . . oh—'

His groan was long and slow when he entered her, penetrating quickly, deeply into the warm, moist welcome her body could not deny him, pushing down on her as if wanting to ensure she could not escape him. He murmured, 'God . . . your heat!' Then, with a savagery that hurt and frightened her, he pounded at her, his breath short rasps of triumph at the taking.

It was over quickly, a sharp cry breaking from his lips as he flooded into her.

Marianne lay without moving, listening to his ragged breathing, unsatisfied and shamed by what she had allowed to take place, for she could not deny she had not done enough to prevent it happening. She thought, too, of Katherine, so that guilt added its burden to the turmoil in her mind.

The bed squeaked when James rolled off her to lie flat on his back beside her, his arm across his face, covering his eyes.

At first she thought he shared her regrets, then she saw his lips spread in a smile. He said, 'God, I've never known such heat!' He touched the flatness of her stomach. 'It'll be better next time, I'll—'

She snatched his hand away and jerked down the remains of her nightdress. 'There won't be a next time, damn you!' she spat out, moving from the bed. She glared down at him, her arms wrapped defensively around her breasts.

He shifted his gaze from hers as he pulled on his trousers. 'Don't try to act high and mighty now, madam,' he said, standing up so that he faced her from across the bed. He fumbled with his trouser buttons.

'You raped me, you bastard.'

'Rape?' His laugh was harsh, mocking. 'Hell, don't try to tell me you didn't want it. You were ready for me, lady. Don't try to pretend otherwise.' His earlier loss of control, when he still had need of her, was gone now. In its place was something akin to scorn, making Marianne feel even more soiled.

'Get out!' she hissed. 'Go!'

His gaze swung back to her. 'All right,' he replied slowly, starting to move around the bed towards her. Marianne shifted back against the wall, tightening the grip of her arms around herself. 'But I'll be back,' James added when he stood before her.

'The hell you will!'

His lips wore a twisted sneer when he reached out to tug at her torn clothing, enjoying her attempts to draw back further still. 'I'll come back, Marianne. I'll take you whenever it damn well pleases me.'

'Never again!'

'Oh yes, I will! And if you don't like the idea, little lady,' he added, his face right up against hers, 'you can always leave. You can go back to your fancy men in Cape Town, and play your games with them.'

'Is that what this is all about, James? What tonight was all about? An attempt to scare me off Ratitāe?'

'No. But if you aren't up to what there is between us, it might be better if you left – if you ran away.' He stared at her for a long time as if expecting a reply. When she gave him none, he turned and went out of the door.

Marianne shut her eyes and slumped back against the wall, feeling desperately sorry for herself, yet at the same time ashamed at how ready she had been for him. She caught sight of herself in the mirror, saw her swollen lips and the bruised skin of her breasts. She straightened up, brushed back her hair. 'To hell with James Quenton!' she said to her reflection, focusing on her sense of outrage as she ripped what remained of her nightdress from her. She slipped on her gown, deciding that the first thing she would do the next day would be to demand that the land be divided between them. Whether he liked it or not, she would have her own birds and paddocks. From tomorrow on, she and James Quenton would be equals.

She had herself under complete control when she gathered together fresh night clothes and headed for the bathroom.

It seemed to Marianne as if James's attitude towards her alternated between hatred and scorn. Sometimes, too, he displayed a tenderness that she was convinced was merely a disguise for lust, in the hope she would allow him into her bed once more.

His hatred had been born of anger. When she'd gone to him the next morning, it was as if he was expecting her appearance, as if he knew she would come to him and talk about what had happened. His smug expression had quickly changed, however, when she made no reference to what had happened the night before, spelling out instead her demands for separate facilities.

James exploded in fury. 'Are you out of your mind?' he shouted from behind his desk. Marianne stood before him, hating herself for appearing like an employee asking something from his master. 'Do you think the few months you've spent here have taught you all you need to know?'

'No, I don't. I'll hire someone if necessary.'

He glared at her. 'Is this some silly notion of spite because of last night, Marianne? If so, you'd—'

'It has nothing to do with last night,' she overrode him, at the same time seating herself so that they faced each other over the desk like two adversaries. Which was what they had become, she reminded herself. 'I've been thinking about it for some time now. It's what I want.'

'You're being a fool.'

'Why? For wanting this, or for not packing up and running away as you'd hoped?'

'Your fancy ideals will prove nothing,' he said, ignoring her question. 'It'll increase expenditure – perhaps even ruin us.'

'What do *you* know about my so-called ideals?'

His smile was thin. 'Kindly inform me then.'

She shook back her hair in an attempt to control her rising irritation. 'I don't agree with your view on high-volume production – therein lies the real threat of ruin.'

'I see,' he said caustically. 'And just what wonderful source of knowledge has led you to that conclusion?'

She ignored the gibe. 'Quality of feathers is going to be the answer. Even in a slump, people will still pay for quality. I want crops, too. Tobacco, in particular.'

The brisk shuffling of the documents betrayed his irritation. 'Do you have any idea what this fanciful quest for pure quality will cost? No, you don't, do you? And I'm damned if I'll stand by and let Ratitāe be turned into a common farm.' He stood up, the gesture an attempt to signal the discussion was at an end.

'I shall not be dismissed,' she said calmly, remaining in her chair.

'Just who the hell do you think you are?'

'The owner of seventy per cent of Ratitāe, that's who. You can't stop me from doing this. I'll carry out my plans – whether or not you consent to discuss the arrangements with me.'

'You bitch!' he snarled, spinning around as though he was about to strike out at her. 'Are you threatening me?'

She gave a sharp shake of her head, determined not to be cowed by him. 'No, James,' she replied softly, 'I'm just prepared to take what I need, the same as you did last night. The only difference is I'm giving you the option. Which is more than you gave me.'

She stood up and moved past him to the door. 'One other thing,' she said as he continued to glare at her, 'I want Outa to work for me.'

'Why?'

'Because he no longer means a thing to you.'

'And he does to you, is that it?'

'He did to Katherine. I need him.'

'Then take him, for what it's worth! Take your ideals and your sentimentality and get out of here! Go!'

She gave him a tight smile as she swept regally from the office, leaving James to slam the door shut behind her.

Eventually, they had discussions on the split, although

these always took place in the presence of their respective lawyers. There were some irate scenes over the selection of ostriches, as if James was trying his best to thwart her goals. In the end Marianne was satisfied with what she had and from then on she wasted no time in putting her plans into action. She consulted with experts when necessary, spoke to other farmers, had the land prepared for crops and purchased a number of top-quality breeding birds for her own paddocks. One of the rooms in the house was converted into an office for herself. Ratitāe now comprised two completely separate ventures.

James's animosity towards her seemed to diminish now that the matter was settled, although he plunged into his own feverish buying splurge. He filled every available space with ostriches, as though determined to prove her wrong, when and if a slump in the market came.

The hard work and sense of independence gave Marianne whatever confidence she had still lacked. For the first time in many years she felt whole and content. She was able to feel at ease in James's company, confident enough to ignore the hostility he still revealed from time to time, almost coming to enjoy her power when she sensed his physical need of her. James knew he could never dare touch her again without her consent and that was not forthcoming. Marianne took pleasure in thinking Sir Anthony would have been proud of what she had become.

Then her comfortable new world fell apart: she discovered that she was expecting James Quenton's child.

At first she was overcome with despair, spending long days confined to the solitude of her office. Was this the end of everything, the failure of her promise to Katherine? That was what would happen if she left and returned to Cape Town, raising her bastard child on her own, an object of scorn. Staying on Ratitāe would be an equal hell, for James would know the child was his. And what would become of Stanley if he removed the boy from her care?

When at last she made up her mind on what to do, she sent Mrs Blake to ask James to meet her in her office. It was the first time since the split that he would come there.

'What is it, Marianne?' he asked, slumping into a chair without waiting for an invitation. 'You in trouble already?' he added with a mocking leer.

She was forced to smile at the unintentional aptness of the choice of words. In trouble – indeed!

His face showed little reaction when she explained the situation. 'I see,' was all he said when she had finished. 'So, what do you now expect from me – marriage?'

'That is one possible avenue.' She curbed a hysterical urge to laugh at the business-like manner in which they discussed what should be a very emotional issue. At least he made no attempt to deny that the child was his.

James was smiling to himself, his fingers toying with the edge of the desk. His own mind was in turmoil: Marry Marianne? He wanted her – he could not deny that. Marrying her would make her his. She would no longer deny him, and perhaps with time he could tame her spirit, persuade her to abandon her fanciful schemes of independent farming. First control her body, then her mind, till she was completely his.

There were other factors to be considered as well. The child was his, he had no doubt about that. He could not, would not, leave it for Marianne to rear it as an enemy of Stanley. The thought of his bastard one day gaining control of seventy per cent of Ratitāe irked him. Then, too, there were already rumours going around town about him and Marianne. There seemed to be no doubt in the minds of the townspeople that the presence of someone as beautiful and alluring as Marianne in the same house as him would lead to sinful complications. James resented his being discussed, and it had already come to his attention that most people would prefer him to maintain a brief period of mourning before marrying his dead wife's cousin, than to have them living in sin in the big house. Marriage to her would be the socially acceptable thing. He shuddered at what they would say about him if he failed to marry her, and they learned that the child was his. He had worked too hard and long at gaining status within the community to have that ruined now.

When he looked up, his face was impassive. 'Marriage,' he said as if thinking aloud.

Marianne watched him closely. Did he think she was now in his power? What if he guessed that her only reason for raising the subject of marriage was because of her promise to Katherine, and for the sake of the children?

'Is that what you want?' he asked. 'Marriage?'

'Yes.'

'For whom, though? You, or the child?'

She hesitated, knowing she could destroy his seeming willingness with what she was about to say. She took a deep breath, then plunged right in, saying, 'I don't love you, James. I don't even like you. Marriage will change nothing between us. It will be a formality only. So, yes, it will be for the children. You and I will be husband and wife in name only.'

He stared at her long and hard, then laughed shortly and rose to his feet. 'All right,' he said as he reached for the door, 'we'll do it for the sake of the children then.' He smiled at her as he went out.

Marianne stared at the open door after he had left. Nothing would change, she vowed.

CHAPTER TWENTY-FIVE

Marianne and James were married that July, 1881, on a crisp and cold morning, when Stanley was seven months old.

The marriage soon lost favour as a topic of conversation. There were things happening in town, more than enough to keep wagging tongues busy. There was the continued rise in demand for ostrich feathers, bringing with it increased prices – almost £8 per pound weight now. The town was bustling with growth; a constant influx of traders brought to its infrastructure coach-building, a jeweller's store, a barber shop, even a liquor merchant. A flow of Jewish immigrants from Russia had started, bringing with it the particular trading skills of the newcomers. In Oudtshoorn it was a time of plenty, and there was plenty to be talked about.

On Ratitāe, Marianne struggled on to make her plans a reality. There were already signs that high-quality feathers seemed to be relatively unaffected by market trends. It was with a sense of increasing excitement that she realised she was on the right track, that in the not-too-distant future she would reap her first crop of feathers.

Life with James was bearable, although at times his frustration at not being allowed access to her body sent him wild with rage and there were moments when she feared he would repeat the event which had led to their present situation. So far he had backed off each time, her victories making her even more confident that he would eventually come to accept the situation. It did not worry her that he was often away at night, sometimes arriving home in the early hours of the morning without bothering to hide the sounds of his horse's approach. It upset her not in the least; neither was she concerned about what the townspeople would say if his extramarital activities became public knowledge.

Her pregnancy suited her. At least, that was what Mrs Blake told her. More than once she studied her body in the mirror, wondering what it would have been like if the child was George's. Yet she never allowed the thought to exist for more than a fleeting moment. By marrying James she had lost George for ever.

As she pushed thoughts of him from her mind, she reminded herself of the mission for which she had sacrificed any chance of enjoying personal happiness: Ratitāe, Ratitāe, Ratitāe. Over and over she said its name, until there was no place left in her mind for anything but the task at hand.

Marianne went into labour two days before Christmas, with a muttered, 'What is it with us Kenricks? Our babies always want to ruin our Christmas!'

James was not on the farm when the first pains struck. He had ridden off shortly after supper, and she knew he would not return till dawn.

'I'll send Outa for Dr Maxwell,' said Mrs Blake after making a peremptory inspection of Marianne's condition. Minutes later there was the thunder of hoofs as Outa raced into the December night, bound for Oudtshoorn to summon the doctor, as well as to search for James as Mrs Blake had instructed.

The doctor arrived alone, with Outa following later. The Zulu shook his head when Mrs Blake rushed into the kitchen with eyebrows raised. 'No one has seen him, madam,' he said, wringing his felt hat in his hands.

The housekeeper's mouth tightened. Probably in some woman's bed, she thought viciously. Damn the man! 'Wait here,' she told Outa, 'in case I need you again. There's coffee on the stove.'

She was down a half-hour later, grinning broadly this time. Outa jumped to his feet. 'It is a son?'

'No, a lovely daughter. As beautiful as her mother.' She

saw the Zulu's face fall. Men, she thought. Only a son counts for anything with them. 'The doctor will be down in a few minutes,' she said. 'Give him some coffee, then see him out.'

'Must I go back with the doctor? To look for the Master James again?'

'No, you've done enough, Outa. Get some sleep.'

Marianne gave a weary smile when Mrs Blake entered the room. 'Thank you,' she said. 'The doctor said you're quite a midwife.'

'Hush, luv. You ladies both need some rest.' She smiled down at the baby's red face, thinking that the child looked just like Marianne. 'What's her name to be, then?'

'Ursula,' replied Marianne, leaned her head towards the child, then glanced at Mrs Blake, seeking her approval.

The woman nodded. 'A fine name for a beautiful young lady!' She tucked the blankets firmly around Marianne, dimmed the lamp, and said, 'Get some rest now – I'll be over here in this chair, so don't you fret about a thing.'

'Where's James? Does he know yet?'

'He'll hear in good time,' the housekeeper replied non-committally. 'Sleep now.'

Mrs Blake positioned her chair in the corner of the room, from where she could watch over both her charges. She set it rocking gently, relieved to see Marianne's eyes droop and then close. Her even breathing followed a few moments later.

Only then did the housekeeper ease herself from the chair and move carefully to the door. Taking the bolt firmly in both hands, she slid it silently home, determined that no one would disturb them that night – least of all James Quenton. When he'd finished with his whoring, he could wait till morning to hear the news of his daughter's birth.

She settled herself back into the chair, both arms folded across her ample bosom.

Laughter rang from the front of the cottage among the trees, the place James had visited so many years ago after he had trapped Jooste into selling his land.

There were three men and three women at Maggie

Lawrence's house, enjoying their drinks in the dim light of the lamp set on the porch. The evening seemed innocent enough, nothing more than a group of farmers relaxing with a few drinks in the company of women. Yet there was a certain unease in the atmosphere right from the start, a sexual tension which the laughter and banal chatter could not disguise.

Although James and Maggie Lawrence had known each other close on eight years, it was only over the last six months that their relationship had resumed after a break of almost four years. As far as James was concerned, he would have had no need to return if not for Marianne's aloof attitude towards him.

'A little party,' Maggie had said earlier that week, when she'd invited him to come around. 'Just a few of us, all old friends, as well as one or two new faces.' She had not elaborated on the event, nor had James asked for more details. It did not concern him that others would be present; he knew the two men who would be there with him, and was confident they would not dare talk.

Like James, they were both successful, wealthy ostrich farmers. He recognised one of the female guests as the eldest daughter of a farmer who was not present in the group. She was in her early twenties, a slim woman with a reputation for providing a pleasant diversion – preferably with more than one man at a time. James had never laid a finger on her, for it was said she frequently thought herself in love with her latest victim, tending to make a thorough nuisance of herself. It was reported that more than one marriage had been ruined by her direct appeals to wives to abandon their husbands for her. James wanted no part of that.

·He had, nevertheless, allowed her to plant a wet kiss on his lips when he entered. 'Hello, Greta,' he grunted, pulling a face at Maggie across the woman's shoulder.

It was the third woman present who started his pulse racing. She was introduced as Clara, an English immigrant who had settled in Grahamstown. 'Clara is on her way to Cape Town,' said Maggie, explaining that the girl's parents were friends of hers. James took one look at Maggie's face and knew she regretted her offer to house the girl for a few nights. He could not blame her.

He guessed that Clara was no older than nineteen. She was tall and full-bodied, with magnificent breasts that threatened – or promised, he was not sure which – to spill from the lace bodice of her low-cut dress. Her skin was pale and creamy, looking soft and delightful to the touch. But it was her eyes, far more than her body, which caused the men to keep turning to her. Of all the women that James had ever seen, none had eyes which promised men so much. They were wise beyond her years, knowing, filled with hints of soft surrender, of surreptitious, pristine delights. Yet there was a hint of innocence, almost one of reticence, which made her gaze appear private and selective. It was a devastating combination, and she had used it to great effect on James from the time he arrived.

He had been busy on his third brandy when Maggie stood up and asked him to help her in the kitchen. He closed the kitchen door on the sound of laughter coming from the porch. 'It's good of you to have us around,' he said, suspecting the reason for her wanting to be alone with him; Maggie was no fool, it was obvious she'd seen the way he and Clara looked at one another.

She tried to smile, to appear at ease, but the attempt failed miserably, serving only to heighten the fragile look in her eyes. 'You want her, don't you?' she said without preamble.

'Maggie, I—'

'Oh, stop it, James! That gentle tone doesn't become you!' Her nail scratched nervously at the back of her hand. 'I'm sorry,' she added quickly, giving a short, embarrassed laugh. 'I've no right to say that.'

'Yes, you have – you're my friend, aren't you? Perhaps the only one I have.'

Her fingers trailed briefly across his cheek. 'Friends shouldn't display jealousy,' she said softly. 'I'm sorry, it's just that . . . Oh I don't know! We've never made demands on each other before – neither of us has. I've always enjoyed you, even though you make me feel guilty.'

'Guilty? Maggie, I—'

267

'I know what you've said. But . . . you've a wife who's expecting your child! I can't help the way I feel . . . It's not as though I'm stealing you . . . I mean, there's no love . . . I'm not even sure I like you all that much! But I can't help feeling guilty when you've been with me.'

She stared at the floor when he made no reply. 'Anyway,' she said after a while, 'that's not why I wanted to talk to you. I can see what's happening. I just wanted to say . . . I won't be awkward about it, James. You can have her – here, in my house.'

He gave her a curious look. 'It's not me you're jealous of, is it? It's her. Clara.'

She worried the back of her hand again. 'I think it's because she's so . . . so damn ripe! Damn her!'

They stood in silence, two people who had loved only with their bodies. Then James said, 'Didn't you know her at all before she arrived?'

'I met her about two years ago, when I visited her parents in Grahamstown. All I saw then was a pretty young girl.'

'And now?'

Her laugh was harsh. 'I was quickly enlightened on that score! You should have seen her when we walked through town this afternoon. That woman gives off a smell, I swear! There was not a man who didn't look at her in that – that certain way. Young and old, they all looked.'

'Maggie, you said it yourself – Clara's a very attractive woman.'

'It's far more than that. It's the way they look at her, I tell you. And how she looks at them. Perhaps that's why I snapped at you just now.'

'What do you mean?'

'You think you want her, that you're going to take her. But you're wrong, so wrong! She'll do the taking – she's already decided that. There's nothing you can do about it – there's nothing I can do! She has full control, only she doesn't let men see it.'

'Do you want me to leave? I can, you know.'

Maggie gave a slow, sad shake of her head. 'That won't prove anything,' she said. 'Stay,' she added. 'Let her enjoy you.'

'Maggie, I think it's best if I leave.'

'No, James, stay. Stay and let the night lead where it will. It's out of our hands now.'

Her warning became obvious once he was outside again and he saw how much attention Clara paid him, hardly noticing the other two men. There was another reason, apart from his desire for her, which occupied his thoughts whenever he looked at Clara. James knew that Marianne was aware of his relationship with Maggie; that she had never discussed it with him demonstrated how little, if at all, it concerned her. Clara, though, might be a different story. She was young, prettier even than Marianne. How would she react if he put the girl up in his town house, made her his mistress? The threat of his being romantically involved with someone might achieve what he had so far failed to do. People would talk, of course, but he could live with that, so long as what he did brought Marianne around to giving in to him. He glanced at the girl when she walked to the kitchen, her hips swinging alluringly. Oh, yes, young Clara could prove to be both an interesting and worthwhile diversion.

The thought of Marianne brought a familiar tightness to his chest. How he'd misjudged her! The damn woman seemed to need nothing from him – not even sexual gratification! Adding to his growing irritation at her independence was the way in which other ostrich farmers seemed to respect her farming endeavours.

The latter aspect was brought home to him once again when one of the men tapped his shoulder to gain his attention. 'That wife of yours,' he said, 'is quite something. Hell, she's showing you up, James! Soon we'll all be following her lead.' The others joined in his laughter. 'You'd better pull up your socks if you want to compete with her,' one of them added, causing a renewed burst of laughter which rankled with James.

Compete? he thought angrily. Was that the way others saw him? In competition with Marianne, with her getting the better of him? He turned away from their taunts and marched into the little house.

Clara smiled at him when he entered the kitchen. Her blatant sexuality tugged at the pit of his stomach, ousting his anger and replacing it with an instant lust. Not since Marianne had he encountered a woman with so much sexual magnetism.

Her look displayed her obvious interest in him, making his body tense at the thought of what the night might bring. She turned to him, hand on hip, her eyes questioning.

'The party's dragging a bit, don't you think?' asked James as he stepped closer to her. He placed his hand gently on hers, stroked the soft skin of her fingers.

'Any ideas on how to liven it up?' Her fingers gripped his, pushed them against the heat of her body.

'Yes, but not here.'

'Where, then?'

'I have a town house. Just the two of us . . . ?'

Her smile was triumphant. She squeezed his hand again and said, 'Let's go.'

Five minutes later they left a saddened Maggie and her guests.

Once Clara and James were in bed, he lost whatever hopes he had had of retaining command over the situation. The girl was expert in a depraved way. She was the master, he the slave. James had never encountered a woman like her before.

He could not resist her demands, could not stop himself from obeying her every wish, finding himself pathetically eager to hear her sounds of satisfaction. When she was silent for too long a time as she worked at him, abused him, drained him of his manhood, he had visions of other men stuck inside her, men who had taught her the secrets she now forced on him. For the first time in his life, James experienced a failure in his erection. He went limp and slipped from her.

'I'm not finished,' she said crisply. Her eyes flashed at him, half angry, half goading, while her tongue darted across his shivering body to find its mark. She was expert there, too.

He was sore when he rolled off her for the last time. He lay on his back, staring at the ceiling while he tried to regain his breath. 'Clara,' he said at last, 'you are beyond belief!'

She lay on her side, elbow propped on a pillow, her chin in her hand. She studied him without touching him. 'I like this house,' she told him. 'If I decided to stay in Oudtshoorn a few more days . . . It would be comfortable for us here, don't you think? Better than with Maggie.'

It struck him that she had spoken the very words he himself had planned. Apprehension edged into his thoughts, but he nodded and reached for his trousers. He fumbled inside a pocket, placed the key to the townhouse in her hand.

'From tonight?'

'Yes.'

'You'll stay here with me?'

He laughed despite his growing anxiety. 'I'm a married man, remember? I have at least to put in an appearance before dawn.'

'Tomorrow night, then,' she whispered, moving her lips along the line of his shoulder. 'I hate being alone at Christmas.'

James was almost thankful to escape the room at last, when Clara had finally fallen into a satisfied sleep. Yet he knew he would be ravenously hungry for her by the time the next night arrived. The challenge would be on him, the need to overcome her superiority, even though he sensed it would be many nights before he achieved that.

The world seemed confined to the tingling pain of his body and the animal who had inflicted it, the beautiful, perverted animal who had never doubted the power she would yield over him.

There was a half-bottle of brandy on the kitchen table. James jerked it to his mouth, drinking straight from the bottle's neck. The liquor burned his stomach, as if Clara had left her mark there, too. He drank again, deep gulping draughts that made him shiver.

Should he tell Marianne? he wondered. No – better if she came to learn of it on her own. The affair would seem more serious then.

The bottle was empty when he walked quickly from the house and drank in the heavy air of summer.

*

271

The sun pushed its way through the half-open curtain to stroke James's face. He opened one eye, groaned aloud, then quickly shut it again. There was a pulsating pain in his head, made worse by the smell of stale brandy fumes when he yawned.

As his mind slowly resumed control, he realised there was no reason for him to rise; it was Sunday, and there were no pressing farm matters to attend to. Nor did he have any desire to go to his wife's bedside to look at their daughter. Of what use was a girl to him? A son, yes, a brother to Stanley, two boys he could train and immerse in ostrich breeding.

The sun moved in deeper, bringing with it its harsh December heat. He kicked off the single blanket and rolled on to his back. The pain behind his eyes added its own agitation to his depression. Anger churned freshly in him when he thought back to his arrival on Ratitāe early that morning.

He had entered the kitchen, seeking coffee to slow his whirling thoughts and emotions. The used cups, pots of water and general disarray of the place told him what had transpired during his absence. He went upstairs, ignoring the urgent need for coffee.

When he stopped outside the door of Marianne's room, he had no idea of the exact time, but sensed it had to be one or two o'clock. No matter; he had a right to see his child any time he wanted to.

The door refused to budge when he turned the knob. Locked? Was he being barred from a room in his own house? He raised his hand to hammer on the door, then slowly lowered it when he heard the bolt slide back.

Mrs Blake appeared in the doorway, looking severe and formidable. 'What are you doing in my wife's room?' he demanded, feeling the old resentment towards the big woman well up inside him.

The housekeeper moved swiftly into the passage, shutting the door behind her. 'I could ask why *you*'re not inside,' she snapped. 'She needed you tonight. She had your child.'

She blocked his path when he stepped forward. 'They're

272

resting,' she said firmly. 'You can see the child in the morning.'

'I'll see my son whenever I damn well please!' He moved again, but Mrs Blake stood firm.

'Then you won't be pleased, Mr Quenton,' she replied, a smirk of satisfaction on her lips. 'You have a daughter, not a son. You can see her in the morning. Good-night.'

James gripped her shoulders when she started to turn away. She reacted with surprising speed, swinging around to face him. With a strength he would not have thought possible in a woman, she gripped his wrists, breaking his hold on her. Pushing him away from her, she flashed him a challenging look before entering the room. The bolt slid back into position.

He had stood there in disbelief, cursing Mrs Blake, Marianne – even his newborn daughter. He hit the wall, his fist carrying with it all his frustration, then made his way to his own room. Despite the liquor he had imbibed that night, it was still some time before he fell asleep.

Now, with the coming of morning, he replayed the scene in his mind. He couldn't even dismiss the housekeeper for her insolent resistance, for Marianne paid her wages. Easing himself from the bed, he rinsed his face repeatedly with cold water. It did not help.

When he left the house and stepped into the warm sunshine, Mrs Blake watched him from an upstairs window. Her body stiffened with distaste as she thought back to his reaction. It was not his obvious disinterest in his daughter which irked her, for that had not come as any surprise. What bothered her more was that James had not even asked after his wife.

The housekeeper had tried to understand Marianne's motives for marrying him, even though she could never agree with them. It was done now, yet Mrs Blake told herself it could not go on like this for much longer.

She turned from the window, snapped the curtain shut in a sharp, angry gesture. Across the room, both Marianne and Ursula slept peacefully on.

CHAPTER TWENTY-SIX

Marianne came to hear of Clara after the girl had been in the townhouse for almost a month.

She heard about it as she left her bank manager's office, while he escorted her to the front door. Two women were about to enter just as he opened it for her. He nodded his welcome at them, at the same time turning to Marianne to say, 'You know Mrs Du Toit and Mrs Fouche?'

She forced herself to smile at the women. 'Yes,' she replied, 'we've met.' She stared at the plump Mrs Fouche, remembering what she'd heard about her relationship with James being the cause of the ostrich chicks being killed so many years ago.

The woman seemed uneasy, as though misinterpreting Marianne's gaze as one of resentment for her past role in James's life. Mrs Fouche's expression of disquiet was there for a moment only, to be replaced by what Marianne recognised as a virulent look when she said, 'It's very kind of you, Mrs Quenton, to house that poor girl in your own home. I believe she was stranded here without money, so she couldn't complete her journey to Cape Town.'

Marianne frowned. What was the woman talking about? What girl? Blushing fiercely, the bank manager tried to steer her towards the door. She moved with him, her confusion clarified when Mrs Fouche added, 'It's kind of James to want to make her feel so much at home. He's at the townhouse almost every night now.' She was walking with them, for all the world like someone chatting to a friend. Marianne knew though, that her goal was not friendliness, but spite.

She realised it was not aimed at her, was instead intended to hurt James. Despite her shock at the news, she thought how easily lost love changed to malevolence.

The banker was pathetically eager to set her on her way now, almost forcing her through the door to her waiting Cape cart. 'I'll take care of the transaction right away,' he said as he helped her into her seat before rushing back inside the bank as soon as he could.

When she reached Ratitāe, she asked Mrs Blake what she knew about Clara. The housekeeper flushed. 'I've heard stories, luv, that's all.' She turned away, pretending to busy herself with preparations for lunch.

Marianne placed a hand on her shoulder. 'It makes no difference to me, Mrs Blake – I feel nothing for him. Is this relationship serious?'

The housekeeper shrugged. 'She's a real little hussy – I've seen her around town in them fancy clothes he buys her. It's a disgrace – the man has no shame!'

That evening, before James left for Oudtshoorn, Marianne knocked on the door to his room. He was unable to conceal his surprise at seeing her there.

She brushed past him, moved to the centre of the room. 'Off to Clara? Again?'

His lips twisted into a lop-sided sneer. 'So, you know.'

'Isn't that what you wanted? For me to find out? So that I'd come running to you, take you into my arms and my bed in order to win you from her?' She was gratified to see his face turn dark with anger, confirming her suspicions.

'Damn you,' he snarled, 'Clara is not just some little—'

'Little what? Oh, I see – you're supposed to be serious about her! Oh well, I won't keep you from her then.' He barred her path when she moved for the door, frightening her with his rough grip on her shoulders.

'Damn you!' he said again, shaking her violently. She broke free, stepped away from him and stood glaring back at him, her eyes daring him to touch her again. Somehow she managed to say sweetly, 'Don't be too late, dear James – you have a farm, or part of it anyway, to run.'

His curse followed her as she went to her own room.

Marianne waited till Ursula was almost a year old before she undertook her journey with the two children to Cape Town.

She would have preferred waiting till the next winter, as the early summer heat and dust would make the journey an uncomfortable one. Yet she had little choice; the reply to her letter to Paris made it imperative she be in Cape Town by the second week of November.

For three weeks she had considered her proposed actions. Only when she was quite certain of the rightness of her decision did she draft her letter to George Laboulaye. Even then, she was not sure of her motivation in writing to the man she had once loved. Was it really the need for his advice and help in setting up a separate distribution network to that of James? Or were there other, more personal, reasons for wanting to see him again?

She had given the reason for her visit as wanting to show the children to her aunt; of George Laboulaye and her distribution plans James knew nothing. Everything had to be finalised before she broke the news.

Her thoughts had been prompted in that direction once the price of feathers edged close to £11. The farmers were going mad and James was worse than most. Ridiculous prices were being demanded for any quality of breeding birds, with hardly a space in and around Oudtshoorn that did not support some ostriches. When she had told James of her fears that the price spiral could not last, he had laughed at her. As if to demonstrate his scorn for her views, he'd immediately gone about increasing his stock of birds, offering prices with which no one could hope to compete.

In direct contrast to his actions, Marianne sold off a quantity of her birds, using the camps they had occupied to plant tobacco and wheat. Even fruit orchards were cultivated; there had to be something to fall back on if the market slumped, even though few others seemed willing to accept that this could ever happen.

One way of preventing personal loss was to establish her own distribution channels, to let customers associate her feathers with the very best quality. Who better to assist with that than George?

She studied Stanley now as he sat beside her in the jolting carriage as it raced across the Karoo plains. He bore little resemblance to James, his fair skin and frail build reminding her more of Katherine. Yet there was something of James in him, as she had learned from the two-year-old's manner. He was prone to sulking, as well as sudden fits of rage. She sensed in him a viciousness she hoped would become no worse as he grew older.

The dusty journey was over at last. Marianne revelled in the green lushness of the Kenrick estate after the harsh brown of Oudtshoorn's Karoo summer. The days passed by slowly, made worse by her growing excitement at seeing George soon. Would he have changed? He would look older, certainly, but apart from that? She had constantly to remind herself he was now a married man – that they were both married!

It did not help.

The brisk wind sweeping across Table Bay plucked at George Laboulaye's greying hair. He was thirty-nine that November of 1882, but appeared older at first glance. It was only when one looked into his eyes and saw the exuberance there that he could be recognised as a younger man.

He smiled to himself as he blinked at the salt-laden air. It was many years since he had last seen the Cape of Good Hope, and now its rising mass beckoned to him from across the choppy waters. Table Mountain seemed to shrug off its mantle of white cloud, like a woman removing her bonnet at the sight of a familiar, if long-lost lover.

A spray of watery mist flung itself against the side of the ship, sending the many passengers lined up for a view of the mountain scurrying back to areas of relative dryness. George stayed where he was, turning his back to the wall of moisture to let it slap against his coat before it passed, its force dissipated by the superior gravitational pull of the grey sea rushing below him.

The thought of seeing Marianne again brought a familiar tightness to his stomach. Although he had tried to put her from his mind, he still thought of her often over the years they had been separated. He had told himself he'd lost her that dark, rainy day when he'd arrived at that same harbour. Yet she had remained his in a way, and the news of her marriage to James hurt him more than he had thought possible. And now? Her letter had not been explicit about her marriage, yet George sensed that things were not as they should be. She had said little more than that she needed his help – enough to bring him to her.

He merged with the throng of passengers eager to disembark once the ship was moored, relieved to escape the confinement of the ship. The land smell, the fragrance of Africa, filled his lungs and soul.

The docks were crowded with workers, anxious relatives, friends and spectators. He was sure Marianne would know of the ship's arrival, but in his letter to her he had said he would make his own way to Sir Anthony's house. The reminder that he would not see the old man again, saddened him as he waved down a hansom-cab.

He climbed into the cab, closing his eyes to let the sounds and smells of Cape Town fill his senses. The clip-clop of the horse's hoofs rang out around him, dulling the cries of the hawkers.

Marianne was waiting on the large verandah when he arrived at the big house. The sight of her swept him back through time, to the days when the little girl with tousled auburn hair would run to him across that same space and fling herself into his arms. He had loved her even then.

Now her face seemed tense, delicate, charged with apprehension as she moved slowly towards him, a beautiful, mature woman who filled him with a sense of intense longing and desire far beyond the physical. She was his, he knew that now – had always been, would always be.

They were still yards apart when the spell of hesitancy

was broken. They moved as one, a last rush before they were in each other's arms.

She was soft and full against him, belonging there. They did not speak, for the discovery of hidden emotions and longing overwhelmed the need for the mundane spoken word. There would come a time for that later.

When she finally spoke, all she said was, 'You came.'

'Of course.' His own voice sounded dry and hoarse. 'I'll always be there for you when you need me.'

She drew slightly away, her arms falling to her sides as she laughed nervously. They were suddenly close to being strangers again. 'I might need you for longer than you think,' she said. 'I doubt whether your wife would appreciate that.'

'There is no wife, Marianne. Not any more.'

She lowered her gaze so that he would not see the relief which sprang into her eyes. 'I'm sorry,' she lied.

George shrugged. 'There's no need to be. It's better this way. Brigette and I were too much alike. It lasted little more than two years.'

'I'm sure,' she replied, attempting to sound gay, 'there are many women who breathed long sighs of relief at your return to bachelorhood.' God, how false her voice sounded!

'I am only interested in the response of one woman,' he replied, then pre-empted a reaction by leading her towards the door of the house. 'Come,' he said, placing his arm lightly around her shoulders, 'I'd better pay my respects to Lady Kenrick. Your aunt always thought I showed too much interest in her brood.'

Later that night, George sat alone in the parlour, pondering the new Marianne he was getting to know. During dinner she had spoken openly of her and James's relationship, as well as her reasons for marrying him, ignoring Lady Kenrick's frequent clicking of tongue, loud sniffs and other noises indicating her disapproval of the situation. He sensed in Marianne a confidence which went beyond that normally provided by motherhood. She reminded him of Sir Anthony in a way.

When at last she rose to settle Lady Kenrick in bed, asking him to wait for her return, George felt a renewed knot of tension at the thought of their being alone.

'A cognac?' she offered when she joined him a few moments later.

'You, too?' he asked in surprise as he saw her arrange two glasses on the cabinet.

She smiled across her shoulder. 'I think you'll find I've changed rather a great deal. I had to if I wanted to beat James at his own game.'

He was unable to keep his disappointment from sounding in his voice when he said, 'So *that's* why you sent for me.'

'One of the reasons,' she replied, smiling demurely. She handed him his glass and sat down beside him on the settee. 'I want my own trading channels, George.' She explained her fears about the market, telling him about James's continued greed. 'I want my own links in case the market slumps – I want to deal with people who recognise the security of trading in quality feathers. I'm concentrating on that – not volume.'

He was silent for a while, then said, 'You'll make an enemy of James once he hears of my involvement.'

Her sudden laugh was harsh. 'Enemy? We're that already!'

'Do you hate him?'

She shook her head. 'I know James for what he is – I even pity him.' She leaned back to let her head rest against the back of the settee. 'I suppose I should be thankful for what he's done – it's through him that I've discovered strengths I didn't know I possessed.'

'I've noticed!' He lifted her hand to his lips, held it there for a brief moment.

She watched him intently. 'How have I changed? Am I harder? Do you think I've become bitter?'

'No,' replied George slowly, 'stronger, definitely more confident. And even more beautiful than I could ever have imagined. Motherhood becomes you.' He was pleased to hear gaiety in her soft laugh.

'*You* haven't changed at all,' she said, squeezing his hand. 'You're as big a flatterer as ever! But I'm glad you believe in me,' she added. 'I think most people are amused by my efforts to become a farmer. My disastrous relationship with James is no secret, so I'm sure they're laying odds on how long it will be before I realise my own limitations – or he puts me in my place!'

George took a small sip of cognac. 'From what you said, or rather, the way you said it, I gather James is not exactly . . . shall we say, being discreet?'

She nodded. 'There've been many women, but now—'

'There's someone special?'

'Yes. He's put her up in the townhouse. It's been going on for about a year.'

'Yet you allow it to continue?'

She told him what she suspected were James's motives behind the liaison. 'I think, though, that he's become dependent on her in a way.'

'Do you know her?'

'I've seen her. She's still a child, but a vicious one. I'm amazed at how long it's lasted. I think she's as corrupt as James and just as selfish. Perhaps that's the reason . . . perhaps he's been unable to make her really belong to him.'

They smiled awkwardly at each other when his hand moved to cover hers. It lay there for a brief moment before they sipped their drinks in silence, afraid of where the next step would take them. When Marianne spoke again, it was about business. 'Will you help me?' she asked.

'Of course. What must I do – find distributors right away?'

She nodded. 'I . . . I'd like you to come back to Oudtshoorn with me, to see the situation for yourself. Perhaps I'm overreacting.'

Unlikely, thought George. Despite his break with James, he had remained involved with the ostrich industry, and agreed with her fears about the future. He wondered how James would react to seeing him again.

'Where will you start?' asked Marianne. 'In Europe?'

'Austria, then America. Those are your major markets so we should consolidate them, with any surplus production going to the other markets. Your plans for quality feathers make good sense, along with limited production. We can hold some private auctions to start off with.'

'Will that work?'

'It will help get distributors to recognise the quality of your produce. Their buyers, in turn, must come to demand it. It'll take time, though.'

'Let's hope we have enough of that left.' She reached for her glass just as the clock chimed in the hallway. 'Good heavens,' she said, 'midnight already! You must be exhausted after your long sea voyage.' She stood up and straightened her dress. George made no move. He stared up at her. 'Is something wrong?' she asked.

He shook his head. 'No . . . on the contrary, everything's going to be just fine – I promise you that. You've a lucky Frenchman on your side, an experienced survivor, although I've a feeling you're quite competent at that yourself. Your children will have their inheritance,' he said softly, moving to his feet.

He had meant only to touch her shoulder, a gentle, reassuring contact, but they had delayed the moment for too long. They moved rapidly into each other's arms. Her cheek briefly touched his before she offered him her lips. As he kissed her, he remembered a long time ago, in Paris, when he'd been amused at the obvious tactic of a young woman discovering her own sensuality. That amusement had rapidly changed to alarm at his reaction to her.

Now, their mutual need was slow and comforting, the end of a weary journey. Her hand was in his hair, gently forcing his lips against hers, without the frantic urgency which normally accompanies first encounters. It was as though they looked back on the past and longed for the future, both wondering if there was some chance they could share it. When they drew apart they smiled gently, and whatever dangers the moment held were past.

She laughed shyly. 'Do you remember—'

'I remember many things.'

'Of course . . . So do I.'

His hands were still on her hips, their bodies touching lightly. She moved gently away from him. 'It's been a long day – for us both. I'll let you sleep till you awake. Breakfast on the verandah?'

'Sounds lovely.'

'Well, you know where your room is. I want to check on the children before I go to sleep.'

'Yes. Good-night, Marianne.'

She hesitated at the door, turned and said, 'Good-night, George. Thank you for being here.' She was gone before he could reply.

Later, he lay in bed and tried to resist his tired mind as it fingered its way through the pockets of his memories. It clutched selectively at jagged visions of stilted moments from his life, of deals made, of women conquered, of opportunities grabbed and lost. A worthless life, Laboulaye, he thought drowsily as sleep made its final onslaught.

But sleep, when it finally came, was not as easily fooled. It stripped him bare of defences to torture him with its ruthless search for the truth.

George twisted and turned beneath his blankets, till even his body lay exposed to the grip of the night.

Across the city, in the harbour area where the wind howled in spitefully from the sea, jerking at obstacles in its path, another man lay awake. He, too, thought of the past, for that was easier than facing the present.

Gert Denker lay on his stomach, for the raw cuts of the cat-o'-nine-tails blazed hotly across his back. It was the fourth time that year the punishment had been meted out to him; he had lost count of the times at the dreaded treadmill.

He was a man alone in the prison, belonging to none of the groups formed for protection or for power. Denker was his own law, feared or hated by many of his fellow convicts, scorned by them all. Few of them realised he preferred it that way.

The air around him was filled with the usual night sounds and odours of the Breakwater: the grunts and snores of men clustered tightly against each other, their stale sweat that no amount of washing seemed able to disperse, the filthy smell of their farts. It was a world which broke some, made others stronger, and embedded Denker's hatred even deeper.

Only two more years, he kept telling himself, only two more years before he could leave the high walls of the Breakwater to go in search of James Quenton.

When the warder stepped into the long dormitory for his

hourly inspection, he saw Denker's eyes glowing hotly in the dim light which stayed on throughout the night. He lowered his gaze and walked uneasily past the rows of men.

The warder was a part of the Breakwater, too, and had been for many years, yet what he witnessed in Denker's eyes he had never seen before.

As always, the sight of Ratitāe filled George with excitement. As he and Marianne drove beneath the nameboard at the entrance to the farm, he sensed the pulsating pace of a growing thing, a living force shaping its own history as well as the very lives of those who attempted to channel its direction.

The house beckoned to them as they turned the last corner, the vines covering its front porch moving in the slow summer breeze. 'I'd forgotten how huge it is,' he said as he helped Marianne down from the carriage.

'Emptiness is always huge,' she replied. He thought it best not to respond.

Mrs Blake appeared, rushing down the steps to help with their baggage. As they stepped on to the verandah, James came out from inside the house. He stared at them with expressionless eyes, making George feel unreasonably like a man caught in the arms of another's wife. There was an awkward silence before he gave Marianne a curt nod, ruffled Stanley's hair, then waved a hand expansively at the front door. 'Come on in,' he said. George noticed that he paid absolutely no attention to Ursula.

'Hello, James,' he said, holding out his hand. James gripped it briefly. 'George,' was all he said, showing no surprise at his unexpected arrival on Ratitāe.

To George, his one-time friend and business associate now appeared flabby, his ruddy face showing signs of an abuse of brandy. There was little resemblance to the young man he had once befriended. James's eyes, too, were different, seeming dull, without depth.

The cool interior of the house was a welcome relief from the stifling heat when they stepped inside, James walking stiffly ahead of his wife's guest, as if he were a total stranger to him. All he said when Mrs Blake offered to lead George to his room was, 'I'll see you at dinner.'

The evening meal was made more bearable by the presence of Owen Cowley, James's lawyer and financial adviser. Although Cowley could not be regarded as a pleasant individual, his presence at least enabled them to talk of generalities instead of trying to explain George's appearance on the farm. It was better that way; he did not relish announcing his new role in Marianne's life, and he preferred delaying the news till he and James were alone.

Almost as soon as dinner was over, Marianne rose and excused herself from the room, pleading weariness from the journey. She looked at George as she spoke, the gesture confining her apology to him alone. He and Cowley both rose to their feet, but James remained seated, sneering as he looked up at her.

George hesitated for only a fraction of a second before making up his mind. He would be alone with James once Cowley left, forced to face the confrontation that would undoubtedly come. He stepped back, pushed his chair against the table. 'I think that's a wise idea,' he said, forcing a smile. 'So, if you'll excuse me as well . . .'

There was a veil across James's eyes as he muttered something unintelligible before turning his attention back to Cowley.

George mounted the stairs beside Marianne. Her voice sounded tense when she said, 'I hope your room will be comfortable. There are spare blankets – although it's so warm at night now.'

'I'll be fine.' There were other things he wanted and needed to say but she appeared edgy; he could see the strain in the stance of her body.

She was still beside him when he reached his room. As he opened the door, turning to her to say good-night, she was right behind him, moving into the room with him. He quickly shut the door. A lamp glowed dully beside his bed, casting its half-hearted light across them.

'You saw what it was like,' she whispered, moving closer

285

to him. 'We hardly talk . . . and the hate in his eyes when he looks at me! He'll want to destroy me when he learns what I'm planning. You as well. Perhaps it'll be better if you leave . . . Let *me* tell him. God knows, he can't hate me any more than he does now that he's seen me with you.'

'Sssh,' he said, drawing her head against his chest, wishing he could drive away her fears with the strength of his arms. 'I'll talk to James tomorrow morning,' he said into her hair. 'Everything will be fine, Marianne. Didn't I promise you that?'

He gently kissed her brow when she looked up at him, the shadows of the lamplight emphasising the taut lines of her face. 'What we don't need,' said George, 'is for him to find you here. You'd better leave.' She clung tightly to him when he tried to release her.

'I don't care if he does,' she said. 'Lock the door, George.'

'Marianne, we can't—'

'Lock it!' She turned and did it herself. 'We can!' she said as she faced him again. 'We've wasted enough time.' When she moved into his arms again, he sensed that this time she sought not comfort from him; she demanded that which she had always wanted and for a time had lost.

The strength of her desire swept away his final hesitancy, caused his maleness to rise to meet her searching urgency.

When at last he touched her naked flesh as they stretched out beside each other on the bed, he knew they would now belong completely to each other.

George found James in the incubation shed early the next morning. They greeted each other warily.

'You know how these things work?' asked James after an uneasy silence.

'You explained them to me on my last visit.'

'Yes, of course. You came with Katherine that time.' He spun around, his face ugly. 'What is it with you and my wives, Laboulaye?' He asked fiercely. 'Did you fuck Katherine as well?'

George managed to restrain himself from striking the malevolent face before him. 'Keep your filthy thoughts to yourself,' he snarled.

James laughed. 'Still playing the innocent, I see. What the hell are you doing here, Laboulaye?'

'I'm going to help Marianne market her own feathers – through her own trading channels.'

The words seemed to have little effect on James, as if he had already guessed that. 'You're a fool,' was all he said.

'I've been many things, James, but not that.'

'Yes, you are. She's mine, Laboulaye – do you understand that?'

'Marianne was never yours, never will be. If not for Stanley, she would have left you a long time ago.'

'She'll ruin herself. And you. Then she'll have to come to me, do you hear? There will be no one else. She's just using you, you stupid bastard. Like a whore!'

George hit him squarely on the nose. James staggered back as blood spurted from ruptured vessels, messing the front of his white shirt. George tensed himself, but there was no retaliation. James shook his head and raised his hand to his nose. His voice was a low hiss when he said, 'That's the only time you'll hurt me, Laboulaye. Now get the hell off my property!'

'Only the part that's yours.' His gaze challenged James as he slowly turned to leave the shed.

As he made his way in a dark rage back towards the house, he heard more filthy invective flowing from the shed. He shut his ears and knew he would have to leave Ratitāe immediately.

His hasty departure would not be because of James, but because he and Marianne would now be forced to act without delay.

CHAPTER TWENTY-SEVEN

Marianne made rapid progress over the next year. Even before her first shipment of feathers was consigned abroad, she had established a reputation locally for producing among the finest quality feather crops. When prices fell, the value of her products was only slightly affected.

James, on the other hand, had suffered financially. Having built up excessive stocks of feathers, he was suddenly left with overflowing warehouses. Fortunately for him, the slump was temporary; within a few weeks it was as though nothing had happened. He nevertheless envied Marianne her success and total absence of need for him or his skills. The way in which local farmers spoke about her achievements added resentment to his emotions towards her.

He became almost totally dependent on Clara, to the point where he even considered leaving Marianne and marrying the younger woman. Even though he knew he did not love her, she was *his*. Yet his greatest fear was of how long she would remain so. What if she tired of her role as his mistress and left him? There would be no one then, for he had come to accept that Marianne would never belong to him.

Clara seemed to toy with the idea when he first broached the subject of marriage, but James had seen the contented gleam that sprang into her eyes. She was not averse to the thought, then, he realised with satisfaction. After all, he was still a man of considerable wealth and influence; becoming Mrs Clara Quenton was undoubtedly a preferable station to the one she currently occupied. God, how he would enjoy showing Marianne he no longer needed her! Perhaps, when she heard the news, she would finally come to her senses.

Marianne did come to hear about James's proposal to Clara. At first she felt a surge of relief – she'd be free, free to be with George, to marry him and be happy at last! Then she thought of Stanley. James would take him from her if he married Clara. She knew enough of the girl to know she was in no way equipped to be any sort of mother towards him. Losing Stanley would amount to a breach of her promise to Katherine. That came first. That, and Ratitāe; her own happiness was secondary.

There were additional rumours about the young woman, that she had been entertaining other men in the townhouse. James obviously did not know about it – or was he so besotted with her that he pretended to ignore it? Marianne doubted it; his pride would never allow that.

It took two days for Mrs Blake to gather the information she needed in order to act.

The farm labourer driving the cart glanced at Marianne when they stopped outside the townhouse. 'Wait,' she commanded him and, taking a determined breath, stepped down.

She stood at the front door, slowly raising her hand. Then she gave an irritated shake of her head; there was no need for her to knock – she had every right to be there! She fumbled in her bag for her key.

The house was silent when she stepped inside, although she could sense the presence of an inhabitant. There was no musty smell as there usually was when the place had been closed for a week or so. There were other smells: a hint of eggs that had been fried; the lingering aroma of freshly ground coffee; the smell of a woman.

Marianne made her way slowly down the passage. Although the main bedroom was empty, it was obvious the bed had been slept in, for it was still rumpled. She stared at the place where Clara and James rutted.

'What are you doing here?' She spun around at the sound of the voice.

The girl stood behind her in the passage. Marianne stared at her, the measuring look a woman gives a rival. It did not help to remind herself the girl was no rival in the true sense; yet, Clara was an intruder in her home and in her life.

The girl held her gaze, frowning slightly. It was already past ten in the morning, but she was still dressed in a white cotton nightdress, her full breasts clearly visible beneath the flimsy material. Her hair had not been brushed; it hung in tangles around her strong shoulders. Loose strands brushed her cheeks and a stray curl dangled over one eye. Marianne could not stop herself from staring. She was so young! The aura of physical robustness, stamina and animal sensuality was overwhelming. She suddenly understood why James had wanted to possess Clara, and was almost relieved she did not have to compete with her for his attentions. 'I am Mrs Quenton,' she said at last.

Clara smiled suddenly, the gesture triumphant. Marianne wondered whether she had made a mistake in coming; it was obvious that the young woman welcomed her presence – even saw it as a victory: the irate wife come to confront her husband's mistress.

'My name is Clara.' A husky voice, unusual in one so young. 'I'm James's . . . guest.'

'Ah! Yes, so he told me.'

'You knew about me?'

'Oh yes! Ever since you moved in.'

'Then why . . . ?'

'Why has it taken me so long to come here?'

Clara clamped her arms defensively across her breasts. Her confidence had dwindled rapidly, so that she seemed even younger now, a sulky little girl. 'You want to buy me off,' she snapped. 'That's it, isn't it? You know James wants to leave you and marry me.'

Marianne did not reply as she pushed past Clara to the kitchen, the padding of the girl's bare feet following her. She studied the kitchen as if seeking something. 'You stupid little tart,' she said more harshly than intended. 'Do you really think I care about what you and James get up to? No, my dear Clara, I have no intention of offering you anything.'

The girl's mouth tightened. 'Then why did you come here? What do you want?'

Marianne turned away and ran a finger across the kitchen cupboard, the gesture more thoughtful than deliberate. 'What I want is for you to leave here. To end this . . . this thing with James. I want you out of this house, preferably out of Oudtshoorn.'

'You *are* jealous, then!' Arrogance crept back into her gaze. 'You know you've lost him, so now—'

'That's not it at all. No, I . . . There are other reasons, reasons which I do not wish to discuss with you. But you will leave here, and leave James's life. That is all which concerns me.'

'Just who the hell do you think you are? I'm marrying James, and nothing you say will stop me!'

Marianne's smile was like ice. 'It's not what *I* have to say, my dear, but what some men *might* say. To James.'

There was a guarded look in Clara's eyes as she struggled to maintain her composure. 'What do you mean?'

'Oh, I think you know very well what I mean. The men you . . . The ones who visit you when James is not here. How do you think he'd react when he learns of them? He's frightfully possessive, didn't you know? He'd see you're ruined, completely finished in this town. I'm at least giving you the chance to bow out gracefully.'

'You're lying.' There was fear in her voice.

'You know I'm not. You – and they – weren't quite as discreet as you thought.'

Clara had slumped back against the kitchen wall, but her anger made her fight on. 'They'd never dare talk,' she snarled. 'They're married – and they fear James.'

'So they do,' Marianne replied calmly, 'as should you. But they'll talk – I promise you that! You see, all of them lost heavily in the recent slump, and just this morning they signed a loan agreement with me, for enough cash to get them back on their feet. They have little choice but to tell James whatever I want

291

them to. Right now their need of me is greater than their fear of him.'

'You bitch,' the girl mumbled, close to tears. 'You utter, utter bitch!'

Marianne stared silently at her, wondering whether she hadn't become just that. Perhaps her circumstances with James had made her so. It was with a sudden flicker of shame that she realised it was the first time she had used money to hurt someone else. Would it also be the last?

She started for the passage. 'James will be here tonight,' she said. 'Tell him whatever you like, Clara, but be out of here – out of his life – by tomorrow morning.'

'I haven't any money to leave Oudtshoorn,' wailed Clara.

'You know how to raise that, I'm sure.' Marianne took sudden pity on the young woman and added, 'All I demand now is that you break with him. Leaving Oudtshoorn can come later.'

She stepped into the passage, turned, and gently said, 'Forget your dreams about being Mrs Quenton. Believe me, it's nothing worth having.'

The air outside seemed wonderfully fresh, helping her to shrug off the sombreness of what she'd done. She smiled at the coachman and said, 'Home, please. Let's get to Ratitãe.'

James paced heavily across the wooden floor of the bedroom. 'I don't understand. Why?' Clara had her back to him. She was packing her things into two suitcases lying open on the bed. Most of the dresses she shoved roughly into them James had bought for her.

She shut the lid of a case, sighed and turned to him. 'I told you – I'm tired of this place. It's such a dull town.'

'It took you three years to discover that?' he asked, his voice a mixture of anger and fear.

She shrugged and sat down on the bed. He really was quite a miserable creature, she thought. Once Marianne had left and her anger had given way to acceptance of the situation, Clara actually came to feel almost relieved at the enforced break with James. It was true she had become bored with Oudtshoorn – with him as well. His love-making did not satisfy her and, like many women similar to herself, she rapidly lost interest in a man once she was confident he was under her spell. Then, too, it seemed to her as if he had lost the aura of power which had surrounded him when they first met.

The thought of becoming his wife admittedly had its appeal: status, wealth, social acceptance . . . No, not the latter – she was aware the citizens of Oudtshoorn would never grant her that, not after what they already knew about her. And what if James lost his wealth the way the others had? She no longer had any doubt about it; the time for a break had arrived. Just a few weeks to raise some money – easy enough to do with her body – then she could leave. Cape Town, perhaps, as she'd originally planned. No one knew her there.

James was watching her, finding her achingly desirable, terrifyingly so, the way a man longs for that which escapes him when he is at his most vulnerable. 'You can't,' he pleaded, 'you can't just leave. I need you, Clara! You said you'd marry me!'

'Oh, James – it was just a thought. But it's not what I want.'

'I'd make you happy! And the town is changing – there's a club coming – I heard that only yesterday. There'll be concerts, theatre. We could go out more often. Just be patient . . . for a few more months.'

'Stop it, you're pleading like a little boy!'

He stepped closer to her, gripped her shoulders harshly. 'Yes,' he said hoarsely, 'I *am* pleading. I need you, Clara. You have to stay! Please – just a while longer.' He realised he had dropped to his knees in front of her, but he could not stop himself or curb the feeling of desolation sweeping through him.

She looked down at him as if seeing him for the first time. 'Go back to your wife,' she said softly. 'Go back to your family.'

His brusque laugh was bitter. 'Since when have you been concerned about my family?' Her response was to shrug indifferently and shake off his hands. She stood up and moved away from the bed.

James suddenly felt ridiculous on his knees. He pushed himself up, started after her, then stopped when he saw the detached way she selected her clothes from the cupboard. At that moment, he realised with a shock that she did not care. She had tired of *him*, not the town. 'Who is he?' he demanded hoarsely. 'Who's been enjoying you, you slut?'

'There's no one, James. You're being childish.'

'Don't lie to me! I know you and your heat too well! Who is he?' He spun her round to face him. The warmth of her flesh beneath the flimsy material of her dress increased his craving for her. He wanted to rip the clothes from her, to throw her to the floor, to force her body to accept his need of her. But the piqued passion of rejection held him in check. He became aware that he was shaking her only when her hair fell across her face and he saw fear in her eyes. Pulling her to him so that her face was against his, he said, 'Tell me! I have to know!'

Her hands were against his chest, her arms caught between his as he gripped her shoulders and shook her again. 'Please – there's no one! I swear!'

He slapped her. The sound of the blow and the sight of her falling across the bed alarmed him at first, then a flush of physical power flowed through him, the last bastion of his hold on her. He reached down to pull her to her feet.

'You little hussy!' he shouted into her frightened face. He flicked a suitcase from the bed with an angry sweep of his hand. Clothes tumbled out and spread across the floor. 'The whore's dresses,' he said, grinning viciously, 'whore's clothes paid for by her master. You want to take that from me as well?' Grabbing her arm, he tugged her from the room. She whimpered with pain and fear, but still he dragged her after him. 'Go back to the streets, you slut!' he shouted as he opened the front door to push her outside, not caring who might pass by and see.

Clara looked up at him from the steps of the porch, holding her hand to her face where he'd slapped her. 'You bastard!' she hissed.

'Go!' he shouted. 'There's the street, you whore! Go peddle your wares where you belong!'

She stared at him for a last, lingering moment, her eyes now filled with hate. Then she swung round and walked through the gate. She did not look back as she headed down the street.

James stared after her, his feelings a mixed cauldron of anger, regret and loss. His body shook, and there was a rigid pluck of anxious pain in the pit of his stomach.

They were all the same – first Katherine, then Marianne and George Laboulaye, now his Clara – all of them slowly robbing him of his strength and power, using him before deceiving him behind his back. They envied him – that was it. They were sycophantic leeches, gaining their succour from his strength, till they thought themselves strong enough to challenge him. They were mistaken – no one could stand up to him – not even all of them put together. He would destroy them, one by one or collectively if necessary.

The pain in his stomach was a molten agony now, almost crippling him as he stumbled through the door and made his way to the kitchen.

There was a bottle of brandy there.

Maggie Lawrence stared down at the girl she had introduced into James Quenton's life. Clara's cheek was swollen from his slap, but it was not that which Maggie studied; she was looking at the malevolence in the young woman's eyes. 'Perhaps it's best if you leave right away,' she said as gently as she could, disliking the smugness she felt at the girl's fall from grace.

James could become hers again – surely he would now realise the worth of friendship as opposed to sexual infatuation? Maggie knew she could never compete with Clara in that respect but she could offer him so much more.

Clara stroked her cheek and said, 'I can't leave. Not any more.'

'What do you mean?'

'The clothes were the only things I owned. I was going to sell some of them to pay for my passage to Cape Town,' she lied. 'But he kept them, the bastard!'

Maggie sighed. 'I'll talk to him, James will listen to—'

'No! I want nothing from that maniac. He can keep his foolish presents.'

'What will you do?' asked Maggie, staring down at her with distaste.

'I'll find the money. But you have to help me.'

Maggie gave a resigned smile. 'I'm sorry,' she said, wishing she had the money to get the girl out of town and out of her life. 'I have barely enough to live on.'

Clara shook her head. 'I don't expect money from you. Just a place to sleep, that's all.'

'For how long?'

'A little while. Till I can raise the money. A month or two.'

'All right, you can have a room, but—'

'But what? I'll pay you for it.'

A bitter smile twisted Maggie's lips. 'Yes,' she said, 'I'm sure you will. And I have a fair idea how you'll be earning the money. I just don't want it taking place under my roof. Do you understand?'

Clara flashed her a challenging look before she said, 'You don't want the competition, is that it?'

The girl's hostility made Maggie feel suddenly old and wise. 'I'd like to think you didn't mean that,' she replied mildly. 'A month. That's all.'

'It's enough,' responded Clara without thanks. 'A month is all I need to pay that bastard back. No man gets away with treating me like a whore.'

'Then stop behaving like one,' Maggie snapped. 'Swallow your hurt pride and forget about James Quenton.'

Clara's smile was knowing. 'That would suit you, wouldn't it. For me to forget about him?'

Maggie contained her anger, then said, 'You might find it suits you, too. James is not someone to have as an enemy.'

'We'll see,' whispered Clara as she touched her swollen cheek again. 'We'll see.'

CHAPTER TWENTY-EIGHT

By the end of 1884, less than three years after she had launched her own venture, Marianne felt she had achieved her goal and assured herself a measure of survival. In December, when feather prices fell slightly to an average of £8, she sold a crop at £105 per pound weight. There were others who exceeded even that, attaining just under £117 for the finest quality available.

It was a time when breeding birds fetched £400 a pair, with the most sought-after fetching four times that price. Marianne sold off large numbers of birds with inferior feathers although she clung jealously to her best breeders. She had every reason to feel satisfied, yet still there was little to make her happy.

She had not seen George Laboulaye since he had left Ratitāe after his clash with James. Although the intensity of her longing for him had not faded in that time, the constant flow of letters between them could not soothe the continuing need – emotional and physical – she felt for him. At times she wished Ursula was George's; then she would have had some part of him, a living reminder to bridge the vast distance separating them.

Unlike James, she still directed a considerable proportion of her production to the local buyers, keeping only her best-quality feathers for her distribution links in Europe and the United States. As for the farmers, she had been amused at their change in attitude towards her over the past year. Where once they had been sceptical of her efforts, her rapid and phenomenal success had changed that. They consulted with her now, sought her guidance and treated her as their full equal.

She knew James hated her even more because of it, but she no longer had any desire to consider the effects of her actions on the emotions of the man who could still legally claim to be her husband. They could neither avoid each other's company within the confines of Ratitāe, nor completely avoid speaking when the situation demanded it. As for the rest, there was no communication between them.

Yet there was a new side to him that troubled her. For some time now he seemed to have regained his old arrogance, often greeting her with a superior smirk on his face. At first Marianne had thought he'd resumed his relationship with Clara for she knew the young woman had remained in Oudtshoorn, descended now to little more than a common whore. A quick investigation reassured her on that score, however. It was something else which provided him his secret pleasure and it bothered Marianne.

Added to her concern was James's sudden interest in Stanley. Every Sunday he would leave the farm with the boy, returning only at nightfall. Marianne never resisted this; James was, after all, his father, and she felt a guilty sense of relief that she could spend the day alone with Ursula.

She had tried hard but unsuccessfully to love Stanley but there was a barrier between them, something solid and impenetrable. There were times when she almost believed her cousin's child hated her as much as his father did. It was impossible, of course; the four-year-old was incapable of understanding what had evoked the present situation between them. She knew, too, that he did not show any warmth towards his father, although he never refused to go with him on their regular Sunday sojourns. Or had James managed to exert some influence over him? She thought not; Stanley was a natural loner, needing no affection and offering none of his own.

Marianne was finally forced to admit that she was powerless to exert any control over the boy she had tried to make her son; his need for isolation was stronger than her commitment to make him her own.

Neither Stanley's attitude, nor her qualms about James occupied her thoughts at the moment when she was taking leave of a burly farmer who'd just purchased one of her breeding birds. 'Are you satisfied with the transaction, Mr Breedt?' she asked as he mounted his horse.

'About as satisfied as a man can be in these times,' replied the farmer, smiling down at her. 'I never thought I'd see the day when I'd pay so much for a stupid bird!'

'It's a good breeder.'

'That it is. But not your best.'

It was Marianne's turn to smile. 'No,' she agreed. 'I explained why I'm holding on to them.'

The farmer rubbed his jaw. 'There are times, Mrs Quenton, when I think it can't go on like this. Then, when I see the prices . . .' His voice trailed off into a light laugh.

'That's just the problem,' said Marianne. 'We're being blinded by price.' She pointed to a field being turned over to tobacco. 'I'm determined to avoid that blindness,' she said in explanation.

Breedt watched her with a curious expression. 'Mrs Quenton,' he said slowly and doffed his hat, 'I think I'd best get going, because right then, when you pointed like that, I had this terrible fear you were right. Good-day, Mrs Quenton. God bless.'

'And you, Mr Breedt.' She watched him ride off in a cloud of dust, a big, burly man whom she had come to like over the years. She hoped her predictions – if they became reality – would not hurt him too much.

As she turned away she spotted Outa supervising the labour on the tobacco field. Marianne smiled to herself; Outa was a man who loved ostriches, not crops. He always seemed unhappy when she gave him instructions to prepare the land, although he always performed his duty with typical thoroughness, a fact that she knew was due to the love and admiration she sensed he felt for her.

He had been James's man, but like so many others, James had turned away from him, treating him almost as a foe. Outa had been miserable for a long time, like a mistreated dog, then switched loyalties when he discovered Marianne's proficiency at ostrich farming.

She started for the field, wishing that Christmas was

past and a new year begun. It had been a sad, lonely year for her, a time of longing for George and the life they were being denied. Perhaps 1885 would prove more kind to her. If only the children were old enough, she thought, she could go to Europe and visit George.

Outa took off his hat, smiling, when she drew near. She listened with half-concentration as he filled her in on progress, thinking that she needed more land, soil which could be turned to crops. Virtually every available parcel in the area was being snapped up for ostrich farming, with prices rocketing to £600 a morgen. 'You've done well,' she said when Outa finished talking.

'Indeed,' came the stock reply. 'Now I must go tend my birds.'

'Outa!' she called as he started off.

'Madam?'

'Tell me a story – a quick one though!' Katherine had told her how much the Zulu loved his tales, so Marianne made a point of letting him relate one whenever she could. In any case, she enjoyed them.

Outa had a mischievous smile on his lips. He studied the ground as if thinking up a tale to suit the moment. Then he looked at her and said, 'The madam knows I can understand the birds?'

'I know that, Outa.' She had often teased him about it.

'And the madam knows how the ostriches always flock together, feed together and so on?'

'Yes, Outa – get on with it now!'

He stroked his chin for a moment, then said, 'Just this morning, I saw one standing all alone at the side of the paddock. Another ostrich ran across to him and asked, "What is wrong?" The first ostrich said, "My friend, I am so sick I just want to die." The other ostrich, he held up his wing and said, "Wait – I shall call the others and we can all die together!" And that is my story, madam.'

Marianne purposely wrinkled up her nose. 'It's not one of your better ones, Outa,' she said.

He was giggling like a child as he walked away. Then he turned suddenly and said, 'It is but a silly story I tell to those who believe an ostrich can talk!' His revenge on her for teasing him made him double up with laughter.

'Heathen!' called Marianne as she started for the house. She glanced back to see him marching off to the paddocks, laughing to himself, still tall and muscular despite his forty-seven years.

Mrs Blake cornered her as soon as she entered the house. 'Ready to decorate the Christmas tree, luv?'

'In a moment – just want to make a note or two.'

The study seemed dark in spite of the bright summer sun outside. Marianne made a few notes on the progress Outa had detailed to her, then snapped the ledger shut and placed it in a drawer. It was time for the Christmas tree.

Sounds floated through the open window of the office, drifting in on the dark, balmy air. She sank back into her chair. The voices were those of the labourers' children, practising the carols they would sing in front of the house on Christmas Eve, as they did every year.

All thoughts of James and Clara were gone now, washed away by the young voices, timid at first, yet growing in confidence and volume as one or two adults stepped in to help. She thought instead of George, and of the brief time they had shared.

As always, the harmonious innocence of the children's voices seemed to filter right through her, brushing aside whatever strengths she portrayed to the world. The music swept gently across her bruised soul and, as always, Marianne cried.

She shed her tears for the spirit of Christmas, for time lost, loneliness, sadness and for hope.

Marianne cried for herself.

James hesitated before he turned the key in the front door of the townhouse. The hinges squeaked as he swung it open. An image of Clara flashed into his mind when he stepped into the stale mustiness. He thrust the old, angry memories from his mind and turned to the boy standing uncertainly on the verandah. 'Come, Stanley,' he said, opening the door wider.

301

Stanley smiled nervously before stepping inside; the silence and emptiness of the place had always frightened him, although James's hand on his shoulder now reassured him a little. He let his father go first before he ventured further down the passage, the floorboards creaking with an eerie echo as they walked. Their first home, his father had once told him, making Stanley glad of the open spaces of Ratitāe.

James led the way through the kitchen, unlocked the back door, and stepped into the bright sunlight. The long green grass of the back yard was familiar and comforting to Stanley, for it was where he always played whenever they visited the house, while James was busy in the small study inside.

Today, however, James took him further out, to the stable at the back of the yard, its doors closed and with traces of peeling paint on its whitewashed walls.

'Don't lag behind, Stanley!' The boy stared fearfully at the wooden stairs leading up the side of the main house to a loft set high in the roof. James was already half-way up. Stanley hurried forward and hauled himself up with one hand clamped around the rail. His father had already disappeared inside when he reached the top.

He hesitated on the narrow landing. He'd not been allowed up before, even though James himself went there every Sunday, carrying piles of documents after his session in the study. Therein lay their secrets, James always told him. Today, at last, his father had promised he would reveal them to him.

Despite his excitement, he shivered when he ducked through the low door leading into the darkness. The dust in the air made him want to sneeze, so he clamped his thumb and forefinger around his nose and shut his eyes.

James was on his knees, cursing as he struggled with a lamp on the floor. He stood up, said, 'Stay here, Stanley, I'll refill it with oil in the house,' and left the frightened child by himself.

Stanley shuddered once he was alone. Sunlight beckoned through the open doorway like a friendly face, so that he vacillated between moving to the landing and staying where he was. After taking an involuntary step towards the door, he opted for the latter, deciding his father would think him a coward if he fled from the gloomy interior of the loft. The memory of James scolding him, just a week ago, was still fresh in his mind.

He'd fallen while running up the steps to Ratitāe, grazing his knee quite badly. Marianne had come running at the sound of his cry and pulled him to her chest. 'It's all right,' she whispered. 'Come, we'll fix it right away.' She took him by the hand and started to lead him inside. 'It hurts, Mummy,' he whimpered.

James stopped them. He stood in the middle of the doorway, frowning down at Stanley. 'Leave the boy with me,' he said softly, but the severity of his voice made Stanley stop crying. He saw Marianne hesitate before she released his hand to push past James. He had no choice but to follow his father to his study.

'Sit down,' said James as he shut the door. The small room seemed threatening, till James's quick smile put him at ease – his father was not angry!

There had been a lengthy silence while James settled himself on the edge of the desk. 'You are not to cry in front of women,' he started.

'But, Mummy—'

'Stanley! You have no mummy, remember that. Marianne is not your mother, she is . . . she's an aunt, sort of. You only have a father – me! Do you understand that?'

'Yes,' whispered Stanley with lowered eyes. 'But Ursula? Ursula is my sister!'

'She is not your full – your proper sister. Perhaps later, when you're older, you'll understand these things.' He moved off the desk to kneel in front of him, gripping the boy's arms in his hands. 'You must not feel any ties to Ursula or to Marianne,' he said sternly. 'You are a special person . . . different from them. Even other children are not like you – you must remember that. You and I are the same, we were born to be different, we don't cry in front of others – we never cry!'

Stanley had been frightened by the strength of his father's voice. He was still confused – why was Ursula allowed to

303

call Marianne 'Mummy', yet he wasn't supposed to? He was too frightened to ask.

'They'll try to make you weak,' James was saying, 'they'll try to make you believe I am evil – Marianne, Ursula, Mrs Blake, all of them! You must fight them, Stanley. Don't listen to them, and never show your weaknesses and fears. Never let them see you feel pain the way ordinary children do. Do you understand me?'

Stanley nodded.

'Say you understand me.'

'I understand you, Daddy.'

James stood up and ruffled his hair. 'Good boy,' he said. 'From now on, you must trust only me. Everyone else is an enemy, wanting to befriend you for what you are and what you have. Beware of them, for they only want your power.' Then he had promised Stanley he would take him to Oudtshoorn and share his secrets with him.

Remembering his father's lecture, Stanley fought down his fears of the dark townhouse loft, even turning his back on the sunlit door. He could discern shapes after a while: an old saddle slumped in one corner; a dirty moth-eaten blanket half covering a wooden crate filled with books; a dusty trunk. He jumped as the light from the doorway suddenly faded, and was unable to stop the small sigh of relief which sprang from his lips when he saw it was James returning with the lamp. 'I wasn't scared, Daddy,' he said quickly.

'Good boy, good boy.'

Stanley stepped back as James moved past him to unlock the trunk. At last – the secrets!

'I said that you and I are special,' James murmured across his shoulder. 'Now you'll see just how special.' Shifting the lamp aside, he spread a large map out on the floor, blowing away dust as he straightened the creases. 'Our farm, son,' he said in a voice deep with reverence.

Stanley felt a stab of disappointment – a farm? They already had one! 'Ratitāe,' he whispered, wondering if the layout depicted on the map was of their home.

James laughed and clutched his shoulder to pull him closer. 'No,' he said, 'not Ratitāe – not the one you know!'

He tapped the map with his finger. 'This will be a much, much bigger Ratitāe, one for you and me alone. There'll be no Ursula and no Marianne with whom to share it. It will be mine, and yours when you're older. We'll be far away from those who want to steal what we've built.'

James's hand forced him down beside him. Stanley's movement cast flickering shadows across the map. He stared intently at the drawing, not understanding the squiggles, yet searching desperately for something to oust his disappointment and allow him to share in his father's obvious delight. But it was only when James reached into the trunk and brought forth a book that his interest was kindled.

'America,' said James. 'That's where our farm is going to be, son. In Florida, America. Soon.'

Stanley's gaze floated over pages filled with words and illustrations as the pages of the large book were flicked over. 'America,' his father whispered again. 'A land far away from here. A land where we'll build an empire of ostriches. What do you think, boy? Just the two of us and our empire, hey?'

The boy was silent, sensing that his father's mind was far removed from the loft and did not require any answer.

James's thoughts had in fact turned inwards. It was as if he was living the moment on which he had focused all his attention and efforts since the day Clara had rejected him, the moment when all his enemies would be destroyed, when all those who had spurned him – Marianne most of all – would find their futile worlds lying in ruins about them.

America – he should have thought of it long ago, that day of his marriage to Katherine, when Sir Anthony had first mentioned the potential threat of America establishing an ostrich industry of its own. He should have started then, before Katherine could wound him with her betrayal.

The investigations he had launched soon proved that Sir Anthony had once again displayed remarkable foresight. America had the right climate, excellent and cheap transport, with easy access to world markets. Once America had produced a sufficient supply of feathers to satisfy demand, the flourishing industry of the Cape Colony would be a thing of the past. It would take time, but it *would* happen! And he, James Quenton, would lead the way.

He had not wasted any time once he'd made up his mind. He formed an association with a farmer in Florida, secretly shipping across some of his choice ostrich chicks. More would follow soon. When James was ready to leave, his departure would be so well planned that even Marianne would be unaware of his absence for at least a day – as unaware as she would be of the loss of her choice breeders which would accompany him.

Stanley, though, would not be that easy. The boy would go with him, of course. He was his son, and he'd lost as much as himself. Betrayed by his own mother, spurned by that bitch with eyes only for her little girl-brat.

Suddenly James became aware again of the boy at his side, watching him with large eyes. 'What do you think, son?' he asked, touching Stanley's face with uncharacteristic warmth.

Stanley felt obliged to say something to please his father. But all he could think of was to ask, 'Isn't Ursula coming with us?'

James slammed the book closed. 'No,' he said as he folded the map. 'Weren't you listening to me? I said it was for the two of us alone! If we stay here, Marianne will try to use Ursula to steal what is yours, the farm I built up for you. They cannot touch us in America.' He shut the trunk, locked it, then straightened up.

Stanley stepped away, concerned now that he had angered his father again. 'I like our secret, Daddy,' he ventured and was rewarded by a fleeting smile.

'Just remember what keeping a secret means,' said James, steering him out of the door before locking it behind them. 'You're to share it with no one. It's just between us two men, do you understand?'

'Yes, Daddy. I won't let Ursula steal our secret.' When James ruffled his hair, Stanley realised he would always be able to win his father's approval by distancing Ursula from himself.

As they started down the steep stairs, he thought that

as soon as they got home he would take back the wire carriage Ursula had taken from his room. He knew she had it; he'd seen her watching him enviously as he played with it in the yard outside the kitchen on Ratitāe. He'd take it back and tell his father about it in the morning.

It would be the last thing Ursula ever stole from him – he'd promise his father that.

CHAPTER TWENTY-NINE

The worst slump the industry had yet experienced seemed to take place overnight, as if the market had suddenly realised there were just too many ostriches. The price of average quality feathers fell by £5 and showed every sign of a further decrease. 'A flash in the pan', people started saying of the industry, sorrowfully surveying the birds roaming their fields. There were 150,000 domesticated ostriches in the Cape Colony in 1885.

The bigger farmers stood to lose the most, although they could survive for a while. They assured one another that things would soon improve, yet their minds kept returning to warehouses piled high with feathers.

The price of ostrich feathers was not the only thing to fall that year. With it came the rain, a deluge such as Oudtshoorn had never witnessed before. It started as a light drizzle on Thursday morning, 13 May, moving in on the chill of a south-west wind. The farmers welcomed it; it would help for a fine lucerne crop after the drought of the past years. But what use would lucerne be now that the ostriches were losing their value?

Thirty hours later, they cursed as the rivers started to flood, sweeping away valuable topsoil as torrents of angry water washed past the farms. Houses were destroyed or at least their foundations sagged, leaving a trail of desolation and homeless families.

The swollen Olifants River swept with awesome power towards the town, smashing the Victoria Bridge which had been opened only the year before. Even the normally placid Grobbelaars River crumbled its embankments as it rushed past Ratitäe. It ripped away the soil, the lucerne, the fences along the riverside. It swept up the fields to swallow the thatched shelters and the birds they could no longer protect.

'Always too much,' said Marianne as she joined James where he stood looking out through the open front door. 'Too much sun, or too much rain. God, but it's a harsh country.' There was nothing she could do except watch the wrath of nature as it ravaged what she had built. What they had both built, she corrected herself. At least the house would be safe enough.

James's face held no emotion, so that Marianne assumed he felt the threat to the farm as severely as she did. His sudden thin smile when he glanced at her told her she was wrong. 'It makes little difference,' he said, returning to his vigil. 'This place is finished anyway. First the drop in price, now this. It's finished. All of it.'

'No, it's not,' she said gently, although his smug manner perturbed her. 'Nothing will destroy Ratitäe – neither the prices, nor the rains.'

'You naïve fool,' he snapped and leaned back against the door. 'This is only the start.'

She was taken aback by his sudden vehemence. 'What do you mean?'

'Your foolish dream of quality feathers, that's what. Even if the industry gets itself back on its feet, you'll be up against ever-increasing production and transport costs. Your feathers will be too damned expensive for the market.'

'The railway line will help.'

He laughed in her face. 'You think so? Then you're even more naïve than I supposed. They've been talking about that railway line for years now.'

'It'll come,' she said firmly.

'I'm sure it will, but it won't be the saviour of the industry as you seem to think. All it will bring is speedier transport to the harbours, but at a higher cost. Nothing can save you now.'

'Me? What about you, James? Or have you no desire to be

saved?' She wondered whether his loss caused by the sudden slump had hurt him more than she estimated. Was that it, was James so depressed he wanted to give it all up? Yet he seemed too complacent, too self-confident.

'No,' he said in answer to her question, 'Ratitāe means nothing to me any more. You're welcome to it, my dear Marianne. For as long as it lasts.' He seemed to be speaking to himself when he added, 'This rain is the final sign. It's time for me to move.'

'Move where? What are you talking about?'

'America.' It was spoken in a low whisper.

'What?'

'America, where I'll establish an industry to swallow yours. A few years, then it'll all be over for you.'

'You can't!'

'Can't?' He laughed at her again. 'Who says I can't? You and those other morons who think all they have to do is sit back and the money will keep flowing in? I already have birds there, and I intend shipping out the rest tomorrow. So don't tell me what I can or cannot do?'

He stepped closer to her, till their faces almost touched. 'Make me an offer for my share of Ratitāe. Isn't that what you've always wanted? Just think of it – you can have it all.'

'You're insane!'

He pushed past her and started up the stairs. 'What about your children?' she called after him. 'Do you intend to ruin their future as well?'

He stopped, turned slowly and stared past her as if seeing something in the wet greyness outside. He wished he could tell her about Stanley, just to see her reaction. But he dared not; it was safer to let her believe that he was leaving alone, abandoning his son. She was sly enough to find a way to stop him if she knew he intended taking Stanley with him. It would be wiser to stick to his plans and allow the men whom he had paid to kidnap Stanley a few days after he'd left to do their job. They'd have the boy with him in time to make the ship on which he'd booked a passage. After that, Marianne could scheme all she wanted – it would be too late.

He forced his gaze to her face. 'You stole Ratitāe from

me – why not take the children as well? I give them to you, my dear.'

'No! You can't!' But he was gone.

Marianne felt an icy numbness, more severe than the cold that drifted in from outside, strike painfully within her. 'No,' she said again as if James was there to hear.

She was shaking now. 'I won't let him do this,' she said aloud. She couldn't allow it; she would have to stop him. Somehow.

Clara shifted on the pillows and studied the face of the man lying beside her. He looked younger now, the lines of his face softened somewhat by the grip of deep sleep. Yet the inner cruelty, the force of him, remained etched on his features.

Her body shivered in a mixture of fear and strange attraction. He had been rough with her, had hurt her, yet his abuse of her body had not been like that of so many other men, who seemed intent on proving their physical dominance over her. They were weak within themselves; this man was his own strength. Violence and brutality were his way, and she had responded to it. He had paid his money, stripped the clothes from his powerful body while he watched expressionlessly as she did the same, then gripped her roughly and taken her as no man had before.

Clara watched him a while longer, then laid her head back against the pillows. The rain splattered noisily against the window-pane. A year, she thought bitterly, a whole damn year wasted.

She should have been in Cape Town a long time ago. Cape Town, where things were happening, where there were prospects awaiting a girl with her looks and body. Yet here she was, stuck in a feather-mad town, providing randy farmers brief moments of self-indulgent pleasure.

Within a few weeks of James having thrown her out of the townhouse, Clara had almost raised enough money to leave Oudtshoorn. All she had needed was a little more time. But

Maggie Lawrence – damn her! – had caught her with a man in the house and thrown her out.

Finding suitable quarters where she could continue her activities had placed an additional financial strain upon her, forcing her to remain in Oudtshoorn longer than planned. Then had come the need for more clothes in order to remain attractive, money for an abortion. Clara's dreams of a fancy life in Cape Town began to fade.

She sometimes saw James in town, although he always jerked his gaze away and pretended he hadn't noticed her. The bastard! Once, when she had been in desperate need of cash, she had curbed her hatred of him in order to try and kindle his old feelings for her. Surely he would help her? After all, he'd loved her! When she saw him coming down High Street on his horse, she stepped out and stood right in the centre of the road. He bore his horse right down on her, his eyes fixed straight ahead as if he had not even noticed her standing there, forcing her to leap aside at the last moment to avoid being knocked down. Oh, how she would make him pay for that!

The man beside her stirred and rolled on to his stomach. Clara felt again the strange blend of repulsion and fascination. What had he said his name was? Gert somebody or other. Daniels? No, a Dutch name. Gert . . . Gert . . . Gert – Denker! Yes, that was it. Denker.

He awoke and looked at her. She shifted her gaze from his and studied the marks on his back, the thick red scars she had felt under her fingers when she lay squirming beneath him.

'What caused these?' she asked, tracing her finger lightly across the hard ridge of angry flesh.

'Cat.' His voice suited him – deep and rough.

'Cat?'

He stared blankly at her for a moment before he said, 'Cat-o'-nine-tails. A whip.'

'A whip?'

Gert Denker rolled away from her, stood up, reached for his clothes and started to dress. 'Prison,' he said across his shoulder. His voice tightened when he added, 'Ten years of the damn place.'

Clara stared up at him with fresh insight. She laughed coyly. 'No wonder you couldn't get enough this afternoon.'

'Little girl,' he replied, his voice devoid of emotion, 'there's nothing on this earth I can get enough of. So don't think yourself special.'

'Are you staying on in Oudtshoorn?' she asked once he was completely clothed and was kneeling down to tie his bootlaces.

Denker shook his head. 'I'm heading for Barberton. I want a share of the wealth lying under that earth.'

'There's talk of gold being found around here as well, near Knysna.'

'Rumours – the world is full of them. Barberton is a certainty.'

'But that's up in the Eastern Transvaal – why are you travelling this way round?'

The floorboards creaked when he stood up. 'I have some business here,' he said. 'Overdue business.' He shrugged into his jacket, opened the bedroom door and turned to her. 'You know where the farms are around here?'

'The ostrich farms?'

He nodded. 'That of James Quenton in particular. You know of him?'

Clara's smile was slow and wide. 'Oh yes,' she said, 'I know James Quenton. Very well, in fact. Are you a friend?'

His eyes told her what she wanted to know. 'Close the door,' she said and smiled again. 'Stay a while . . . Let's talk about our mutual friend. I'll tell you all you want to know about him.'

The rain stopped that night, but a watery mist still rose from the ground early the following morning. A grey shroud of cloud hung menacingly overhead, shutting in the cold and damp below.

Marianne looked up when she sensed the early morning sun trying to burn its way through. She hoped it would succeed.

The clinging wet of the soil slurped around her long boots as she stepped through the muddy fields on her way

313

to where the river still surged along its new banks. She passed by two ostrich carcasses, unable to find the courage to stop and look at them. She bit her lip and thought how arrogant and foolish she had been to build some of the paddocks so close to the river. Anyone who had been through one drought in the Karoo should have realised how dangerously high the waters could rise once the rains came. At least her breeders were in separate paddocks on high ground. She still had to check on them as well as the labourers' cottages, although she would have heard by now if there were any significant damage to either.

Her feet were sucked into the wasted ground. She pulled up the collar of her coat as tendrils of damp lifted into the saturated air and wound through the thickness of her hair.

It was very still around her, the sinister hush that often comes once violence has passed. The only movement was that of the birds which had survived the floods. They picked their way through the mist, clawing anxiously at the ruined ground in search of pebbles.

There was plenty of food in the barns, lucerne that had been cut before the rain started, but the stones the birds needed had either been washed away or now lay hidden beneath layers of mud.

Marianne stopped when she came to the river. She turned her back on the rushing water and stared across the fields at the house almost concealed by the haze of vapour.

James was wrong, she thought; it was not over. The land would resurrect itself, as would the market for feathers. The real threat lay in his plans for America. It had almost overtaken Austria as the major market for feathers, and she had known for quite a while that the Americans had received ostriches from the Colony, even though local farmers disapproved of those who supplied them. How could James have done such a thing! Even though America did not as yet have an organised industry or even a major producer of feathers, someone with experience could change that. Someone like James.

She felt her flesh tingle at the idea and for a moment thought she imagined the flicker of movement in the mist some distance away from where she stood. Then she saw it again, the bulky figure of a man in the chick paddocks, bending over as if scratching at the earth. One of the labourers? Outa, perhaps? But they would still be clearing out the mess that the flood had driven into their houses.

The figure straightened up just as the mist swirled and cleared around him, allowing Marianne to recognise the breadth of shoulder beneath the bulky overcoat. James! What was *he* doing there? Ratitãe was no longer of concern to him, so why would he be interested in what damage the flood had wrought? And at this early hour?

Then the fact that he was in the breeding paddock – *her* paddock! – registered, and she recalled what he had said the previous afternoon. He was selecting the ostriches he wanted to take with him, and chicks would be the best and easiest to transport. He would obviously select from *her* brood, the very best the region had to offer the world. Fury bubbled up inside her, ousting the cold. She started forward, frustrated by the sucking grip of the mud which slowed her down.

The sweating ooze stretched the short distance into a seeming eternity. It tired her, enriched her anger, so that her hands clamped themselves tightly around the top rung of the wire fence when she finally reached the boundary of the paddock.

James had moved further away now, his figure a hazy blur in the surrounding mist as he made his way carefully through the flock. An adult bird, a female, hissed and kicked frenziedly against the wooden barrier dividing the paddock from the breeding area. The bird's own nest still contained some eggs, and her quivering body displayed the anger and fear she felt at the sight of the shrouded figure she perceived as a threat to her offspring. She spotted Marianne, adding confusion to her emotions as she charged up the length of wall at the new menace.

Marianne stepped back, knowing of the power and rage which would crash against the fence. The protective bird would ignore the pain of the impact and be unheeding of any injury it might cause itself. The charging bird stopped short of the fence, as if deciding that the first threat was the greater. It turned and ran back along the wall.

Marianne's own mind was spinning as she stepped through the wire strands to enter the paddock. Her body seemed to move of its own accord when she made her way along the boundary wall, bent low so that the crazed ostrich would not see her. The clamour of its rage pierced through the surging noise in her mind as the bird fluttered and kicked further along the wall, its attention now focused fully on James.

When she reached the sturdy gate joining the paddock to the breeding area, her heart pounded wildly as she noted the wire that kept it securely closed. It would be so easy – a mere flick of the wrist. Then the bird would be through, charging at frightening speed, bent on destruction.

Her eyes burned in her skull. So easy. She could end it all then – the years of animosity, of personal sacrifice, the threat to the farm and the children. Opening the gate would release the bird and free them all.

Her hand seemed to move of its own accord. She watched as her tensed fingers found the wire rung and started to lift it. Sanity fought wildly against the ambush of blankness filling her mind. The bird spotted her and charged once more at the renewed source of its confusion.

The only movement was that of the ostrich. Marianne's pulse seemed to pause, she drew no breath. Only her eyes lived as she watched the movement of her fingers.

The crash of the ostrich against the gate sent her reeling, instantly bringing reality back to her wildly spinning thoughts. 'Oh God,' she whispered and glanced to where James stood. He remained oblivious to her presence.

She was suddenly hot, her body drenched with the sweat of realisation of how terrifyingly close she had come to murdering her husband. Then the trembling started, so that she was barely able to make it through the fence wire. She almost fell into the mud as she struggled in the direction of the house, fighting the horror which had surged up into her throat, threatening to spill like an evil spirit from her body.

Behind her, the ostrich vented its growing rage against the wall.

*

Denker had watched, his gaze at first curious, then entranced by the woman's action. It was the wife, he realised when she turned and scrambled through the fence. Clara's description of the woman had been surprisingly accurate, he thought with grim satisfaction.

He moved from behind the cover of the breeding house and watched Marianne stagger across the field. The little bitch – she had come so damn close to cheating him of his revenge. And he had almost let her.

He stooped and moved easily and silently through the wire strands of the fence. His chest constricted at the thought that he and James Quenton were at last together. Little more than a hundred yards separated them. He glanced towards where his enemy knelt, a young chick wriggling between his hands.

Denker smiled. He would move silently closer, then reach down and wrap his huge, powerful hands around that hated throat, the way he had imagined it during those long years in the Breakwater. His fingers would close and pinch and tear the life from James Quenton as he squirmed face down in the mud, not knowing who or what was choking him. Only then, at the very last moment, when recognition was still possible, would his face be turned around to stare for the final seconds into the eyes of his executioner. Denker shivered. He had waited so long for this.

The ostrich smashed into the gate again. Denker turned and looked at the bird. He felt hatred as he stared at the ugliness of the creature, resentment for what they had given Quenton while he, Denker, was forced to struggle endlessly with a society that had turned its back on him. The ostrich and James Quenton – they were both responsible for his suffering.

Denker hesitated one more instant, then crouched against the wall, out of sight of the ostrich. He was denying himself the pleasure of physical revenge, but even in the narrow, twisted tunnel of his mind there was a sense of simple poetic justice. He reached out and flicked the wire catch from the gate.

James turned in that instant, and was blinded suddenly as the sun tore through the layer of mist. It seared through the air, casting a prism of light, as it bounced across the wet ground, stretching and clawing its way through the vapour

317

as it spilled over the mountain tops to hurl its vengeance at the low clouds.

Even through the quick squirt of tears as the dazzling light hit his eyes, James saw it all at once, as if a mighty curtain had been raised, revealing the set upon which he had to play his part. He saw the sun, Denker, and the ostrich. He saw death, for on that stage it was his final role.

His eyes met those of Denker for a brief moment, a tell-tale interjection of time which could no longer be held in check. He saw the irrevocable movement of Denker's hand, the slow swing of the gate as it fell open under its own weight. Then only the initial charge of the ostrich filled his vision.

The female hurtled into the paddock, a plumed beast intent on nothing but the preservation of her offspring. Pent-up frustration carried her cloven feet like wind over the oozing earth.

She came out of the sun, a blurred kaleidoscope of colour and movement as her mighty hoof swung up, splattering James's face with mud before the impact of her kick shattered his chest. Her long, curved, chisel-like toenail cut a swath through flesh and bone, driving splinters and fragments through his lungs and deep into his heart. His mouth opened in a last, silent scream of terror.

He fell back into the mud. The bird stepped on top of him, pounding furiously, oblivious to the lost life that already seeped from his broken body to mingle with the glutinous mire of wet earth.

There was an abrupt stillness broken only by the squeak of wire as Denker ducked under the struts of the fence and headed across the fields to the trees where he had left his horse.

The mist lifted rapidly now, creating its own silent music. A voice called from somewhere near the labourers' cottages still partly shrouded by cloud. Someone answered. There was a laugh.

Ratitãe was awakening. It was coming alive.

CHAPTER THIRTY

Marianne started at the shrill cry of a child and relaxed as the sound turned to an excited laugh. She recognised Ursula's boyish giggle.

The ten-year-old had become a little terror on the farm, with a demanding thirst for knowledge about everything concerning the ostriches for which she displayed a great affection. Marianne often reflected – not without a certain relief – that Ursula's fascination with the birds seemed to be the only thing she had inherited from James.

The memory of James seldom plagued her these days. Even the guilt, the thought that she might have actually loosened the gate and released the ostrich, which had killed him close to six years ago, now haunted her far less often.

When it did come, it was at night, in disturbed dreams during which her mind replayed the scene in the paddock. Then she would see again her hand reaching for the catch on the gate, actually feel the breathless agony of the conflict within her as she tried to stay the movement. And all the while James would stand there, close to her as he had not been on that fateful day, his face taunting her to find the courage to complete the deed.

Had she actually done it? Had her mind perhaps blotted out for ever the final action as her trembling fingers lifted the latch? How else could the bird have escaped?

She tried to shrug off these thoughts as she headed for the front door of the house. Ursula, with thick bundles of auburn hair like her own, bounded up the steps towards her.

319

The little girl fell upon Marianne and hugged her tightly. Her frail body smelled of sweat and the boyish clothes she wore were darkly stained. Marianne wondered what morning adventure had wrought its havoc upon her.

'I rode an ostrich, Mummy! A big one!' Marianne went cold at the thought of the inherent dangers her child had faced. One slip, one kick . . .

'You mustn't do such a thing again, Ursula,' she said, trying to mask her alarm. 'You're still too little and—'

'Stanley rides! Why can't I?'

'He's a boy. And he's older than you.'

'By only one year. And I ride better than he does.'

'I don't care how well you ride,' Marianne said sternly. 'I don't want you to do it again. Not ever! I'll talk to Outa about his carelessness.'

'It wasn't Outa,' replied Ursula, lowering her eyes and kicking idly at a step. 'It was Stanley who put me on. But I asked him to.'

Marianne's alarm turned to anger. Stanley – he seemed to take pleasure in putting his sister's life at risk. 'I'll take it up with him, then,' she said tightly.

Her expression softened when she saw the look on Ursula's face, as though the child regretted having landed her brother in trouble. 'Go into the house,' she said, pushing her in the direction of the door. 'You can ask Mrs Blake for a slice of bread – but wash your hands first!' she added, giving the little girl another push which was more of a light slap on the buttocks.

She wiped a hand across her face and started down the steps. The sight of George standing in a nearby field drove all thoughts of Stanley from her mind. They had been married five years already, a time that seemed to have wiped out all the loneliness she had suffered while they were forced to remain apart. It was as though they had always been together.

George seemed to sense her gaze, for he turned and waved. He was too far away for her to tell, but she knew he was smiling. How different her life was now, how full! The burdens – Ratitāe, the children – could be shared now. And love. Even the ostrich-feather industry had surged forward from the temporary setback of low prices. The future looked promising again.

Her thoughts were broken by a horse streaking past in front of her. She stepped back and was covered by a thick cloud of dust. 'Stanley!' she shouted, but the boy was already past. 'Stanley!' She knew he had heard her the first time, but he stayed at a gallop until he was some distance down the road. Only then did he slow and turn in the saddle to stare back at her. His reluctance to obey showed in the grudging manner in which he steered the horse back to where she stood.

'What is it?' he demanded. The grey mare seemed to sense the irritation of her rider, for she moved nervously, raising more dust as she circled Marianne.

'Keep that horse still! Stanley! Get down! I'm trying to talk to you.'

The boy stayed on the horse, but he smoothed the mare's mane and whispered something in its ear. It stopped moving, although it snorted uneasily. 'I'm busy,' he said. 'I've got to fetch some kaffirs back from the roadside paddocks.' He did not look at her as he spoke.

'Stop calling them that!' snapped Marianne. 'How many times must your father speak to you about that.' She resented being forced to look up at the boy – especially when he obstinately avoided her eyes.

'My father is dead,' replied Stanley. He looked at her now, his eyes a pale, hard blue. There was an intensity there, although it was frigid, the passion of indifference he fought so determinedly to maintain. Yet there were times, more frequently these days, when Marianne saw not indifference but loathing. Then she would know with complete certainty that he hated her and George and even little Ursula.

Stanley had been only four when James died, so he could not have known much about what his father stood for. Yet Marianne knew he had retained some image – she could not describe it as romantic, for such an emotion would be foreign to him – that James was a good man who had suffered at the hands of his second wife and the man who was now her husband. There were times when she felt Stanley resented Ursula for carrying some of James's blood within her.

321

She decided not to pursue the matter of George's status at that moment. 'Where is your saddle?' she asked instead.

'I don't need one. Saddles are for children and townspeople.'

Marianne sighed with exasperation. 'Another thing, young man,' she started. 'I want you to take better care of your sister. How could you let her—'

'I don't look after girls.' She could scream when he interrupted her. It was a habit of his now, for he knew it infuriated her.

She managed to keep her voice calm when she said, 'Ursula is your sister. She needs looking after.' She wished now she had let him ride on by, but she felt obliged to finish what she'd begun. 'If you want to be treated as a young man rather than as a child, you'd better start acting like one. That means you must learn to accept responsibilities, including caring for Ursula.'

'She'd better start looking after herself,' he snapped back. 'She'll have to know how when I leave here.'

Marianne frowned. What silly talk was this of leaving home? Did he consider it a new way of annoying her? 'And just where are you planning to go, young man?'

He smiled, the gesture thin and superior. 'America,' he announced. 'Just like my father told me.'

She knew her face must have revealed her shocked reaction to his words, for Stanley's eyes glittered with a sudden awareness of his power. He tugged at the horse's reins while she stood in shocked silence. With a last insolent glance at her, he dug in his heels and galloped away.

There was an anxious knot in her chest as the child's words floated across her again. America. So James had spoken to him about it. But would Stanley have understood – and remembered? He'd been too young, then, too much of a child to grasp or be at all interested in his father's dreams. She decided it could be nothing more than a vague memory of something that James had said to him, of something which even then he had been able to understand as intentionally hurtful to her. Now he was trying it out for himself – that had to be it.

Yet, as she turned away, she was unable to shrug off the apprehension flowing through her. She hesitated at the

322

door and glanced up at the craggy peaks of the Swartberg Mountains. A cluster of white cloud scraped across the highest outcrop of rock, broke apart and hastened past the cliff face to become one again.

For a brief moment, Marianne wished she was a part of it, soft and almost weightless, free to scurry across the face of the earth with nothing more than a glimpse at the human problems far below.

She sighed, suddenly weary at the thought of having to fight through another struggle, with James's son this time.

A short distance down the road, Stanley dismounted and led the mare in among the trees. He let her graze freely as he leaned back against a tree, sliding his body slowly down the trunk till he sat on the ground.

He shut his eyes tightly for a while, watching the little bright spots of flashing colour dance before his eyelids. His pulse thumped loudly in his ears. He'd made a mistake, he thought angrily – he should never have revealed his secret to Marianne! But he'd wanted to shock her into silence – who was she to give him orders?

He smiled as he thought of her expression just before he'd ridden away. Still, it had been a mistake; they knew of his plans now and would try to stop him. If only he was old enough to leave immediately!

The first few years after James's death had been strange and lonely ones for him. His father's last instructions had weighed heavily on the little boy. He was to trust no one, James had said – least of all Marianne and Ursula. He had gone about distancing himself from them, still not fully understanding the threat James had stressed, but sensing nevertheless that his father's lecture on his being a special person demanded aloofness.

It was only a year ago when Stanley had sneaked into the kitchen late one night, lifted the townhouse key from behind the door, and then ridden into Oudtshoorn the next morning.

The trunk in the loft had revealed even more treasures

323

than those James had shown him. There were more books on America, and Stanley was old enough by then to appreciate where and what the land was. The contracts, though, the records containing details of transactions of ostriches sent across, the reports of conditions there – these were all still beyond his grasp. So he had carefully replaced everything, locked the trunk and shifted it deeper into the shadows of the loft. He would return for it some day.

He snapped open his eyes when the horse snorted. Stanley gave a low whistle and the animal moved slowly closer. He frowned when he saw George and Outa in a paddock across the road. How could they ever expect him to accept that man as his father? James had been his father; there could never be any other. George was nothing more than another of 'them', those whom James had warned him about. Stanley took a scornful pleasure in resisting all of George's attempts at friendship.

He pushed himself to his feet, reaching for a handful of the mare's mane. As he mounted her, he wondered how best he could punish Ursula for telling her mother about her ostrich ride. He'd told her to keep her mouth shut. Marianne would have known about it if she'd been hurt, of course, but that would have been worthwhile. But – damn the little brat! – she had ridden the bird with a skill that made the watching labourers cheer in admiration.

The area was known as Millwood Forest and, like so many other regions in the developing country, it had undergone dramatic changes. By coincidence, it was the ostrich which acted as a catalyst for the transformation.

It had started when a farmer, J. J. Hooper, entered the mountains near Knysna to collect pebbles for his ostriches. He found more than he searched for: a glittering nugget of gold. This set off a government-sponsored investigation which yielded a sprinkling of nuggets and gold dust all over the mountains. Yet it took ten years before there was a request for the area to be thrown open for pegging.

While the government hesitated, hopeful diggers from all

over the world, including those who had tried and lost at the Barberton fields in the north-eastern lowveld, streamed into the Millwood Forest, only thirteen miles' ride from the coastal hamlet of Knysna.

Apart from the diggers who ignored the dilly-dallying of government, there was the usual complement of ladies of the night, as well as men with get-rich-quick schemes. By the time the area was finally proclaimed in 1886, the village of Millwood had already dug its roots.

It had three newspapers – the *Sluice Box*, *Millwood Eaglet* and *Millwood Critic* – and within the space of a further two years it gained six hotels. By the end of 1889, when the Barberton fields had dwindled to almost nothing, Millwood boasted more than seventy wooden and brick structures and was home to four hundred people. It was a typical gold-rush town, a mushroom town.

Gert Denker arrived in Millwood only in March of 1891. Like a few others, he had clung desperately to his hopes of finding a strike at Barberton. Long after the majority of diggers had left, after the dozens of canteens and liquor shops and music halls had shut their doors, and the madams had moved their girls to richer pickings in places like the Witwatersrand, Denker and other die-hards continued their digging. He managed to find enough scraps of gold to keep him alive, but no sudden riches awaited him. At last he, too, packed his tools and left the ghost town, heading back for the Cape and Millwood.

He entered Millwood on a grey, humid day and headed directly for Morgan's canteen. After two tankards of beer which barely quelled his thirst, he took a room at Howell's Hotel. He had been recommended to try Holt's Temperance Hotel, but the very name of the establishment discouraged him. Howell's would do fine for a start. Carefully keeping his grub-stake money aside, he paid for three days' board and lodging.

That night he drank and spoke with the miners, both those who had rushed to Millwood in the early days and stockpiled their riches, as well as the ones who had followed later with their hopes of still discovering a fortune. It was a typical night in a rough mining town, filled with bustling sound. The thud of the stamp batteries mingled with the tinny tonk of pianos and the raucous laughter of dancers and pleasure seekers. Later, Denker delved into his precious hoard and went with a young girl of indeterminate breed and an even more confusing name of Mulligan Mary. The energetic Mulligan worked at him with a passion that reminded him of Clara. For the first time in many years, he wondered what had become of her.

By the end of the second day he'd spoken to enough diggers to know the fields weren't as rich as they had been made out to be. Most of the gold appeared to be alluvial, and many shafts that had been sunk in a desperate rush were not payable.

'It's the same old story,' a bearded old-timer told him in Morgan's. 'They find one or two good strikes an' all an' sundry rush in like madmen. It's the first ones in who grab the pickin's. After that, the rest of us all live on hope. We just don't wanna say "die".'

Denker knew what he meant. 'Why are you hanging on then?' he asked.

The old man gave a toothless grin. 'Again it's the old story. I'm holding' out for a fresh grub-stake. Wanna try my luck at a newer field.'

'Witwatersrand?'

The gold-digger shook his head. 'Across the mountain at Prince Albert. Reckon that's the place to be. They're bound to throw it open to the public one of these days. Got to be there when it happens. Some fellows I know already are.'

Denker sipped his beer thoughtfully. He had heard of the Prince Albert find while on his way to Millwood. It was not the first time there had been talk of gold in that area; in 1871 an aardvark had dug out a nugget weighing two and a half ounces. No further gold was found till recently, when a shepherd stumbled across a nugget on the farm called Klein Waterval. The news was spreading rapidly. Denker knew he would have to make his decision soon.

The old man beside him said, 'Thinkin' 'bout it, are you? Would be movin' that way if I was you.'

Denker gave him a cold look while he drained the last of his beer. 'Just rumours,' he said, scraping back his chair.

326

He studied the people on the streets as he made his way to Howell's Hotel. He could smell it, he thought dismally – the smell of failure. Didn't he know it well? It was here, too, starting its rot before most people could sense it. Another few years and it would have taken over. It would be Barberton all over again.

He stomped into Howell's, announced he was leaving at once and demanded the balance of his lodging moneys back.

By sundown he was already on the road to Prince Albert, the small village situated on the other side of the Swartberg Mountains, the wedge of ancient, solid earth separating the town from its affluent neighbour, Oudtshoorn.

CHAPTER THIRTY-ONE

The Swartberg chain was one of the country's great mountain ranges. Stretching from deep inside the western Cape, it sprawled eastwards for hundreds of miles, a magnificent natural barrier which repulsed the rain clouds and ensured that the vast plains of the Great Karoo remained a harsh, waterless expanse of earth.

The mountain was at its most impressive between the towns of Oudtshoorn and Prince Albert, standing five thousand feet above sea level at its summit. Once the intense heat of the Karoo summer had passed, winter storms swept over its peaks and slashed at its many valleys, plunging temperatures to way below freezing, blanketing its surface with deep layers of snow. It was a place where careless men and animals froze to death.

For many years, a simple track for pack-animals – the steepest in the country – was all that linked the inhabitants of remote valleys to the nearby towns.

It was only in January 1888 that a pass was successfully completed over the Swartberg. Under the guidance of the surveyor Thomas Bain, eighteen convict gangs braved the heat and cold and stubborn will of the ancient mountain. When it was finished at a cost of eighty thousand pounds and many lives, the Swartberg Pass was the steepest and most awesome in the southern region of the African continent. The pass provided a transport link for Oudtshoorn farmers to their nearest railway line. Produce was transported across the mountain, through Prince Albert lying in the foothills of the range at the start of the Great Karoo, and on for a further twenty miles to the tiny railroad station designated Prince Albert Road. A coach drawn by six mules left Oudtshoorn every day before dawn, arriving at Prince Albert Road station in the late afternoon. The passenger fare was thirty shillings.

As far as Gert Denker was concerned, it might as well have been thirty pounds, for his diminished financial reserves were scarcely sufficient for a start on the new gold fields. He could not afford the luxury of a journey by coach.

'Thirty shillings,' the coach driver repeated firmly, turning his back on the big man. Denker resisted the impulse to plant a kick on his broad buttocks. Swallowing his anger, he headed down the road, walking aimlessly at first, his head filled with acrimonious thoughts and hatred towards all those better off than he. It was only later that he remembered the girl, Clara. Would she still be in Oudtshoorn? She'd have money – surely she'd lend him some?

It was almost six years since he had extracted his revenge on that grey, wet day in May. The town had developed since then, but the tiny house where he had first met her was unchanged.

The years had been unkind to Clara. 'So,' he said when she opened the front door, 'you didn't get to Cape Town, after all.' Denker knew she must be around twenty-five, but thought she looked nearer forty.

Her eyes were narrowed, as if trying to place the big man among the many who had passed through her empty life. Then recognition dawned, and she smiled sardonically before stepping back. 'Well, well, if it isn't the murderous Dutchman! Come in . . . People around here don't approve of my being seen from the street. They say I corrupt the morals of their children.' She laughed – a harsh, dry sound, more like a cough – and led him along the dark passage. 'If they only knew,' she added over her shoulder, 'how some of their precious sons slip over the fence at night, paying for their lessons with money stolen from their upright fathers.'

Denker shut the door, thinking he had made a mistake in coming there; things could not be going well if Clara was taking in boys. There would be little chance of extracting money from her.

He studied her once they were inside the kitchen. The firm, full body which had filled so many men with wild desire had turned flabby now. Her skin, once the colour of cream, now had an unhealthy pallor. Denker thought that, like the inside of the house, she smelt of decay. He wanted to leave, but the thought of the money he needed made him sit down and smile at her.

'So, big man, you want coffee or a drink? Or do you prefer to get down to business right away?' Her bitter smile told him she had seen the revulsion in his eyes. 'Yes,' she said, taking the seat opposite him, 'time can be cruel, can't it?'

He shrugged before studying his massive hands lying on top of the table. 'Six years is not that much time,' he said slowly.

'Argh! What do you know about time and events?' she spat out. 'Tell me, Denker, did you do it? Did you kill James Quenton?'

His eyes were hooded. 'Quenton was killed by an ostrich,' he replied after a while.

Clara laughed. 'Yes,' she said, when her heavy breasts had stopped shaking. 'Death by misadventure, according to the officials.' She was silent for a while, then said, 'I thought you'd have had the guts to do it yourself. Instead you used a bloody animal.'

Denker's fingers twitched. 'Keep your thoughts to yourself, woman,' he growled.

'Oh, are you going to kill me to keep me quiet? Is that it?' She leaned forward to laugh into his face. 'Is that why you came here?'

Her taunting expression changed into fear when his hand snaked out, gripped her hair, and pulled her face down to the table. 'Listen to me, you soiled bitch – I came here to offer you a chance at making some money. Do not play games with me, or I might well end your miserable life.' He jerked his hand up and threw her back into her chair.

She tried to blink away her fear, but it showed in the trembling of her shoulders. 'What money?' she asked hoarsely.

'Gold. At Prince Albert. That's where I'm headed.'

She seemed to have overcome the worst of her fright at his violence, for she snickered sarcastically and said, 'Gold? Didn't you find that at Barberton?'

'It ran out. There wasn't much to start off with. Prince Albert will be different – provided I get there *now*.'

'And where do I fit into these fancy plans?' She was frowning now, cautious and curious at the same time.

Denker's thick lips twitched into a semblance of a smile. 'A little investment on your part. Just to get us started. A few tools—'

Clara laughed at him, although she leaned far back from his reach. 'Money? You fool! What makes you think I'd have any money? And that I'd risk it on you?'

'Laugh, you filthy bitch,' he said, slamming the chair back against the table. 'Laughter is all you've got left, and soon that'll be lost to you as well.' He started down the dark passage.

'And you, you bastard?' she shouted, following him. 'You don't have anything at all! You're a loser and you know it. You lost at Barberton, you'll lose at Prince Albert. You even lost to James Quenton!'

He spun around, gripped her wrist, and thrust his face up against hers. 'I beat Quenton, damn you! I took his life!'

Clara was terrified, but she had gone too far to stop now. 'His widow—' she said through gritted teeth. 'Let go, damn you – ah!' He forced her down on to her knees, but relaxed his grip on her arm a little. 'His farm is doing better than ever,' she continued. 'He has a son. Please, Denker, let go!'

'What about his son? Tell me!' He released her so suddenly she fell back against the wall.

Clara rubbed her bruised wrist and looked up at him with hate-filled eyes. 'His son will take over one day. James Quenton will live on. He's beaten you. Again.'

Denker looked down at her for a long time, then said, 'Quenton is dead. I killed him, and I'll take care of all of his family when the time comes. That name will be wiped from the face of this earth.' He reached for the door.

She pushed herself from the floor and grabbed his shoulder, forcing him to turn back to her. 'You're a loser, Denker,' she spat at him. 'You'll always lose. And I'll tell you something else, you dumb bastard . . . James Quenton was more of a man than you could ever hope to be – in or out of bed!' Her lips were pulled back in a vindictive snarl as she clung to his shoulder, her long nails clawing into his skin through the coarse texture of his shirt.

Denker felt the familiar steely cold rush through him to clutch at his mind. A vein throbbed angrily on his forehead.

He was not even aware he had slapped her. He stared, almost bemused, as she spun away from him and hurtled against the wall. Her body seemed to spin like a top, smashing from one side of the narrow passage to the other before she fell to the floor, sliding into the kitchen.

The breath slowly returned to his body as he stared down at her limp form. He let out a long shuddering sigh, glanced at his hand, then at Clara again. She did not move. He went slowly into the kitchen and bent over her. She stared sightlessly back at him. Then he noticed the acute angle of her neck. Damn!

He felt no remorse at the woman's death, only an added frustration. He could not leave the house now in case someone spotted him. Had he been seen entering? It did not matter; he would be gone by the next day.

He locked all the doors before dragging Clara's body into her bedroom. He dumped her on the bed, then started searching for money, finding ten pounds. Pocketing the cash, he settled down to wait for nightfall.

Once, shortly after sunset, someone knocked at the front door. Denker stayed in the room till he was sure that whoever had wanted Clara's company had assumed she was already occupied. Then he went to the kitchen, found a bottle of brandy, sat down and drank straight from it.

Just another hour or two, he told himself, then he could slip out of the back door and leave town. The nights were still reasonably warm, so he would sleep quite comfortably on the veld. In the morning, he would make a final effort to get more money, and he knew just where to try. Then he'd head for Prince Albert and gold.

*

Marianne was busy brushing Ursula's hair when Mrs Blake entered the room. 'She looks quite the little lady, doesn't she?' Marianne said, adding under her breath, 'For a change.'

'That she does,' replied Mrs Blake, smiling at the little girl before turning back to Marianne. 'There's someone to see you,' she said.

Marianne sighed. 'Can't George help?'

'He's out in the fields. Besides, you were specifically asked for.'

'Who is it? A farmer?'

'This one's no farmer,' replied Mrs Blake with a quick shake of her head. 'Says he's a friend of James Quenton. A rough-looking type.'

Marianne frowned. 'All right, I'll see him.'

Gert Denker was waiting in the large hallway when she came downstairs. He held his hat in his hands as he studied the interior of the house.

'Good morning,' said Marianne. When he spun round, she felt an involuntary tug of apprehension at the sight of him. There was something evil about him, something dark and menacing. Marianne told herself she was being unfair towards a total stranger, yet she could not shrug off her feelings of unease. 'I'm Mrs Laboulaye,' she said without offering her hand or inviting him to sit down.

'Mrs Laboulaye?' he echoed, and Marianne sensed the surprise in his voice was faked. 'I was hoping to see Mrs Quenton. Mrs James Quenton.' She shuddered as his gaze ran over her body.

'I am . . . was James's wife. He died some years ago.'

'Yes, so I heard. My condolences.'

Marianne gave a curt nod. 'What can I do for you, Mr . . . ?'

'Denker. I worked with James on the roads.'

'I see. That was a long time ago.'

He shrugged. 'I never forgot James, though,' he said, smiling, the grimace failing to touch his eyes.

'He . . . he never mentioned you.'

The sudden frown, like so much else, seemed false. 'That's strange. We met again once in Cape Town when James was already quite successful. He made me promise to visit him here.'

Marianne stared at him and wished she could rid herself of the tension his presence caused. 'Anyway, Mr Denker,' she started, 'if you knew that James was dead, you must have some other reason for coming here. What can I do for you?' If only George would come into the house.

Denker lowered his gaze and laughed softly. 'Well now, Mrs Quenton, you're making me feel quite embarrassed. You see, James said that if ever I needed . . . well, help . . . I should come here. He and his family would always assist me.'

Marianne had the measure of him then. 'You want money,' she finished for him. 'How much?'

He shuffled his hat between his hands. 'Well, I'm on my way to the gold fields . . . Some tools to get started. James said that—'

'Would ten pounds buy your tools?' Although she was under no obligation to give him anything, she just wanted him out of there, away from the house.

Giving her a mock bow, he said, 'Ten pounds would be a great help.' His lips twisted into a mocking smile. 'Just to get started, you see.'

'Yes. So you've said. Please wait here.' She felt his eyes on her back as she moved down the passage. Her hands trembled when she unlocked the top drawer of the desk and reached for the small cash box. Withdrawing the money, she slipped it into her hand. How would she explain it to George? He would be annoyed at her having given such a large amount to a perfect stranger.

Denker was still smiling when she returned and thrust out the money. 'Good day,' she said firmly. His eyes shone when he took it from her, and Marianne knew instinctively that everything he had told her was a lie. But why?

'Thank you,' he said. 'I knew that James's woman would understand.'

Marianne bit back a retort at the sudden familiarity. Denker walked heavily behind her to the front door. 'These gold fields,' she asked once he was outside. 'Would they be at Prince Albert?'

He nodded, the smirk in his eyes telling her that he'd guessed her unspoken wish that it was somewhere far away. Like the Witwatersrand.

'Just over the mountain,' he said, driving home the fact. 'I'll return the money as soon as I've found my first nuggets.'

'There's no need, Mr Denker. The money is a gift. From James.'

'Then I'll not be bothering you again, Mrs . . . Laboulaye.'

Marianne nodded, but as she watched him start down the steps, she knew with complete certainty that that too was a lie.

CHAPTER THIRTY-TWO

The utter silence of the Karoo veld was broken only by the whine of a bleak August wind which seemed to spring from the dry, rutted earth itself. It whipped itself up from the ground, scratched at the dust, then subsided again. The silence reigned supreme once more.

Despite the cold, Denker felt the grit collecting against the sweat on the naked skin of his chest. He lowered his shovel and reached for his water canteen. While he drank, his gaze took in the broken veld over which men had once crawled, their picks and shovels ripping into the innards of its surface in search of gold. They were gone now, moved on to try once more in another place, where perhaps this time they would find the riches they sought so desperately.

Like them, Denker had lost again.

He shut his eyes against the rising wind, imagining for a brief moment he could hear the sound of tools and laughter. For a while, over five hundred prospectors had worked more than a thousand claims on the Prince Albert fields. But that was four years ago, when no one thought the biggest find by any one person would be only a hundred ounces.

The surface of the Prince Albert field was mainly sandstone, with crevices rarely dug deeper than two feet. All a prospector needed was a crow-bar, pick and shovel, a pail and pan.

When Denker arrived on the fields, it was at a time when a new town, already named Gatplaas, was being planned. Carts and coaches rumbled in from the Prince Albert Hotel every second day, bringing more and more diggers as the news of the find spread. The nearest shop, L. H. Bosman, was crammed with mining equipment supplied by George Findlay & Co. of Cape Town. As with any new field, there was excitement and joy, violence and pain.

Then the gold ran out. Most of the men packed their goods and moved on to the seemingly endless gold reef on the Witwatersrand, while some decided to give Millwood a final try. Denker stayed on, as he had in Barberton, finding enough snatches of gold to keep body and soul together. But he was an embittered man, tired of losing.

Corking his canteen, he wiped his parched lips and began digging again. The strenuous working of his muscles drove the sights and sounds of the past from his mind.

He concentrated instead on tomorrow, for that was when he would start work as a driver on the coach which ran between Prince Albert and Oudtshoorn. The work would not be easy, for during winter the Swartberg Pass was often covered in snow, making the road slippery and even more treacherous than usual. Denker was aware of all this, but he was in desperate need of money, and it would be good to get into Oudtshoorn again. He needed a woman.

That thought made him wonder whether the investigation into Clara's death had been closed. It surely had to be by now; he was in no danger by going back there.

He lifted his pick, then decided against working and threw the tool to the ground. What reason was there for him to slog at the sterile ground? There would be money coming in now. The hated, barren claim could wait for a while.

A few yards away stood a tattered canvas lean-to, shielding his single blanket and soiled knapsack from the elements. He reached inside and withdrew a bottle containing a few swallows of brandy. What better time than now, he thought smiling, to finish it?

Denker had been right in assuming the journey would be formidable. The pass was filled with snow, with more still falling, carried along by a bitter, raging wind. At least there were no passengers on this, his first trip.

He knew enough about mules not to drive them too hard. He rested them once he had passed the toll-house, drawing the coach off the road into a clump of trees. Although he knew he would not make Oudtshoorn at the scheduled time, he nevertheless unharnessed the fatigued animals. Rather that, he decided, than have the mules die and he be stranded on the lonely mountain in the fierce blizzard. When he was sure the mules were secure, he went in search of wood to light a fire for coffee.

It was an hour before Denker was satisfied that the animals were rested; only then did he harness them and start the coach going up the last steep haul to the summit.

From there on, it would be downhill all the way.

It was dark when the coach rolled into Oudtshoorn. Stanley watched it come to a halt, experiencing a flush of disappointment when he saw it contained no passengers.

He should have been home hours ago, and knew that Marianne would be furious with him. Her scolding did not really bother him — it never did — although he always found it less irritating when there'd been interesting passengers in the coach.

At fourteen, Stanley was small for his age. His pale skin raged red when he'd been in the sun too long, something the other children in town teased him about. Their childish barbs had little effect on him, however. How could they; he was above them, a special person with a special purpose in life. Like his father had been. The children who taunted and beat him would one day lose their tenuous hold on him. He would leave them behind, just as so many discarded aspects of his life to which he would never return.

He shifted his weight on the concrete step of the coach station and hugged his knees to his chest. The wicked cold made him shiver uncontrollably, yet he did not want to make his way homewards. So he sat in the growing night and thought of James Quenton.

His father's face had been a vague blur for so long, till he had once again gone back to the trunk hidden in the attic of the townhouse. Taking out everything this time, he'd been thrilled to find copies of the *Oudtshoorn Courant* containing photographs and articles on James. A special person, James had called him. Stanley understood then what his father had meant; the records of his achievements were the ones he wanted his son to follow. He was now old enough fully to understand the yellowed documents and notes which gave life to James's dream of a new feather empire, a dream which Stanley decided to make a reality.

That was why he was at the coach station almost every day; the coaches brought passengers who had often travelled from distant places – including America. They were amused by the youngster's curiosity and humoured him, answering his many questions, misreading them as being nothing more than a child's need for romantic mental adventures. But tonight there was no one to respond to him.

Stanley watched the coach driver, noticing that the man was not one of the regulars. He stood up and ambled over to the big man.

'No passengers?' he asked. Denker gave him a sour look before unloading the bags of mail from the coach. Stanley was not perturbed by the lack of response. 'I talk to the passengers,' he continued, 'especially the Americans. I like Americans.' Denker grunted, almost bowling the boy over as he gripped two heavy bags, one in each hand, and stomped towards the stage office. Stanley strolled behind him to the door, waited till he had dropped the bags on the floor, then followed him back to the coach for the next load.

'Is this your first trip?' he asked, sticking his cold hands inside his trouser pockets. 'I know all the drivers, and this is the first time I've seen you. Will you have passengers tomorrow?'

Denker swung round angrily. 'Listen, you little brat, I don't have time for silly questions. Now get the hell home!'

Stanley glared at him, his frail body stiff and erect. 'I'm not your brat,' he replied, his voice filled with umbrage. 'I am Stanley Quenton, and I own the biggest ostrich farm in the district.' He trembled with outrage.

The big man had started to lean into the coach, but now

339

he turned slowly and stared down at the youth. 'Quenton, you say? James Quenton's son?'

Stanley nodded, and a smile wiped the frown from his brow. 'You knew my father?'

Denker sank on to one knee. 'Very well,' he said. 'We worked together, but that was many years ago. You say you own the farm now?'

The boy lowered his eyes. 'Well . . . not quite. Not yet, anyway. I will, though, when I turn twenty-one.'

'All of it?'

Stanley hesitated, then said, 'Half.'

'Well, that's certainly a big responsibility for a young man. No brothers or sisters to share it with?'

'The other half will go to my sister. She's not my real sister, though, and I'll take it from her. What do girls know about farming?' he added with a derisive snort.

Denker rested a big hand on the boy's head. 'You're right – they know nothing. Perhaps you should go home now. I'll bring some interesting passengers for you next time.'

'Will you?'

'I'll try.' He patted Stanley's shoulder, making the boy smile in gratitude before he turned and ran off.

Stanley's horse was tethered behind the coach station. He leaped into the saddle, still smiling widely as he rode around the side of the station, waved at Denker and galloped off.

Despite the big man's feigned friendliness, which had not fooled him in the least, he was strangely attracted to him. He sensed Denker was like himself, alone yet not lonely, the way he imagined James had been. There was something treacherously dangerous about the coach driver, which filled Stanley with a sense of excitement, making him look forward to their next meeting.

Denker watched the youngster disappear into the night. A vague plan started to form itself in his mind. It would take time, but if he was patient and clever, the final revenge might be that much sweeter. Stanley Quenton might just provide the way to take it all from his old enemy.

*

'I want Stanley to go to a Cape Town school,' said Marianne. 'As from next year.'

George Laboulaye lowered his *Oudtshoorn Courant*. 'And Ursula?'

'She'll have to go as well, or else Stanley will see it as favouritism once again.'

George smiled and reached over the arm of his chair to lay his hand on her shoulder. 'It's Stanley we need to discipline, but we're expecting Ursula to share the punishment as well. Is that fair to her?' He stroked her hair gently and added, 'I wonder whether it would make any difference to him if his sister goes or not.'

'Probably not, but a refined school wouldn't be a bad thing for that young lady. She's acquired far too many mannish traits as it is.'

He laughed. 'Don't look at me as if it's my fault! I can recall someone else who displayed similar inclinations at her age.'

'Nonsense! I'd already started flirting quite successfully by then!'

'Hmm. I'd forgotten!' He leaned across to plant a kiss on her cheek. 'Have you spoken to her yet?' he asked, quickly adding, 'About school, I mean – not flirting!'

'No. Nor to Stanley.'

'Perhaps if we'd been stronger,' said George and sighed, 'if we'd been firmer with him, then—'

'I don't think it would have helped at all. If anything, it would probably have placed an even greater distance between us.'

'Perhaps strangers and new friends might change him.'

Marianne could not stop the harsh laugh which escaped her. 'Friends?' she blurted out, 'I wonder whether he'll ever have any, whether he even wants them?'

George gave a little shrug. 'He has one, so I'm told. A coach driver.'

'A coach driver? Why would a grown man want to befriend a boy? And Stanley of all people?'

'I have no idea, my love. He's probably being nothing more than amicable.'

341

'Hah! Those are rough men. I don't like it at all.' She suddenly knew why Stanley often arrived home long after dark and seemed indifferent to her remonstrations.

'I wouldn't interfere,' George advised her. 'It's only a few more months before the new year starts. Let the boy be till then.'

'I'll talk to Ursula about school right away,' she said and stood up.

His voice stopped her as she was about to pass through the door. 'And Stanley?' he asked.

She turned slowly, smiled down at him. 'I think I'll leave him till the morning. I'll have more energy then.'

The resigned way in which George turned back to his newspaper told her he had had enough of Stanley for the moment. She could not blame him; he had tried long and hard enough to offer the boy affection and friendship, only to find it scorned with increasing bitterness.

She went in search of Ursula.

Marianne caught the thirteen-year-old Ursula studying her budding breasts in the mirror. As she pushed open the bedroom door and Ursula swung around, she was angry with herself for not having knocked; she was forgetting her daughter was no longer a little girl.

She need not have worried; Ursula was not in the least bit embarrassed. She smiled and said, 'Look, Mummy – they're growing!' Without waiting for Marianne's response, she turned back to face the mirror side-on, lifting her hands to cup her budding breasts. The incongruous womanliness of the gesture made Marianne smile as she leaned back against the wall. 'They are absolutely beautiful, my darling,' she said softly. 'Like all of you.'

She studied her daughter's long limbs in the soft glow of the lamplight. She would be tall, she thought, tall and slim. Although Marianne had retained her youthful figure, she felt a sudden yearning for her own young womanhood.

'Will they be as big as yours, Mummy?' asked Ursula, studying herself from all angles. The short skirt hanging low about her hips twirled as she spun right round in front of the mirror.

'As big – even bigger!' replied Marianne, trying hard not to let her amusement show. 'Now get dressed, little lady – I want to talk to you.'

Ursula reached for the blouse lying on the bed. 'Am I in trouble?' she asked impishly, taking a last look in the mirror before buttoning up the blouse.

'For a change, no. I want to talk about school – a Cape Town school.'

Ursula's face fell. She seated herself on the bed and said, 'I don't want to leave Ratitāe, Mummy. I love it here. I love being close to you and George.'

'I know, my sweet,' whispered Marianne, seating herself beside the young girl, gently running her fingers through her daughter's hair. 'We don't like the idea of your being far away from us either. But—'

'Little girls don't grow into gracious ladies on a farm, do they?' interrupted Ursula with a disarming smile. 'I understand, Mummy – I really do!'

Marianne kissed her forehead. 'Thank you, my angel. We women must put up with these things, you know. The world expects us all to be refined ladies of good breeding and education.'

Ursula gave an exaggerated sigh. 'Yes, it's such a burden, isn't it?'

The mischievous look in her eyes made Marianne laugh. 'Oh, Ursula – I love you so!' she said when her daughter hugged her.

'What do you want – why didn't you knock?' Stanley lay on his bed, his hands cradling the back of his head against the pillows as he glared at his half-sister.

'I did – you must be deaf!' Ursula snapped back and shut the door. Ignoring his obvious resentment at her presence, she moved into the room and sat down on the bed. 'We're off to Cape Town, the two of us,' she announced without preamble, 'where we'll learn how to act like civilised human beings.'

343

Stanley studied the ceiling. 'I'm not going,' he whispered, although the sound of it was harsh.

'Why not? It'll be fun! New friends, a big city, lots of—'

'Don't be so stupid! Can't you see what they're trying to do? No, of course not! You wouldn't understand – you're just a silly girl!'

Ursula ignored the insult; she was used to them. 'We'll be in separate schools,' she continued as if he had not spoken. 'A boys' school for you, one for young ladies for me. Mummy tells me they're quite close together, though – perhaps we can see each other at weekends!'

'Oh, shut up, will you?'

Ursula stared at him. 'You'll have to go – so why not try to make it exciting?'

He pushed himself on to his elbows and glared at her. 'Can't you see I'm busy thinking? Can't you see I want to be alone? This is *my* room – it's not for silly goody-goody girls! Leave me alone!'

Ursula sighed and got to her feet. Stanley's antagonism towards her no longer bothered her the way it had when she was younger. She wished he was nicer to her – wished they could be a loving brother and sister – but she was tired of trying.

She fluttered her hand at him before she left the room, closing the door softly behind her.

Stanley slumped back against the pillows and covered his face with his forearm. Tears of anger stung his eyes. Damn them! They wanted him away from Ratitāe, far away so they could plot in safety! Did they think that distance would sway him from his goal, from completing his dead father's dream?

He would go to their damn school, he thought sullenly – he would have to! But they were wrong if they thought it would make any difference.

CHAPTER THIRTY-THREE

As with any war, the Anglo-Boer War that finally broke out in October 1899 sparked off a vast range of varying opinion throughout the world.

It was seen by many as a bullying tactic in Britain's continuing drive for imperial expansion. The Netherlands, France and Germany passionately condemned the move. Many other countries were equally appalled at the conflict, although less vociferous in expressing their displeasure.

Britain, then the most powerful country in the world, had no reason to heed or fear any of those who disapproved her action. Her only real rival was Germany, with the strongest army, but she was undoubtedly still mistress of the seas.

The British considered it a just war – those who did not at least called it necessary – and one which would be soon ended. Apart from a small group of isolationists, the country rallied round its government. Soldiers departed the country in a spirit of music-hall militarism, intent on smashing what they considered the uppity and inferior forces of President Paul Kruger's Boers.

The Boers considered themselves guided by the divine hand of God, a nation about to fight for its very survival. They rode to join their commandos, varying in number from three hundred to three thousand. They wore no uniform; most were dressed in boots, corduroy trousers, a broad-brimmed hat and khaki shirt, over which was slung a cartridge pouch. Each man brought to the war his own horse, saddle, ammunition and enough supplies for eight days.

The officers and NCOs wore no distinguishing badges of rank, and each man under his command had as much say in things as the highest general. Once in battle, it was expected of the Boer soldier that he should display a high degree of personal initiative. This was an attitude at which their British foe scoffed; it was considered a lack of discipline, a battle flaw that would make a British victory somewhat easier.

They were wrong.

The Boer brought to the field outstanding marksmanship, masterful camouflage, and a breed of pony trained to stand still in battle while its rider jumped off, discharged his rifle, then galloped swiftly away before the enemy had time to recover. The Transvaal ponies were accustomed to the climate and immune to the diseases which struck down the British horses. They carried light loads and were capable of travelling long distances for days on end.

The Boer women, too, played a vital role at the start of the conflict. They were the army's supply line, following their men in large canvas-covered wagons drawn by strings of oxen. When supplies were scarce, the Boers lived off the land or off the enemy, whichever was the easier. Food, luxuries, weapons, cannon – even uniforms were taken from the British who seemed quite helpless in the face of a mobile, deadly foe.

The battle front spanned an area of more than a thousand miles from the Cape to the northern border of the Transvaal, and about five hundred miles from the Kalahari desert to Delagoa Bay. It was terrain the Boers knew well.

The British, on the other hand, possessed useless maps and an inadequate intelligence service. Tactics which had worked at Waterloo now brought tragic results. The only concession their leaders had made to the vastly different terrain was to change the traditional red uniform to khaki. It was turning out to be a very different war from the one they had envisioned. By February of the following year, there were some frantic discussions at very high level – both on the war front and back in Britain.

At Ratitāe, George said, 'I feel we have to do something!' Marianne smiled as he sank into a chair, but she did not reply.

346

At the outbreak of war, sympathies in the Cape Colony had been divided, for there were many who verged on open rebellion, choosing to ignore their allegiance to the British and to side with the Boers whose blood coursed through their veins. Even now, eight months into the war, passions still ran high; George's, like those of most Frenchmen, lay firmly on the side of President Kruger's men.

'More and more troops are arriving,' he muttered from his chair. 'The tide of war *has* to change in favour of the British.'

Marianne sighed. Walking over to him, she eased herself on to his lap and placed her arms about his neck. 'Will you ever lose the adventurer in you?' she mocked, kissing his forehead.

George smiled. 'You're putting on weight,' he said and patted her rump. 'Then again, it becomes a woman of—'

'Of what?' She made as if to rise, but he held her securely to him.

'Of maturity,' he finished.

She kissed him, for she knew that he was teasing. She had turned forty-one that January, yet looked far younger, and her figure still drew admiring glances from men of all ages. 'Now,' she asked, 'what's this nonsense about wanting to get involved in this dirty war?'

When she felt him tense beneath her, she wished she had not raised the subject again. 'You're right,' said George, 'it *is* a dirty war. And I have to do something to help.'

'It's not our fight! Sorry, I know how you feel about it. I just don't see what you can do.'

Apart from a few heated arguments and one or two incidents of fisticuffs, Oudtshoorn had remained relatively untouched by the hostilities. Ostrich feathers were still considered the height of fashion and production continued unabated. But the British had taken no chances with one of the Cape's major sources of income; a strong presence of soldiers had been established in the town.

'I want to go to France,' said George. 'I can get some help there.'

'France? What kind of help? What are you planning?'

He placed his finger over her lips. He smiled and said, 'Just a visit. I want to check on the strength of their sentiment, that's all.'

'Nonsense!' Marianne's sudden outburst startled even herself. She knew he was not telling the truth; George regularly received newspapers posted to him by business acquaintances in France. The illustrations and cartoons adorning the front page of the *Petit Journal*, in particular, made it very clear where French sympathies lay. 'Tell me what you have in mind,' she demanded.

He smiled sheepishly. 'Weapons,' he answered her.

Marianne closed her eyes for a moment, then glared at him. 'You damn fool Frenchman,' she said without rancour, 'you'll get yourself locked away!'

'Nothing will happen to me. All I want to do is set up channels for the Boers to send in their own men to negotiate for arms.'

'Will the French agree to that?'

'Not the French,' he replied, 'the Germans. But I'll have to work through my connections in Paris. Kruger will have to get more guns – especially cannon – if he wants to stop the British advance. The only chance he has is by talking to the Germans.'

She shifted from his lap, faced him with her hands on her hips. 'I might be mature,' she said slowly, 'but I'm beginning to think you're senile. The only problem is that I love you, you damn fool.' She sighed and moved back towards him. 'When are you planning to leave?'

He cocked an eyebrow. 'Does that mean I may go?'

'Did you think I could stop you? When?'

'I don't know. It'll take time to make the arrangements. A few months, I'd say.'

Marianne was thoughtful for a moment, then said, 'Take Ursula with you.'

'What? How can you suggest such a thing?'

'Think, George! It's a perfect cover. You'd be taking your daughter over there to expose her to feather marketing. Visit the auctions, let as many people as possible know you're there and why.'

George tugged at his lip. 'You're right, but I can't put her at risk.'

'You won't. Not if you're both careful.'

'You mean we'd tell her the truth?'

Marianne smiled indulgently. 'In case you hadn't noticed, my dear husband, Ursula is eighteen years old and she's rather astute. Do you honestly believe you'd be able to keep her in the dark for long?'

'Right again,' he said and laughed. What Marianne had suggested made sense; he'd be able to move across borders without raising as much suspicion as he would on his own. He could even arrange for his contacts to meet with him in Austria! No one would think anything strange of an ostrich breeder being in Austria, still a major market for feathers. 'What about Stanley?' he asked suddenly.

Her quick frown answered him. Could Stanley be trusted? It saddened him to realise they were obliged to consider that about their charge. But the young man's bitterness would be a security risk.

'We'd have to invite him to go along with you,' Marianne said at last. 'Just to keep the peace. But only as far as France.'

'I could suggest he goes on to America from there. On his own. He'd love that – he's always been fascinated by that country.'

'He might not want to go along at all. He doesn't seem to be very interested in ostrich breeding – in anything at all, for that matter.'

She sighed, stood up. 'Where are you going?' asked George.

'To talk with the young man. It's time he decided what he's going to do with his life.'

He gave a slow shake of his head. 'I spoke to him yesterday. It seems he's no desire to go on to university. I don't think he knows what he wants.'

'He'll be legally entitled to his share of Ratitāe in two years' time. He'd better have made up his mind by then.'

'We don't seem to have that problem with Ursula. I don't know whether to be thankful or not!'

'She was born to be a feather baroness,' replied Marianne with a laugh. 'Perhaps that's why Stanley isn't interested in ostriches. He realises his sister will show up his shortcomings.'

George was lost in thought for a moment. Then he looked up and said, 'Good luck. You'll be needing it.'

'And you,' replied Marianne. They smiled at each other before she left the room.

Marianne found Stanley seated in the shade of the patio alongside the house. He closed the book he was reading and glanced at her with expressionless eyes. What demons drive you? she thought as she sat down opposite him.

Her stepson was nineteen years old, slender and pale, although he had become quite tall over the years. He had finished his schooling the previous year, and for the past two months had stayed on at Ratitãe, a morose, brooding figure who revealed nothing and showed no sign of needing or wanting anything from any of them.

Her hopes of boarding school and the company of boys his own age changing his introverted nature had come to nothing. If anything, he had returned home more withdrawn than ever, and reports gleaned from the school's headmaster revealed that Stanley showed no inclination to form any kind of intimate relationship with his peers.

'Have you had tea?' she asked, forcing a smile.

'Yes. I was busy reading.'

'Anything of interest?'

He shook his head. 'Not to you.'

Marianne bit back her angry retort and said instead, 'Are you pleased to be finished with school?'

'You asked me that same question some weeks ago,' he snapped. 'I told you then, I don't have particularly strong feelings about it.'

'Do you have feelings about anything?' she asked harshly, unable to take any more of his insolence.

'Yes, I do.'

'What are they, Stanley? Why don't you share them with us?' There was no reply. Marianne pressed on, saying, 'George tells me he spoke with you yesterday. About going to university.'

'Yes. I told him I wasn't interested. I can't see that it has anything to do with him.'

'How dare you talk like that about your stepfather! George is concerned and—'

'He is nothing to me! He's your husband, that's all.'

She was glad of the table between them, for otherwise she knew she would have slapped the boy. Her hands wound themselves in a vice-like grip around the arms of the chair. 'You're impertinent,' she said in a low voice. 'Ungracious and impertinent. Towards me as well as George.'

Stanley looked away from the anger in her eyes. 'I'll be staying on at Ratitāe for a while,' he murmured.

Marianne waited till she had her anger under control before she said, 'George is planning a trip to Europe. We thought you and Ursula might like to go along.'

'Whatever for? I went in June, remember?'

His arrogant response irked her, but she managed to remain calm. 'That was with school-friends, Stanley,' she said. 'What George has in mind is an . . . call it an educational tour, if you like, one concerning the marketing of feathers.'

'I'm not interested.'

'Not interested? Even though you'll get your share of Ratitāe quite soon? Have you given any thought to that?'

'Why? Are you hoping I'll give it up and leave it to darling Ursula? Is that what—' He gave a sharp gasp as Marianne's hand swept across his face. She was leaning half-way across the table, so that the distance between them made her slap do nothing more than graze his cheek. Even then, her fingers crashed into his nose, causing a quick, sharp spurt of blood to run down over his lips. He stared at her in shock. All he said was, 'I'm bleeding!'

Marianne's face was white with anger. 'I'm surprised,' she said in a thick, low voice. 'There are times when I wonder whether you're human.'

He stared back at her, outrage spreading into his face. He lifted his hand to his nose, studied his bloodied fingers. 'You've no right,' he hissed at her. 'How dare you hit me? You're not my mother!'

'I'm your guardian, damn you! And I'm sick and tired of your insolence. Do you hear me? Answer me!'

He wiped the back of his hand across his face and glared back at her. 'I hear you,' he said softly, 'but I owe you nothing. As far as I'm concerned, the lawyers could have been my guardians. You have only two years left, anyway.'

Marianne's legs trembled so much she was forced to sink back into her chair. She stared with something akin to hatred at the man-child sitting opposite her. She heard her quaking voice say, 'My God, Stanley, how can you say such things? You're the one who's spurned everything – love, interest – everything we've ever tried to offer you! You're the one who's done the rejecting. What kind of person are you?'

'My father's son,' he said, his tone challenging. 'I am James Quenton's son.'

She shut her eyes, and her voice was low when she said, 'Yes . . . yes, I can see that.' She heard his chair scrape back and opened her eyes again. He was standing, a thin sneer tugging at the corner of his mouth.

'As for my share of Ratitāe,' he said, 'I'm sorry to disappoint you, but I'll be taking it up when the time comes. All fifty per cent of it.' He hitched up his trousers and added, 'Till then, I feel I'm as much entitled to stay on Ratitāe as anyone else.' He started to turn away, but Marianne's voice stopped him.

'Thirty per cent,' she said softly.

His shoulders tensed, and he turned slowly back to her, denying her words with a shake of his head. 'No,' he said, 'half of it. It's always been half. You're lying!'

Marianne could not stop the surge of triumph rising within her. At last she had been able to reach him, even though it had taken thinly veiled malevolence to achieve it. 'Only thirty per cent,' she repeated. 'All your father owned when he married your mother was twenty per cent. He purchased a further ten from the lawyer, Abraham Isaacs. That was all he owned, Stanley. Nothing has changed since then.'

He stared at her with his mouth agape. 'But—'

'Yes, I know we always spoke of you and Ursula each getting half, but I don't see why you should.'

'You can't do this,' he screamed at her. 'It's—'

'I can and I will! Your mother left me her seventy per cent, and I'd always intended sharing it all between you and Ursula. Your attitude has made me change my mind.'

His face was pale and ugly. 'I suppose Ursula gets it all now. You're such fools – can't you see how she's twisted you both around her little finger?'

Marianne gave a slow shake of her head. 'Ursula will get the same as you. George and I will retain the remaining forty per cent in the hope that time will make a decent human being of you. I have my doubts, though.' She was through trying; if brutality was what Stanley thrived on, he had better learn to accept it as well as he handed it out.

He took a step forward, stopped and shook his finger almost in her face. 'You can keep it,' he snarled, 'all of it except what is rightfully mine. That's all I need!'

'To do what?'

His finger was still pointed at her, accusing and warning at the same time. 'Wait,' he spat out, 'just wait and see! I'll make it all mine before I destroy it!'

'Destroy? Stanley, the only thing you'll destroy is yourself. You'll do that with your own bitterness and senseless hatred.'

His voice turned into an angry shout. 'Just wait!' He spun around and ran from the patio.

She sat still for a long while before she leaned forward and placed her head into her cupped hands. She remained like that till George's soft voice made her look up. 'I heard most of it,' he said. 'What do we do with him, my love?'

She shook her head inside her hands. 'I don't know,' she whispered, 'I honestly don't know.' She brushed back her hair. 'I can't throw him off Ratitāe. He has a right to be here.'

He nodded and moved in behind her. His hands reached for her neck, gently massaged her tense muscles in slow, circling movements. 'You realise, of course,' he said into her hair, 'that one day Ursula will have to face him on her own.'

'Yes,' she whispered hoarsely, 'I was thinking the same thing. I just hope there'll be enough time for her to find sufficient strength.'

'She already has it,' came the laughing reply. 'She's your daughter, isn't she?'

The mare's sweating body was covered with foam by the time Stanley reached Oudtshoorn. He tugged brutally at the reins as he galloped in behind the coach terminus. The exhausted animal snorted with irritation and resentment when he jumped down and walked off without bothering to remove her saddle and bridle.

The sandstone building was deserted except for the coach-station superintendent who glanced up when he saw the boy. 'You're too early, lad,' the old man said, hauling out his pocket watch. He tapped the glass. 'Almost an hour to go if they're running to schedule.'

Stanley ignored him and moved into the bright sunlight outside the small building. He sat down on the steps as a fresh shudder of anger and resentment coursed through him. They were hoping they'd rid themselves of him, of course – that bitch and her French lover who'd stolen his inheritance from his mother and father. It was fear – he knew it! But only thirty per cent?

There was a sharp stab of pain in his chest. He breathed deeply to rid himself of it, but it clung stubbornly to him, spreading into his shoulders and upper arms, as intense as his hatred and suspicions of those who called themselves his family. They were nothing to him, and he would beat them. They could steal and cheat and scheme, but he would vanquish them in the end. Denker would know how to help him.

He glared when he heard the superintendent cough behind him. The old man seemed oblivious to the look as he sat down beside Stanley with a loud groan and a creaking of his joints. He struggled to light his pipe, then studied the young man. 'I can still recall the times,' he said, 'when you'd arrive here in short pants and bare feet,' He chortled and added, 'Guess I kind of missed you while you were away at school.'

Stanley ignored him. He squinted into the bright sunlight,

354

pretending to study the houses in the vicinity. 'What'll you be doing with yourself now?' the old man asked.

Turning slowly to focus cold eyes on the man's face, he said, 'Why is everyone so damn interested in what I'll be doing?'

The superintendent reared back at the vehemence in the youngster's voice. 'No need to be huffy about it,' he said. 'Just wondered if you'd be staying on at the farm, that's all.'

'I shall,' Stanley replied coldly, wishing the man would leave him alone. What was keeping Denker?

The superintendent sucked noisily at his pipe. 'Hear your sister's breaking quite a few hearts,' he said after a while.

Stanley gave him a sidelong glance. 'What do you mean?'

'Now hold on, don't go snapping at me again! All I meant was she's a pretty girl, and half the young men in the district fancy the idea of courting her. Seems she's not really interested, that's all I meant.' He looked offended as he sucked his pipe again.

Stanley sneered at the man's mistaken interpretation of his response as having been defensive towards Ursula. He had hoped he could glean some interesting news from the old man, some rumoured indiscretion on Ursula's part. Perhaps there was something, he thought and decided to probe, saying, 'She's very popular with men, isn't she?'

'No, lad, I said—'

'I know, I know! Even at school there were always boys wanting to get to know her.' He was pleased to see the look of interest on the other man's face, then realised it was nothing more than a normal male response to the possibility of some juicy details about a woman. He decided to drop the subject and shut his eyes, wishing the coach would arrive from Prince Albert.

As if in answer to his prayer, there came the clatter of horses' hoofs as the coach rounded the corner in a thick cloud of dust and bore down on the station.

Denker removed his hat and slammed it hard against his leg. An equal amount of dust wafted from the harsh khaki

355

cloth of his trouser leg as from the hat. He settled it back on his head and smiled when he recognised Stanley. He felt satisfaction at the thought that even the years away at school had not weakened the hold he had over the young man.

His plans with Stanley were still a vague outline in his mind, for he was a man who reacted impulsively, instinctively, and he was not given to much forethought or planning. Yet from the time he had first met the youngster he had known he would be useful to him. James Quenton's own son would provide the means for ultimate revenge. Through Stanley Quenton, he would be able to destroy Ratitāe and all who profited from her.

He jumped down from the driver's seat and stretched out his hand to the young man. 'What's the matter?' he asked when he saw the anguished look on his face.

Stanley glanced furtively at the passengers disembarking from the coach before he led the Dutchman to one side. 'It's the farm,' he whispered. 'They're trying to take it away from me. They're stealing it.' Denker frowned, placed a hand on Stanley's shoulder, and asked him to explain.

He listened carefully, then said, 'I don't think you need worry.'

'But . . . they're doing it to ruin me, don't you see? They don't care what it costs to get rid of me!'

Denker gave his shoulder a sympathetic pat, but what he felt was scorn for the youngster's perception of self-importance. Did he really think James's widow feared him? 'Thirty per cent is enough to start off with,' he said.

Stanley was not reassured. 'I'll need more if I'm to finance my activities in America.'

Denker laughed harshly. 'Forget America! That's just an idle dream.'

'The hell it is!' Stanley shouted with such force that Denker held up a hand in a conciliatory gesture, warning himself to be more careful with the highly strung youth.

'All right,' he said, 'but I still think you needn't worry about it. We'll take care of your sister when the time comes.'

A sneer tugged at Stanley's lips, causing a hint of his usual self-assurance to return to his face. 'You'll help me, then?' he asked softly.

'I always said I would. But you have to help yourself, too. Be patient! It won't be long before you have your share. Till then, learn all you can about the farm, how it operates. You'll need to be an expert if you want to achieve your goals in America.'

'But my sister! You promised you'd take care of her!'

'When the time comes, I said. Your stepmother and that Frenchman as well. You'll get your farm. Just be patient.'

'What shall we do – how shall we destroy them?'

'When you inherit your share, you appoint me as your farm manager. Just over your portion, you understand. They can't stop you doing that.'

'And then?'

Denker smirked. 'Then it's just a question of time, my impatient young friend. We'll ruin your sister – a sudden disease among the ostriches, perhaps. It happens from time to time.'

Stanley was smiling now. 'Then we force her to sell to me for next to nothing, is that what you mean?'

The Dutchman nodded. 'Except that you don't use force, you use your head. Don't ever let her suspect how you feel. When the time comes, appeal to her to sell to you, to keep the farm in the family instead of letting it go to outsiders. Then you can sell at whatever price you need to get started in America.'

'And you, what will you get out of it?'

The Dutchman stepped closer and pushed his face up against the youngster's. 'You'll leave the farm to me when you move to America. You'll have no need of it then.'

Stanley threw back his head and laughed. 'What use will that be?' he said. 'Within a few years after I start up there, there'll be nothing left of the local industry – I promise you that! You'll be left with worthless land!'

Denker curbed his resentment of the young man's arrogance. 'It won't happen overnight,' he said. 'There'll be enough time for me to make what I need out of it.'

Something sinister in the big man's eyes made him step away, but he extended his hand and said, 'All right.'

Denker placed his own big hand around that of James Quenton's son.

CHAPTER THIRTY-FOUR

Ursula studied herself in the full-length mirror of her first-class cabin aboard the *Kildonan Castle*. A steamship of the Union Castle Line, the *Kildonan Castle* had first come into service in 1899, when it was used to ferry three thousand British troops to the war in South Africa.

From the time they had left Cape Town with a thunderous blast of the ship's whistle, gay bunting fluttering in the wind, the pomp and splendour had made Ursula's head spin, filling her with visions of finding glorious romance on the voyage which awaited her and George.

Added to the excitement of the cruise itself, was the special treatment afforded them once it became known that they were ostrich breeders. The tall Frenchman and his beautiful daughter were sought after as dinner companions among the tables of the very wealthy, all of them eager to talk to the producers of the feathers that adorned the elegant ladies aboard ship.

On the second night after leaving Cape Town, they were invited to be seated at the captain's table, an event which made Ursula feel quite faint with pride and elation. Even the leers she received from the elderly gentleman sitting opposite did not diminish the thrill of the evening.

The memory of her excitement made her glance in the mirror again. The evening gown fitted her perfectly, hugging her full breasts and narrow waist tightly before flaring out over her hips to cascade in reams of satin down to the floor.

Her thick auburn hair fell in a wild tumble across her

shoulders. Was she beautiful? As beautiful as her mother? She smiled at her reflection, trying to form a mental picture of Marianne at her age as she turned to give herself a sidelong glance in the mirror. A good *derrière*, she decided.

Watching her every move in the mirror, she slowly stripped off the dress. Her skin was dark and smooth, and she let the satin caress it as she slid out of the material. The feeling taunted her, caused a shiver of sensual delight to ripple through her, making her wish it was already night so that she could wear the garment to the ship's ball.

Stepping from the last restrictions of the dress she laid it carefully across the bed. The image in the mirror emphasised her near-nakedness, flat stomach, the tautness of her breasts.

There were a number of eligible young men on board, but so far none had stirred within her that special response she longed to feel. She had been friendly to them all, danced with most, and allowed a very few to kiss her while moonlight sparkled on the ocean. Yet for none did she feel any real attraction. Something was still lacking.

She sighed, thinking it would take a very special man to live up to her ideal of what constituted an idyllic romance. No, she corrected herself, idyllic was not the right description – Marianne's and George's romance had certainly not been that, not in the early days at least. Perhaps she was wrong to expect – no, demand! – the same intensity from a relationship as her mother had experienced. And she was too practical to dream of some grand romance, even though it would be nice to discover it, to feel that special flutter she read about in novels.

Her thoughts turned to their destination: France, George's home, the place where he and Marianne had first discovered their feelings for each other. Ursula felt a fresh flush of gratitude towards them for having treated her like an adult and taken her into their confidence. France – and intrigue! Absolutely gorgeous! Her only regret was that Marianne had not accompanied them. Conversely, she was relieved at Stanley's insistence that he sail on his own to America.

She had come to learn of Stanley's clash with Marianne, and it had been she who had gone to him, urging him to

359

swallow his pride and accept their offer to go abroad. He had pretended to pay no attention to her entreaties, but Ursula had not missed the gleam in his eyes when she drew mental pictures of what he would experience there. America seemed to be the only place he cared about, she had thought then, wondering at the same time whether she was pleading with him to go for his own sake, or that of Marianne, for she had felt uneasy at the thought of leaving her mother alone with him on Ratitāe.

Even though they had been at separate schools, Ursula had made a point of seeing her half-brother as often as possible during the years they spent away from the farm. As was the case with George and Marianne, she, too, had hoped Stanley's manner would change. But she found his company tiring, her efforts at building a relationship completely one-sided, so that eventually she had despaired of him and gone about building her own life.

It was the same once they had finished school and returned to Ratitāe. Ursula threw herself into the task of learning everything about the farm's operations, for she was determined to be of support to her mother. Under Marianne's watchful eye, her childhood interest quickly developed into a mature passion for everything affecting the ostriches and the marketing of their plumage.

Marianne and George encouraged her in every way, often involving her in decisions as well as forward planning. Ursula knew she wanted no other way of life and she longed for the day when part of Ratitāe would become hers. Perhaps all of it, she often thought; Stanley seemed to have little interest and she might buy him out one day.

She realised Stanley was irked by the manner in which her parents involved her in the farm, that he saw it once again as favouritism towards her. But she had long passed the stage of being concerned about what he thought and felt.

As she slipped on a light, sleeveless summer dress, she felt relief again at Stanley's not being with them. Now, she would at least have George all to herself. Dear George – he should have been her real father. Ursula thought him very romantic, enjoyed his company and being seen with him, for he was an elegant, handsome man. She felt a mixture of pride and possessiveness when they walked into the first-class dining room and women looked with interest at the tall grey-haired man at her side. Often their curious glances made her wonder whether they saw her as his daughter or as his young mistress. The thought amused her, as she knew it did him, too.

Sometimes, when they walked on the promenade deck after dinner, her arm tucked inside the crook of his, she would sense his thoughts were on her mother. Then Ursula wished that some day she would find a man who would love her as deeply. Once, when George was particularly subdued, she teased him, saying, 'If I didn't love Mother as much as I do you, I could really resent your ignoring me like this!'

He had laughed and gripped her tightly. 'I'm sorry, my sweetness, but it's your very presence which at times saddens me.'

'Saddens you? Why?'

'No, no, it's just . . .' He sighed, kissed her hair, and said, 'you remind me so much of her, you see. I can't help but think of the years we . . . I wasted. We never shared times like these, a walk on the deck, a ball, so many things we should have.'

Ursula knew all about those early years, for Marianne had never tried to hide them from her, telling her everything about her life with James, her promise to Katherine, the way she sometimes felt guilty at not having included George's feelings in her act of self-sacrifice. It had served to reinforce Ursula's view of the romance associated with their relationship. Now, for the first time, she began to understand the pain.

'Have you always loved her?' she asked as he gently rested his arm around her slender waist.

'I was too much of a fool at the start,' he replied sadly, then laughed, forcing his mood to lighten quickly. 'But now I have her beautiful daughter beside me. Ah, but life can be good!'

Ursula moved closer to him. 'Was she very beautiful?'

'As much as you are,' he replied. 'That's why I have this sudden desire to dance with you, to feel other men's envious eyes on me! Come, sweetness, just one whirl before

361

I go to bed and put young men's heaving hearts at ease!'

Her eyes glittered when she stared at him. 'I might well dance with those young men you speak of, but I already know *he's* not aboard this ship.'

George frowned. 'He?'

'Him! The one I want, the young man that you once were!'

He laughed delightfully, relieved that he had not missed being aware of any involvement on her part.

'Now for that dance!' Ursula said gaily, throwing herself into his arms, allowing him to twirl her around the deck as if she were a little girl again.

An elderly couple strolling by watched them, glanced quizzically at each other, then back at the grey-haired man with the excited young woman held tightly in his arms, and wondered.

The ship was five days from Southampton when, for the first time, Ursula thought she saw the man she dreamed of meeting. It was early morning, a grey, blustery day, and she rose early, eager to escape the confines of her cabin and make the most of what remained of the voyage.

She dressed warmly before starting her stroll down the still-empty expanse of the promenade deck. One of the junior officers, a freckled young man named Mort Eagleman, who from the start had not bothered to hide his passion for Ursula, spotted her, called out and barely managed to refrain from running to be at her side. Ursula was polite, almost frostily so, but she hugged her coat tightly about her and kept returning her gaze to the horizon while he chatted away. She hoped Eagleman would be sensitive enough to realise she wished to be left alone. For once, the young man was, for after a few minutes of one-sided conversation, he flashed her a lame salute before sauntering back to the sanctuary of his post.

She continued on to the end of the deck from where she could look down on the area utilised by the tourist-class passengers. At first she thought it was as deserted as the first-class section, but then she spotted a man leaning against the railing, his gaze focused intently on the waters rushing past the ship.

Slim and not very tall, there was something in his stance which made her study him more closely. He was very neatly dressed, his clothes seeming tailor-made, emphasising his broad shoulders, narrow waist and hips. She could not help focusing on the tightness of his buttocks as he stood spread-legged, his hands thrust deep into his trouser pockets. Ursula almost willed him to shift his gaze sideways, just to enable her to see his profile.

It was as though her desire was transmitted telepathically to the stranger for he turned then to glance along the promenade as though he sensed he was being observed. She caught a brief glimpse of his face, saw that he must be in his late twenties, before he looked up, staring directly at her.

She found herself mesmerised by the mocking familiarity in his expression. It was almost a look of arrogance, as if he was enjoying her discomfort at having been caught in her scrutiny of him.

He smiled suddenly, a slightly lop-sided grimace which caused her stomach to tilt. It was a feeling Ursula had never experienced before. She felt herself blush, her body seemed to move of its own accord as she spun away to head back along the deck, torn between escaping the sweet agony of his gaze and the need to see more of him.

The vision of the stranger preyed constantly on her mind, and the thought of him never failed to bring back a delightful tremor, as intense as the moment when he had first looked up at her. Despite repeated sojourns on to the promenade deck at varying times of the day; she failed even to glimpse him again. Once, disguising her need as one of curiosity, she asked George whether he would accompany her to the tourist-class section. He refused gently, saying that if the purchasers of that status ticket were not allowed to enter first class, it would be wrong for them in turn to take advantage of their station aboard ship. Ursula swallowed her frustration and continued her vigil, but to no avail.

When the *Kildonan Castle* steamed into Southampton, she tried one last time to spot him as the passengers disembarked. Her young man continued to elude her.

She and George spent a brief stop-over in England, attended a feather auction in London, then sailed on to France. Her depression deepened upon their arrival in Paris, where bad news in the form of a telegraph awaited them at their hotel. It was from Marianne, informing them of Lady Kenrick's death. Although Ursula had never developed a close affection for her, she knew that Marianne felt differently and would grieve at Lady Kenrick's passing. Anything that touched her mother had its effect on her.

'She was not a warm woman,' said George as he drafted a reply, 'yet she was always kind to me.' After that there was little time for thought of Lady Kenrick or much else apart from the task at hand.

They spent a week in Paris, days filled with tension as George went about his dangerous mission, making contact with parties prepared to lend more than mere moral support to the Boer cause. He was ably assisted by his marketing agent, a jovial Frenchman named Philippe Bruyère, who had a good idea of who could be trusted to respect the confidentiality of the subject, even though they might not be prepared to provide support. Both George and Philippe were aware that the British anticipated aid for the Boers to come from European sources and that there were bound to be agents in France.

Although he kept Ursula informed of his progress, George was adamant that she refrain from being present at any meetings or discussions.

'But that's why I'm here with you,' she protested, 'to ensure your safety!'

'Your presence is support enough,' he replied firmly. 'There's no need for you to take unnecessary risks. Your mother and I agreed on that. It's enough that you accompany me from place to place, that we're seen together.'

'Do you think we're being watched?' she asked then, knowing there was no point in pursuing the argument any further. George had made up his mind and that was that.

He was silent for a while, then said, 'No, I don't think so. But it's best not to take chances.'

Despite the circumstances of their visit, George was, however, not insensitive to his stepdaughter's needs. After the first few days of negotiations, he insisted on showing her round the city, taking her to places he and Marianne had visited when she had first come to Europe, speaking freely about how disconcerted he had been by her presence. But Ursula's thoughts kept turning to how she would have enjoyed those same places with the man who had escaped her.

Apart from George's clandestine activities, they paid visits to all their regular distributors, at which Ursula participated as her stepfather's business associate, enjoying the way men's gazes changed from admiration of her beauty to respect for her knowledge about the market.

At one such meeting, the elderly chief of a major distribution network remarked, 'I once had the privilege of meeting your mother, when I visited the Cape Colony. I'm glad to learn her forward vision on quality was not limited merely to the production of feathers.' Having made the comment, he immediately went on discussing business, as if emphasising that his remark had been not simple flattery but a sincere and objective comment. She felt grateful to the old man for having impressed upon her that she was not just a child with a passing interest in the family business, but a concerned and professional participant. She felt rightly proud of herself, and became even more determined to support George in any way she could to make his covert mission a success. Yet she was unable to forget the face that continued to haunt her.

From Paris they went to Switzerland and Germany, then on to Vienna, where George had arranged meetings with a group of Germans who had responded to his subtle signals from Paris. Ursula visited massive warehouses filled with feathers, attended auctions where buyers vied for the best-quality feathers, and still found time to explore the old city, in the process falling prey to the beauty and charm of Europe.

'Everything's been arranged,' George told her towards the end of their stay in Vienna.

'They'll supply what is needed?'

'That's not for me to negotiate, little one. The Boer republics will send in their own man to conclude things. He's already in Paris, waiting for word.'

'But how could they have been so certain the Germans would agree?'

He shrugged and said, 'They weren't. But time is of the essence, so they decided to risk sending someone. A wise decision in retrospect, no?'

Ursula nodded. 'Do you know him?'

He hesitated, then smiled shyly. 'He came to Paris on the same ship as we did, crossed over to France on the same day.'

She stared at him in shock. 'My God – we stopped in England! He could have—'

'He had false papers, Ursula – don't be alarmed.' George wondered whether her anxiety was for the Boer representative or for him. Or both. Perhaps he should have kept her informed about everything. 'The man's father was German,' he explained, 'so some of his identity is real.'

Whatever Ursula felt about the matter was overruled by her curiosity. 'Who is he – did you meet him secretly?'

'Only once. It was too dangerous. He kept pretty much to himself during the voyage – just in case.'

Ursula nodded slowly, feeling no resentment at how George had kept some things from her for she knew he had acted out of concern for her safety. She formed a mental picture of a bearded man with stern eyes, wide-brimmed hat and ragged, home-spun clothes, for that was how the newspapers depicted the Boers.

They returned to Philippe Bruyère's offices on their first day back in Paris. The Frenchman was overjoyed to hear of the success of George's negotiations, flirted merrily with Ursula and then made sure the door to his office was securely closed before saying, 'He is ready to move.'

'He's safe?' asked George, making Ursula wish they would tell her more about the Boer, the mysterious 'he'.

'The people who are housing him,' Philippe explained, 'are completely trustworthy. While you were away I had his papers checked as well. They're excellent. As an added precaution, though, the right people will be on duty when he crosses the border.'

'You've done well, Philippe. I'm in your debt, old friend.'

366

Philippe gave a Gallic shrug. 'I share your sentiments on this war. Do you wish to meet with him one last time?'

'Gentlemen.' They both turned to stare at Ursula as if noticing her for the first time. 'That's right,' she said caustically, 'I do speak, see and hear.'

The two men glanced at each other, Philippe questioningly. Then George laughed. 'We apologise,' he said. 'It's just—'

'I know, I know!' she interjected, smiling to show she was not really offended. 'It's for my own good.' She stood up and reached for the door. 'The point I wanted to make was that if you have no real need for me here, then I'd much rather chat to Philippe's secretary about the best places to buy clothes before we leave.' She smiled sweetly at George and added, 'Better not to take chances, no?'

'Chances?'

'Really! Don't you think it would arouse suspicion if a woman, especially one involved in fashion, visited Paris and left without buying any clothes?'

George and Philippe stared at her, then at each other, knowing she was right.

'You will be taken to Worth's,' said Philippe, and was rewarded by Ursula's satisfied smile, for it was every young woman's dream to visit that establishment. Once a poor Lincolnshire boy, Worth had become one of Paris's most famed couturiers. 'We supply them with feathers,' continued Philippe. 'Mireille,' he added, referring to his secretary, 'will be thrilled to accompany you.'

Ursula smiled sweetly at both of them, waved in farewell and left the room.

CHAPTER THIRTY-FIVE

The day after their meeting with Philippe Bruyère, George asked Ursula to accompany him to a feather auction taking place that afternoon.

She had planned on seeing some more of the delights of Paris now that their mission was completed. There were only a few days left before they were scheduled to return to the Cape, and she had hoped to persuade George to take her to the opera. Now, she sensed he was tense and uneasy, so she readily agreed to escort him to the auction, suspecting he was not going there for the sake of the event itself. She vowed to keep her eyes and ears open.

The hall they went to was large and filled with more people than Ursula had ever seen at any auction before. Prospective bidders inspected feather stocks, discussed quality with their colleagues.

There were a surprising number of women present, unlike the feather auctions in England or Austria. Dressed in the height of fashion, they appeared to stroll aimlessly around the vast hall. Their practised eyes, however, were taking stock of who was wearing what and in whose company.

The pitch of feverish activity and excitement within the hall was high, and a babble of voices filled the air as French buyers argued about the quality and price of the latest batch of ostrich feathers.

'Will there be any of Ratitãe's crop among this?' asked Ursula. George kept his hand firmly clamped around her elbow to avoid being separated from her by the crush of the crowd.

'There most likely is,' he replied, his gaze moving constantly across the crowd as if searching for a specific face. He's here! she thought triumphantly – their Boer agent was at the auction, to meet with George! At last she would see him, meet him. She was so excited she hardly heard George finish replying to her question, 'The feathers that aren't earmarked for our distributors could end up at any auction.'

The next moment there was no sound, no sensation other than the electrifying wave of pleasure that seemed to engulf her entire body. There he was, just a few yards away – her young man from the ship! Was it possible? But it was him, staring back at her with that same mocking smile. His gaze shifted by only a few inches to settle on George. Ursula glanced quickly at her stepfather and saw him give a slight shake of his head. The tremor which gripped her then was one of shock, for she realised who the young man was. Their Boer – but could it be? He was too young, too . . . civilised?

When she turned her gaze back to where he had been standing, he was no longer there. She scanned the crowds, but he had disappeared.

At that same moment her attention was drawn by another, very different, face, standing some distance from them, a man who jerked his gaze away when she looked at him. He was very tall, towering over the shorter Frenchmen. His features were unusual, finely sculpted, yet containing a hint of cruelty. A dangerous man, she realised instinctively and felt a spasm of alarm when he glanced at them again, trying to make the gesture appear fleeting. *Them* – she realised with a shock – he had looked at *them*, not *her*!

George's grip on her arm was suddenly firmer. 'Is something wrong? You're shaking!'

'We – we're being watched! At least I think so. That man over—'

'Don't look! Describe him to me.' He held her arm tightly, as if fearing her legs would not support her.

Her heart seemed to beat in her throat. 'He's . . . he's very tall, slightly bald, standing there . . . on your right, on the far side of the hall. Oh God!'

'Don't panic – it might be nothing.' George changed

position, shifting so that his scrutiny of the area where Ursula had seen the man would not seem too obvious.

'The other one, the Boer, he's here, isn't he? The young man you nodded at just now?'

'Yes.'

Even though her mind still reeled in disbelief, she felt George's tension transmit itself through his fingers clamped tightly around her arm. Throughout their travels she had found their situation exciting, almost a childlike game of make-believe. Now it was very real, very frightening.

George's grip tightened, hurting her with its force. 'You're right!' he hissed with frustration. 'We've been betrayed!'

'What now? Is—'

'You must leave,' he interrupted. 'Our man will take you back to the hotel. Wait for me there – No, pack our things, contact Philippe and leave with him when he arrives to fetch you. Go now!'

'And you? I can't—'

'Just go!' His expression softened and he squeezed her arm, gently this time. 'I'll be safe, little one. I'll join you soon.' He looked over her head and nodded at someone, indicating Ursula with a roll of his eyes. The Boer?

Her protest was lost in the sudden swelling of noise as the crowd surged forward when bidding started at one side of the hall. Someone jostled her from behind, forcing her apart from George.

She was caught up in the human stream, forced along on its urgent tide. Her body went along with the flow, unable to resist. The bright colours in the hall – ladies' fashions, soft feathers, the pungent mix of tobacco and expensive perfumes – all joined in a vicious assault on her confused senses, adding to her terror. 'George!' she shouted in vain.

She was jostled again, so hard that this time she almost fell down. Strong hands gripped her shoulders and held her on her feet. 'Come with me!'

As she swung around she looked up into the face of the man they had come to meet. 'It's safe,' the Boer agent shouted above the din. 'Just come with me.'

'But George!'

'He'll be fine – trust me! Come!' He held on to her and started to move backwards, using his body to force a path through the crowd, ignoring the verbal abuse of the Frenchmen as he elbowed them roughly aside.

Ursula was torn between being hauled to safety by the young man and trying to get back to George's side. She tried to glimpse him, could not at first, but then saw him join the crowd struggling for good positions. The stranger she had identified to him moved closer, removing any remaining doubts she might have had about his true purpose there.

Suddenly she and the young man pulling her along behind him were at the exit. She glanced back one last time, but could see only the backs and shoulders of people as they pushed closer to the auctioneers, pens raised to scribble the latest prices in the small notebooks clutched in their hands.

The grey afternoon light had given way to night, making the bright light in the hall appear harsh as it burst through the open door when they stumbled out on to the pavement. Crisp air slammed into her, so that she reeled back and would have lost her balance if not for the firm grip around her wrist. 'Take a deep breath,' the Boer said, signalling a cab at the same time.

He bustled her inside, settled himself in his seat, then smiled at her. 'George will be all right, I promise you. They won't dare harm him.'

'What will they do?'

'Nothing, except watch him. Fortunately he'd planned for such a possibility – my instructions were to get you out of there if things went wrong.'

She stared at him in the dark, trying to get a better look at the face that had had such an effect on her when she first saw it. She still found it hard to comprehend that this young man, well dressed and groomed and speaking English without a trace of an accent, could be an agent for the Boer republics. 'Who are you?' she asked in an unsteady voice.

He smiled again. 'Henry Ritter. The rest . . . well, I gather you're fully informed on that.'

'Henry Ritter? That's your real name?'

He laughed softly. Ursula found the sound comforting, his calm reassuring her somewhat. 'Yes, it's my real name, my authentic name. Although I must confess it does appear on some not-so-authentic documents.' He leaned closer, so that she saw the whiteness of his teeth. 'And you,' he said, 'are Ursula. You see? We Boers are not so barbaric that we don't first establish the identity of a pretty woman before that of our enemy.'

Ursula smiled at his attempt to relieve her anxiety. 'And who is this enemy, the one there with George?'

Ritter shrugged. 'English, I suspect. Or a Frenchman on their pay-roll. He probably heard something about George's discussions, that's all, and thought it might be worth while keeping an eye on him.'

'Not on you?' Despite her fears for George, she felt herself relaxing. She was not sure whether the rapid pounding of her heart was from their risky situation or from Henry Ritter's presence.

'No, I am unknown to them. Or I should be – I've not made any kind of contact apart from with George and Philippe Bruyère. George is the one who did all that, he's the one they'd like to know more about. Even if our spy saw us leave – which I think he did – he'd stay with George.'

When they reached the hotel, Henry repeated her step-father's instructions that she should pack their things in readiness to move out. 'I'll contact Philippe to find out where we should go. He's provided a safe house in case of a situation like this. You'll stay there till you leave.'

'And George?'

'Once he's rid himself of the fellow watching him, he'll contact Philippe and meet you there. Probably tomorrow morning.' He stared intently at her, smiled and said, 'I'll look after you till then.'

Ursula jerked her gaze away before he could see how this affected her. She felt almost relieved to escape to her room to pack.

An hour later, Philippe arrived to escort them to safety, adding his own reassurances regarding George's well-being.

The place to which he took them was situated in the

back streets, a small but well-maintained suite of rooms above a bakery. 'You will be quite safe here,' he told her before rushing off again to await word from George.

Henry seemed restless now, constantly peering down through the curtains at the dark street below.

She used the opportunity to study him more closely. As she had first noticed, he was not a big man, just slightly taller than herself. Apart from the wide spread of his shoulders, his body was lean, even slight, yet he exuded a strength which was more than just mental. Nor was he particularly good-looking, she thought; not until those eyes smiled in that certain way, containing both amusement and fervour. But somehow the package deserved closer inspection.

A woman's flirtatious laugh drifted up from the street, answered by a man's voice speaking in low tones. The woman laughed again, the sound filled with excited anticipation.

'I saw you on the ship,' she said lamely, wanting to break the silence reigning between them.

He turned from his vigil to stare at her, his gaze intent, mesmerising, the kind women were either drawn to or else ran from. 'Yes,' he said slowly, leaning back against the curtains, 'on that cold, grey morning.'

Ursula lowered her eyes. 'Have you ever been to Oudtshoorn?' she asked when he said nothing more.

Henry smiled then, the gesture releasing some of the tension from the room. 'No,' he replied thoughtfully, 'although I'd like to. Perhaps . . . if someone invited me to come.' He raised his eyebrows and his smile spread.

She felt her cheeks glow. Was he just teasing her – or was it more than that?

'Perhaps after the war,' he said, releasing her from the need to respond.

'Yes,' she heard herself say, 'I'm sure George would love to have you.'

'I'd like to have thought it would be his daughter who extended the invitation. Not only is she very beautiful, but brave also. I admire her.' He came to sit beside her as she sank on to the couch, unable to trust her legs any longer. Her entire body tingled at his nearness.

'I – I admire you too. For what you're doing.' If he touched her now, if he laid so much as a finger on her . . .

But he had moved away, rising to his feet again. 'There is some cognac in the kitchen,' he said. Why was he changing the subject – did he think she was too young for him? Or had he merely been amusing himself with her, a way of passing the time while he waited for George to arrive?

'No, thank you,' she replied crisply.

'It'll help you relax.'

'I'm quite all right.'

'Well, I'm not!' he called out from inside the kitchen. 'Tonight gave me quite a fright.' He came back with the bottle and two glasses in his hands. 'Quite sure?'

'All right – a small one.' Was he pretending to be unsettled by the night's events just to make her feel better?

She sipped the drink slowly, enjoying the feel of its warmth spreading rapidly through her body. She could feel his eyes on her, and kept her own fixed on the floor at her feet.

'Another small one,' he said, standing before her. 'To help you sleep.'

'I don't want to sleep – I want to wait for George.'

'He won't be here till day-break. It's best that we both rest. Come, one more sip.'

She handed him her empty glass and felt a shock pass through her when his fingers accidentally touched hers. 'When are you leaving?' she asked, her voice throaty.

'For Germany? After tonight, the sooner the better. I'll speak to Philippe, try to arrange it for tomorrow.'

Tomorrow! She'd never see him again after tonight. But what did it matter? He was nothing but a not-too-handsome yet dashing stranger, a man to whom she meant nothing. Just an insignificant attraction, that's all. Her mental reassurances did not help; Henry Ritter was the only man she ever wanted to see again.

'And now,' he said, taking her hand in his, 'you should try to get some sleep. I'll be just outside your door, so don't be scared.'

She allowed herself to be led to the tiny bedroom like a child, hating herself for accepting it, yet unable to pull free from his touch. He let go of her hand when he reached the door. 'Good-night,' she said, sorry that her time with him had ended so swiftly.

'Ursula?'

'Yes?'

He stood close to her, his eyes smiling, yet free of any sign of mockery. 'I might be gone by morning, and I – I just wanted you to know I meant what I said about visiting Oudtshoorn when the war is over. But it's not the town I'm interested in.'

Her pulse seemed to beat right through the skin of her neck. Did he really mean it?

'Will I be welcome?'

'I – yes,' she said and felt her own smile form. 'Yes! We – I'd love to have you there.'

They stared at each other for a long while before he smiled again, gently touched her cheek, then left the room.

The morning chill woke Ursula at the same time as the sound of footsteps on the wooden floor outside her room. She tugged the blankets tightly around her and thought sleepily of Henry Ritter. Had she dreamed it or had he really spoken those words to her? No, it was no dream! No dream could form as clear a picture of his eyes as she had seen them last night. He had looked at her the way a man looks at a woman he wants. It's happened, she thought happily. That *something* she always knew was missing had taken place.

The soft knock on her door brought her reeling senses back to earth. George? Had he come yet?

'Ursula?' Thank God – he was safe!

'Come in,' she called out and sat up in bed, keeping the covers up around her neck in case Henry should follow her stepfather inside.

George was on his own. He rushed to her side, gripped her tightly when she reached out for him. 'Oh, you're safe!' she whispered. 'You're safe!'

'Yes, little one – the British agent made the mistake of assuming I was a stranger to Paris.' He laughed, appearing in no way alarmed by his experience. 'It was simple losing him in the alleys. An amateur!'

She joined in his laughter, relieved just to have him back with her.

'Your Mr Ritter took good care of me,' she told him. 'I have still to thank him properly.'

'There'll be no opportunity for that, I'm afraid. Henry left after I arrived. About five o'clock this morning.'

George misread her crestfallen expression and said, 'There's no need to be concerned. Henry is a capable man. He knows how to look after himself.' He kissed her forehead and stood up. 'I've some coffee on the boil. Stay in bed – the air's very cold. I'll bring it to you.'

'George?'

He turned at the door. 'Yes?'

Ursula pushed back her tousled hair. 'He's the one.'

George leaned back against the door frame and studied the young woman he loved as if she were his own flesh and blood. He nodded slowly, acknowledging what she said. 'Yes,' he said softly, 'I can understand how he could be. But you will have to be patient, my sweet one – Henry's first love is to his fatherland. Although, now he's seen you, that might change. Henry Ritter is no fool!'

He smiled and went to fetch their coffee. As he busied himself in the kitchen, he thought anxiously how Ursula's and Henry's situation paralleled that of his own and Marianne's. In their case it had been Marianne's promise to Katherine that had kept them apart. Ursula and Henry had to overcome a war.

'Please, God,' he whispered aloud as he took a cup in each hand and headed back to the room, 'let it be over soon.'

As he handed the cup to Ursula, George wondered whether his own recent efforts had not perhaps helped to extend it.

CHAPTER THIRTY-SIX

Stanley arrived back on Ratitāe two weeks after the return of George and Ursula. He seemed less restless now, although he carried with him an air of confidence which troubled Marianne. She tried telling herself it was possible that his travels had, in some miraculous way, matured him – a woman, perhaps? – yet still the sense of unease gnawed at her.

She tried more than once to get him to talk about his experiences in America, but he divulged nothing other than that he had found his visit very interesting. Marianne gave up, concentrating instead on her enjoyment at having George and Ursula with her once again, heaping all her attention on her daughter, who struggled with the new-found sensation of thwarted love.

If Stanley appeared calm on the surface, inside he trembled with nervous anticipation. His visit to the United States had been far more than the holiday Marianne had intended for him.

Using the notes he had found in James's trunk in the attic above the townhouse, Stanley had gone about tracking down the farm to which James had been sending ostriches before his death. After only two days in New York itself, he headed for Florida.

The few ostrich farms he encountered during his travels were a disappointment, little more than experimental ventures, often only an unimportant side-line to other farming activities. The feathers were of inferior quality, far removed from the double-fluff variety which had made Oudtshoorn famous for its produce. There existed no organised system for buying and selling of feathers and he came to the conclusion that the Americans were riding the crest of a wave, at a time when anyone with a minimum knowledge of the birds could make money from them. Nowhere did he come across any attempt to plant lucerne.

When he eventually found the farm he sought, it was even more of a disappointment than those he had seen before.

The farmer's name was Grant Tyler, a large-boned man with skin made leathery by the sun. 'They're *your* birds, son,' he told Stanley after extending his condolences on James's death. 'Wondered why I'd had no further word from him,' he added gruffly.

Tyler grabbed at his hat when a sudden gust of wind rasped across the dry land. 'Your pa sent 'em to me to take care of, that's all,' he went on, blinking away the loose dust blown into his eyes by the wind. 'Ain't paid nothing for 'em. He said I's to keep the money from whatever feathers they produced in the meantime, though. Can't say there's been much of that. You come to set up your own place?'

Stanley shook his head. 'Not yet,' he replied, struggling to fight down the misery he felt. He tried to look on the bright side, telling himself the place was wide open for someone with knowledge and vision. *He* was that person.

He knelt to scoop up a handful of sand. The wind snatched it away when he slowly released it. 'No pebbles,' he said, wondering what the ostriches used to triturate their food.

'The ostriches make do with the sand,' explained Tyler. 'I give 'em bone-meal when I can lay my hands on some. But, hell – it gets damned expensive!'

Stanley took his leave of the farmer with the promise that he would send word when he was ready to come to America. 'Help you get set up,' offered Tyler.

The prospects awaiting him occupied Stanley's thoughts for most of the remainder of his travels. There was nothing he couldn't do once he'd got started: set up his own organisation to buy and sell; import the right ostrich stock to enhance

378

quality with the minimum of delay. He had to move fast, though, before someone else got a head start.

In December – just ten months away – he'd turn twenty-one and receive his thirty per cent share of Ratitãe. What would it be worth, he wondered – enough to get started?

He thought of his agreement with Denker, sure now that it would take too long to achieve what they wanted. Then, too, it would not be as easy as the Dutchman thought to ruin Ursula and Marianne. He had to concede that his half-sister had become too proficient in ostrich breeding to be easily fooled. Denker's plan of introducing a disease into her flocks would not work. No, it had been a childish goal. Let the Dutchman find his own way of gaining whatever it was he wanted from Ratitãe!

In any case, Stanley had not seen Denker for some time, not since the outbreak of the war. There had been no word, just the sudden appearance of a new coach driver in his place. Denker's replacement was unable to tell him what had become of his predecessor. He wondered whether perhaps the Dutchman was dead, the thought bringing with it a measure of relief.

By starting in America without delay he would make his father's dream become a reality that much sooner. Ursula and the others would suffer so much more later. When he was ready, not all the knowledge and skills in the world would help them survive. Ratitãe would be ruined, although that no longer mattered to him – not since they had stolen it from him and his father.

By the time Stanley returned to Oudtshoorn, he was ready to implement his plans. The only obstacle he faced was how to sell his share to the highest bidder without Marianne stopping him. He would have to wait, be patient for a few months, till it was too late for them to try and rob him again.

The Laboulayes decided October was a good time to hold a party on Ratitãe, for no other reason than to celebrate the coming of spring and an unprecedented demand for quality feathers. Also, both George and Marianne were delighted at

Ursula's sudden happiness after many months of moping around, with her fears for what had become of Henry Ritter etched on her taut features. For the first time since meeting him in Paris, Ursula had received word from her love.

It was only a short note written on a crumpled piece of paper, hastily scrawled somewhere on the open veld of the Orange Free State where Henry rode with a commando. She had read the words over and over again, trying to smooth out the creases without further damaging it. It was a miracle it had reached her.

All that mattered were his stated intentions in regard to her, and that he would be coming for her as soon as the war was ended. There was little apart from that; no mention of the status of the war, which Ursula knew was going against the Boers now that the British were pouring in more and more resources. But at least she now knew that he was alive.

More than a hundred guests attended the party, all of them comfortably catered for on the spacious lawns in front of the main house. The evening air was warm enough to remain outdoors, although arrangements had also been made in the house in case the night turned cool.

It was not an ostentatious event, yet those in attendance were pleased to have been invited, as it was considered an honour to attend a social function on the great farm.

An orchestra played on a bandstand beside the specially assembled dance floor, raised some feet above the ground and positioned in the centre of a circle of gaily bedecked tables. Ursula danced with any man who asked her, enjoying life for the first time in months. She was quite exhausted when she finally took her seat beside George. She kissed his cheek and whispered, 'It's wonderful – just what I needed!'

Stanley sat at the same table, almost directly opposite her. Her show of happiness made him scowl darkly. So, he thought, she had a lover. It had been Ursula herself who told him, although she did not add that Henry was a Boer soldier.

He had wondered whether the relationship might yet prove to be a blessing in disguise. If Ursula married, she might well find her desire for a family overruling her passion for farming. Perhaps her husband – whoever the man might be – would even take her away from Ratitāe. But why worry about that, when he had made up his mind he had no desire for the farm?

His scorn for her was replaced by the lurching of his stomach, caused by the volume of wine he'd consumed. A further spasm of giddiness gripped him, making him shut his eyes in an attempt to control his nausea. Stanley had been drunk only once before, with Denker behind the coach station. He'd stayed sick for days after.

He raised his glass to his lips, but his elbow slipped from the table, causing red wine to splash on to the stark white table-cloth. 'Shit,' he muttered loudly enough for the guests at the table to hear. They shifted in their chairs and stared at him.

'Stanley,' said Marianne, leaning forward, 'don't you think you've had enough?'

He stared back with red-rimmed eyes. 'Yes,' he agreed. 'But enough of what?' He pointed at the glass, then waved his hand in the direction of the general assembly. He turned back to Marianne with raised eyebrows. 'Of what?' he asked again.

Her mouth tightened, but she made no reply as George rested his hand gently on her arm. 'It's a party,' he said, smiling at the guests. 'A man has a right to have a little too much to drink. I know I have!' He laughed, and some of the others joined him, although they still stared strangely at Stanley.

He glared at George, hating him for having tried to reduce the tension. Always the do-gooder, he thought bitterly. He drained his glass, stood up and staggered away from the table. There was a visible relaxation all round.

Ursula glanced at her mother. 'I'll talk to him,' she whispered. Before Marianne could respond, she headed after him.

He was standing among the group of assembled carts, coaches and wagons when she caught up with him. He held on to the side of the cart, swaying so much she thought he would fall over at any moment. The drivers watched with amusement.

'Stanley,' she said softly, touching his shoulder. He jerked away from her. 'Oh, Stanley,' she tried again, giving a sad shake of her head, 'why are you always so bitter? Can't you try to be nice to George and Mother for a change? You're always so—'

'Just leave me alone, damn you!' He lurched dangerously but managed to grab hold of the cart again.

Ursula turned away with a sigh of disgust. Stanley's voice stopped her.

'You want my – my share, dear sis-ster?' He hiccuped loudly.

'What do you mean?' She moved back to where he stood, alert to the viciousness in his voice.

'M-my share of Ratitãe. You want it?'

'No one wants what's yours,' she replied calmly. 'Go to bed, Stanley. You're very drunk.'

'Can have it . . . you can. Just pay what Eben Du Toit . . . what he's prepared to. Happy then. You . . . me . . . both happy.'

She watched him in silence, his gaze trying to maintain its focus on her. Did he want to sell his share in Ratitãe? But what was that about Eben Du Toit? Would Stanley go so far as to sell his part of the farm to an outsider? It had to be!

'Does Eben want to buy your share?' she asked, thinking about the pompous Eben Du Toit. Marianne would never permit it. But could they stop him?

He snickered and lurched when he let go of the side of the cart. Quickly he reached out again. 'Lotsa money. Worth lots.'

'But why sell, Stanley? And to an outsider? Mother would have lent you money if you needed any.'

His guffaw was so loud it turned the heads of the guests nearest them. 'Lend?' He laughed again, more controlled this time. 'No, no – not for – for what I want to do.'

'And just what is that?' She noticed a thin stream of saliva flow from the corner of his mouth.

'Go to 'merica,' he slurred. 'Start there. My own.'

She stiffened. 'You're mad,' she said softly. 'Your bitterness has made you quite mad.' She swung round and walked rapidly back to the tables.

She heard him start to speak, but the sound broke into a rasping cough. When she turned he was being sick, bent double while he clung to the cart. You poor man, she thought with sudden pity. If only you could as easily disgorge the hostility within you.

America. Had it been merely a threat, or more? She had to speak to George and Marianne. Not right away though; it could wait till morning, for Stanley was in no condition to be of any danger to them just then.

Stanley glared at Marianne across the desk. He was slouched in his chair, yet his face revealed his tension. George stood at the side of the study, resting his hands on the wide window-sill.

'You have no right to do this,' Stanley snarled, although he did not raise his eyes to look at either of them. 'It's *my* share – I can sell to anybody I want.' Damn Ursula, he thought morosely, but he was equally angry at himself for having allowed liquor to betray his secret. A brief moment of enjoyable spite towards her, and now his careful plans were to be thwarted. Even though Eben Du Toit had kept his mouth shut about the intended sale, Marianne would stop it going through now that she knew of his plans. She had enough influence – but could she legally do that?

Marianne watched him closely, her own expression one of complete calm. 'Even if you do sell to Eben Du Toit or anyone else,' she said, 'you're naïve to think I'd allow the money from the sale to leave the Colony.'

'What you wish to allow is of no consequence,' he spat back, but his tone lacked confidence. She would do it, too, the greedy bitch!

'Over the years,' continued Marianne, 'I've made sure every farmer involved in ostriches is fully aware of the threat America poses to our industry in the longer term. You can be sure no ostriches – and certainly no money – will move from here to America. Not again.' She glanced at George, then pressed on. 'One word from me and those farmers will employ their own methods to ensure Mr Du Toit refrains from taking up your offer. Do you understand?'

He looked up at last, his eyes blazing with frustrated hatred. Marianne met his gaze evenly. 'You've no right,' he hissed. 'No right!'

She allowed herself a small grin of satisfaction. 'Right doesn't enter into it, Stanley. It's power – influence – and right now I'm the one who possesses both. You have neither.'

He spun from the chair and reached for the door. 'Stanley!' The strength of Marianne's voice stopped him. He turned slowly back towards her.

'I'm prepared to make it easier for you,' she said, indicating he should resume his seat. He acquiesced in spite of his outrage.

'I will pay you what your share is worth,' she said slowly, pointedly. 'I'll even let you take the money out. To America. But not one bird, not a single chick.'

'I'll not—'

'Let me finish!' She waited till he had subsided back in his chair. 'I'll let all that take place, on condition you're out of here within a month. So you see, I'm even being gracious by letting you have your money almost two months before your inheritance is due.'

Stanley glared at her but made no response. He knew he would accept her offer – but to have her beat him this way, demean him like this . . .

'Once you have left,' continued Marianne, 'you will never again have contact with us, with Ratitāe, or with anybody connected to the ostrich industry in the Colony. Is that clear? If you do, I'll find a way to ruin you. I promise you that. When you leave here, you will cease to exist as a member of this family. Do you accept my terms?'

He rose stiffly to his feet, feeling as though his legs would not carry his weight when he stepped towards the door.

'Do you accept, Stanley? I'm not so gracious as to allow you time to think it over. You must give your answer now. Do you accept?'

He stopped, his body seeming about to snap from tension. He felt their eyes on him, felt their power holding him in its grip.

384

'Yes.' It was a whisper, a sigh. Then he managed to walk out of the study.

Marianne's head ached, threatened to burst. She let out her own sigh, one of pain and humiliation at what she had been forced to do. It did not help to tell herself it had been done for Ratitāe, that Katherine would not have blamed her. Stanley had never been her cousin's child – he could not be! – he belonged to James in every sense. Even while Katherine's body was forming him into human shape, he had borne the stamp of the man who had not truly loved her.

She felt George's hand on her shoulder, the touch gentle and reassuring. She reached out her own and placed it on his. 'Do not feel guilt, my love,' he said softly. 'It would have been James all over again, but this time Ursula would have been the one to suffer the hatred. You could never allow that.'

'No,' she whispered and laid his palm against her cheek, his skin warm against the cold of her tears. 'No,' she said again. 'I couldn't, could I?'

Yet, when the day came for Stanley to leave Ratitāe and their lives, Marianne could not help wondering again whether her actions were not a betrayal of the promise she had made her cousin.

But it was too late to change that now.

CHAPTER THIRTY-SEVEN

It was a long, rugged valley, a pit in the earth carved a thousand feet down from the high mountains shrouded in mist. Bare walls of vertical rock scrambled up to scratch at the sky, so that its very inaccessibility secured its sanctuary over the centuries.

The first people to seek the protection of its isolation were the Bushmen who made their homes in its caves. The white man's guns, in the hands of other men of colour, the Hottentots, drove them out at last. But the canyon remained unchanged.

Then the white man came, a few families determined to escape British officialdom. They grew wheat and fruit sufficient for their simple needs, hunting with superb skill when dietary demands warranted it.

The valley was their home, the mountains their protective wall against the world. They named it Gamkaskloof, others called it the Hell.

A frenzied wind churned its way up the crags of rock to twist and tug through narrow fissures and granite funnels. It plucked furiously at a solitary figure battling up the slope as though it sensed he was not one of those the valley safeguarded. Just twenty-four hours ago, a band of intruders had penetrated its protective fringe. Now, one of them defied the authority of wind and rock on his own.

Henry Ritter cursed as he stopped to regain his breath. Blood flowed from the gashes and scratches inflicted on his hands by the sharp rock, some of the wounds raw from the previous day's descent. The jagged hole left in his leg by an English bullet throbbed angrily as he gently massaged the protesting muscles surrounding it.

They had chosen well, he thought, recalling how he and his fellow Boer riders had practically stumbled across the hidden valley.

Theirs had been a long journey. They had joined up with the column of Jan Smuts at the end of August 1901, when the Transvaal Boers had cut the barbed wire of the British, slipped past the patrols and entered the Orange Free State. The leaders of the embattled Free State commandos had added their men to the column intent on reaching the Cape itself, to harass the British and save the Boer supporters who had been branded rebels by the Empire. It was a final, desperate attempt to turn the tide of the war.

The men under the command of Jan Smuts travelled light and lived off the land. They had no uniform, although some of them sported khaki jackets and leather boots taken from captured British soldiers. Their saddle-bags held a single blanket, a small canvas to ward off the worst of the rain, some rusks and biltong and a small three-legged pot. And a Bible.

They faced bitter cold and wet on their travels, their tough ponies suffering as much as the men, sometimes pushed to do sixty miles hard riding in one day. Dozens of them died from exposure while others struggled on as their riders tumbled out of their saddles from weariness and hunger. There was no turning back; there was nothing to return to except farms devastated by the British and the Boers' wives and children held behind the barbed wire of concentration camps.

When the Boer forces finally stopped near Algoa Bay on 4 September 1901, only 250 of them faced the concentrated attention of 35,000 British soldiers.

As the forces seeking to destroy them escalated, Jan Smuts split his tiny army into separate commandos for easier movement. Henry stayed with the commando of Deneys Reitz as it slipped from the coast and sought the open plains of the Karoo to rendezvous with Smuts once again. The hazards of the journey faded from his mind as he thought how close he was to Ursula. So close, and yet so far.

For days they managed to elude the British who dominated the Little Karoo, bypassing the heavily guarded Meiring Poort. Further west, they had to turn and flee eastwards again when they came across a strong force of British near the Seven Weeks Poort. It was during this skirmish that Henry had been shot in the leg.

At last they entered the daunting Swartberg Mountains, commencing their climb when the sun was at its zenith. For three hours they battled with the mist and uncompromising terrain. As they began their descent, they broke through the cloud layer to see a canyon and a ragged cluster of huts far below them. The riders started forward, thinking that there would be natives to guide them to safety across the mountains.

They were forced to abandon the horses after a while, leaving them untethered in the shadow of a deep ravine, and it was dark when they reached the canyon floor. They approached the huts with rifles at the ready.

They found not natives but white people who welcomed them in a strange form of Dutch and served them goat's meat, milk and wild honey. The Boers were assured they were the first soldiers – Boer or British – to have ventured into the secluded valley.

It was early the following morning when Deneys Reitz took Henry to one side. 'You won't last with that leg of yours,' the commando leader said with a gentle smile. 'It'll get worse, and we'll be forced to abandon you.' Henry nodded, knowing that no single man would be allowed to slow the commando's progress to the southern Cape.

'There's little chance of your making it back to the Free State,' continued Reitz. 'It might be best to give yourself up to the British. At least they'll care for your wound.'

'No! I won't surrender to them. Not now! I'll try to make it to Oudtshoorn – I have friends there.'

'You realise there's a good chance you'll be captured, don't you?'

'A chance,' agreed Henry, squinting into the rising sun. 'But there's also a chance I can disappear in Oudtshoorn, assume life as an ordinary citizen. I'll come back when the war's over – we'll all have to help rebuild our country.'

Reitz smiled at his unspoken reference to a British victory. They had been in the saddle long enough to have lost the patriotic zeal which had characterised their earlier actions in the field. He studied the man beside him, sorry to be losing him. When Henry had joined the commando shortly before they left for the Cape, Reitz had known he had no battle experience. He also knew of how Henry had served the Boer republics on a different front. Reitz admired any form of courage, so he had welcomed the young man into his ranks. It did not take long to determine that Henry's courage extended to physical battle as well.

'We'll be guided out this evening,' Reitz said. 'We'll spend the night where we left the horses, then head for the northern plains at day-break.'

'I'll pray for you and my comrades,' replied Henry, staring up at the towering cliffs. 'I'll leave this afternoon. If the Khakis catch me, I'll tell them I deserted you west of Seven Weeks Poort. They won't think of searching for you north of here.'

They stood in silence, taking a wordless departure from each other as their minds flitted over the past and reached tremulously for the future. Reitz said, 'I'm sure we'll meet again . . . whatever the outcome of this war.'

'I'll be back.' They shook hands before Henry moved off to collect his gear. The men watched him, then slowly stood up and said farewell. There was neither time for explanation, nor any demanded of him.

He could no longer see them from his present position. He envied them the sunshine warming them while he shivered in the cold and damp of the overhanging rocks. Taking a deep breath, he forced himself to his feet; there was no time to waste, for a long journey awaited him.

The inhabitants of Gamkaskloof had told him it would be safer to travel along the reaches of the Swartberg Mountains than to follow the easier and quicker route of the coastal belt. It meant he would have to walk his horse for a good part of the journey, as the terrain would be too rugged for riding. His leg wound would not help matters, yet if he could just last out the journey – if he could just avoid being spotted by a British patrol . . .

Once he made it to Oudtshoorn, he would be indistinguishable from any other farmer. He must obtain suitable identity papers, though. George Laboulaye would help with that.

He cursed when he lost his footing and slid back a few paces. The Mauser rifle slung across his back slammed painfully into him.

It took him a further hour to reach the ravine where they had left the horses. His quick check told him they were all still there; the men had been fearful of attacks by leopards during the night.

The small troop was restless and unnerved by their isolation, so that he was forced to approach his own horse with slow and patient caution. The animals shifted nervously, nostrils flaring, eyes stretched wide with fear and panic, their hoofs trampling up a layer of fine dust lying just below the grass and moss. Henry spoke softly as he inched closer, his hand outstretched to stroke the young mare's neck.

It took a few moments for her to accept his presence, then she followed him as he crossed to the rocks where the men had stored their saddles and excess gear. The equipment was cold and clammy, and the mare shied away when he attempted to place the saddle across her. He let her find her own sense of ease before he tried again, successfully this time.

He gave his saddle and gear a final check, then glanced down at the Mauser clutched in his hand, wondering whether he should leave it there for his comrades; he would in any case have to abandon it before he reached Oudtshoorn. Yet the weapon gave him a sense of security and, after a few moments of indecision, he shrugged and slung it across his back. Then he led the mare from the ravine.

The sudden warmth when he emerged from the cliffs was comforting, but an hour later he was suffering from the heat. He struggled on, trying to ignore the throb in his leg, riding his horse whenever the terrain permitted it.

He spent a cold night tucked into a crevice of overhanging rock, sleeping fitfully, plagued by pain and hunger. He needed warm food desperately, but did not dare make a fire.

The first inkling of morning light came as a welcome relief. Henry stirred stiffly from his hard resting place, his muscles and joints cramped, so that it was close to an hour before he had gathered enough strength to push onwards.

The terrain at least permitted him to ride now, although he was so weak he had to call regular halts to overcome the increasing bouts of nausea which threatened to topple him from the saddle.

By the fourth such stop, Henry realised he had lost so much time he had little chance of reaching Oudtshoorn by nightfall. Even though he considered whether it might be safer in the dark, he had to restrain himself from the natural impulse to urge the mare on at greater speed.

His ride took him across the plateaux of the Swartberg range as the sun weakened its grip upon the day. It reached out for him, a soft golden touch which caressed man and horse. Their passage trailed fragments of fine dust that lingered in the balmy air before settling back to the earth.

The dwindling daylight turned red now. It swirled around the cracks and hollows of the ground and among the low hills, performing a kaleidoscopic ballet with the evening shadow. Together they danced across the earth, bringing a placid beauty to a land which only hours before had glistened harsh and ugly under a callous sun. It was the time of day when man and beast turn languid, the juncture where work ceases and the mind anticipates the calm awaiting at home.

The same sense of anticipation filled Henry, for in a way he, too, was going home. But what if he had been wrong – what if his assumption about Ursula's feelings for him were incorrect? He was acting like a love-struck youth, someone who believed in the romantic notion of love at first sight. Yet he *did* believe it! It had been there when their eyes met for the first time aboard ship, again when they shared that agonisingly short time together in Paris.

He tried to force the doubts from his weary mind, thinking instead of what George Laboulaye had told him about Ratitāe, and tried to imagine himself with Ursula on the great farm.

The ache he felt for her strengthened him, so that he drove his heels into the mare's flanks. The animal responded eagerly, although her sense of urgency was a natural one. For her there was no thought of a farm or a home, merely the need to make the most of the remaining light before darkness settled, bringing with it hidden dangers which could snap her legs as her master drove her on.

The mare sensed the tension and renewed energy in the man upon her back, and knew he would not halt till they reached their destination. She sensed, too, that it was a different strain to the one they had shared over the past few months. This was no flight from danger, no retreat from other men on horseback who sought to destroy them. Yet she missed the sight, sound and smell of the other horses. At least they had shared her qualms.

The earthly ballet diminished around them. A new music took its place: the silence of the evening veld. Henry saw the signs of change which the day's cycle had brought. Hares scurried across ground where before there had been only heat and dust. A large antelope on the ridge of a nearby slope lifted its head to gaze at the man and horse as they passed.

A last red ray of sun reached across the veld and brushed the pair as they rose from the low ground to canter over a ridge. It touched the long barrel of the Mauser, making the metal explode in a glitter of reflected light.

The gleam flickered for an instant, catching the eye of a young British soldier standing beside his horse on the mountain slope some miles away from where Henry rode. He touched his companion's shoulder, pointing at the spot where he had seen the flash of light. 'I saw something,' he said, quickly raising his binoculars. 'A man on horseback,' he confirmed a moment later.

The other soldier shrugged and busied himself with lighting his pipe. They were watching for groups of riders – not for some farmer. He reached for his horse's bridle when he had the pipe going. They had already left it very late for the long ride back to the barracks in Oudtshoorn, and now he silently cursed his young companion's sense of diligence. 'Let's get going,' he muttered, but the youngster continued staring through the binoculars, his forehead creased in concentration. 'I'm sure that reflection came from a rifle,' he said.

They were both relative newcomers to the country and the

war, a part of the final wave of reinforcements shipped in to bring it to its conclusion.

'It *is* a rifle!' The soldier held out his binoculars. 'Here – take a look for yourself!'

'So? Probably a farmer out hunting.' The man sighed before reluctantly lifting the binoculars to his eyes. The dark was settling in fast now, so that all he could discern was a blurred blob of movement as the rider galloped at an angle towards them.

'But his clothes!' the other persisted, 'his saddle-bags! That's a Boer, I tell you!' He grabbed the binoculars and concentrated again on the figure far below.

'And I'm telling you we should get back to the garrison,' his companion replied. 'I don't fancy getting lost in this damn place after dark.' He pulled himself into the saddle, and with a last glance at the other soldier, dug the heels of his boots into the horse's flanks and started off.

The younger man hesitated, then thrust the binoculars into his saddle-bag and mounted. 'He's heading for the pass,' he called out when he caught up. 'We can cut him off at the foot of the ridge.' His face glowed in anticipation of combat.

As soon as they arrived at the designated spot, he dismounted and moved for the cover of the brush. His companion called him back, saying, 'We'll wait for him in the bloody road. I've had enough of playing soldiers for the day.'

'But—'

'It won't do to ambush one of the locals,' the other interrupted. 'You know the regulations.'

'That's no local,' the youngster grumbled, although he moved back into the road. He slammed a round into the chamber of his rifle.

'We'll wait fifteen minutes – no bloody longer, you hear?' the older man said, studying the shadowed track of the Swartberg Pass, 'I don't trust this trail.' He remained in the saddle as he readied his own rifle.

The two men waited in the narrow pass, chilled by the thin air cloaking the craggy mountain. They shivered, and it was not just from the cold.

CHAPTER THIRTY-EIGHT

The two British soldiers heard the rider coming just as the fading light was balanced by a huge full moon rising over the mountain top. The veld was soft and silent, so that the sound of the horse's hoofs carried clearly to them. Their own steeds trampled nervously.

Suddenly, their quarry was upon them. The three men and their horses filled the narrow trail, the shock encounter making the animals rear and whinny in fright.

Henry saw only the outline of the helmets in the dim light. Despite his weak state, he slipped the Mauser from his back with practised speed. It was in his hand even as his knees worked to turn the mare. The sound of the bolt sliding home clicked harshly in the gathering night.

The young soldier had lifted his rifle, but his hand seemed locked around the stock, inches away from the trigger. The man and his horse seemed immense and threatening.

It was the other soldier who moved first, sluggishly raising his rifle as he cried, 'Bloody hell – it's a Boer!' The action broke the momentary trance which had held all three men in its grip. It also cost the soldier his life.

Henry saw the rifle come up, pointed directly at him. His strained nerves knew no hesitation, for the past months had denied them that luxury. He fired as the mare turned and he was too close to miss.

The helmeted figure tumbled from his horse with a dull cry. Even as the soldier plunged to the ground, Henry worked feverishly at the Mauser's bolt. The mare was positioned badly now, forcing him to turn in the saddle to sight the second soldier.

He straightened his rifle with one hand, grabbed the reins with the other. Jerking cruelly, he tried desperately to turn the mare back towards the danger.

The rifle barrel came up. At the same time as he pulled the trigger – firing from the hip – there was a flash from mere feet away as the soldier managed to overcome his fright. As inexperienced as the young Englishman was, the Boer, struggling to right his horse, presented so large a target that his bullet could not fail to strike home.

Henry felt the dull thud as his rifle recoiled into his hip, but the next second there was a tearing pain that ripped into his side and left him breathless.

His limbs turned heavy and useless. He was unable to stop his slide from the saddle as he plummeted powerlessly to the ground. He lay suddenly in the hard dust, sore and dazed. He heard his own voice talking soothingly to the mare – or was it the soldier?

The silence grew. Not even the horses stirred. Overhead the moon was in full control now, its cool, mild light casting the scene of violence and death into a mocking repose.

Henry stirred, surprised and relieved to find that his body could still move. He raised himself on to one elbow. There was no soldier looming over him, no final echoing shot being prepared, no foreign accent calling for his surrender.

He reached out for the mare which stood loyally alongside and pulled himself carefully upright. The pain was not too bad, but he knew it would soon get worse. He had seen that often enough with other wounded soldiers.

The Englishman he had shot from his horse lay curled on his side. Henry knew he need not check; the man was dead. The other soldier lay on his back in the middle of the road, his helmet beside him in the dust, its dull khaki flecked with wet blood. He was groaning softly.

Henry fought off the dizziness which gripped him as he knelt beside the youngster. 'Where are you hit?' he asked when he saw the soldier's eyes flicker.

'Please – my stomach – oh dear God, help me . . . please!'

Henry studied the neat jacket, as perfect as if it had just been pressed. He glanced at the stained helmet, then at the young man's bloodied head. He would have had a chance if it was a stomach wound, he thought sadly, wondering why it was that so many severely injured men thought they had been hit in places other than the actual wound.

'You'll be all right,' he lied, then saw there was no longer any need for it. Reaching out for the helmet, he placed it over the young soldier's face. He would have to leave them both where they lay; he had hardly enough strength left to lift himself into the saddle.

He rested atop the mare for a while and tried to slow his thoughts. He was badly wounded – the rest of the journey could kill him. Even if he survived and made it to Ratitāe, he would now be a great risk to George and Ursula. Yet there was no other way out; no way but forward, on to Oudtshoorn. Perhaps the British would capture him and give him medical treatment. At least he had a chance of staying alive that way, and to live meant being with Ursula one day.

Henry turned the mare and headed her down the pass. He gave no thought even to his rifle which still lay in the dirt.

The mare snorted as they shifted past the dead men and the other horses. Henry glanced down at the helmet hiding the distorted face. So young, he thought, and then reminded himself of the many youths who had died while riding with the Boer commandos, of the women and children virtually starved to death in the concentration camps of the British.

The anger of the memories helped still the fresh pain in his side and he tried to feed it with recriminations at his own negligence in riding so easily into the soldiers' trap. So keen was his longing for Ursula that he had foolishly forgotten he was still a soldier. Now meeting her again was threatened by the wound which pumped the strength from his body.

He reminded himself he was still a soldier, albeit a weakened one. But the pain pulled and tore at his side, making him groan aloud.

Beneath him the mare moved on, tired now, for there had been little rest during the past two nights, and the day which had passed had been full with ferment. She felt the changed weight of the man upon her back and knew he was no longer in control. She trod carefully onwards, studying the track glistening in the moonlight.

Around her the night was alive and chilling. The moon spread its beams across the mountain slopes, bringing to play a host of darting shadows. They mocked her, terrorised her, but whenever she hesitated they slipped away to lie in ambush further along. The man's weight slumped more heavily upon her, spreading itself across the breadth of her strong back.

She shook her head as if flicking away the fears that tormented her and steadfastly moved on.

The English sergeant climbed the three wooden steps and jerked open the office door. He fingered the magnificent moustache which twirled up the sides of his cheeks, waiting for the duty officer to finish writing and acknowledge his presence. Bloody pompous twit, he thought, and sniffed loudly.

Lieutenant John Crosley ignored him for a few moments longer. Then he sighed, recapped his pen and looked up. 'Yes, Sergeant Brown? Oh, of course – the missing men. Well, did you find them?'

'They're nowhere in the barracks, sir. And no one's seen them in town.' He fingered his moustache again, wishing he was back in combat.

Sergeant Brown was a big man, a veteran of the war. It was only the vicious wound in his abdomen that had removed him from the front, placing him in the relative calm of the Oudtshoorn barracks. He studied the much younger lieutenant, annoyed at the indecision he saw on his face.

Brown had little regard for the new arrivals of recent months. The army was sending them freshly trained officers with no knowledge of warfare or the terrain in which they would operate. They were like the first batch to be sent in, he thought, remembering the farewell parties in England before they had boarded the troopships. Like bloody celebrations they were, he recalled bitterly; no one had believed the war could last longer than three months. How could a rag-tag army of uncouth Boers withstand the might of the British Empire? Almighty Christ – how wrong they'd been!

'We'd better send out a search-party,' said Lieutenant Crosley, cutting into his thoughts.

Brown stared at him, thankful that one of the bastards had at least been kept from a combat unit; a few hundred men could owe their lives to that. 'A search-party, sir?' he asked, keeping his thoughts from showing on his face. 'At night?'

'Take care of it, sergeant. But make it a strong party. There are reports of contingents of Boers heading towards the mountains.'

Sergeant Brown shut his eyes for a brief moment. 'Begging your pardon, sir, but that's the reason we've had patrols in the area all day. They were both new men,' he added patiently, 'raw recruits. The bloody fools probably got themselves lost in the mountains.'

'No need for crude language, sergeant,' snapped Crosley. 'Why on earth did you send new men out on their own?'

Brown took a deep breath. 'Because,' he said through gritted teeth, 'the experienced men are patrolling further inland. The only men left in the barracks at the moment are all new recruits. They've been here only a few weeks – about as long as you. Sir.'

Lieutenant Crosley stared up at his subordinate, then got to his feet. Even so, he had to raise his eyes to look the sergeant in the face. 'What do you suggest then?' he asked, pretending suddenly to find an item of interest on the bulletin board.

'That we wait till morning before we mount a search. If there are Boers out there, our men wouldn't stand a chance in the dark.'

'And your missing men?' Brown did not miss the subtle shift of responsibility. 'Are you prepared to leave them to the mercy of the Boers?' added Crosley.

'If they've run into Boers, they're probably dead by now,' replied Brown. 'I wouldn't like to sacrifice more men just to find that out. If they're lost, I hope they have the good sense to find a comfortable spot and sit tight for the night.'

Lieutenant Crosley's shoulders tensed, but he did not move from the bulletin board. 'Very well, sergeant. Put together a search-party to leave at first light.' He turned only when he heard Brown's soft 'Sir,' and the bang of the door. He made a mental note that there had been no salute.

The early morning chill made the coloured youth shiver. He yawned and grumbled softly as he pulled down the sleeves of his tattered jersey. The cuffs were frayed from years of wear, but he stretched them till they covered his hands so that he could grip the ends between his fingers.

He closed the door of his parents' shack and stood blinking in the faint light of dawn. Rising early was always a difficult task, and all too often he had succumbed to the temptation of shirking his duties by spending an extra half-hour huddled beneath the warmth of the single blanket which covered him at night. It had happened again only a few days ago, and his ears still smarted from the clouts his father had dealt him.

He yawned again as he stumbled sleepily towards the paddocks. The gate squeaked when he passed through. Wary ostriches watched him from their thatched shelters. They were used to his presence, so merely gave a habitual hiss prompting the usual muttered response from the youngster.

He tugged at the jersey again when he came to a smaller enclosure housing a brood of young chicks. They were waiting anxiously for his arrival, for he was the symbol of their first meal of the day. The young boy was also their foster father, the human who took on the role of the parents the incubator-bred chicks had never known. It was he who fed them bone-meal and crushed barley, providing them with suitable pebbles and their supply of water. When he moved, they followed, for he was their protector and they adored him.

This day, however, the ostrich chicks would have to wait. Although the boy was on time, he had failed to cut a batch of lucerne from the adjacent field the previous evening. He kicked at the excited chicks, scattering them for a moment before they moved in again. They followed him all the way to the fence, treating his kicking and cursing as an invitation to play.

The short-handled scythe hung where he had left it, on a roughly shaped wire hook attached to the fence. He grabbed it, jumped the fence and moved into the lucerne patch. The jersey slipped back across his wrists as he readied himself for the first swing.

The scythe never slashed at the lucerne. It remained poised above his right shoulder as he stared at the horse standing at the far side of the field. It stood, head bent, grazing idly, the slumped figure on its back swaying as the horse moved. The boy lowered the scythe and walked warily towards the animal.

He stopped a short distance away. The horse raised its tired head to stare at him. Then it moved slowly closer, the human load on its back jerking as the horse lifted its legs high to cross the thick lucerne.

The youth took a backwards step when he saw the blood on the man. '*Mijnheer?*' he said softly, hoping to stir some life into the rider. He was scared; he had never seen a dead person before.

The horse nudged him with its nose. The youngster pushed it away and leaned closer to the saddle. He touched the man, then jerked his hand away when he heard a low groan.

'*Mijnheer?*' he said again, then quickly glanced across the field to see whether anyone else had arrived at the paddocks. Only the ostriches stared back at him.

The rider groaned again and moved in the saddle. The youth stepped closer to prod the limp form. There was no response. He reached out, raised the man's head with trembling fingers. The youth sighed with relief when he saw his eyes flicker open. He said, '*Goeiemôre!*' – Good morning! – and smiled.

The smiling face and the first touch of the rising sun on the green pasture brought a glimmer of reality back to Henry, dissolving the confused nightmares of his mind. He tried to focus on the boy, to convince himself that what he saw was real, that somehow he had survived the night.

The cold had stiffened his body, making him gasp with pain

when he gripped the pommel of the saddle to raise himself. He felt the youth's hands on him, helping him into a sitting position. The pain in his side took on a fresh intensity when he moved. He tried to speak, but nothing more than rasping noises crossed his parched lips. 'The master wants water?' the boy asked, still smiling fixedly at Henry, who nodded briefly.

The tin can the boy brought had jagged cuts along the rim. Henry ignored the smart of his bleeding lips as he pushed it roughly to his mouth and greedily downed the cold water. The boy took the can back with a satisfied grin. 'More?' he asked.

Henry shook his head and wiped his right hand across his mouth. He noticed his fingers were covered with dry, caked blood, and realised he had been clutching his wound while unconscious. 'Ratitāe?' he asked, relieved to see the youth bob his head in understanding, pointing at the same time to the east. 'How far?' asked Henry. The boy raised two fingers.

The hoarse laugh which broke in Henry's throat made him wince. Only two miles! The relief he felt brought new strength to his body. Only two miles before he could rest – and see Ursula again. He reached down and stroked the mare's neck.

The boy was chattering now, his arms flailing as he rattled out directions. Henry managed to decipher enough to learn that the road lay not far away. He would have to risk it; he was too weak to try making his way through the veld.

As he nodded his thanks, he wondered how long it would take for the news about the youth's encounter with a wounded man to spread. He realised there was nothing he could do to stop that, and jerked on the reins. The movement caused a fresh spasm of pain, so that he clenched his teeth to stop himself groaning.

The mare moved reluctantly at first, then felt the new force in the man who rode her. She shrugged off her exhaustion and flexed her muscles. The land ahead lay soft and gentle; he would surely let her rest soon.

The boy watched them slowly move off. What should he tell his father and the others? he wondered. Would they believe his tale of coming across a wounded man in the lucerne field?

Probably not; it would be fobbed off as his excuse for not feeding the ostriches on time.

The thought spurred him into sudden action. He slashed at the lucerne with the scythe, swinging his arms as if demons were chasing him. He soon built up a sweat, and had a sufficient pile of lucerne to keep the chicks busy for a little while at least. He raced back and threw the food across the fence. He was running into the lucerne field even before the anxious chicks fell upon their breakfast.

If anyone saw him now, he thought, he would say he had miscalculated the amount of feed needed when cutting it the night before, and was quickly gathering some more for the ravenous chicks. That oversight would extract little more than a few harsh words.

As for his strange visitor, he decided, as his arms rose and fell in a practised rhythm, it would be better to say nothing at all.

The sun warmed Henry's back as he crossed under the signboard at the entrance to Ratitāe. The boy had been optimistic when he said two miles, and his weakened condition made the journey seem even longer. How far still to the farmhouse?

The thought of the farm set his mind working again. Could he just ride up to the house in his present state? He glanced at his bloodstained jacket. Even his trouser leg was streaked with blood, caused by the opening of his first wound. His hat had been lost sometime during the night and his thick hair was coated with a mixture of early-morning dew and dust. It would be better to find a labourer who could summon Ursula. No, not Ursula; it would be best if first he spoke to George Laboulaye.

The road seemed endless now. Once or twice he thought he heard voices in the fields, yet when he slowed down to check, there were only ostriches grazing contentedly in the patches of lucerne.

Each time he spurred the mare on the animal seemed to falter. She stumbled once as if about to fall but quickly righted herself and staggered on with an almost apologetic snort.

When Henry heard voices again, he ignored the urge to stop and check. He imagined he could even hear the sound of hoofs and carriage wheels, and forced his eyes open to assure himself of his madness.

The road stretched out ahead, and there, less than a hundred yards from him, a light buggy stirred up the dust as it hurtled in his direction.

It did not matter to Henry that it was an illusion. The sight was so welcome, so reassuring, that he dug his heels into the mare's flanks with a hoarse cry of triumph.

The mare knew it was no illusion. She felt the thrill pass through her master as he spurred her on, willing her to respond.

She tried one last time to serve him as she had done throughout the long night. But her legs had suffered enough, and her heart could no longer pump enough blood to her demanding muscles. She went down in an exhausted heap, throwing up a cloud of dust as she plunged heavily to the ground, dragging Henry with her.

The mare was powerless to counter the sense of failure flooding through her. She lay on her side, her legs kicking defiantly at the air, yet unable to find the strength to raise herself and regain her dignity.

Henry lay beside her in the dust, his left leg pinned beneath her, his arm crushed awkwardly under his own body.

He heard the illusion more clearly now – could even feel the hands trying to free him from the horse. And then, the sweetest torture of all: he heard Ursula's voice.

I'm dying, he thought. He closed his eyes and let the blackness roll in behind them.

CHAPTER THIRTY-NINE

The house was silent, touched only by the stillness of midday. Or, thought Ursula, it appeared to be so because of the man lying critically ill upstairs.

She glanced at the ceiling, as if the gesture would transmit her own strength and will through it and into the room where Henry Ritter fought for his life. Concern for his welfare made her shudder, yet at the same time she felt ashamed at her selfish joy of having him with her at any cost.

The morning's events still seemed unreal to her: leaving the house in the open carriage driven by Outa; the sight of the bloodied man slouched in the saddle of his horse; then recognition – disbelief, at first, followed quickly by alarm when Henry tumbled to the ground as his mare collapsed beneath him. She had no memory of helping Outa lift him into the carriage, or of the race back to the house. She recalled only her mumbled prayers for him to live.

The bullet fired by the English soldier had lodged itself deep within the flesh and muscle of Henry's side, chipping a place in the bone from where it spread its slow, metallic poison. Its task was made easier by the weakened state of its human target; Henry's earlier leg wound, loss of blood, weeks of hard riding with continuous tension and irregular meals had all undermined his resistance to its deadly intrusion.

A doctor should have been summoned hours ago, except that the nature of his injury prohibited such action. The treatment of a gunshot wound was no everyday occurrence as all doctors were under strict orders to report such instances to the authorities. While Ursula had been more than ready to run that risk for the man she loved, she also forced herself to consider the consquences to George and Ratitāe.

She glanced at the ceiling again. Mrs Blake was a competent-enough nurse, but she did not possess the skills or instruments necessary to remove the bullet which would eventually kill Henry.

Marianne's voice made her look up. 'We have to come to a decision about what to do.'

'I know. But—'

'All we need do,' said Marianne hurriedly, 'is to report the presence of a wounded soldier on the farm. There's no reason why the authorities should suspect we're aware of his identity.'

'It would incriminate George!'

'Why? They have no reason to connect the two of them. As long as they don't see your reaction to Henry's being here, his appearance on Ratitāe might not cause suspicion. A wounded soldier who appeared on the farm, that's all.'

Ursula worried a fingernail. 'Surrendering Henry to the authorities would mean his being interned for the rest of the war.'

'It would also mean saving his life.'

She stared at her mother, knowing she was right. 'Will you let them know?' she asked after a while. 'Tonight? Soon – please – he *must* live!'

Marianne stepped closer and placed her hand on her shoulder. 'He'll live,' she said firmly. 'Go to him now, be with him when the fever drags him from his sleep.' She waited till Ursula pushed herself from the chair and started for the door, then said, 'You need to get some sleep yourself. Let Mrs Blake stay with him. She'll call you when he wakes.'

Ursula smiled sadly, then gave a small shake of her head.

Marianne was thoughtful, remembering her own circum-stances when she had been Ursula's age. She, too, had wanted someone whom fate seemed determined to keep from her. She thought of all the wasted years before she and George were together at last; now it threatened to happen to Ursula as well. Giving Henry up to the military would undoubtedly save his life, but would also serve to take him from Ursula. Yet there was no other choice. She would ask George to ride into town; he would know how best to approach the British authorities.

Turning to the window to see whether she could spot George in the fields, she saw the labourers returning to their work after the noon break. They chatted idly before slowly moving on again. There was no sign of George, although Outa appeared, scolding the labourers severely for their reticence in returning to work.

She smiled as she realised how old he had become; the Zulu was in his sixties already. They were all getting old. Soon she and George would have to give up Ratitãe to Ursula. Once it had been for Stanley as well, she recalled painfully – but who would Outa give up to?

She sighed as she turned away from the window, knowing there would never be another like Outa.

In the lucerne fields, George's thoughts too centred on the young man dying in the house. He knew it was foolish, but he could not shrug off a feeling of responsibility for what had happened to Henry.

He had taken an instant liking to the Afrikaner when they had first met in Cape Town, just a day before they all – he, Ursula and Henry – were due to sail. George had known instinctively that the Boer republics had sent him the right man. Educated in England, Henry was bright and charming enough to move in European circles without arousing suspicion. George had sensed an inherent toughness within him, all too necessary for the negotiations he would have to face.

What appealed to him most, however, was Henry's pragmatic approach to his task. He had been afraid he would be sent some emotionally patriotic individual following a mission of blind allegiance; Henry Ritter was certainly not that.

His arrival on Ratitãe had shaken George. The man his stepdaughter loved, the man who had helped his own goal of German aid to the Boers to become a reality, would die unless they summoned help.

A new thought struck him and filled him with alarm: what if the British were able to tie both of them to the arms supply? Would he, George, be hanged for treason? It was not impossible, for that was the fate awaiting the Cape burghers who still supported the Boer cause. After all, it had been that exact threat which had caused Jan Smuts and his forces to embark on their first daring raid into the Colony.

He glanced over the fields, saddened at the possibility of being removed from the loveliness of Ratitäe. 'No sense in postponing it,' he said aloud, as if the calamity had already befallen him. He sighed and started for the house.

George stopped suddenly when his mind, searching frantically for a way out of the predicament they were all in, found a possible solution. No – he couldn't do it – he was mad even to think of it! Marianne would never permit it! But he had already started for the incubator room, hoping Outa was there and thinking that the gloomy prospect of being hanged outweighed the risk attached to his new idea – even when combined with his lovely wife's anger if he carried it off.

When the workers remaining in the fields saw him coming, they immediately put an extra effort into their chores. They feigned great surprise at seeing him there, their greetings containing the right mixture of warmth and respect. The response was not feigned; there was not a labourer on Ratitäe who had not at one time or another been exposed to a tongue-lashing as well as some act of kindness from George.

He nodded vaguely at them, while they frowned and paused in their work after he had passed. They sensed that something was amiss and glanced knowingly at one another. Since that morning, the news of the wounded man had been discussed at great length among themselves.

George wrenched open the door of the incubation room. A young labourer stared back at him with anxious eyes. 'Where's Outa?' George barked. The young man had been on Ratitäe only two months, and it was the first time he had come so close to the master. Tales of his anger when things went awry flashed through his mind as he lifted a trembling hand and pointed to the nearest warehouse.

George let the door slam shut. Outa came out of the

warehouse when he was still a few yards away, his body straightening at the sight of his employer. He smiled, for his heart held no fear of George. He saw the troubled look on his face, and like the other workers, guessed its cause.

'Walk with me,' said George, heading away from the warehouse and out of earshot of the others. Outa fell in step beside him. 'You were with the carriage this morning?' George asked after a few yards.

Outa nodded. Seeing the mare give way beneath her rider was a sight he would always remember. He had seen horses fall before, but never had he witnessed in an animal such defiance towards its own exhaustion. He had tended the mare himself once the wounded man was in the house. Later, he slipped into the stables again to check on the animal's condition. Talking gently to the mare and with respect, the way he sometimes communicated with the ostriches, he led her slowly from the stable, stroking her softly and talking reassuringly as he led her around the yard, letting her test her legs, showing her with words and gestures that her greatness had not deserted her.

'What do the workers say of this man?' asked George.

Outa gave a slight shrug. 'There is only so much they can think and say,' he replied. 'Just two kinds of people shoot at each other these days – the Boer soldiers and the British soldiers. The man with the wound is definitely not a British soldier. Everyone knows that. I have spoken to them, told them to still their wagging tongues.' He lifted his shoulders in another shrug and added, 'There are so many young ones on the farm these days – they seek their place in life with tales that impress others. I fear what they will say when they see other youngsters in the town.'

'That will be no fault of yours,' George said softly, studying the lines on the Zulu's face, the eyes which once were forceful, now gentle with life's experience. James had been the poorer, he thought, for letting this man grow away from him. 'The bullet lies deep inside the man,' he said after a while. 'It lies there and poisons him to death.'

Outa nodded in understanding. There was no need for him to ask why a doctor had not been called. He smiled when George asked, 'You remember telling me of the Xhosa woman? The one with the snake stone?'

He laughed. 'Yes, I remember well. I still have the stone. I also told how the witch removed a broken knife point from a man's stomach. He still lives today.'

'And the woman . . . the witch? Is she alive?'

'She is still in the mountains.' He lifted his gaze to look up at the imposing might of the Swartberg range. 'It is but a short ride,' he added.

George was silent for a while. At last he sighed and said, 'Take the best horse. The hours of daylight are few.'

'I will take the Boer's mare. The ride will cause her courage to return.'

There were no other words between them, for none was needed. George watched the black man resolutely stride off in the direction of the stables. Only when Outa had disappeared inside did he head for the house, deciding he would not tell Marianne – not till it was too late.

The brave mare followed the trail again, nervously at first, then with growing confidence at the feel of the old Zulu's weight on her back, his legs firm yet gentle around her girth.

What helped, too, was the presence of the other horse. Even the path was less threatening, for there was neither darkness nor tormenting shadows. The earth was filled now with a warm richness which clung to her hoofs as they flicked its crust aside.

For Outa, the ride diminished in pleasure the further they climbed towards the shadows of the towering mountains. His years among Europeans had not entirely removed the many superstitions of his African culture, and he was fearful of meeting the woman. How would she receive him? With anger at his intrusion into her isolated domain? What if she cast a spell on him? He would fail George then. The mare felt his sudden trembling and snorted with unease.

The warmth of the fading sun gave way suddenly to a deep, damp shade as the man and two horses moved into the heart of the mountains. Cold air swooped out to embrace them with icy fingers. Gigantic ferns, damp with moisture that had never been challenged by the sun, parted reluctantly to let them pass. Tall trees grasped tentatively at the light high above, selfishly smothering everything beneath in dank darkness.

It was not a place suited to the fears of men and horses, and it seemed to sneer at them as its tight enclosure of leaf and branch snapped shut behind them.

As if in amnesty, after Outa had travelled less than a mile, a parting appeared in the dense growth. It revealed a rough wooden hut that stood askew on its foundations with a thin tendril of smoke rising from a crude hole at the side of the roof. Outa stopped the horses and waited with pounding heart.

At last there was a dim flicker of movement as the door of the hut opened. A black woman of colossal proportions stepped out. A loose cotton wrap, stitched together from a variety of bits and pieces of old dresses, tried vainly to conceal the rolling mounds of her flesh. Her breasts, the size of melons, overcame the futile restraints of the cloth to rock jerkily as she stepped away from the hut. Outa stared in amazement as they swung like a pendulum across the distorted splurge of her misshapen navel. Her mound, he thought in spite of his fear of her – imagine the size of her mound! His fleshy assegai would disappear in there!

'What does the old Zulu seek on my mountain?' Her voice befitted her size. She took a step closer, making Outa's legs tremble across the width of the mare's back.

His own voice sounded thin and frightened. 'He seeks the help of the Wise One,' he said. 'Not for himself, but for his masters,' he quickly added.

The woman guffawed loudly, so that her breasts and rolls of fat bounced grotesquely. 'Your masters? Do they seek the *muti* to make the man hard and strong all night?' Outa felt resentment creep into him when she gave another scornful laugh.

'My master has a strong member,' he said, 'and my mistress has legs and hips strong enough to take him. For hours on end I hear their love noises from their room.' The lie sounded good to him, so much so that he stared defiantly down at the woman.

Her snort was derisive. 'The old man still remembers the sound?'

Outa forgot his fears as he continued to glare at her. Witch or not, he thought, he would plunge his thick shaft into her fat quivering lips, pierce her so deep and so rapidly that she would have to call on her own medicines to heal her afterwards! Why, only three days ago he had felt the early-morning lust pound when he passed water!

'Where is your respect?' the woman snapped suddenly. 'Do not dare to talk to me from atop your horse, old man! Get down before I cast a spell on you!'

The chill of fear thrust deep into his heart. He slipped from the mare's saddle without even thinking, and stood with trembling legs on the wet grass, his shoulders bunched.

'Speak, old one,' commanded the woman. She let Outa explain the situation, then said, 'They will have to pay me well, for it is a long ride . . . and the man is a Boer soldier.'

'If you heal him,' Outa said slowly, keeping his eyes lowered to the ground, 'if you remove the bullet and he becomes well, they will pay whatever you ask.'

'Do not make terms with me, senile one! I heal whatever I want to heal! They will pay me before I leave there.'

'It will be as you wish,' said Outa, swallowing loudly. He still did not look at her when he added, 'I have brought a horse to carry you on the journey.' He was pleased he had displayed the foresight to bring one of George's biggest and strongest animals, for the beast's burden would be a heavy one.

The woman studied the horse, then looked at Outa again. 'I must prepare my *muti*,' she snapped. 'Go back to the foot of the mountain. Wait for me there. Wait as long as it takes me to ready myself.'

Outa turned the horses round with a sense of relief, but it was only when he felt the late afternoon sun touch his shoulders that he was able to relax once again.

He let the horses roam freely among the lush grass, hoping the witch would not take too long. George was depending on him.

411

'Are you mad?'

George turned away from the anger in Marianne's voice. 'The thought had crossed my mind,' he muttered softly, then quickly added, 'but she's here now – let's see whether she can't help.'

They were in the room next to the one in which Henry lay. 'You think I'll allow that hag you call a witch,' snapped Marianne, 'that filthy, smelly creature – to touch him?'

He stared back at her, understanding her shock and anger. 'It's the only alternative to handing Henry over to the British,' he replied. 'I've no fear of what might become of me – please believe that! But . . . I feel responsible for Henry. I don't want to see him in prison. Neither does Ursula, I'm sure.' His eyes pleaded with her.

Marianne was silent as they stared at each other. At last she said, 'She'll have to wash – I won't allow her to touch him till she's cleaned up, do you understand?'

Relief flooded to his face. 'The water Outa put on the stove should be boiling by now.'

'You are mad,' said Marianne again with a shake of her head. 'We are both mad!' Then she stepped forward and threw her arms around his neck. 'Just don't let Ursula know,' she added before she kissed him.

Together they sneaked the Xhosa woman up the stairs, bringing Mrs Blake – who did her best to dissuade them – into their confidence, and using the housekeeper to keep a watch on the door to Ursula's room. At least Ursula was asleep, exhausted by the events of the day.

Marianne felt a last moment of hesitation when the gargantuan Xhosa woman knelt over Henry, mumbling to herself as she threw a handful of dry, reeking bones on to the floor. Her eyes were shut, and a spasm jerked her huge shoulders. As suddenly as she had started her ritual, she stopped and chortled hoarsely. 'The Boer will live,' she declared. Marianne and George glanced at each other, neither of them feeling entirely reassured.

George shrugged, turned to the Xhosa woman and said, 'Get on with it.'

412

The woman withdrew two long needles of bone from a goatskin bag slung around her waist. 'You will clean those!' insisted Marianne, and was surprised when the woman agreed, asking for boiling water to be brought to the room.

After some time – which seemed like hours to the anxious watchers – the hag gave a cry of triumph and showed them the jagged piece of metal clutched between her bloody fingers. She let it fall to the floor with a dull thud before reaching inside her bag. Pulling out a smaller pouch, she threw its contents – a mixture of herbs and leaves – into a clay crucible. Then she added a little water and pounded at the pungent mixture.

It was a while before she gave a satisfied grunt and, scooping up the mess with her fingers, smeared it gently into the raw flesh of the wound. Then she covered it with more leaves extracted from the goatskin bag.

George lifted the blanket and pointed at the wound in Henry's leg. 'There, too,' he said, thankful there was no bullet lodged inside the flesh. The Xhosa woman hesitated, grunted, and started applying her *muti*.

At last she was done. 'What do we owe you?' asked George. The woman cackled. 'Twenty pounds. You must pay me now.'

He nodded. 'Help me get her out of the house,' he told Mrs Blake, who seemed amazed that Henry was still alive.

When they had the woman outside, George handed her the money, but the Xhosa demanded the horse she had ridden in on. 'Take it,' he said, willing to give whatever was necessary to get rid of her.

At last she was gone from the farm. George went back inside and, finding Marianne, said, 'Promise me that if something like this happens to me, you'll send for a real doctor. If I came to and saw some witch hovering over me, I'd die of shock!'

She laughed with him, her earlier anger replaced by relief at the successful removal of the bullet. 'I promise,' she said softly. She gently touched his cheek and added, 'Things seem to be all right now.'

George nodded, but they both knew that only time would tell whether or not the crude surgery had left unwanted complications to replace what it had removed.

'We'll have to move him as soon as he's well enough,' he said. 'It will be some while before he can make the long ride back to the Transvaal. It won't be safe to keep him here.'

'What makes you think he'll want to go back to the Transvaal? He came here, didn't he?'

George sank into a chair. 'You could be right, of course,' he said and sighed. 'My God, trust Ursula to fall in love with a man who's a danger to us all.' He wiped his hand across his eyes.

'You're the one who arranged his visit to Europe,' Marianne reminded him, but her voice was gentle, without recrimination. 'And it's apparent your Mr Ritter had no hesitation in opting for the same emotional state as Ursula.'

Despite his quick laugh, his face was creased in concern. 'The British will be looking for him – Henry must have become separated from his commando during a battle.'

'Commandos? Around here?'

'There are a few groups headed for the southern Cape. I heard about it some days ago. Perhaps there'll be news in town.'

'Be careful. If they *are* looking for him, you'll arouse suspicions by asking questions.'

'Don't worry – an old spy like me knows how to handle these things.'

Marianne made no response to his attempt at humour. 'Wait till morning – Henry might be strong enough to tell us what happened.'

'You're probably right, but we still have to get him away from here. As soon as possible.'

'What about the labourers?' Marianne asked after a while. 'They saw Henry.'

George thought it best not to repeat what Outa had told him. Instead he said, 'All they saw was a bloodied man being carried into the house. If the British ask questions, we'll say he was attacked by a leopard. We treated him and he went on his way again.'

'Where should they go?' she asked.

'They?'

'Of course. Henry will need someone to look after him,

414

and I doubt whether Ursula will let you send him away from her.'

George scratched the side of his jaw as Marianne settled herself on his lap. 'The cottage,' he said. 'The British won't search as far as Knysna, and there's still plenty of time before the farmers head to the seaside for Christmas.'

She realised he was right; the seaside cottage they owned would be the safest. 'We can't let them go on their own . . . I mean—'

'I know what you mean. But would it be wise for one of us to leave the farm right now, just to act as chaperone?'

'I don't know.'

'Outa.'

'What?'

'Outa. He's a trusted friend, Marianne. He just proved that once again.'

'I know, but wouldn't he feel awkward about it?'

'Outa? He's been bossing Ursula around ever since she could walk! He'd take his role very seriously, and both Ursula and Henry would be aware he'd report everything to us.'

She played with her lower lip while she thought about his suggestion. Then she smiled and said, 'All right, Outa must go with them. For how long?'

'Till the British have lost interest. Perhaps the war might even be over by the time they return.'

'And Henry can stay on Ratitāe to look after Ursula.'

'You're matchmaking, my dear,' he scolded with a wag of his finger.

'Only because I know Ursula feels the same way about Henry as I felt about you when I was her age.' She smiled when he feigned surprise at her statement.

'He's a fine man,' George said. 'He'll be a great help to her when it comes to the running of Ratitāe.'

Marianne studied him closely, saw the nervous tap of his fingers on the arm of the chair. She shifted so that he could no longer avoid her gaze and said, 'You're talking about us retiring, aren't you? If Ursula gets married, we can—'

415

'Go to Austria,' he finished for her, smiling sheepishly. 'We've discussed it before.'

'Well . . . not discussed exactly. It was just a thought.'

They sat in silence for a few moments, glanced at each other, then looked away again. 'Just a thought,' repeated Marianne.

'An interesting one. We'd still keep our fingers on the pulse of things, of course. After all, Austria is still a major market. But there'd be time for the theatre, going to operas, time for—'

'Do you think she's ready?' interrupted Marianne, feeling herself entranced by his description of the life they would lead.

'She's learned everything there is to know. With the right man at her side, she'll be more than ready.'

Without knowing it, they both thought momentarily of Stanley. But it was George who said, 'She would have beaten Stanley, you know. The only difference his leaving has made is now she'll be spared the agony of doing so.'

When Marianne made no reply, he took her hand in his and said, 'Woman, let's hope that Xhosa witch of Outa's performed a miracle tonight! If she did, I'll get Henry to safety, and you get Ursula married to him. Austria we'll do together.'

'Since when have we relied on miracles?' she whispered, moving closer to kiss his forehead.

CHAPTER FORTY

Lieutenant John Crosley shifted in his chair and stared with distaste at the man on the other side of his desk. He studied the large head and the scar tissue at the side of the eyes.

Crosley knew from the file in front of him that his visitor was sixty years of age, yet he still looked fit and strong enough to take on men far younger than himself. He decided this was a man who fought for the sheer pleasure of it. Clearing his throat, he said, 'I'm still not quite sure we'll be needing your services, Mr Denker. At this very moment my men are—'

'Lieutenant,' interrupted Denker, 'it's not your decision to make. I've been officially summoned by your headquarters to undertake this task. You need a professional for this. That's why your superiors retain men like me.'

Crosley bristled with outrage. The nerve of the man! How could he talk about himself as though he were an extension of Her Majesty's armed services? There were no bounty hunters in the British army – never would be! It was only now, when all available troops were being directed north for the final onslaught on the Boer republics, that men such as Denker were being used to track down the many Boer soldiers who had deserted.

Some of the deserters had formed themselves into small bands which criss-crossed the countryside and plundered outlying guard posts. The army could not spare soldiers to hunt them down, so they tended to use colonials such as Denker, whose consciences were no hindrance when it came

417

to the Boers. It went against all of Crosley's deeply ingrained principles and perceptions of honour.

He glanced at the file before him. There was a brief record of Denker's spell on the postal coaches before he had offered his services to the British when they established a garrison in the Dutch Reformed church in Prince Albert. The file revealed that Gert Denker had tracked down and captured ten Boer soldiers within a year, and had also provided information on farmers who had sheltered Boers or were sympathetic to their cause. Crosley's distaste for his guest increased as he closed the file.

Denker flicked a single-page document on to the desk. 'If you'll just sign that, lieutenant, I'll get going. No sense in wasting more time.' Crosley lowered his gaze and studied the document. His signature would authorise Denker to operate within the area under the authority of the garrison, and to capture the Boer who had killed the two British soldiers. He gave a sigh of exasperation before scrawling his name with a flourish, then pushed the document across the desk.

The Dutchman sneered. 'Thank you, lieutenant. I'll bring you your man – dead or alive.'

'There's no need to kill him,' Crosley retorted, not bothering to hide the outrage he felt.

'It's easier that way.' Denker moved to his feet without shifting his chair back against the desk. 'I'll be in touch,' he said as he started for the door.

'I want continual reports,' uttered Crosley, surprised at the strength in his voice.

At first he thought Denker had ignored him, but the big man turned slowly, a dark, ugly look in his eyes. 'You'll get your report when I bring the Boer in,' he replied. 'I'm not one of your men.'

The English lieutenant swallowed the sudden fear Denker's glance had instilled in him. 'I have no desire to interfere with your methods, but I am not prepared to let you disturb the good relations this unit has with the citizens of Oudtshoorn.'

'I won't be arresting your dear citizens,' snarled Denker. 'A few questions, that's all.'

'That's what I mean. I can't stop you asking questions, but

I want to know if you suspect the man is hiding out on one of the farms. There are some prominent people around here, and I don't want you barging in on your own.'

The two men stared at each other, the one with hostility, the other with a look of forced strength. At last Denker said, 'If I think it's necessary, I'll let you know.'

He gave Crosley a last hard look, then left the office.

As on any other Friday afternoon, Oudtshoorn was busy with labourers from the ostrich farms. They came in on wagons borrowed from their masters, their mission to purchase the weekend liquor supplies for their employers as well as the quota supplied by them to each labourer. Apart from this official function, they also brought a substantial share of their weekly wage packets, including their fellow labourers', in order to purchase extra supplies of liquor.

The streets hummed with their laughter and loud greetings. Their voices contained excitement at the thought of the weekend awaiting them, even though most of them would still be hard at work the following morning.

While the entrustment of fetching the supplies of liquor was a desirable task, it was also a hazardous one. It often happened that a fair proportion of a labourer's own stock was consumed within the town itself while chatting to friends, or trying to persuade some hesitant maiden into opening her mouth to the bottle and her legs to a different kind of warmth. This, in turn, frequently led to the 'loan' of someone else's liquor, resulting in ferocious brawls back at the farm where the supplies were scrutinised.

Behind the liquor merchant lay an open plot, an ideal place for meeting others and quenching a week-old thirst. A group of eight men stood huddled together, chatting excitedly as they uncorked their bottles, testing the contents with a deep sigh of satisfaction and a fatalistic shiver of delight.

Their enjoyment was stifled, however, when a big man rounded the corner on his horse. They hastily slapped back the corks before wiping their hands across their mouths. The man's size, as well as the sight of a rifle snuggled in the scabbard of the horse's saddle made them cringe and bow fearfully while they uttered flowery words of greeting.

There was added confusion when he smiled at them. They stepped back as he climbed down from the saddle with a loud creak of leather.

Gert Denker smiled again, just enough to hide the sneer which automatically sprang to his lips whenever he encountered those whose skin was darker than his own. A useless breed, he thought to himself; a bastard race whose only aim in life was to drink, sleep and fornicate. They meant nothing as workers. They would rob you blind unless you watched them all the time. And the only logic they understood was that of a fist.

Denker hated them. That on numerous occasions he had, often violently, enjoyed the favours of their women, did not change the way he felt towards them. But now he widened his smile, letting it reach his eyes as he felt inside his saddle-bag for a bottle of cheap, fortified wine.

The setting sun cast its shadows across the town, its pink hue softening the derelict plot of land where the group stood apprehensively. Its refracted rays picked at the minuscule particles of dust raised by Denker's boots as he stepped closer to the men.

'The heat dries out a man's insides,' he said as he raised the bottle, plucking out the cork with his teeth and spitting it to the ground. A dozen bobbing heads indicated the group was in full agreement with his statement.

They watched enviously as he tilted the bottle and took a slug of wine. Some of those who had started to slink away moved stealthily closer, their eyes on his bobbing throat as he swallowed noisily.

With a grunt of feigned satisfaction, Denker lowered the bottle and wiped his lips with the back of his hand, smirking when he saw the envy on the faces before him. He held out the bottle to the nearest man. 'It's good stuff,' he lied, but he knew the labourers were used to a lot worse.

One of them timidly took hold of the bottle and raised it carefully to his lips, watching Denker to see whether he had not misunderstood the gesture. When the white man gave an encouraging nod and a wave of his hand, the labourer did not delay any longer. Two gigantic gulps diminished the contents of the bottle before he stopped to reassure himself that Denker had been sincere in his offer. The big man was still smiling when he indicated that the bottle should be passed round. This time there was no hesitation; the bottle hardly touched a set of lips before it was torn away by anxious hands.

Denker removed a second bottle from the saddle-bag. He threw it towards the men. It was caught before it had travelled a few feet.

There was suspicion on their faces again, and Denker decided it was time to announce the reason for his generosity. He withdrew a third bottle, uncorked it, and moved closer to the group.

'There are three more bottles in there,' he said, indicating the saddle-bag with a jerk of his thumb. Their eyes followed the movement. He let his words prickle their curiosity for a while longer before he said, 'You can have them all, so long as you give me what I want.'

They glanced furtively at each other. Three bottles of wine – plus the three he had already produced! Whatever it was Denker wanted, it had to be very important.

The Dutchman waited, enjoying their bewilderment. He crouched on the ground, indicating that he was in no hurry. 'I want to know,' he said, 'whether there have been any strangers on the farms.'

The men glanced at one another again. 'A Boer soldier,' he added. 'Possibly wounded.' He took a small sip from the bottle in his hand before passing it on.

They fidgeted nervously, each of them busy with his own thoughts of how best to capitalise on the opportunity of earning a few bottles of wine.

Almost all of them had, at some time or another, seen a stranger on horseback pass through their farms, so now their imaginations went to work, convincing them that the stranger had seemed in pain. Yes, they assured Denker, all trying to talk at the same time, they had seen such a man. The names of a dozen farms were rattled off at him.

He stood up, gave a tight grin and kicked lightly at the

ground with the toe of his boot. 'So many wounded Boers,' he said, 'riding over so many farms!' He gave the ground a last hard kick before turning away. 'I do not give away wine for a bunch of lies!' he snapped.

The men were silent as Denker pulled himself into the saddle. He caught the eye of an older, ugly man standing towards the rear of the group. He had been silent when the rest clamoured to tell their tales, and Denker sensed he would be worth talking to. He gave the man an almost imperceptible nod before he turned his horse.

The rest of them watched with despondent faces which lit up with smiles of surprise as he stopped, dug inside the saddle-bag and threw a bottle at them. They called out their thanks, not realising the gesture was not one of generosity, but merely meant to keep them occupied; it would make it easier for the man Denker wanted to slip away from the group.

He gave the labourer one last glance before he started his horse forward. Passing by the front of the store, he rode a short distance up the street before stopping beside a clump of thorn trees.

The labourer appeared within a few minutes, nodding respectfully. 'Master?'

'What's your name?'

'August.' Denker stared down at the ugly face with its long scar running from eye to chin. He patted the saddle-bag. 'No lies or fancy tales, you hear?'

August bobbed his head vigorously. 'No, master. I know of the man you seek.' He glanced at the saddle and added, 'I do not even want the wine. I have more need for money. The master can decide the worth of what I tell him.'

Denker stayed in the saddle, towering over the short man. 'Where do you work?' he asked.

'On the farm Ratitāe.' He pointed in the general direction of where the farm lay.

There was a quick narrowing of Denker's eyes, but he remained silent.

'The man you talk of came to the farm this week,' August continued. 'He was bleeding here and here.' He patted his side and leg.

'What happened then?'

'They took him inside, into the house.'

'Who's they?'

'Master George and Miss Ursula. I was working in a nearby field and watched them.'

'You think it was a Boer?'

'Yes, master. He had the clothes of a Boer.' He pointed at Denker's rifle and said, 'There was a place on his saddle for a rifle, but there was none. He had bullets, though,' he added, describing a bandolier.

Denker's wide smile was one of satisfaction. The military's report had stated that a Mauser had been found alongside the dead British soldiers. 'Is he still on the farm?'

August shrugged. 'The people no longer talk of him,' he replied, 'so I do not know. I never go inside the house.'

'Do not speak of this to anyone, do you understand?' said Denker, digging into his jacket pocket and dropping a few coins into the labourer's outstretched hands. 'All right, August – get on your way. And remember what I told you. Speak of this to no one!'

August bobbed his head in anxious assent.

Denker watched him amble off, pleased to see that he did not rejoin the group behind the store. He had no desire for the information he had just acquired to be spread around. That meant he would have to conduct a search of Ratitäe without delay.

The thought of James Quenton's widow being involved in illegal activities brought a smile to his face. Then he was reminded of Lieutenant Crosley's demand to be kept informed. The owners of Ratitäe were prominent people and they would no doubt cause a hue and cry about his appearance on the farm. He decided it might be better if Crosley were to accompany him after all. The capture of the Boer soldier was no longer of importance; what counted most was that James Quenton's family be socially embarrassed – perhaps even gaoled. It would be better if the military were there to see things for themselves.

He thought suddenly of Stanley. Would he also be involved in providing sanctuary to a Boer? Denker thought not. Would the bitter young man still be on Ratitāe? He knew it was only a matter of months before Stanley took up his share of the farm. A few more months during which he, Denker, would have to continue working for the British. When Stanley received his inheritance, he would appoint him to act as manager of his portion. Then would start the beginning of the end for the family of James Quenton. Denker realised he had been foolish not to maintain contact with Stanley; the youngster was volatile enough to change his mind about their agreement.

His thoughts returned to his immediate priority, making him smile in satisfaction as he spurred his horse in the direction of the British garrison.

Lieutenant John Crosley brushed his hand across the bright red of his dress jacket. He was pleased to see that very little dust clung to the thick material. As he and Denker, with four soldiers trailing a short distance behind, rode through the entrance to Ratitāe, Crosley tugged at the chinstrap of his helmet, hoping the headpiece was on straight. He had heard that Ursula Laboulaye was rather beautiful, so he wished to appear the perfect military man, his attire immaculate, his bearing erect.

During the ride to Ratitāe, he had sensed Denker's impatience to increase the pace at which they rode, but he had stubbornly refused to advance the party beyond a light canter.

He was angry with the Dutchman for having the audacity to think that a family such as the Laboulayes would harbour a fugitive Boer. Marianne Laboulaye was a pillar of the community, a woman who had set milestones in the ostrich industry! It was unthinkable that such an august family would associate themselves with one of the enemy. If the Boer soldier had indeed entered the farm, George Laboulaye would have immediately notified the military. Hadn't the garrison's commanding officer himself been a dinner guest at the farm on more than one occasion?

It was mainly because of the latter reason that Crosley decided he would accompany Denker to the farm early the next morning. The Dutchman was an insensitive brute, with no inkling of diplomatic subtleties, and the colonel would be furious when he learned that he had searched Ratitāe. He, John Crosley, possessed the necessary tact with which to conduct the search.

He frowned when Denker suddenly stopped his horse at the entrance to the great farm. 'What is it?' he snapped, brushing his jacket again as the dust swirled around them.

'Leave two of your men here,' came the reply.

'Good heavens, man? This is not some Boer stronghold. You're being absolutely—'

'Lieutenant,' interrupted Denker, 'you said yourself you didn't like the idea of coming here with a display of force. And it'll be good to have them here just in case there is a Boer who tries to escape.' He started forward without waiting for Crosley to respond.

The lieutenant stared open-mouthed after him, reluctantly admitting that what Denker had said made sense. He gave his men the order and spurred on his horse. 'I'll do the talking when we get to the house,' he said when he had caught up with the Dutchman.

They were shown inside the house by Mrs Blake, who settled them in the large, airy sitting room while she went in search of George.

He entered the room a few moments later, tall and distinguished-looking. Denker felt the familiar flush of resentment which always invaded him whenever he was confronted by those deemed to be of higher social standing than himself.

'Good morning, lieutenant,' said George, giving Denker a curt nod.

Crosley shot to his feet and introduced himself. 'This is Mr Denker,' he added almost in apology. 'He's on assignment to the garrison.'

George nodded at Denker again, but did not offer to shake hands as he had done with the lieutenant. Denker's mouth tightened at the corners.

Turning back to Crosley, George said, 'Is there something I can do for you?'

The lieutenant cleared his throat. 'Well . . . I'm afraid this is extremely embarrassing, Mr Laboulaye. I assure you that—'

'Why don't we talk in my study?' suggested George. 'You appear to have weighty matters on your mind.'

Before he shut the study door behind them, George offered the men tea. Crosley declined, saying, 'Thank you, sir, but we don't wish to cause any more inconvenience than that we are about to.' He clutched his helmet tightly under his arm.

George laughed. 'You certainly appear troubled, lieutenant! Out with it – am I to be arrested?'

'Oh no, sir! Nothing like that – no, of course not!' He gripped his helmet even more tightly and sat down stiffly once George had taken a seat behind the desk. 'It's just that . . . well, sometimes duty imposes the most unwanted tasks upon one.'

'Of course it does,' agreed George, amused at the English lieutenant's uneasiness.

Crosley started to explain, stressing that they were obliged to conduct routine searches of all the farms in the vicinity following reports of a wounded Boer in the area.

'It's possible he's hiding out on a farm without the owner's knowledge,' he added. 'I beg you to indulge our duty, sir. It certainly gives me no pleasure to have to search the homes of law-abiding citizens. A most embarrassing task, I assure you!'

'Calm down, lieutenant! No one can take offence at an officer of the Crown performing his duty. My house is open to your scrutiny. I'll accompany you myself – that is, if you have no objection?'

'I would deem it an honour!' Crosley blurted out, beaming with relief at George's favourable reaction. 'The task will be less distasteful with your presence.'

'Good! Let's start with the house first, then we can cover the outbuildings.' George rose to his feet.

Crosley moved with him, thinking that the colonel would surely receive a favourable report from George Laboulaye as to his diplomatic manner.

When Denker followed them, George swung around, his eyes cold. 'An officer of the Crown is one thing,' he said, 'but this man wears no uniform. I see no reason for him to inspect my abode. Unless you care to provide a reasonable explanation as to why I should consent to it, lieutenant.'

Crosley's face reddened. 'There is no reason for him to accompany us,' he said rapidly, glaring at Denker in warning.

The Dutchman ignored him. 'I have papers which say differently. The finding of the Boer is *my* task.'

'Only when Her Majesty's forces deem it necessary for you to act in that regard,' snapped Crosley, his voice thick with outrage. 'This is not one of those occasions, and I can assure you there is no Boer on these premises. The mere thought of it is appalling – an insult to Mr Laboulaye!' Despite his anger, he was terrified Denker would whip out the document which proved that he was in essence a bounty hunter, and flaunt it in front of George.

All the Dutchman said was, 'Why bother with a search if you're so convinced there's no Boer?'

'For the simple reason,' Crosley replied, glancing apologetically at their host, 'that I cannot be seen to skip certain farms because of the character of their owners. Others could then accuse me of shirking my duty. You will wait here,' he finished and followed George as he led the way from the study.

Denker cursed softly once they had left the room. Crosley was a bloody idiot, a pompous, snivelling little brat!

He paced the room angrily, while he waited. He felt sure the Laboulayes were guilty of hiding the Boer, that the labourer named August had told him the truth. But what if the man had already left, smuggled away with their help? Crosley would be unable to pick up tell-tail signs of his stay on Ratitãe.

During the journey to the farm he had wondered whether he would bump into Stanley, and how the young man would react upon seeing him again. It wouldn't do for the others to learn that they knew each other. But they would have to meet again soon, thought Denker; there was much to discuss. Yet capturing the Boer soldier and embarrassing the Laboulayes was the first priority.

After a while the walls of the study seemed to close in on him, heightening his frustration. The Boer had been there – he knew it as surely as he had known he would revenge himself on James Quenton one day. But how to prove it?

Denker could stand the confinement of being indoors no longer. Snatching up his hat, he strode into the passage. There was no one in sight as he started for the front door.

The bright sunlight dazzled him, so that he stood on top of the steps for a few moments before heading for the open fields where he spotted a group of labourers at work.

He was still some distance away when August noticed him for the first time. The labourer's heart leaped, and his first instinct was to try to move away across the fields. He saw it was too late; Denker had already seen him, was beckoning him closer. August shuffled towards him, trying to fight down his fear at the sudden appearance of the man. Did his employers know what he'd done? He also wondered what explanation he could give his fellow labourers for Denker's singling him out.

'Morning, master.'

Denker ignored the greeting. 'The Boer,' he snapped, glancing around to see whether anyone was watching them. 'Any more news of him?'

August wished he could stop the fearful flutter of his heart. He gave a violent shake of his head and said, 'No, master. Nothing.'

'Could you have been mistaken? Did you lie to me?'

August took a backwards step, terrified at Denker's expression. 'No – he was here! I swear, master! I saw the Boer with my own eyes!'

'Then where is he now? Tell me that! Or did he disappear the way he came – in a flash of your imagination?'

The frightened labourer thought rapidly. What had become of the Boer soldier? None of them had given any more thought to the matter after Outa had bullied them into silence. But Outa was not there right then, had been away for a week already. Was that it, then? Had Outa and Mistress Ursula taken the Boer with them?

August raised his eyes, smiled and said, 'Perhaps I do know where he is. There is a cottage, near Knysna, where the family goes for holidays.'

He was relieved when Denker returned his smile and said, 'Tell me exactly where, August.'

Denker was waiting near the front door when George returned with Crosley in tow. Neither man commented on his having left the study.

George once again offered tea, and again Crosley declined. 'We've taken up enough of your time, Mr Laboulaye. You've been very patient.'

The heat stung them once they were outside. Crosley mounted and adjusted his chinstrap till the headpiece sat snugly across his forehead. 'Please convey my respects to Mrs Laboulaye,' he said. 'And to Miss Ursula,' he added, pleased that the rim of the helmet placed his eyes in shadow. It had been a disappointment not to have seen the beautiful young woman about whom he had heard so much. He flashed George a smart salute before leading the way from the farm.

Denker did not speak until they reached the main road. 'Lieutenant,' he said as he stopped his horse, 'I've obviously been fed false information. I'll have to spread my search away from the town.'

'Good,' responded Crosley, relieved that the Dutchman would no longer pose a potential embarrassment. 'Let's get back to the garrison and file your report.'

Denker stared at him, then started to laugh. 'Report?' he asked, his voice scornful. 'What's there to report? You just go ahead and write whatever you like. I've a Boer to catch.' He turned his horse and galloped off without a backward glance at the English officer.

Crosley watched him go with an expression of repugnance on his face. 'What a boor of a man,' he said to the soldier near him. 'I hope he doesn't cause the Crown any further embarrassment.'

He hoped, too, that Denker would find the Boer soldier before long. The sooner the garrison was relieved of the unsavoury affair the better.

At least the Laboulayes weren't affected, he thought with relief.

CHAPTER FORTY-ONE

It was more than ten years since Denker had crossed the towering Outeniqua Mountains on his way from Millwood to the gold fields at Prince Albert.

He passed through the town of George at the foot of the Outeniqua, ignoring the tight dryness in his throat at the thought of the comforting drink and warm welcome a tavern would provide. A great deal of rain had fallen during the past week, with signs of more to come, making a night out in the open an uncomfortable prospect. He pushed the thought of cosy accommodation from his mind; a stop-over in George was a delay he could not afford.

When night fell, he was still half a day's ride from the cottage he sought. Denker stood at the edge of a promontory which towered over a narrow strip of white beach sand. Beyond lay the Indian Ocean; to his left, lakes sprawled into the distance, their immensity concealed by islands and twisting gorges.

The wind from the sea plucked at his clothes, warning him with its moisture. He turned away and went in search of a suitable spot to spend the night.

Moments after he had rigged a piece of tarpaulin to ward off the worst of the elements, the wind turned, spun and then hovered for a confused instant before the first drops of rain began to fall.

The rain ceased early the next morning. What had been a valley of lakes the day before was now a plateau of thick white mist. It seemed to stretch from Denker's crude camp in a thick carpet, enticing him to walk the endless miles to where the sun stirred on the eastern horizon.

He flipped back his soaked blanket and rose stiffly to his feet, his stomach crying for the warmth of food and coffee. But there was little chance of finding dry wood with which to make a fire, so he packed his horse and mounted.

An hour later, only a few isolated pockets of mist remained as Denker rode by the flawless waters of the lakes. A vast variety of bird life fluttered joyously among the bulrushes where the waters lapped and sucked softly against their muddy shores. A flight of flamingos winged their way silently overhead, heading for the eastern mud-flats to feed upon the worms and crabs scarring the wet sand with their scurrying tracks. Yet Denker was oblivious to all this, for he was not a man to ponder on the beauty or intricacies of nature.

It was midday when he reached the isolated group of cottages. They lay strung out along the shoreline, the nearest one only yards from the sea. Recalling the description August had given him, Denker gave a grunt of satisfaction; he was in the right place. He dismounted, then moved in behind the slope of a sand-dune from where he could study the buildings.

There were five cottages in an uneven row, spaced a few hundred yards apart, all of them facing the sea. The beach ended a short distance further on, where sand changed to dark rock standing resolutely against the punitive pounding of the rising surf. On the beach itself, a stream trickled into a U-shaped lagoon, separated from the breakers of the Indian Ocean by a narrow strip of sand.

Denker studied the houses again. There was no sign of life except for two horses grazing contentedly among the trees near one of the cottages. A small wagon stood at the side of the house. That was where they would be, he decided, studying the cottages one by one. The rest seemed deserted. A small distance from the buildings, close to the start of the trees, stood a series of huts which he assumed to be the servant quarters. He sat down on the warm sand and planned his approach.

He watched the windows closely, searching for movement

which would indicate occupation. Yet the house seemed as empty as the others.

With a start, Denker realised that he might be exposing himself to the couple; it was possible they had gone for a walk and would spot him lying against the dune when they returned. He spun round to scan the expanse of beach behind him, but only the jerky movements of tiny birds criss-crossing the sand met his gaze.

He nevertheless led his horse into the brush, then studied the house from his new position. There was little doubt now that there was no one inside the cottage. Tethering his horse, he removed his rifle from the scabbard, checked and oiled it, then slid a bullet into the breech. He slotted fresh bullets into his belt before settling down to wait.

While travelling to the cottage, he had decided it would be simpler to kill the Boer rather than try to take him back to Oudtshoorn alive. His body would be all the British needed to confront the Laboulayes with their treachery.

He shifted into a more comfortable position, his mind busy with the ways in which he could go about his task. He could fire from where he lay, but that would not be as satisfying as seeing the look of fear in the Boer's eyes. Also, the girl could run and make it to the bushes before he was able to catch her. It would be best to wait till they were inside the cottage. They would be unprepared for him there, and he would have them both where he wanted them.

Just as he shifted his body on the sand, digging a depression in it for greater comfort, he heard a squeak as the door to the nearest hut opened. Denker cursed his carelessness at not having considered the presence of servants. His thoughts were angry as he watched the big black man make his way towards the cottage.

Outa stopped near the cottage door. He stretched, relishing the feel of the early-spring sun on his body. Although he enjoyed the opportunity to relax and be with Ursula and Henry, he was concerned at how things were going at Ratitäe during his absence. He would personally flog the hide off any labourer who had not performed to satisfaction while he was away. George would tell him who the culprits were.

Ah, but his birds – his beloved ostriches – how he missed them! He stretched one more time before entering the cottage.

As always, the kitchen was tidy, with little left for him to do. Outa smiled, thinking how Ursula seemed to enjoy playing housewife. Then, too, there was something else, the love which glowed on her face and that of the man with her, the glow that only comes from a man and woman sharing the same bed.

It amused Outa how they tried to hide it from him, how the rumpled bed in Henry's room had been carefully arranged to mislead. He knew he should feel ashamed and guilty at having failed in the mission George and Marianne had entrusted to him. Yet Ursula's happiness made the knowledge easier to bear. How could a man such as he, a man who understood better than most the yearnings of the fleshy assegai and the sheath which longed to hold it, come between such a force? No, it was better to share their happiness – even though in subtle ways he had let the couple know what he suspected.

He had enjoyed the consternation on Ursula's face when, just the morning before, he had made up her bed and arranged the pillows for two people. Let her worry about what he would report to his master! He chuckled to himself and stepped back into the sunlight.

The arm that surrounded his throat from behind was awesomely powerful, cutting off his breath. He threw himself back, using his weight to throw his assailant off balance. He knew then that the man holding him was as big as himself and immensely strong. Outa tried again to break free, using the remaining breath in his chest to keep his mind thinking. It was useless, for his attacker moved with him, so that they swayed like a drunken couple, smashing against the side of the cottage before Outa felt his head start to spin from lack of air.

Even in his weakened state he knew the threat to himself was directed at Ursula. The thought gave him a spurt of superhuman strength, so that with a mighty heave of his arms he broke free and swivelled around to face his assailant.

His quick intake of breath changed to a short gasp of pain as he felt the cold, sharp thrust under his ribs, and he knew he had been stabbed. His body was still in motion, carrying him through his turn, so that his gaze met that of Denker as he fell forward against the white man. Again there was a thrust, deeper this time, making Outa feel as though he stood on air, as if he had no legs.

'Die, kaffir! Die!'

The words, hissed at him as he felt himself slide powerlessly to the ground, seemed to come from a great distance. Live, Mthembeni, live! he shouted silently, the noise louder in his mind than the words his assailant had spoken. Could he hear him, could the man hear him refuse to obey? Live, Mthembeni – be the one who can be trusted. Live for Miss Ursula! Live . . . live . . . li . . .

Denker looked down at Outa, satisfied there was no longer any life in him. He rolled him over, gripped his shoulders and, with a grunt at his great weight, dragged him towards the bushes. A thin trail of blood marked the spot where the Zulu had fallen.

After he had hidden the body, Denker raced back to the cottage and pulled up the grass smeared with blood. Quickly he scanned the terrain for other signs of their struggle and, giving a satisfied nod, moved back to his hiding place.

He checked his rifle one last time while he tried to bring his ragged breathing under control.

Ursula laughed gaily and clutched Henry's arm as she struggled to maintain her balance on the uneven rock. Waves crashed yards from them, stinging with salt spray.

'That one was close!' she cried, glancing warily at the sea as it tossed back from the rocks. She placed her arm carefully around Henry's waist, taking care not to touch his bandaged side. The wound had healed far faster than she had expected, and Ursula realised that the time spent as a soldier had strengthened his body. Even so, he suffered considerable discomfort at times. She could see that his leg wound, too, bothered him after the long walk.

'I don't know about you,' she said gaily, 'but this walk has finished me!'

Henry laughed. It had been he who had insisted on their daily exercise. 'I intend to do double the distance tomorrow,' he told her, 'along the beach this time. I might even go for a run!'

'Listen to the hero! You're overestimating your capabilities, my love.'

He tapped his side gently. 'I'm almost healed. Didn't you notice last night?' He stopped walking and drew her to him.

Ursula blushed at his reference to their love-making. This was how it should be, she thought happily, remembering her girlish dreams when George and Marianne had brought the family to the cottage during the summers. She had often sat on the beach by herself, wondering what it would be like to be in love, to have a man to herself at their seaside retreat. Now she knew, and it was more fulfilling than any of her wildest dreams.

She reached up to kiss him. 'Let's get back,' she whispered into his neck. 'First, we'll have some lunch . . . then we'll see just how much you've recuperated.'

Henry smiled and tugged at the thick ridge of bandages plastered to his side. 'If you'll just let me take these off,' he said, 'we can give it a real test. Before lunch, if you like!'

She laughed, pulled free and started across the rocks. 'Not with Outa around, you won't! Not during the daytime.'

'You really think he knows?'

Ursula nodded, but her smile showed she was not unduly concerned. 'He will do nothing to hurt me,' she said, breaking into a run towards the cottage.

'Be patient, woman,' Henry called out as he started after her, but the effort brought a gasp of pain to his lips, forcing him to stop and grasp his side.

By the time Ursula realised he was not behind her, he had managed to mask the discomfort on his face. 'Having second thoughts?' she teased him, feeling as if she would burst with happiness.

The cottage was not large, but George Laboulaye had ensured his family would not have to endure primitive conditions during their vacations there. A huge black coal stove filled one entire wall of the kitchen, for George was determined that his womenfolk and servants would not be inconvenienced when it came to cooking.

Ursula called out to Outa through the open door, then turned to the stove. 'Probably gone for a walk,' she said, stoking a fire into life while Henry rested in a chair. She quickly prepared the ingredients for their meal: six eggs, slices of rich brown bread, a strip of sausage and some mutton chops. After getting the coffee going, she filled another pot of water and placed it on one of the stove plates. It would be boiling and ready for Outa to wash their eating utensils by the time they were finished.

Henry watched her while she worked, enjoying the easy grace of her movements. He still found it hard to believe he was with her. His experiences since leaving the commando were a vague blur in his mind, so that when he had regained consciousness for the first time and George had questioned him about where and how he had been wounded, he was at first unable to answer. It was only later that some of the images returned: the long ride, the sudden appearance of the British soldiers on the pass. The killing. Of how he had made it to Ratitāe he had no recall.

None of it mattered now; he was with Ursula and it was all that concerned him. Even though they were fugitives, Henry was confident they would soon be able to commence a normal life together. George would send word when it was safe to return to Ratitāe. And the war would not last much longer – he was sure of that.

The possibility of the war ending did not distress him as much as he had thought it would. He was satisfied they had fought valiantly, even though it might have been in vain. Better to refrain from emotional despair, to start building again and come to terms with the situation. He would have to go back then, just for a while, to see for himself what could be done, as well as what role he might play.

'Why so serious?'

He looked up and smiled. He would have to tell her about his plans for going back, but not just then. 'Tell me about your family,' he said. 'During one of the few conversations I had with George, he told me your real father started the farm.'

'I was only five when he died, so I don't remember much about him.' She stood in front of Henry, her hands resting on his shoulders. 'There was never any love between him and my mother . . . It's a long story.'

'An unpleasant one?'

Her fingers stroked the skin of his neck. 'Most of it. Apparently he always felt she'd stolen Ratitāe from him.'

'He was killed by one of his own ostriches, wasn't he?'

She nodded. 'One of my mother's birds. She caught him in her paddocks, selecting chicks to take with him to America. She once admitted to me she came very close to setting loose the ostrich. It still haunts her, I think, the doubt that perhaps she did unlatch the gate holding back the bird.'

'Tell me about him – if you want to, that is. What kind of man was James Quenton?'

Ursula opened her mouth to speak, but it was the booming voice of a stranger which answered Henry. 'James Quenton,' it said, 'was the biggest bastard I ever knew.'

They spun around to stare in fright at the big man leaning against the doorpost, the rifle looking almost toy-like in his huge arms.

'Who the hell are you?' demanded Henry, starting to rise from his chair.

The barrel of Denker's rifle shifted ominously. 'Stay where you are, Boer.' He smirked with savage satisfaction as Henry sank back in the chair.

Ursula had been rooted to the spot, but now she clutched Henry's shoulder tightly. 'We've hardly any money,' she said in a frightened voice, 'but you can take it all. It's in the bedroom.'

'I'm not after money, little woman – it's your soldier boy I want.'

'He's not a soldier!' she cried. 'He's – he's my fiancé.'

Denker stepped closer. 'Take off your shirt,' he ordered

437

Henry. 'Now!' He jabbed the rifle barrel into the wounded man's chest. 'Do as I say, boy!'

Henry glanced at Ursula, then slowly started undoing his shirt. Denker saw the strip of bandage and smiled. 'Not a soldier, huh? How did he get wounded then? Or did you claw him that badly when he was piling his Boer sausage into you?' He laughed loudly at his own crudity.

Henry's face flushed with rage, but he knew he had no chance of reaching Denker before the other man could pull the trigger. He gently removed Ursula's hand from his shoulder, thinking that he would stand a better chance if he could get her to move away from him.

Denker saw what he was up to and lashed out with the barrel again. 'Don't get clever, soldier boy,' he snapped. He stepped back and let his gaze rove across Ursula's body. Then he looked her in the eyes. 'Your mother wanted to kill him, you know. I saw her try, but she lacked the guts. I finished what she started. Oh, yes,' he added when he saw the look on Ursula's face, 'I killed James Quenton. I killed him for all the suffering he caused me, the bastard! He's paid, but the rest of his family must still settle the debt. I'll start with you.'

Ursula had moved closer to Henry again. 'But why?' she asked hoarsely. 'What did he do to you? Why punish us?'

Denker ignored her and swung the barrel back towards Henry. 'I thought a Boer was never without his rifle,' he growled. 'Where's yours, soldier boy?'

'There is no rifle.' The next moment Denker jabbed the barrel into Henry's chest with such force he toppled backwards from the chair, falling to the floor with a cry of pain.

Denker stepped around the table as Ursula gave a small, anguished whimper and knelt down beside Henry. 'There's no rifle,' he mimicked. 'Fancy that – a Boer without a rifle!' He laughed and lashed out with the butt this time. The weapon struck Henry's ribs with a sickening thud. Ursula screamed.

The Dutchman reached down, grabbed a handful of her hair and hauled her roughly to her feet. 'The rifle, woman,' he snarled, pulling her to him. 'Where is it?' He slid his hand from her hair, cupped it with cruel hardness around her breast. She struggled futilely in his grip before he slung her aside. She fell against the stove, burning her hand on a plate and upsetting the pot of coffee which streamed to the floor. Crying out with fear and pain, she sank to her knees, her eyes fixed in terror on Denker.

The big man's lips pulled into a snarl as he looked down at her, before stepping across Henry's writhing figure. He stamped downwards with the rifle butt so that it struck the exposed part of Henry's neck. The Boer stopped moving and lay still.

'Please!' cried Ursula, 'it's in the bedroom. Please stop!' She was sobbing as she crawled across the floor to where Henry lay unconscious.

Denker pushed her back against the stove with the toe of his boot. 'Why don't you show me, woman. Come . . . show me where you pleasure your body with this Boer.'

Using the side of the stove, she pulled herself to her feet. 'Your brother, woman,' snarled Denker, 'where is he?'

She was terrified of him, but relieved that he would at least leave Henry alone for now. She cringed back when he lunged at her. Gripping her wrist harshly, he pulled her to him. 'Where is he?'

'In America,' she said hurriedly, confused by Stanley's being brought into things. 'He – he left some weeks ago! Please – you're hurting me!'

Denker's mind seemed to explode. America? The little bastard! He'd been cheated – there was nothing for him now, nothing but destroying what remained of James Quenton. He felt the girl squirm within his grip, shaking him from his angry trance.

He slapped her, a short, sharp blow, then threw her to the floor. Grabbing her by the hair, he started to drag her across the floor till she managed to move on to her hands and knees and crawl after him like a dog on a leash.

Booting open the first door he came to, Denker glanced quickly inside the room. 'The rifle?'

'In the corner,' whimpered Ursula, but he had already spotted the rifle which George Laboulaye had lent them. He released his grip on her hair. She remained cowering beside the door, terrified of what he would do next.

It started even before her raging thoughts could formulate the worst. She saw him place his own rifle against the wall before grinning wickedly at her as he kicked the door shut.

His hands seemed monstrously huge when he reached forward and grabbed her arms. He lifted her effortlessly to her feet before raising her to the level of his face, so that her feet dangled off the floor. She smelled his stale, sour breath. 'James's little girl,' he said thickly. 'Who would have thought the bastard could sire anything as pretty as you?'

'No – please don't!'

'Please don't what, woman? You'll be crying for more in just a while.' Ignoring her kicks and struggles, he laughed madly and threw her across the bed. When she tried to rise, he slapped her face with two brutal blows which dazed her and sent her reeling back on to the bed.

Denker stared down at her. Her dress had ridden high across one leg, exposing the smoothness of her skin. He swallowed loudly, his rage at Stanley's betrayal replaced by lust.

The bed creaked as he climbed on. Ursula groaned when his hands touched her legs, spreading them wide before he knelt down between them. He sucked in his breath as he raised her dress over her hips. 'What a woman!' he whispered drily and tore away the flimsy silk of her underclothes. He groaned in anticipation when he had her exposed.

The shock of his hand on her private parts brought Ursula back to full consciousness. Her cry of outrage came from deep inside her before she bit down on her bruised lips. She tightened her legs, but the brute kneeling between them growled and thrust them apart again. She reached for his face, her nails tearing at his rough skin.

She felt a deep barbaric thrill when he cried out and clutched at his torn and bleeding skin. Jerking her knees upwards, she tried to spin off the bed, but he yanked her round, grabbed her throat and forced her back against the mattress. This time he slapped her so hard that specks of blood flew from her broken lips to splash on to the wall. Her head snapped back against the bed, and for brief seconds she saw only speckled blackness.

When she opened her eyes again, he towered above her, his hands pressing down on her shoulders as he lowered himself on to her. He had pulled his trousers down across his buttocks, and his tumescent organ swung across her exposed abdomen. She screamed.

The sound broke the glassiness which had formed across Denker's eyes. 'Not yet, woman,' he said, 'not yet!'

He threw himself upon her, his weight crushing her scream, making it fade into a horrible gurgle in her throat. Revulsion curdled its sickening way from her stomach into her mouth. He lay completely on top of her now, grunting like a wild animal as he tried to enter her. The nightmare seconds dragged past as Ursula struggled desperately beneath him.

She bit down on her bloodied lip and dug her nails in behind his ears as he lowered his head against hers. Denker pulled away with a curse.

The shift of his head was enough for her to claw at his face again. This time her fingers gouged at his eyes, her sharp nails digging in so that he screamed loudly and jerked back. He slipped off her and from somewhere she found the strength to pull back her knee to slam it into his testicles. The sound of the blow was like a soft slap. Denker bellowed and rolled on to his side.

Ursula was off the bed in an instant. She lunged for the door. Denker grabbed hold of her wrist. Her flight was so desperate that she pulled him after her, dragging him half off the bed. He tried to stand, but his trousers were half-way down his legs now, so that he tripped and fell, releasing his hold on her.

Her eyes flashed to Denker's rifle propped up against the wall, but he lay between her and the weapon. She yanked open the bedroom door and fled towards the kitchen. She heard him call out after her. There was a dull thud as he tripped and fell again.

Henry still lay prostrate on the kitchen floor. Ursula's mind raced as she tried to cope with her terror as well as find a means of escape. Denker would kill them unless she could get them both out of there. But how? She could not carry or even drag Henry from the house before Denker

441

caught up with them. She fought to curb the panic threatening to overwhelm her. A weapon! She had to find a weapon! Where were the knives?

On the stove, the pan of sausage she had set cooking before the terror began was sizzling angrily. The pot of water had started boiling over. She scrambled for the drawer where the eating utensils were kept. From down the passage came the heavy thuds of Denker's footfalls.

He loomed large in the doorway, clutching his pants around his waist with one hand. 'I'm not finished yet, you bitch!' he snarled and stepped towards her. She jerked open the drawer, but Denker grabbed her. She managed to break free and backed away, almost falling over Henry's inert form.

She kept moving till she was up against the stove. Globules of boiling fat spat out of the pan and stuck to her arm. She jerked away and in that instant knew how she could defend herself.

Denker saw her reach for the pan. He hurtled across Henry with an angry cry, but the blackened sausage and boiling fat struck his neck when she hurled the pan at him. He yelped in anguish, reared back and fell heavily against the wall. Ursula scampered back to pick up the pot of boiling water.

He was on his knees now, whimpering as he tried to scrape away the burning mess from his skin. He looked up at her, cursing vilely. There was a madness in his eyes as he shrugged off the pain and struggled to his feet.

Ursula stepped closer till she stood before him, her legs spread as she struggled with the weight of the pot. She saw Denker's sudden look of fear when he raised his hand and cried, 'No! No – don't!'

She threw the boiling water directly into his face.

For one brief moment she watched the results of her action. Then she shut her eyes and ears to the horror and fled from the kitchen.

She grabbed Henry's rifle from the bedroom, knowing it was loaded and ready for firing. It felt heavy and evil in her hands as she raced back to the kitchen. She heard herself moan: 'Please – dear God, forgive me – I can't allow him to live!'

Denker was whining like a stricken animal on the floor. His face was a mass of red blisters, his ruined eyes bulging sightlessly from their sockets. The pink remains of his lips blubbered as he cried out his pain.

Ursula's hands shook when she levelled the rifle. Raising its weight to her shoulder she took aim at the man who had tried to defile her. The barrel swayed as her finger curled around the trigger. The weapon was suddenly too heavy for her to keep steady. It sagged downwards, away from Denker.

It was as if he suddenly sensed her presence, for he stopped crying and stared sightlessly in her direction. An animal-like moan escaped his lips. He lunged forward, fastening his hand on to the hem of her dress. He dragged himself closer, almost pulling her off balance as he clung desperately to the cloth.

'No!' Ursula tried to break free, but his other hand shot out and grabbed hold of her ankle. His grunts had a ring of satisfaction to them now. 'No!' she cried again and slammed the rifle barrel against his head, weakening his grip enough for her to break free.

She shivered and tried to raise the rifle. This time she was able to hold it, to keep it steady as her finger curled around the trigger.

'No . . .'

The gasp made her turn in fright. She stared in shock at the sight of Outa leaning against the doorframe, the front of his shirt stained brightly with blood, his eyes glassy. 'Outa!' she screamed. 'Oh God, Outa!'

The Zulu staggered into the room and crashed into the table. Ursula thought he would fall, but somehow he made it to her side, his breath coming in deep, ragged bursts.

In front of them, Denker's groans and whimpers mingled with the sounds of Outa's pain and her own terror. His hands flailed the air, seeking a hold on her.

Ursula recoiled against the stove. 'I must kill him, Outa – I must!'

The Zulu shook his head and staggered again. 'No, Miss Ursula,' he whispered, 'No . . . not—not you. It . . . it must be me . . . must be me.' He held out his hand and tried to take the rifle from her grasp.

Somehow the proud Zulu managed to hold the rifle, although he swayed so much Ursula had to steady him with her hands. She shut her eyes tightly at what was to come.

Denker was suddenly silent on the floor. He raised his ruined face and stared at Outa with his sightless eyes. 'Kaffir?' The sound of his voice was like the ripping of cloth. 'Kaffir?' he said again. 'So, you are not dead.' His hand snaked out and gripped Outa's leg.

The shot was loud in the confines of the kitchen, masking the clatter of the rifle as it slipped from Outa's hands and fell to the floor. Denker's death-grip stayed firmly around his ankle.

'It is done, Miss Ursula,' Outa whispered, sinking to his knees. She threw her arms around him, unable to look at Denker's remains. She sobbed with relief and love for the man who had refused to let her live with a death on her conscience.

'I shall live,' Outa said, 'for what is a knife wound to a little bitty Christian?' He managed a weak smile before glancing to where Henry lay.

Ursula scurried in a crab-like crawl towards Henry. Blood caked the back of his head, and the wound in his side had started bleeding again. He groaned when she lifted his head on to her lap. She gave a small cry of relief; she had not known whether he was still alive!

She sat there on the floor, cradling him in her arms till at last he opened his eyes, confused at first, then focusing on her face. 'Ursula?'

'Ssh . . . it's all over now . . . it's all right.' Tears streaked her face, but her voice sounded steady to her own ears. 'It's all right now,' she repeated as if soothing a child.

She saw his eyes move from her face to Outa, then to the bloodied pulp that had been Denker's head. When he looked back at her broken lips and torn dress, he was instantly fully conscious. He struggled to his knees. 'What happened?' he asked, taking her face in his hands. 'Did he—'

'No,' she said quickly.

Henry took her into his arms. They stayed on the floor,

clutching each other tightly in an embrace that was a mixture of relief and delayed shock.

The cloud layer hung like a dark, ominous curtain before the waning sun curled into its resting place beyond the sea's horizon. A few last, stray rays of ochre light broke through the rearguard of the day to stab defiantly at the approaching night.

Near the beachfront cottage, the sea moved with an eternal power, its force grudgingly altered by the changing day and accompanying whims of ebb and flow. Churning water crashed on to the rocks where the couple stood in the gathering dusk. It slipped back hissing, rebelling against a forced retreat from the reaches conquered earlier that afternoon.

'The tide is moving out,' said Henry. Ursula shivered and nodded. Neither of them looked at the bulky shape concealed beneath the blanket lying beside them on the rocks.

'Let's do it,' she whispered hoarsely. Her fingers clamped tightly around Henry's arm. She glanced at the blanket, shuddering again as she thought of how they had dragged its weight from the kitchen, across the grass and sand to its present position. From there it would be a short roll to its final resting place.

Henry placed his hand on hers while he continued to study the surging ocean. 'We must wait a while longer,' he said, 'till the tide pulls strongly.' She knew he was right; the last thing they wanted was Denker's body washing up on the beach the next day.

The afternoon had dragged by with agonising slowness. Now, at least, she felt as if the disposal of the body would relieve the sombre and threatening atmosphere which had invaded their cottage retreat. Even though they had covered the corpse, once Outa's wounds had been seen to and Henry fully recovered from Denker's attack, she had been left with the reminder of violence.

Henry went in search of the Dutchman's horse. 'He must have one hidden somewhere,' he had said. 'I'll set it free, bury the saddle and equipment.'

'What if the British know he came here?' she had argued. They had come across the document signed by Lieutenant Crosley, but Henry doubted that Denker would have worked closely with the authorities. 'There would have been soldiers with him if they knew of our whereabouts,' he had said. 'And this creature made it clear he was more interested in some personal revenge on your family. Did your mother ever mention him?'

'No,' she replied, 'it must have been something between him and my father. He knew Stanley, too,' she added with a confused shake of her head. 'What do we do now, my love? We can't stay here!'

'I'll have to, but you must get Outa to a doctor. I'll come as soon as it's safe.'

'And then?'

He had taken her face in his hands, smiling with a gentleness that belied the ordeal they had just been through. 'Then,' he told her, 'you and I'll be married and have children and live happily ever after.' He kissed her.

'You'll stay then? With me on Ratitāe?'

His hesitation was momentary. 'If you want me.' They would talk about his other responsibility later, when their senses were back to normal.

As she sank into his arms, they clung to each other for a while, their closeness momentarily obliterating the violence, which still cast its ugly shroud over the cottage.

Later, they spent some time discussing how Denker could have traced them, both agreeing that he had been informed by some disgruntled labourer. 'Quite a few of them know of the cottage,' Ursula said, 'and I suppose it was easy enough for him to track us down to the exact spot.'

The wind swept in from the sea now, cool, angry and spiteful. It tugged at the frightened couple, adding its own gloom to the deed they still had to perform. 'Please,' said Ursula, 'I can't stand it any longer!'

Henry pulled her close to him. 'You go to the cottage and see to Outa,' he told her. 'I can manage on my own.'

'No! We'll do it together.' She knelt and grabbed one end of the blanket while Henry took the other.

After Denker's body had slipped into the churning water, they stood wrapped in each other's arms as the tide went to work. Ursula kept her face pushed into Henry's shoulder, till at last he said, 'It's all right. He's gone now.'

Only then did she turn to look at the dark waters, but the sea concerned itself with its own altered strength and seemed unaware of the gruesome burden they had added to its restless movement.

'Come,' said Henry as he turned her towards the cottage. 'Let's go home.'

CHAPTER FORTY-TWO

On Saturday, 31 May 1902, the Boer leaders finally accepted the British conditions of surrender. The Anglo-Boer War was brought to an end.

An uneasy peace also prevailed on Ratitāe. 'Do you still plan on going back?' George asked Henry when news of the surrender reached Oudtshoorn. Henry looked at him for a long time before he gave a slow shake of his head.

When Ursula had left with the wounded Outa, they had agreed it would be safer for Henry to remain at the cottage on his own. He had stayed there till the end of November the previous year, when George considered it safe for him to return to Ratitāe.

The months spent on Ratitāe since then had made Henry realise he could never leave Ursula, not even for the land that had been his home. He could not risk losing what they shared by returning to that which was already lost.

The two men sat in the late afternoon sun which still danced lightly on the walls of the house. 'Where are our women?' asked George.

'Out for a walk.'

'Ah!' He gave Henry a sidelong glance, for he suspected that he and Ursula had arranged for the two of them to be alone for a while. George could guess why.

'George?'

'Mmm?' He enjoyed witnessing the young man's obvious discomfort.

'I . . . well . . . you've been very kind in letting me stay for so long.'

'Well, we knew you had to wait till the war was over. Then there was your uncertainty about returning to the Transvaal. It's been a pleasure having you here.'

'I appreciate your hospitality.'

George glanced at him again, a light smile on his lips. 'A pleasure, really.'

The silence dragged on till finally Henry said, 'Well, I was thinking . . . Ursula and I . . . We—'

'Yes?'

'We want to marry.' It came out in one quick burst.

'Ah.' George scratched the side of his nose, pretending to give the statement considerable thought. 'Ah,' he repeated. 'Yes, marriage.'

Henry sensed he was being teased. 'Do I have the blessing of Mr and Mrs Laboulaye to proceed?'

'Proceed with what? To ask Ursula, or with marriage itself?'

'Marriage,' replied Henry, for he suspected Ursula had already told both Laboulayes about the plans they had discussed while still at the cottage. He was sure that, despite what George had said, his lengthy stay on Ratitāe would have met with some disapproval if they had not been aware of his hopes for a life together with Ursula.

'I should think,' George said slowly, 'this constitutes sufficient reason to open a bottle of my finest champagne. Shall we go inside?'

Henry smiled and stood up with him. 'Does that mean we have your blessing?'

'It does.' As they entered the warmth of the house, George decided to wait till later before telling Henry how the request for Ursula's hand in marriage suited his and Marianne's plans for retirement to Austria at the end of that year. He knew that Marianne would be telling her daughter about them.

The two women walked arm in arm beside the paddock. 'I'll miss you,' said Ursula, pulling closer to her mother.

'There'll be visits . . . We'll want to see our grandchildren, of course.'

'Oh, Mother – I don't even know whether Henry's worked up the courage to ask George yet!'

Marianne smiled to herself. 'Henry's a fine man, my darling. He'll make a good husband. And father. You have such an exciting future to look forward to.'

Ursula stopped, turning to face her mother. 'I have you to thank for that,' she said, 'you and George.'

Marianne leaned closer to kiss her forehead. She thought briefly of what it had taken to protect that future – the pain, loneliness, the strength and even cruelty which had been demanded of her. That was over now, yet she would do it all again just to enjoy the stage they had now reached.

'The other future,' asked Ursula, as they drew apart and faced the paddock, 'will that also be exciting?'

'The ostrich industry?'

She nodded. 'Things seem to be going very well, but for how long?'

'Who knows what could happen? Overproduction could cause another slump or the growth of rival industries might break our hold on world markets. Or feathers could simply go out of fashion!'

'You think that could happen?'

'At any time. The ostrich will soon be worth its weight in gold, but it could also become totally without value.'

'And the rival producers? America? Stanley?'

Marianne smiled wistfully. 'Yes,' she said softly, 'but he won't be the destructive force he thinks he is. It will take many like him, but it will happen. Yet they will suffer the same way if fashion deserts us.'

There was a flutter of movement from within the paddock. A large cock strutted arrogantly about the hens, starting his moves to separate the one of his choice from the others. His booming roar rang out, carrying clearly to the watching women.

Marianne placed her arm around Ursula's waist. 'Come, let's go in. It's cold, and our men will be missing us.'

'The industry might flounder,' Ursula said softly as they

walked away, 'but there will always be ostriches on our farm. They are Ratitāe, and Ratitāe will always be theirs.' She felt Marianne's grip tighten about her.

As if he had heard her, the ostrich cock turned to watch them go. He extended his wings, displaying the finery of his feathers. He roared again: once, twice, and then a long third cry which lingered on the stillness of the approaching night.

He was Ratitāe, the flightless one.

Not even in the early centuries, when the earth was young and pliant, and flight granted a greater degree of subsistence, had his forebears possessed that power.

Neither had time changed him, except to instil in him the deepest sense of survival. That inner compulsion, so strong that his offspring possessed it at birth and practised it without any form of instruction, ensured that the ratites roving the elastic surface of the earth would continue to exist in a future world.

The earth grew hard with passing time. It flexed and creaked, its inner core stirring with molten savagery as opposing forces escalated, collided, then subsided again. In one such seething shrug, the immature plates crusting its surface cracked and split apart. Masses of water flowed where once there was land. As the earth was broken, so was the family of ratites scattered apart. Separated by the oceans which now defined the new continents, each formed their own family type and adapted for survival in their new worlds. Even their physical structure changed. After aeons of time had passed, man would one day classify them as ostrich, emu, rhea, cassowary and kiwi.

But Ratitāe's descendants, who would be known as Struthio camelus, the African ostrich, changed not at all. When the restless earth gave rise to its continents, they already knew how to survive in their known world. There was no need for change.

This day, Ratitāe roved in the form by which the earth had known his forebears. He stood eight feet tall, and his mass was near three hundred pounds. His small-set head moved idly atop the thin length of his lead-grey neck. When he turned to survey his domain, his long eyelashes fluttered against the hot breeze disturbing the dust of the land they now called Egypt. His overhanging brows twitched while his large eyes quickly scanned the shimmering horizon. All was still.

Ratitāe moved forward, a mincing walk on down-pointed toes. His legs, like his neck, were deceptively thin. His shins glowed a dull, light red which flashed more brightly whenever his anger or sexuality was aroused. Between his muscular thighs and his neck lay the only aspect of what could be termed beauty. A dense plumage, so intensely black that it glistened in the bright sun, covered the mass of his body. Only at the tips of his wings and his tail was the blackness broken by a stark white. He was the Ratitāe. The king of his tribe.

Around him the desert glowed hot and bright and parched. There was a time, centuries ago, when his ancestors dwelt in another region, a land of succulent grasses and abundant water. But the great dinosaurs had decimated their number, till at last their instinct for survival forced them to move to where the giant beasts would not follow. Their cloven feet carried them with relative ease across the thousand-mile trek. The ratites entered the desert lands, adapting to the absence of water by learning to survive off aquiferous plants.

Their flight from the dinosaurs did not bring complete sanctuary, for the passage of time brought new enemies with which to contend: the lion, leopard, jackal and hunting dog – all kept the growth of their number in vicious check.

Ratitāe survived all these, but for some time now he had faced an enemy who threatened the continued existence of his clan. It was for this enemy that he now restlessly scanned the horizon.

Man . . .

How long had they sought him now? Years? For was he not the greatest ratite of all?

This time, he knew, they hunted him in earnest. For two days now they had followed him, the tips of their killing sticks glinting evilly in the glare of the sun. For two days he had evaded them, leading them away from his tribe. He knew it was he they wanted, but he knew, too, that a slaughter would follow if they found him among his family. A senseless slaughter, for Ratitāe had learned that was the way of man.

He shut his eyelashes against the rising dust and recalled the rotting carcasses which covered the windswept plains of his travels. The birds were all males, weaker and slower than he. They lay in their hundreds – thousands – ruined bundles of flesh ruthlessly stripped of their feathered finery. Ratitāe's shins flushed red at the memory.

Man . . .

Ratitæ knew not why they hunted him so remorselessly, only that with this enemy, there would be no survival. He did not know that man sought his feathers for adornment. He was unaware that the vexilla of his feathers was of equal length on either side of its shaft, making it a symbol of equity and justice for man. He had no way of knowing that some emperor had acquired a taste for the flesh of the ratite, or that another had served the brains of six hundred of his kin in a festive dish. He knew nothing of the plumed feathers that travelled along the dark corridors of death within the pyramids of the mighty pharaohs.

Ratitæ was ignorant of these things, yet he knew that man would destroy him and his kin.

Man . . .

He could sense them now. Soon he must meet them, and his death.

Ratitæ was no stranger to man. Many times he had run from them with incredible speed, using the stoutness of his heart to take gigantic strides of ten feet and more as he steadily outpaced his pursuers. He had even killed man once, charging at an unwary enemy who approached his nest, crushing his fragile bones with a massive kick. He had tasted their blood, and now they meant to taste his.

Man . . .

Ratitæ saw them now, coming in vast numbers from the west. He knew they had seen him grazing up against the low hills and that, even now, more of them would be moving in from the other side. Still Ratitæ did not run.

He shifted his head to stare out to the east, to a distant spot he could not see. There his family would gather with the other clans as he had instructed. They would start their trek the following dawn, moving away from this enemy to whom they could not adapt.

Ratitæ knew there would be dissent, for all would know their king was dead. Some would want to move back to where they believed the grassy plains survived; others to the north, or even west.

His sons would obey him. They would gather his family – perhaps six hundred or more – and start the long trek south. They would follow his wishes, moving ever southwards till they came to the breaking of continents. If they survived the journey and the land which lay there, they would survive for ever.

Man . . .

Ratitāe looked up sharply. He heard them now, a soft clink as they made their way through the rocks at the foot of the hills. It was man; he could sense them and smell them, those who called him the camel bird, ignorantly thinking he lived in the arid regions by choice. It was those who thought him a silly creature, foolishly plunging his head into the sand, thinking himself safe if he could not see the danger facing him. Even after all the killing, man had still not realised he laid his head on top of the hot and stony ground, thereby reducing his bulk and the chances of discovery. How many hunters had passed him by in this way?

There! They were closing in now! Ratitāe's body shuddered in a reaffirmation of his presence and stature. He raised himself to his full height, his head erect and eyes alert, his entire being an immense spectacle of pride and defiance. Every magnificent feather stood on end. The plumes along his wings opened like a gigantic fan.

He turned to face his enemy. Shutting his beak, he expelled air up into his mouth, from where it was forced back into his gorge. Simultaneously, his cardia compressed, shutting the escape route of the air to his stomach. His long neck swelled and his defiance boomed out across the plains like the grunt of a lion.

Man heard his roar: once, twice, then a long third cry, which reverberated across the dry and dusty earth.

Then Ratitāe ran.

He fled across the ridge of the hill, heading for the open plains where he would produce his greatest speed. He ran, knowing he would not escape death this day.

He reached the dusty plain, his huge heart pounding strength into his body, his legs taking gigantic strides across the hot earth as he outpaced his pursuers. He would continue to run, leaving the horses of man far behind, till he could run no more. Then he would fall, never to rise again.

Of the many things Ratitāe did not know – the kings, the feasts, the value of his feathers – none was as significant as the flaw in his pattern of flight: he, like all of his kind, ran in an immense circle. Of greater import than his ignorance of this trait was man's knowledge of it.

In the two days of their pursuit, the pharaoh's hunters had constantly manoeuvred their forces to intercept his path. But the circle run by the king of the ratites was of so great a diameter that they failed to be in position when he crossed by.

454

This day, a small group of hunters struck out at right angles to his flight, racing their horses headlong across the desert till they came to a cluster of boulders at the base of a hill. There they concealed themselves and waited for the king.

Ratitāe saw them just as he felt the last strength pour from his tired body. For a brief moment he faltered, his instinct for survival urging him to change direction. But it was too late for that, and too late for a king to deny his destiny. His feet found their pattern again as he rushed onwards in twelve-foot-long strides.

Man rose to meet him, the overhead sun glistening on the tips of their killing sticks.

It was a last, silent rush, for the great bird's body would not permit a final roar of defiance while in motion. The only sound was the thrashing of his feet across the sand, and the deathly swish of the javelins spinning through the tepid air.

One of the javelins entered Ratitāe's body, piercing the soft fleshiness below the protective strength of his armour-like breastbone. He stumbled and rolled across the pebbled earth. The scattering dust seeped through his tear-stained eyelashes.

Man was all around him now, shouting their glee as they raised their killing sticks for the final death thrust.

Ratitāe's eyes seemed to smile beneath the tears, for he thought of his sons and their long trek south. They would find another world, other men, a different future.

The barbed spikes of the javelins reached for his unprotected body as Ratitāe lay his bruised head upon the hot sand. His eyelashes, thick now with tears of waste, fluttered once and then closed.

Man . . .

They thought it was ended.

But it was only the beginning.

All Pan books are available at your local bookshop or newsagent, or can be ordered direct from the publisher. Indicate the number of copies required and fill in the form below.

Send to: **CS Department, Pan Books Ltd., P.O. Box 40, Basingstoke, Hants. RG21 2YT.**

or phone: 0256 469551 (Ansaphone), quoting title, author and Credit Card number.

Please enclose a remittance* to the value of the cover price plus: 60p for the first book plus 30p per copy for each additional book ordered to a maximum charge of £2.40 to cover postage and packing.

*Payment may be made in sterling by UK personal cheque, postal order, sterling draft or international money order, made payable to Pan Books Ltd.

Alternatively by Barclaycard/Access:

Card No.

Signature:

Applicable only in the UK and Republic of Ireland.

While every effort is made to keep prices low, it is sometimes necessary to increase prices at short notice. Pan Books reserve the right to show on covers and charge new retail prices which may differ from those advertised in the text or elsewhere.

NAME AND ADDRESS IN BLOCK LETTERS PLEASE:

Name

Address